SACRIFICING THE QUEEN

LEGEND OF THE DRAGON LORD
BOOK 2

PETER WACHT

Sacrificing the Queen
By Peter Wacht

Book 2 of Legend of the Dragon Lord

This book is a work of fiction. Names, characters, places, and incidents are the product of the author's imagination or are used fictitiously. Any resemblance to actual events, locales, or persons, living or dead, is coincidental.

Copyright 2025 © by Peter Wacht

Cover design by Ebooklaunch.com

All rights reserved. In accordance with the U.S. Copyright Act of 1976, the scanning, uploading, and electronic sharing of any part of this book without the permission of the publisher constitute unlawful piracy and theft of the author's intellectual property.

Published in the United States by Kestrel Media Group LLC.

ISBN: 978-1-950236-66-4

eBook ISBN: 978-1-950236-65-7

Library of Congress Control Number: 2025905362

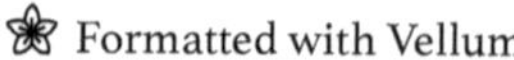 Formatted with Vellum

ALSO BY PETER WACHT

THE REALMS OF THE TALENT AND THE CURSE

LEGEND OF THE DRAGON LORD

A Painful Truth (short story)*

Stealing the Light

Sacrificing the Queen

Roar of the Broken Bear

Rise of the Dragon Lord (Forthcoming 2026)

THE TALES OF CALEDONIA

(Complete 7-Book Series)

Blood on the White Sand (short story)*

The Diamond Thief (short story)*

The Protector

The Protector's Quest

The Protector's Vengeance

The Protector's Sacrifice

The Protector's Reckoning

The Protector's Resolve

The Protector's Victory

THE TALES OF THE TERRITORIES

(Complete 8-Book Series)

Stalking the Blood Ruby (short story)*

A Fate Worse Than Death (short story)*

Death on the Burnt Ocean

Monsters in the Mist

The Dance of the Daggers

Bloody Hunt for Freedom

A Spark of Rebellion

Shadows Made Real

Shadow's Reach

Storm in the Darkness

THE SYLVAN CHRONICLES

(Complete 9-Book Series)

The Legend of the Kestrel

The Call of the Sylvana

The Raptor of the Highlands

The Makings of a Warrior

The Lord of the Highlands

The Lost Kestrel Found

The Claiming of the Highlands

The Fight Against the Dark

The Defender of the Light

THE RISE OF THE SYLVAN WARRIORS

Through the Knife's Edge (short story) *

THE FALLEN KNIGHT SERIES

The Death of the Dragon (short story) *

The Dragon Awakens

Duel With a Dragon

Beware the Dragon

The Dragon Returns

* Free stories can be downloaded from my author website at PeterWachtBooks.com. My books are also available on Amazon and other online retailers.

YOUR FREE STORY IS WAITING...

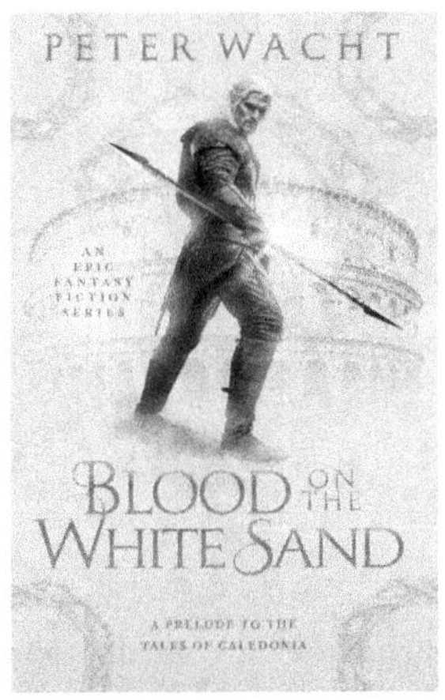

This eBook is a prelude to the events in my epic fantasy series *The Tales of Caledonia* and is free to readers who receive my newsletter.

Join Peter's newsletter and get your FREE short story.
PeterWachtBooks.com

1

ICY FORETELLING

"Where do matters stand between you and the Queen of the Crux?"

Mikel didn't have the chance to answer the question. He was too busy diving to the side and then sliding across the crusted snow to avoid the scythe that sang through the air where he had been standing.

It was a beautiful weapon. Mikel would be the first to admit that. The haft was made of the smoothest and strongest stone, the blade crafted from a steel that was easily mistaken for ice and never lost its edge. But that didn't mean he wanted that weapon cutting so close.

Mikel was back up in a flash, the steel spikes on the soles of his boots giving him a grip on the icy surface that allowed him to move with his customary speed. The only hindrance slowing him down was his damaged knee that tightened and ached in the cold of the Frozen Waste.

"Matters are no different than they were when last I saw her," Mikel finally answered. "Why?"

Mikel frowned as he slashed with his scimitar, the steel glowing dimly, and not because of the bright sunlight reflecting off the white of the Maze. He shook his head, trying to clear it of the woman sitting on the throne of the Crux.

He needed to keep his focus on his opponent. Otherwise, the Frost Lord would make him pay for his lapse in concentration.

He had little expectation of gaining the touch that he wanted. The best he could hope for was that he kept Cadmus on his toes, making his friend hesitate before he attacked again.

The Giant of the Rime held a distinct advantage. Since Cadmus stood almost twice as tall as Mikel, he enjoyed a much longer reach. He didn't need to risk getting in tight to Mikel to gain the touch that would give him the victory. Cadmus could poke at him from a distance for as long as he desired so long as he didn't make a mistake that Mikel could use against him.

However, for Mikel to gain the touch that would end this practice combat, he needed to get in close. A risky tactic, though a necessary one. And on this day a challenge he had yet to meet.

"Are you certain of that?" Cadmus asked, his deep voice rumbling off the circular wall of the hollow that was carved out of the snow and ice.

The Frost Lord had led Mikel to the Maze that morning. Supposedly seeking more of a test as part of his training regimen than he could gain against his Defenders while offering his friend a unique honor. To hone his skills as the Giants of the Rime did.

Rather than take on the many obstacles situated throughout the Maze that the less-experienced Giants needed to master before the final combat could begin -- tricks and traps, perils and hazards that changed regularly, from shifting walls and hidden pits to tusked mastodons and snowcats larger than draft horses – Cadmus had led Mikel right to the center of the training ground.

The Circle.

Bridges crafted of ice allowed the Rime Armsmasters to look down on all that occurred in the practice ring so that they could evaluate their students as they sought to pass the required tests to become a Defender of the Rime.

Neither Cadmus nor Mikel felt the need to add to the level of difficulty of that morning's exercise, preferring to climb down the ladder at the end of the bridge to take their places. Having little doubt that their adversary would test them in ways that no other challenge or opponent could. And the last hour had proven them right.

The Frost Lord and Mikel displayed an innate and ingrained ability that few could match. Since the practice combat began, neither had gained a winning strike, though it had been a near thing for each on a few occasions.

At the same time they engaged in a conversation that started with their mutual business interests and now had taken them to more delicate topics. Matters that Mikel had little desire to discuss.

Mikel stepped back a few more feet, wary of Cadmus' scythe as he circled around to his friend's left, the Frost Lord having taken up a position near the center of the Circle. Before he attacked again, Mikel wanted the sun streaming into Cadmus' eyes, the glare worse coming off the ice and snow.

"Why wouldn't I be?" Mikel asked. He frowned again at his friend's comment. What was Cadmus implying? It seemed as if the Frost Lord wanted to say something, but he wanted Mikel to say it first.

"Because I would think that after all that has happened circumstances between the two of you have changed."

"How so?" They had. Mikel couldn't deny that. How could they not after what had conspired on the Crux?

But he didn't need to admit that to Cadmus. If he did, he'd never hear the end of it. When Mikel felt the heat of the sun on the back of his neck and saw Cadmus squint, he rushed forward, slashing toward the Giant's hip.

The Frost Lord moved faster than someone his size should be able to. Pivoting, the Giant took one big step backward. Then he ducked, allowing Mikel's blade to cut through the air above him.

Cadmus was about to push himself back up, wanting to target Mikel's vulnerable back leg, sensing that his victory was close, when he stopped abruptly. Or rather the touch of cold steel at his throat stopped him.

The Frost Lord growled. Furious. Though not at Mikel. Rather at himself. He had fallen for Mikel's feint, not even seeing his friend pull the dagger from the sheath at his hip.

"You saved her life, Mikel," Cadmus rumbled, accepting his friend's hand as he regained his feet. Sighing. Disappointed once again. The same result as every other time he brought his friend here.

Cadmus had yet to defeat Mikel in a combat. More than frustrating. And that was the reason he preferred to train with Mikel on his own.

Nevertheless, a good result in his opinion. His failure helped to keep him humble, and it meant that he had a goal to strive for the next time the two stepped into the Circle.

"And because of that you believe that she's in my debt?" Mikel asked in a soft chuckle. He sheathed his dagger, sword still in his hand. "I doubt the illustrious Queen of the Crux sees it that way. She's been quite clear about what her expectations are with respect to my business dealings. She's made quite a few pronouncements, in fact, about what I'm supposed to do and what I'm not allowed to do. Not even a conversation. Simply our great and august Queen of the Crux issuing a host of rules and requirements that are supposed to define the link between the Crown and the King of the Underworld."

"Do you intend to follow these rules?"

Mikel didn't even need to think about it. "Of course not. There'd be no fun in that. Besides, I have a reputation to maintain."

Cadmus laughed, expecting just such a response. "You can't really blame her. She feels the need to exercise her authority. To solidify her position as quickly as she can because she does not want to rely on you to hold her throne. It only makes sense."

"Agreed," Mikel replied with a nod, "so I'm not taking issue with her motivation. I'm taking issue with her constant stream of orders. You would think that she would demonstrate at least a modicum of delicacy with respect to her approach."

Cadmus frowned again, this time his expression more a question. "You do understand that she doesn't just see you as the King of the Underworld, right?"

Now it was Mikel's turn to frown. "Why would she see me as anything else? That's what I am. What little interaction we've had since she ascended to the throne of the Crux has been focused solely on how she expects the City Above to interact with the City Below. As I said, what I am and am not permitted to do. All of it is more than just a little aggravating because it doesn't have to be this way between us."

"That's all that's been happening between you two?" Cadmus prompted with a raised eyebrow. He was certain that Mikel's unsaid complaint only partially had to do with the business he had with the Queen and the role he played behind the throne.

Mikel had a ready reply, though he didn't offer it. Instead, he thought about what his friend was implying. Had his relationship with Celindria Dengannon changed since he helped her claim the throne after her father's murder?

It was Cadmus' turn to chuckle. "You see it now, don't you?"

"I don't know what I see," Mikel grumbled, feeling the need

to be stubborn at least for a little while longer. Not yet ready to acknowledge what Cadmus was hinting at.

"You do know. You just don't want to put it into words. If you do then it becomes real."

Drin had assumed the throne just a month past, and in that time Mikel had been busy. Not only with his own many businesses and dealings, but also in helping the Queen with some tasks best left to his particular expertise.

Mikel's expression changed then. Becoming harder. His frown solidifying and threatening to become a permanent fixture on his brow.

"You don't like it when I'm right, do you?" Cadmus asked, having little trouble reading his friend.

"In this case, no," Mikel growled, realizing how his friend trapped him. Nevertheless, he didn't want to give Cadmus all the satisfaction that he was seeking. "Although in truth I'm more surprised since you're so rarely right."

The Frost Lord's eyes tightened. Flashing once. Then he shook his head. "Always pushing, even when you know better."

"One of my better and more appreciated traits," Mikel replied, giving his friend a smile that did little to improve his rough appearance.

Cadmus snorted, then admitted the truth. "At certain times, yes it is."

"I've enjoyed my start to the day, Cadmus, but weapons training out in the middle of nowhere and then you grilling me about my connection to the Queen," Mikel refusing to use the word *relationship*, "wasn't the only reason, the primary reason in fact, that you asked me to join you here today."

Mikel motioned with his free hand at their surroundings. The snow-capped peaks that separated the Frozen Waste from the Kingdom of the Crux were several leagues to the east. The Icehold, Cadmus' capital, was a few miles to the west. Besides the Maze that the Giants had carved out of the ice and snow on this frigid plain there was little to see other than the drifting white that danced and swirled at the whim of the gusty wind.

And there was little to feel other than a bone-breaking cold. Although Mikel was grateful that he avoided the worst of the chill thanks to the clothes Julia had gifted to him several years before, Cadmus' daughter displaying a somewhat unsettling interest in him.

Made of the unique material that the Giants of the Rime wore, though in a smaller size, the thin layers allowed Mikel to conserve his heat and, since he didn't need to wear a heavy parka – several heavy parkas when the worst of the cold came during the darkest nights of the winter, not limiting his movement in any way. Best of all, the mix of white, blue, grey, and random specks of black allowed him to blend into the colors of the Frozen Waste. It served as a natural camouflage if he didn't move hastily.

Cadmus smiled. His bright blue eyes sparked as he ran a hand through his long white hair that resembled icicles. "You need to learn more about the scimitar. You also need to practice using the weapon."

"That's why we're really out here?" Mikel nodded knowingly. He had assumed as much. In fact, he hadn't expected Cadmus to take so long before inviting him into the Frozen Waste.

And that was a key point. Only those invited into the bleak, wintry landscape were permitted to enter. To do so without an invitation ensured a quick death. For the Giants of the Rime had only one punishment for intruders.

Cadmus nodded. "In large part, yes. I did want to put you through your paces, although it seems the opposite occurred. You put me through mine."

"I was happy to help in that regard."

"I bet you were," Cadmus confirmed, ignoring the grin Mikel gave him that was designed to get under his skin.

"Moving beyond that, you need to learn how to partner with the Blade of Light."

"Partner?" Mikel had been hired to steal the scimitar from the very depths of the Citadel.

And he had.

But he had refused to relinquish it the instant his fingers touched the steel.

Mikel never broke a contract. And he didn't view holding back the ancient weapon from the person who hired him as doing that. Because the woman never revealed prior to their agreement that she was a Dark Magus. He found that out on his own, and to his way of thinking that voided the deal.

He didn't do business with people touched by the Curse.

Ever.

He understood the cost of doing so.

Cadmus nodded. "Partner."

Thinking about what his friend was telling him, partner made sense to Mikel. The few times that he had used the power contained within the Blade of Light, he hadn't demanded it from the ancient weapon. Rather the blade crafted by the Giants of the Rime had gifted him the potent energy. As if they had come to a meeting of the minds.

Perhaps that was the trick. Just like any good business deal, two parties coming together based on mutual interest or need.

"The blade and I work together," Mikel mused. "Based on the little experience I have, it's strange. It's almost as if it has a consciousness all on its own."

"Exactly," Cadmus confirmed. "In fact, some believe that the Blade of Light does have a consciousness just as you said."

"But you don't know?" That was a line of thought that piqued Mikel's interest. It would make learning the properties of the ancient weapon much easier.

Cadmus shrugged, shaking his head sadly. "We have lost a great deal of knowledge over the centuries, in large part because of the War of the Brothers. My father was a historian of sorts, and even he couldn't tell me much about the Blade or many of the other artifacts that my Giants shaped and infused with the Talent millennia ago."

Mikel snorted. "So what you're saying is that I'm on my own. There's not a lot of guidance you can give me other than the fact that the Blade is designed to connect with the Bearer and form a partnership of some type. And because you're not sure how it's supposed to work or what the results might be if I try to do as you suggest, you brought me out here where I couldn't hurt anyone and I could cause the least amount of damage if I made a mistake while you put me to the test."

Cadmus smiled broadly. "Exactly."

"Not really a recipe for building my confidence. You do realize that, don't you?"

Cadmus shrugged. "I've never known you as one who has lacked confidence."

"I'll take that as a compliment."

"If you must," Cadmus allowed. Then the Frost Lord became serious. "I didn't bring you out here to play games. I don't know all there is to know about the Blade of Light, but I know enough. The artifact has selected you. Why? I don't know. But when a weapon crafted with the Light and the Talent chooses you, it is not something to discount or ignore. Until you learn how to work with the Blade of Light, you're a threat to yourself and anyone around you."

Several pointed comments immediately came to mind. Mikel kept them to himself. Cadmus was trying to help him. At least he thought he was. "Not very comforting."

"It wasn't meant to be, Steelheart." Cadmus clapped his friend on the back, though not so hard as to knock him to the ground. "We still have a few hours before we need to head back. Let's begin. Let's see what you can do with that ancient blade that doesn't involve you swatting me with it."

2

POKING AT SHADOWS

Finn sat on the terrace that extended along the top floor of the abandoned building he had claimed as his personal residence. The seawall was just below. The clash of the four rivers meeting at the Crux a muted roar, the whitewater of the Churn surging and flowing in a rhythm all its own and granting the Magus a welcome, comforting familiarity.

At his age, he preferred the routine. He didn't like surprises.

Although there was one surprise that made him smile right then.

He didn't know where Mikel had found her, but Natalya truly was an uncut diamond.

Every time he trained her in the use of the Talent, he learned something new about her.

Still rough around the edges, his efforts to polish her skill were working. Of course, it helped that she was a fast learner and more determined than most.

Driven.

Committed.

And perhaps most important of all, she hated to fail.

He couldn't have asked for a better student.

He just needed to make sure she understood that there were certain paths to be avoided, no matter how curious or confident she might be. Paths that led only to darkness and worse.

Finn grimaced. Distracted from his thoughts. The pain that shot down his spine and then out into his extremities much too familiar and much too frequent.

In this one respect, he would have liked to get away from his routine. The constant of the agony that ravaged his body.

Unfortunately, there was little that he could do other than suffer through it. Punishment for his mistakes. And a penalty he gladly paid, understanding the cost of surrendering to what was consuming him.

The Magus scowled, forgetting his pain if only for a moment as he sensed the power that was approaching. His best student ...

He turned around slowly, identifying the tainted presence who had joined him and not happy about the interruption.

"Why are you here, Assindra?" Just as always the woman's appearance disoriented him. Her hair leaning toward black flashed in the light, giving her a glow that was at odds with her true self. Her nature colder and more tumultuous than the waters of the Churn buttressed by a cunning and greed that mirrored the darkness lurking within the Magus.

"The thief escaped me, Finnelaus. That was not part of the agreement."

Finn snorted. "The only thing I promised you was information. How to contact your thief. No more than that."

Assindra took a step closer, then stopped when she realized that Finnelaus had taken hold of the Talent. He was weaker than the last time she had visited him. But still she knew that he would be a formidable and treacherous opponent if she pushed him too far, and she wasn't quite ready for that clash. Not with more important matters preying upon her mind.

"The King of the Underworld refused to hand over the artifact he acquired for me. You never told me that could be a possibility. You never told me that I needed to worry about him."

"Good for Mikel," Finn replied with a broad smile, obviously pleased. "Then again, not altogether surprising. I told you that he could be difficult at the best of times."

"He stole from me, Finnelaus." Assindra's eyes flashed dangerously, the power within her awakening, desiring to be set free. The Dark Magus required a target for her fury.

"He stole for you. No more. No less. That's how he sees it."

"I will have that artifact," Assindra promised.

"And all you need to do to make that happen is take it from the King of the Underworld." Finn offered his former student a grin that he was certain would aggravate her even more than she already was. Just as he intended. What better way to go to the other side than challenging the Magus responsible for his affliction. "Good luck with that."

"You don't think I can?" Her tone was menacing. Her preferred method of communication when events weren't working out as she wished.

"I think you didn't listen to what I told you. I think you underestimated Mikel. And because of that I think that you might have missed your chance."

Assindra didn't reply right away, thinking about what the Magus said. "You don't think that he can actually ..."

Finn shook his head. "No. He doesn't have the ability despite his heritage. But he is uniquely qualified to be a constant burr under your saddle. Therefore, you antagonize him at your own risk. I can tell you that from experience."

"Your latest advice is proving to be just as helpful as all the other advice you gave me," Assindra said tartly.

"I answered all your questions, Assindra. I told you all I knew about him. And just as I said, he was the right thief to steal the artifact. The fact that he didn't actually give it to you ..." Finn shrugged his bent shoulders, the movement suggesting that he had no control over Mikel's actions. He had done as asked and felt no compunction to do any more. Nor would he. His loyalty stronger to Mikel than to his former student.

Assindra was about to offer the Magus a sharp reply when her expression turned shrewd. She studied Finnelaus for a time. Once one of the strongest of the Order of the Magii. Now failing. Weakening. No more than a shadow of his former self thanks to the Curse burrowing through him. "It's almost like you wanted the thief to gain the Blade of Light."

"Why would I want that?" Finn snorted in disbelief. Then he coughed. Bent at the waist, he needed several seconds to recover once the fit passed. "You're poking at shadows, Assindra."

"Perhaps. Perhaps not." The Dark Magus gave Finn a devilish smile. "How are you feeling, Finnelaus? Have you accepted that the end is near? All because of your stubbornness and lack of vision."

"I will never accept it, Assindra. Never."

"Then more's the pity," she tsked. "So much offered. So much to be gained. If you weren't such a stubborn fool."

Finn ignored the taunt. He was angry. Not with Assindra. Rather with himself. Because he was the one to blame for his affliction. His arrogance and foolishness getting in the way of his reason. "You didn't come here just to irritate me, Assindra, or berate me for your own failure. What do you want?"

For once, Assindra offered an honest response, done with picking at his scabs. "Testing you, Finnelaus. Wanting to see if you betrayed me in any way."

"You were my greatest success, Assindra," Finn murmured softly, ignoring her assertion. "Also my greatest failure."

"Come now, Finnelaus. This isn't like you. Blaming me for your own frailties."

"I gave you what you wanted, Assindra. Your failure to get what you believe you deserve is your problem. Not mine."

"I see it differently," Assindra challenged, her blue eyes turning icy in a heartbeat as a black mist began to drift out from her fingertips.

Finn didn't care. "Kill me now, Assindra. It will cut short the inevitable, so I certainly won't complain."

A quiet descended between the two Magii. Both staring at one another like the gladiators of old who used fight in the Colosseum in Caledonia.

"No, I don't think I will," she said finally, giving a good bit of thought to her favorite instructor's suggestion. "Not today. I will allow you to enjoy your suffering for a little while longer. Besides, the artifact will be mine soon enough. And I have little doubt that you will experience even greater pain than you are now when the thief is no more."

Finn couldn't maintain his stoic composure any longer. Hearing the threat and promise in the Dark Magus' words. "What did you do, Assindra?"

3

NOT JUST STEEL

S teelheart.

His Caledonii name translated to the common tongue. One that Mikel rarely used.

Instead he employed Stahlherz to eliminate any potential questions and issues, and likely discrimination, when he was within the Realms, which was most of the time.

For the Giants of the Rime, Mikel's last name meant a great deal more.

Mikel smiled. "Strange, don't you think, that few in all the Realms view someone like me as an equal other than the Giants of the Rime."

"Not strange at all considering the history of the Caledonii," Cadmus rumbled, "and how the people of the Realms view us."

Mikel couldn't dispute his friend's logic. The Giants of the Rime were tolerated because they demonstrated a craftsmanship that couldn't be matched by anyone else within the Realms, whether weapons, glasswork, or a host of other items. If it could be crafted in a forge, the Giants shaped it, and they did it better than anyone else.

That and the fact that the Giants rarely strayed from the

Frozen Waste and their other sanctuaries, ensuring that the people of the Realms had little cause to interact with them directly. Their keeping to themselves and rarely leaving their homeland made the rulers of the Rime more ephemeral than real. So though they might not care for the Giants themselves, those with means cared for their products.

The same could not be said for the Caledonii. One of the original twelve tribes to settle the Realms, for a time they were revered. Every Caledonii was born with the Talent, and they used their natural magic to help make the world what it was.

Yet with that power came a growing fear and envy among those who could not exercise the secrets of the natural world, that bleak and fearful perspective exacerbated when some few of the Caledonii strayed to the Curse.

A natural failing.

A human failing.

Unavoidable most would say.

Nevertheless, it was what the people of the Realms remembered first and most often when they thought of the Caledonii. The terrible tragedies that came about because of those few Caledonii seduced by the Curse.

That bias became ingrained within the Realms, turning those who had once been heroes for their good works into pariahs. Thereby keeping most of the Caledonii to their handful of remaining mountain enclaves, unwilling to risk the hatred the people of the Realms were more than happy to release upon them when presented with the opportunity.

Thus, Mikel's desire to keep his heritage hidden. He didn't want to deal with the possible repercussions, particularly since he was the only Caledonii who could not touch the Talent. That failing left him vulnerable in a way that the rest of his people weren't.

"Not surprising when most in the Realms view the Caledonii through the lenses of fear or envy," Mikel admitted. "Nevertheless, there's no reason to spend our time on topics that serve only to depress. I can see by the spark in your eye that you're desperate to share a lesson with me."

"It's that obvious?" Cadmus asked.

"I've known you for a long time, Frost Lord. Besides, I always wondered why you were named the leader of the Giants of the Rime. Not that you don't deserve the position and rule well. It's just that there are times when it seems like your true calling is that of a teacher."

"In that ..." Cadmus shrugged. "There are times when I agree with you. But as you know from experience, we cannot always choose our fate. We must ..."

"Learn how to live with it." Mikel chuckled, shaking his head slowly from side to side. "One of your first lessons. I remember."

"And relevant to what we discuss now, because I believe fate had a hand in the burden you now bear."

"I require more clarity, Cadmus. I'm not in the mood for sussing out your meaning."

"I've been thinking about why the Blade selected you."

"Any conclusions?"

"Just one. I believe the Blade of Light chose you because you are Caledonii."

"Really? Why? I can't use the Talent. That makes me less than Caledonii. That's why I'm an outcast."

"Perhaps in the eyes of your tribe," Cadmus admitted, "though perhaps not through the perception of the essence used to craft the artifact. Perhaps it's because you are Caledonii and you can't touch the Talent on your own that the Blade chose you."

Mikel scowled, not knowing what to make of his friend's theory. "Your hypothesis is resting on very thin ice."

"Perhaps. Perhaps not." Cadmus said it with a confidence that was lacking in Mikel.

"You'll need to explain."

Reaching the end of the bridge, Cadmus waited for Mikel to pass him by before swinging the gate closed. With the touch of his hand, ice formed around the bars, locking them until another of Cadmus' brethren ventured out to the Maze for training.

One of the abilities unique to the Giants of the Rime. Shaping the landscape – ice, snow, water, though not rock – with just a touch and a thought. The strength and skill of the craft dependent on the innate potency within each Giant.

Then they began the long hike across the wintry plateau back toward the Icehold, Cadmus' seat of power. Winding their way through the many crevices the Giants carved out from beneath the surface of the plain that allowed the sun to stream in but kept out the howling wind that swept across the icy tundra.

"I will. Do you have the necessary patience?"

Mikel snorted at that as he and his friend navigated the paths reserved for the Giants who ruled this land. The trail was never straight, rather always curling or twisting. The crafters worked with the ice and snow while listening to the rock, taking from the various natural materials what they gifted. The Giants' patience and understanding merged with a skill that created beautiful walkways. Each one unique.

The last one was a twisting staircase made of ice as clear as glass that was no thicker than a piece of paper yet stronger than stone. Next a passageway curled to the left and right then back again, disappearing within a tunnel before descending into an icy chute that Mikel and Cadmus could traverse only because of the spikes on their boots.

Another wondrous sight always just a little farther along the trail. The one coming up a huge though delicate ice sculpture that resembled an overlarge flower through which they needed to turn sideways to pass. Its petals almost as thin as a hair and sharper than a blade.

"You seem to be suggesting that I don't."

"You are not always known for your patience, my friend," Cadmus chuckled.

"I'm wounded," Mikel replied, his emotion clearly feigned.

"No you're not."

"I'm not," Mikel agreed with a quiet laugh. "I can be patient so long as you don't jump into one of your longwinded explanations that takes up most of the afternoon."

"I'll try to contain myself," Cadmus promised, not rising to the bait Mikel threw his way.

"Then I'll listen and withhold my judgment until the end."

"Very kind of you," Cadmus muttered. With a spark of pleasure in his eye, he dove into his theory, seeking to make the most of this opportunity since he so rarely had the chance to teach these days with all that was required of him as the King of the Rime. "You are familiar with how my Giants shape the weapons and tools that the Magii have requested from us over the millennia."

Mikel nodded. "I am. You know that."

"I do. Now stop interrupting. That wasn't a question."

"I'm sorry, it seemed like a question," Mikel apologized, although clearly he wasn't.

"No, you're not." Before Mikel could dispute his claim, Cadmus continued. "You have revealed a skill working in the forge that no one else but a Giant of the Rime has ever demonstrated."

"That's very kind of you. Thank you."

"Mikel." Cadmus was not amused. He did not view this conversation as a give and take despite his statements sounding much like queries.

"Sorry, I just wanted to note my appreciation."

Cadmus started again, taking a deep breath first. He refused to allow his friend to knock him off track. "As I was saying, you have demonstrated a unique skill in shaping the materials that are used to craft a weapon of power. A weapon that can be infused with the Talent just as the Magii require. Perhaps not with the dexterity of a Giant of the Rime, but close to it."

Catching Cadmus' warning glance, Mikel held up both hands, not saying a word although he was tempted.

"Steel is only one part of that process," the Giant continued. "The Magus will add the power of nature at the end. And as you know there is another ingredient that is absolutely essential. An ingredient that can only be incorporated in a Giant's forge."

"Light."

"Exactly so," Cadmus smiled. He nodded with satisfaction, unbothered by Mikel's interruption. "Not just any light as you know. Light intensified ten thousand-fold by the special mirrors Giant smiths employ in their work."

Cadmus didn't feel the need to say much more about that crucial invention. It had taken just a single lesson before Mikel had mastered that unique skill. Truly remarkable for one who was not a Giant of the Rime. Though Cadmus felt no need to offer that compliment and give his friend the chance to interrupt again.

"Weaving the Light into the steel. Making the two one. That's what allows us to craft weapons and other artifacts that can withstand the demands that the natural energy of the world makes upon these essential items. As an example, when it comes to a blade like the one scabbarded across your back, it is with the Light that we create an edge that can never be blunted. We create a substance that is more than just matter. In fact, whatever we create takes on a life all its own."

"Wait a second." Mikel held up his hands again. "You seem to be implying that Giant-made weapons that are used by the

Magii are more than just weapons. You make it sound almost as if they're alive. That they have a spirit unto themselves."

"I'm more than just implying it, Mikel," Cadmus replied, not minding this interruption because it would help him get to his point that much faster. "I am stating it for a fact. Light and steel shaped into a new material. Because of that, the weapons we make, such as the sword on your back, are more than weapons. They are receptacles as well. Repositories. Yet even that does not give them their proper due."

"You're not just talking about the Talent now, are you?"

"I'm not," Cadmus confirmed, certain that his friend already had made the jump. "The Talent is added well after we have done our work."

"When you say repository, it's not just for the Talent. It's for the Light as well."

Cadmus smiled broadly. "Correct, because the Light that I speak of is power just like the Talent or the Curse. In fact, stronger than the Talent when employed in a certain way with precision. Yet that skill is rare. The last Giant capable of making use of the Light much as a Magus does the Talent went to the other side centuries ago."

Cadmus' silence of a few seconds revealed his secret.

"Your father." Mikel nodded. He should have assumed as much. "I am sorry, my friend, to bring up a memory like that one."

"There is no need to apologize. The memory of my father who ruled before me is not all of loss. Have no fear."

Mikel recalled some of the story. Not all.

The War of the Brothers.

Cadmus' father was challenged for the title of Frost Lord by his younger power-hungry brother. The conflict almost destroyed the masters of the Frozen Waste. To prevent that fate from befalling them, Cadmus' father Karolingan sacrificed himself to ensure that the Giants of the Rime remained free from the touch of the Curse. "Why so few Giants with the skill your father displayed?"

"An excellent question," Cadmus replied as he and Mikel hiked up a path that curled to the left then dropped down precipitously on steps made for Giants, Mikel jumping down from one to the next rather than walking. "Unfortunately, I don't have an answer. It is a question that has plagued us since my father's passing."

"You do have a theory, though."

Cadmus smiled. "Why do you say that?"

"Because you always have a theory."

"You know me too well."

"Maybe I do," Mikel admitted.

"You say that as if it's a bad thing," Cadmus replied, a hint of offense in his voice.

"You didn't let me finish, Cadmus. Maybe I do know you too well. But you know me too well also. As a result, we are more than friends."

Cadmus understood and he agreed. "Brothers."

Mikel nodded, acknowledging the importance of their shared belief. "Now what is your theory? Why so few Giants with the skill your father demonstrated?"

"My father believed that it went to the very heart of the individual."

"Meaning?"

"Character," Cadmus explained. "My father believed that the ability to make use of the Light, to employ it as a Magus might the Talent, depended upon the Giant's character."

Mikel thought about that, mulling the proposed concept. "That seems a bit farfetched."

"How so?"

"The Giants are known for their character. Their forthrightness. Their honesty. That would suggest more of you should have the skill your father had."

"Maybe. Then again ..." Cadmus shook his head sadly. "Remember, the War of the Brothers lasted for more than a decade. Many atrocities were committed. Most by my uncle and those loyal to him. Even so, my father's side was not blameless. All who fought in that conflict were tarnished in a way that still remains a burden upon us to this day."

"You believe that the stain of that civil war has stayed with you for more than five centuries?"

Cadmus shrugged. "Who can say? I do believe that the character of the individual carrying the weapon you have is essential to its use."

"Then why would you also believe that the scimitar picked me? You know what I am."

"I do," Cadmus replied. "The blade does as well."

"Exactly. So that fact tears your theory to shreds."

"Not necessarily."

"Not necessarily?" Mikel's expression became one of disbelief tinted with challenge.

"The blade determines the individual's character. The blade makes the judgment. Likely based on a standard that we cannot comprehend."

"I feel like you're grasping at snowflakes, Cadmus."

"And perhaps I am. However, I am basing my theory not only on what my father told me and what I have learned on my own since taking the throne of the Rime, but also on what the Magii who have come to the Frozen Waste have told me."

"So you believe that the Blade has picked me because it sees something in me that no one else can?" Mikel's distrust for that conjecture was quite apparent.

"I do, because I have no other reason to explain the selection. The Blade of Light has never left the grasp of a Giant. Ever. Until now. Until you claimed it."

"Until I stole it," Mikel corrected.

"Until you retrieved it."

Mikel had a few pointed comments to offer his friend. He kept them to himself instead, finding the entire conversation disorienting. Worrisome as well, because he had no facts with which to discount Cadmus' argument. "Now you're just playing with words."

"Perhaps," Cadmus admitted. "And perhaps not. Why do you think we call you Steelheart?"

"Because it's my name in Caledonii."

Cadmus grunted. He had walked right into that. "No one in the Rime knew that. Not until you told me after I bestowed the name upon you."

"Just a quirk of fate, my friend."

"Doubtful. I named you Steelheart because of your integrity. You have kept faith with us always even at great cost to yourself."

"I just like to make sure that our deals are fair. And I keep my word." That was all that Mikel was willing to say on the matter. He believed those were two of the keys to his success, in business and in life. "Often that's all I have."

"You do not give yourself credit where credit is due," Cadmus countered. "Much like the Giants of the Rime, for you, honor comes before all else. That is a rare trait in the Realms."

"I still believe that you're searching for something that isn't there."

"You simply don't want to admit to the possibility, Steelheart. But you need to. Ever since the Giants of the Rime came to the Frozen Waste – more than three thousand years and counting -- only a Giant has been able to shape steel with the Light. Until you. Only a Giant has claimed the Blade of Light. Until you. The Blade itself confirmed the truth of its selection in a multitude of ways. The most obvious how it sized itself perfectly solely for you."

Mikel frowned. He had no good argument to offer. Because it was true. He didn't know why. He couldn't explain it. But when he stepped into Scipio's forge for the first time, he felt as if he had come home. It was as if he belonged there.

He had spent several weeks in the fire, heat, steam, and ash. Practicing. Learning. Mastering. And by the end of his time there, he crafted with the Light better than any of the smiths working there except perhaps for Scipio himself, a master with more than a century of experience.

And then when his fingers first touched the hilt ...

Aggravated that he had no good rebuttal to Cadmus' theory, Mikel fell back on a response that sounded flimsy even in his own ears. "Despite all that you say, Cadmus, we cannot ignore the fact that I'm a thief."

"We can't. You're right. You are a thief." Cadmus leaned down as if he was sharing a secret with Mikel. "Yet even so you follow a code that is unique. It is obvious in all that you do. It is obvious in how you approach the world. So I would argue that you are much more than just a thief."

"Fine. Let's say you're right, except for the part that I'm more than a thief." Mikel was feeling distinctly uncomfortable. Cadmus' words were hitting too close to home. "If I am who you say I am, if I'm the one the Blade has selected despite not being a Giant, how am I supposed to partner with it if I don't understand how to do that?"

Mikel waited as he and Cadmus hiked through a tunnel carved from the tundra, the passageway perfectly smooth, the surface covered in a frosty sheen that dazzled at the touch of the light streaming through the few narrow slits above them.

Not only was he curious about how Cadmus was going to respond, but he was searching for any piece of information held close by the Giants that could aid him. Because Mikel didn't understand how he could use the Blade. Why the Blade would even select him. He had no skill in the Talent, a rare and disappointing truth that ate at his very identity. Nonetheless, a truth that couldn't be ignored.

"Some things we are not meant to understand," Cadmus intoned in as wise a voice as he could manage.

Mikel stared at him. Then he snorted out a disappointed laugh. "You're full of it, aren't you? You don't know how to do it."

"I do know. I was just having a little fun with you."

"Now isn't the time to have fun."

"You can have fun at my expense, but I can't have fun at yours? You don't need to be so serious." Cadmus stopped, he and Mikel reaching the end of the tunnel. From there, it was a journey of a little more than a quarter mile to the covered and hidden pass that would lead them through the knolls to the west and then to the Icehold. First, though, they would need to make their way along the far edge of the Barrows. "You are Caledonii, and you're right. It is more than rare to be Caledonii and not be able to use the Talent. Unheard of, in fact. Totally unthinkable."

"You're not making me feel any better," Mikel grunted as he took in the broad white expanse that waited before them.

The plateau appeared to be perfectly flat. It wasn't. It was simply a trick of the light. A few hundred yards farther on they would dip down among the snow-covered mounds.

"Mikel, I understand, at least in part, what it has meant for you to be Caledonii but not Caledonii. I am simply suggesting that perhaps there is a reason why. Perhaps there is a reason that you are the rarest of the rare."

"That's what you believe? Because from my perspective it seems like you're still grasping at snowflakes."

"It doesn't matter what I believe. What matters is that the Blade of Light believes."

"What do you mean?"

"The Dark Magus sent you after the weapon. Did she tell you what it was that you were seeking?"

"Just an old scimitar that had some value to her."

Cadmus grunted. "Did she tell you that if the Blade did not

believe you worthy to wield it, you would die at the first touch of flesh to steel?"

"That part must have slipped her mind," Mikel growled, disliking that uncomfortable revelation.

"Maybe it did or maybe she didn't know. You think that what I have told you so far is supposition. I have little in the way of fact to support my theory. I won't argue with you about that. But you can't argue that the Giants of the Rime don't know a great deal about the Blade of Light. Most of what we know lost to the passing centuries. One truth we do know, however, is that anyone who is unworthy who touches the Blade dies. Painfully. Quickly. Always. Without exception."

Mikel's frown deepened. "Why didn't you tell me that at the beginning?"

"I was getting to it, but we got off on a few tangents."

"Really? That's your excuse?"

Cadmus ignored the barb, acknowledging that his friend was irritated because he was having a harder and harder time explaining away what he couldn't explain away. "You touched the Blade. You didn't die. You even used it. Somehow. Without even knowing how. Not well, mind you. Still, you formed some kind of connection with the Blade of Light that worked. That tells me one indisputable fact."

"And what would that be?" Mikel was afraid to ask, but he couldn't help himself, understanding that's what Cadmus wanted.

"You're the catalyst the Blade requires."

"The catalyst?" Mikel didn't understand.

"Yes, the link to the power of the natural world. You can't draw on it yourself. You were not born with that ability. But linking with the Blade links the Blade to the power of the natural world. It links you to the power of the natural world."

"It allows me to make use of the Talent?" That possibility

pleased him like nothing else ever could, years of self-doubt potentially lifted.

"A power more ancient than that."

"Older than the Talent?" Then Mikel got it, reviewing all that Cadmus had revealed as they hiked back from the Maze. "The Light."

"Precisely," Cadmus nodded, pleased that they had reached this point in the lesson so quickly. He had thought Mikel would prove more difficult than he had been. "There is a power in the Light. And from what I have learned, both in my studies and from quite a few Magii, there is a strong belief that the Talent comes from the Light. The Light an older and more potent force."

"So similar but different, the Talent and the Light."

"Yes, the theory strengthened because the principles of using both essences are the same. Or so my father said before he died fighting my uncle."

"That would mean the same concerns apply as well."

Cadmus confirmed Mikel's conclusion with a nod. "You will need to be careful. Because the Blade of Light does not see distinctions. It sees only power. Energy. The soul of the natural world. That is what it draws upon. That is what you draw upon now that the Blade has bonded with you. Therefore, intention is key."

"With great power comes great responsibility," Mikel quoted, recalling one of the strictures stated by the Kaisari, a key lesson in the first book he gave Nat to read.

"Something like that," Cadmus confirmed.

Mikel pulled the Blade of Light from the scabbard on his back, taking a few seconds to study the scimitar.

It looked like any other blade. Clearly old. Clearly made by the Giants. Yet he sensed the power within. The ... possibility. "How much of this power, the Light, can I harness?"

"I don't know. You will need to discover that on your own."

"And how am I supposed to ... partner with the Blade of Light?" Mikel didn't quite understand how to describe what would be required of him.

"That I can answer."

"Finally some clarity." Mikel stared at Cadmus expectantly. Waiting.

"Right, sorry," Cadmus chuckled. He was distracted for a moment. He thought he glimpsed a flash of movement across the top of one of the barrows a half mile distant. There then gone just as quickly. "You already know how."

"Cadmus ..."

"Think of what you did while working in the forge. Think of how you fused the Light with the steel."

Mikel took his friend's advice, remembering that experience as if it had occurred only yesterday. None of the Giants in the forge wanted him there. They didn't understand how a human could do what they did and were insulted that he would even attempt to do what only they could. Until they saw the quality of his work.

Scipio had allowed him to stay. The Giants' Master Crafter saw some aspect in him that no one else did.

Scipio hadn't offered him any advice after Mikel explored the forge, taking note of how the Giant smiths used the various mirrors to redirect the sunlight streaming through the large hole in the center of the roof that was never covered even in the worst weather. That sunlight reflected by dozens of mirrors, each one of a different quality and design, created different beams of energy that the smiths manipulated as they worked the steel.

Then he had taken up a position at a forge at the very back. Scipio tasked him with crafting the scythe that Cadmus now claimed as his own.

Mikel had some experience as a smith, learning the trade when he was a boy. But what he did then was something else entirely. The mirrors complicated his task. Not because of the need for their use. Rather because of the almost innumerable possibilities they opened to him. The infinite options available. So many that it was almost impossible to begin.

Until he decided that rather than trying to control the process he needed to surrender to the process. He needed to allow the steel and the Light to guide him. Not the other way around.

Doing so had felt incredibly uncomfortable when he began his work. That sensation fled swiftly. After an hour, it felt right.

He took the same approach now. Closing his eyes, he concentrated on the scimitar he had pulled from the scabbard across his back and held loosely in his hand.

He allowed his mind to drift.

His thoughts taking him where they would.

Seeing nothing in his mind's eye except for the Blade.

The steel that glowed even in the sunlight.

The steel that was more than steel.

The steel that was also Light.

The steel that was greater than what it appeared to be.

Mikel smiled. He sensed it then. The connection. The link between him and the ancient weapon.

The remarkable reservoir of power contained within the Blade of Light that waited for him if he dared to reach out and dip his fingers into the surging magic.

Then he realized that he wasn't just looking at the Blade through his own eyes. There were others there with him. The consciousnesses of all the Giants who had once had the honor of wielding the Blade of Light.

A dozen all told.

The artifact thousands of years old.

Knute Frost Lord, father of Karolingan, the last. A source of knowledge that Mikel could draw from.

And he did.

He learned how they had worked with the Blade of Light.

How they manipulated the Light.

He discovered that the Light was heat. Energy. Fire. And so much more. Faith. Belief. Hope. Resolve.

Blinding.

Illuminating.

He discovered what the Light offered him.

The ability to destroy. To burn.

The ability to create. To build. To heal.

He learned what the previous Bearers of the Blade had accomplished.

How they had failed.

The dangers that he needed to be wary of.

Mikel understood then.

What it meant to partner with the Blade of Light.

The weapon had a sentience all its own, that consciousness crafted by all those who had been selected by the Blade to wield it.

He added his consciousness to the mix. Or rather the Blade reached out and linked to his.

A meeting of the minds.

A meeting of purpose.

A connection formed in just a heartbeat.

One that could only be broken in death, and then only partially.

He learned as well that he could only ask so much of the Blade. That to ask it to do certain things would go against the artifact's very essence and the Light used to create it.

Then, at the request of the Blade, Mikel did the hardest thing that he could possibly do.

He let go.

He gave himself to the Giant-crafted weapon. Just as the Blade gave itself to him.

A marriage of sorts.

A bond.

A contract.

A promise.

Opening his eyes, the scimitar glowed with an intensity that Mikel had never imagined possible. That energy pulsed. Expanded. Enveloped him until Cadmus was forced to turn away.

The white light blindingly bright, Cadmus lost sight of his friend. Impressed by what Mikel had accomplished so quickly. Worried as well. He understood what Mikel's success meant even if his friend had yet to do so. A topic they had not discussed but would need to. And soon.

Then just as quickly as Mikel disappeared, the light surrounding him flared and dimmed. The Blade glowed softly just as it always did when released from its scabbard.

Because Mikel realized as he and the Blade got to know one another that the connection between them was more than that.

It was also a means of communication.

A way to share.

The Light offered Mikel a new perspective on the world around him. Sharper. Almost painfully so.

Nevertheless, he was grateful for what the Light granted him.

Thanks to that gift, Mikel sensed that all wasn't as it should be. His skin prickled as he saw what he couldn't see before.

Releasing his hold on the energy that had been coursing through him, Mikel turned to Cadmus. The Giant was about to congratulate him on his success. He didn't after taking in the dark expression on Mikel's face.

"What is the matter, Steelheart?"

"We're not alone."

4

DANGEROUS TRACKS

"What is it?" Cadmus asked.

"I don't know. It just doesn't ... feel right."

"Not very helpful, Mikel." Although the Frost Lord couldn't mistake his friend's unease. And he wasn't about to ignore it.

"I'd offer more detail if I could. It's just a hint of warning in the back of my brain. No more than that." That was the best that Mikel could provide, not sure how to interpret in greater detail what he was experiencing other than the fact that he and Cadmus were in peril.

"You trust it? This feeling of yours."

"I do. And it's not just me. It's also the Blade of Light. Warning me. But ..."

Cadmus glanced down, noting how the scimitar in his friend's hand mirrored Mikel's concern, gleaming so brightly that he could barely make out the steel. He couldn't argue with the warning as he and Mikel walked in among the Barrows, Mikel leading them along the trail that he believed would take them to the source of his escalating discomfort. In the Frozen Waste, better to come upon the threat on your terms rather than have the threat come upon you.

"But what?"

Mikel shook his head, not really certain how to explain. "It seems like the Blade is eager. Like it wants me to use it."

"Not surprising at all," Cadmus grumbled. "Giant-crafted weapons are made for a distinct purpose."

"Fighting those touched by the Curse," Mikel murmured. The sense of approaching doom was drawing closer. Yet he could identify nothing that offered a hint as to what it might be.

"Exactly."

"Not really what I wanted to hear." Mikel stopped. Cadmus did as well, gripping the haft of his scythe with both hands rather than spinning the weapon from one hand to the next as was his habit. He could feel it now as well. A touch of evil on the wind. And a smell that reminded him of the crypt. "It's coming closer."

The King of the Rime was certain of it. But where? And what could it be that made him feel this way? As if his own land was no longer a place for the living.

"Take a look at this." Mikel knelt, touching with his fingertips the edge of the prints in the snow. Cadmus examined the tracks over his shoulder.

"They're just polar bears," Cadmus scoffed. "They usually don't bother us if we don't bother them."

Mikel pushed himself up. His eyes went to the trail between the mounds that rose several dozen feet above them and placed them in shadow, the sun already setting to the west because they were so far north. "So many together? Two or three perhaps. A mother and her cubs. But not this many."

Cadmus looked down at the snow again. Mikel was right. Not just one bear. Quite a few, in fact. More concerning, the tracks were deeper than he would expect for this kind of snow, which was packed down hard. That realization turned Cadmus' spine to ice. Because that meant ...

"Cadmus!"

Mikel stepped forward and to the left, giving the Frost Lord the space he needed to swing his scythe. And he would need to swing it.

Just a hundred yards farther down the path between the barrows came a sight that was a first for Mikel. One that he really didn't care to see.

"I was right to worry," Cadmus muttered. "I should have known."

Mikel wanted to ask his friend what he was talking about. But he couldn't, instead focusing on the Giants charging toward them riding on the backs of polar bears.

A terrifying sight.

Made worse by the fact that the bears and Giants weren't alive.

They had been at one time. No more, however.

They were remarkably well preserved because of the cold.

The flesh of both was shriveled and blue with empty eye sockets, a strange, haunting black where their eyes had been. Their bones were visible or protruding from the wounds and injuries they had died from, though those gashes, tears, and breaks scarcely impeded them.

Draugr Giants.

Riding on the backs of undead polar bears.

Definitely not a discovery that he had ever wanted to make.

Mikel didn't have the time to wonder how this was possible. He didn't even want to think about how it was possible.

He needed to think about how to survive an attack by monsters that were already dead and now only fifty yards away from him and closing the distance between them much too swiftly.

Because he and Cadmus had nowhere to go.

They couldn't climb the barrows on either side to escape their attackers. The polar bears would have little trouble catching them on the slope.

And they couldn't stand against the creatures charging toward them, the polar bears' sharp claws digging up the ice and snow and creating a spray of white behind them. The undead animals would trample them, leaving the Draugr with little to do.

"We cannot hold against these blighted beasts!" Cadmus yelled. "We must ..."

The Frost Lord never got the chance to finish his thought.

Mikel acted swiftly. Just as he always did.

Relying on the connection he had established with the Blade of Light, the fiery energy surging along its length with even greater intensity, eager to be released, he knelt and pounded the hilt of the ancient weapon against the frozen tundra.

The effect was instantaneous and devastating.

A wave of ice and snow rolled out from the Blade, crashing into the charging Draugr and their undead mounts and halting their attack in a heartbeat. Several were buried in the snow, forced to dig themselves out from the small avalanche.

Before any of the monsters touched by the Curse regained their feet, Mikel was in among them. Cadmus not too far behind.

Yet even with their momentary advantage, the Frost Lord found the battle to be a difficult one. Despite being a master of the scythe and inflicting several terrible wounds on Draugr and polar bear alike, still the monsters came for him regardless of broken bones or lost limbs.

The undead creatures were unaffected by most of the injuries he inflicted. His only success came when he took off a Draugr's head with a single swipe of his blade, and a lucky one at that. The undead Giant had placed himself unwittingly within the arc of the Frost Lord's scythe when Cadmus was targeting another of the Draugr. The headless monster dropped to the snow and didn't rise again.

Mikel's efforts proved to be a great deal more effective, though he refused to take any of the credit. He believed that his success resulted primarily from the ancient weapon that had chosen to join with him.

With every touch he earned with his blazing steel, a flash of fire erupted. Whether Draugr or undead bear that fire burned with a blinding intensity, consuming the creature and turning them into pyres. Destroying their bodies, the Light broke the hold of the Curse that had pulled them from their graves, allowing the dead to return to the other side for good.

Despite the horror of what he faced, Mikel fought with a discipline earned from hard experience. Dodging a swipe from a polar bear, the creature's claw passed just over his head. His move to evade brought him in close to the undead creature's maw, the stench of the grave almost too much for him.

Rather than pulling back, Mikel pushed forward. Rolling beneath the bear, he trailed his Blade along the creature's underside. The deep slice, biting through desiccated flesh and fat, opened up its belly.

The slash, though a terrible wound, meant nothing to the undead animal. The creature's end came because the fire released by the blazing steel ate hungrily into the frozen flesh. Charring it. Consuming it.

The undead bear crashed into the snow just a few feet past Mikel, never to rise again, as a cloud of ash and smoke drifted up from the burning corpse.

He turned then, sensing the lull in the battle.

His part of the battle.

Not Cadmus'.

Two Draugrs, one having regained his mount, were pressing the Frost Lord. Hard. His friend facing a difficult test.

The Draugr forced Cadmus to place his back against a barrow. Trapped.

Worse, the Frost Lord slipped, avoiding the snapping maw

of the undead polar bear when he dropped down to one knee because of his misstep. The Draugr on the other side, quick to make use of the opportunity, stabbed with its spear, targeting Cadmus' chest.

Before the rusted weapon struck home, Mikel was there. Knocking away the steel he removed the Draugr's head with a backhanded slash, the Draugr's body collapsing to the frozen ground.

Mikel continued his motion, slicing across the polar bear's front paw and severing it. The undead animal stumbled then crashed face first into the barrow, the Draugr thrown from its mount.

Cadmus shouldered into the Draugr before it could push itself off the side of the snowy mound then slashed with his scythe. A slice born of anger and desperation, he removed the undead creature's head with a clean cut. Cadmus glad to confirm that fire wasn't the only way to dispatch these monsters.

Mikel challenged the polar bear. Although severely wounded, flames licking up its damaged limb, the undead animal turned faster than should have been possible. But Mikel wasn't there.

Instead, he had shifted to the bear's blind side, driving his sword through the creature's neck. The flash of energy that burst from the Blade ripped through the beast.

The undead animal crumpled. The evil essence that had resurrected it destroyed, its remains swiftly turned to ash.

Mikel wasn't pleased with his success, however. A cold chill that had nothing to do with the frigid temperature swept over him upon hearing a growl from above.

Mikel turned, knowing that it was already too late.

He had made a mistake. He had focused so much on the bear that he didn't notice the threat approaching from behind.

Another Draugr.

The last of the undead.

Just a few feet away from him.

He cursed himself for a fool.

He thought that the bear that was now no more than a pile of cinders was the last creature he needed to put down.

He was wrong. And he was going to pay for that error because though he was fast, he wasn't fast enough to bring his scimitar up in time to defend against the battle axe singing through the air toward his scalp.

Yet before the rusty steel could bite through his flesh and bone, another shriek that made his teeth hurt erupted above Mikel.

He watched in amazement as a stream of icy fire streaked right over his head. The blast slammed into the Draugr that had been about to kill him and punched the monster back against the side of the barrow.

Not one to waste good fortune, Mikel already was moving. Racing forward, he slashed through the Draugr's neck before the undead could rise again. Though that was unlikely to begin with. The dragon fire proved just as effective as the Light.

That task done, Mikel turned swiftly. Wary. He wanted to avoid making the same mistake again that had almost cost him his life. Scanning all around him, he was certain after his quick inspection that the clash had concluded.

Mikel nodded to Cadmus. Pleased to see that the Frost Lord made it through the fight unscathed.

Then he looked up into the sky, a large shadow draping itself across him for just a split second.

He smiled warmly.

Eisa.

The ice dragon shrieked one more time before flying off toward the mountains far to the north.

She had grown since he had last seen her, and it had only been a few weeks.

Then she had been as big as a draft horse. Now she was four times that size and still not yet full grown.

"Lucky to have a friend like that." Cadmus walked up to Mikel and clapped him on the back. Grateful to be alive and willing to admit it had been a closer thing than he would have preferred.

Surveying the battlefield, the Frost Lord shook his head in wonder. All that was left of the Draugr and undead polar bears were piles of ash. And even that evidence wouldn't last for long. The gusts of wind whipping between the barrows already were scattering the cinders far and wide.

"I can't argue with that."

"Lucky to have the Blade of Light as well."

"I won't argue that either." Cadmus was right. If the ancient weapon hadn't selected him, and he and the Blade hadn't come to an understanding before these monsters from the grave appeared, then both he and Cadmus would be dead ... or undead. He didn't like either possibility. The latter worse in his mind. "Those were Draugr I take it?"

Cadmus nodded. "I'm afraid so."

Mikel didn't know what to think. He was familiar with the legends of the Frozen Waste. He just never anticipated coming across one of those legends in real life. "You're going to need to explain to me how it's possible that Draugr are roaming the Frozen Waste."

"I will as soon as I can explain it to myself."

"Fair enough," Mikel replied. He could tell from the slight waver in his friend's voice that the Frost Lord was just as unnerved as he was.

"Let's get moving," Cadmus suggested. "I feel the need to get behind the walls of the Icehold."

Mikel wasn't about to disagree, falling in step with the Frost Lord. "These Draugr ..."

Cadmus cut him off. "Let me talk to some of the elders.

Then we will talk. Draugr have not appeared for centuries. Not since the War of the Brothers when my uncle broke our traditions and made an alliance that has tainted our kind ever since. When I have useful information, I will share it with you. To speculate now would do neither of us any good."

Mikel nodded his thanks, finding the entire experience both surreal and terrifying. He had come up against quite a few difficult opponents during his time. It was inevitable considering his occupation.

Yet nothing quite like Giants and bears risen from the grave. And he did not relish the prospect of facing them again, though he feared that this had only been his brief introduction to the undead. The Blade of Light still singing in his ear hinted that the worst was yet to come.

"Out with it, Cadmus. I know you're not done with your lesson."

The Giant chuckled, the deep sound echoing off the sides of the barrows. "As I said, you know me too well." He picked up his pace, the urge to get back to his capital stronger now that the shadows were lengthening. He had no desire to be beyond the Icehold when night fell. Not after this clash. "One last piece of information for you regarding the Blade, which you seem to have taken to like a narwhal to the Winter Sea."

"Can I stop you?"

"No."

"Then as I said, out with it." Mikel swept his gaze from left to right, looking over his shoulder and then starting again. He didn't get the sense that they were being hunted. Not anymore. The feeling of menace had faded as they moved away from the battlefield. Likely just the last of his nerves, which only made sense.

"You used the Blade of Light in the most obvious and direct fashion."

"It worked."

"It did," Cadmus confirmed, "and I'm grateful for that. But there are subtleties with respect to this weapon that are worth learning."

"Such as?"

"The Blade of Light is linked to you now. Essentially a part of you just as you are a part of it. If someone with the skill to use the Talent or the Curse attempts to take the steel from you, if you know what you're doing, you can drain them of their ability to use magic. Because that's what the scimitar does. The Blade of Light takes the power offered to it and then uses that power. A two-edged sword in a very literal way."

"And if you don't have the ability to use the Talent or the Curse?"

"Now there's a good question, because it applies to you." Cadmus caught Mikel's eyes, wanting to ensure that his friend understood the importance of what he was about to tell him. "If you're not careful, if you're not in balance with one another, the Blade of Light can drain your vitality. It will draw the strength it needs from you. One way or another."

"Meaning a painful death."

"I'm afraid so."

"You didn't think to tell me that before I used the Blade?"

Cadmus shrugged. "I didn't have the chance. Besides, you survived the battle unharmed, so there's that."

"Cadmus, I really should ..."

The Frost Lord interrupted Mikel before he could give free reign to his rising anger. "That being said, well done, Lightcrafter. You should feel good about what you accomplished. I would ask, however, that you keep in mind that there is a great deal more that you will need to learn if you hope to take full advantage of the potential the ancient weapon offers you. Therefore, I would advocate for persistence and patience on your part."

"I'm not exactly known for the second of those traits," Mikel mused.

"Persistence, yes," Cadmus agreed. "Patience ... well, I can hope." He nodded toward the ice dragon that was now nothing more than a speck in the sky far to the north. "That ice dragon certainly is attached to you."

"I'm glad she is," Mikel said with a broad smile. "She's probably just returning the favor."

"I think it's a little more than that."

"What do you mean?"

Cadmus didn't reply right away. He knew his friend was referring to the ice dragon valuing Mikel's assistance when trappers sought to cage her and taking an interest in her rescuer. That, in itself, was remarkable, because ice dragons tended to stay away from Giants and men whenever they could.

But now with polar bears and his Giants coming back from the dead?

There was more going on here than Cadmus could see. That worried him on a visceral level.

What bothered him even more was that he didn't yet know what it meant. Other than the fact that change was coming.

A big change.

And whether that change would be good or bad for the Giants of the Rime, he didn't know yet.

Though he got the sense that how the scales would tilt depended a great deal on the Steelheart. Now the Lightcrafter as well. Which would require even more of an education for Mikel if he was to reach his full potential.

"It means the Blade of Light coming back into the world ... was meant to happen."

"I stole it, Cadmus. That's why it's back in the world."

"Yes. *You* did. The Blade wanted *you*. That's why *you* were able to acquire it."

"That's ridiculous." Mikel didn't have much more of an argument to offer.

"It doesn't matter whether you believe, Mikel."

"Why?"

"Because it's the truth. You stole the scimitar because the scimitar allowed you to steal it."

"Again the theory that it's alive."

"Isn't it?"

"All right. Fine." Mikel didn't want to waste a lot of time arguing the merits of Cadmus' theory. Because at least in that respect, his friend was right. In some ways, the Blade of Light -- linked to Mikel, linked to the consciousnesses of its previous Bearers --was alive. "Why now? Why me?"

"You? A good question we discussed in large part. Now?" Cadmus nodded back to where they had fought Draugr and undead polar bears. "I don't know for certain. All I can assume is that a great evil stirs. An evil connected to you now because of the Blade."

Mikel shook his head. "This isn't what I wanted."

"When do we ever get what we want?" Cadmus asked.

"I'll agree with you on that at least."

"One last warning."

"I can't wait to hear it."

"You just experienced it. You are a catalyst for the Blade of Light. If you can master it, you will exercise a power against which few can stand."

"I sense the bad news coming."

"Simply the reality of what that truly encompasses. The Blade of Light functions like a lodestone."

"Meaning?"

"It attracts the Curse and creatures made of the Curse."

"Wonderful," Mikel muttered under his breath, closing his eyes as he shook his head in resignation. "Just wonderful."

5

PORTENTS IN THE GREAT HALL

"I didn't want this father. I told you that many times. Yet still you did what you believed was necessary, and now it has fallen to me," Cadmus said quietly, alone in the flickering light.

He stood in the back of the Great Hall, staring into the fire, the hearth taking up most of the wall. He couldn't escape his memories, scenes from the War of the Brothers passing before his eyes in the dancing and crackling flames as if it were only yesterday rather than five centuries past.

The Night of Broken Ice, when his uncle, Kronin, rose up against his father. Giant fighting Giant in the Icehold. The very floor he stood upon covered in bodies. No space to walk between them, the fighting so fierce. The blood so thick that it was like wading through a shallow pool, Kronin's surprise complete. Cadmus was forced to leave the city to his uncle so that they could regroup and continue the battle in the Rime.

There were countless clashes on the Frozen Waste. Lightning attacks with Cadmus leading the effort to keep his uncle's forces off balance and uncertain. Then the larger battles when it came time to press Kronin.

Polar bears charging.

Giants fighting and dying on the plateaus, the crags, in among the barrows.

Friends, brothers, and sisters becoming enemies.

Families breaking apart.

The memories continued to flood Cadmus' thoughts, leading him to the most painful. Discovering the truth about Kronin. How it was possible for him to enjoy so much success at the beginning of the war.

His uncle had turned to the Curse to aid his insurrection, a hidden hand guiding from the shadows.

Facing dire straits, Cadmus and his father gained the aid of the Magii, using the weapons that only they could help craft to take back what his uncle had stolen from them. Breaking Kronin's hold over the realm, they set the stage for his father's ultimate victory. His ultimate sacrifice as well.

But not before his father imprisoned his brother and his followers. For what Cadmus hoped would be all eternity, not wanting his father's sacrifice to be in vain.

Yet now, after what he and the Steelheart had just experienced ...

Cadmus shuddered involuntarily, fearing that his desire to keep the atrocities and terrors of the past in the past was no more than that. Desire. Not reality.

"And I will do as I promised that I would," Cadmus murmured, for just a moment seeing the spirit of Karolingan in the flames. "No matter how much it pains me, no matter how much it costs, I will do as I promised."

Cadmus turned away abruptly. He could not ignore that afternoon's clash against the Draugr. More pressing, he needed to ensure that his Giants were ready.

He could hope that what he feared would come to pass wouldn't. However, doing that would be a disservice to the bond he had made with his father those many centuries before.

Besides, better to be ready and not have to fight than not be ready and have to fight.

That thought consuming him, he strode toward the dais a hundred yards distant. Insulated by a thick layer of snow and ice on the outside, the Great Hall was constructed of stone and oak, massive beams crisscrossing above him in a mesmerizing design. Oil lamps hung down on long chains that cast shadows on the ceiling designed to reveal the ancient and valued symbols of his kind.

Yet Cadmus had eyes only for the throne that was carved from a massive slab of white marble. An incredibly uncomfortable seat, Cadmus had learned. Physically and otherwise. Made so for a reason.

Cadmus hadn't wanted to rule the Frozen Waste. At least not when he was forced to assume the throne. He wanted to pursue his other interests until he no longer could.

It wasn't meant to be, however, his father's bravery demanding that he accept the kingship much sooner than he anticipated. Not ready. Not willing. Not having any choice.

Stepping up onto the dais, he moved past the throne after running a hand along the armrest, just like his father had done every time he assumed his seat as the King of the Giants of the Rime, staring at the several examples of what only his best smiths could do.

More than a dozen battle-tested weapons glittered in the light.

All Giant-crafted.

A few spears. A couple swords. A trident. A whip made of steel links with a spike at the end. A battle-axe. Morningstar. Flail. War hammer.

All with histories, both bloody and heroic.

Some sized for Giants. Some for humans.

All infused with the Talent when the Order of the Magii

determined that there was need. All returned for safekeeping in the Great Hall when their use was no longer required.

And perhaps the strongest of them all now in the possession of a human. Caledonii, true, but still a human.

Cadmus still didn't know what that truly meant, and he feared that he never would.

The Blade of Light.

An ancient artifact thought to be lost. Yet not lost. Lying dormant instead. Hidden. Until the Lightcrafter found it.

Lightcrafter.

Cadmus shook his head, finding it difficult to believe that Mikel demonstrated the skill to do what only a select few Giants ever had been able to accomplish. So few that through the entire history of the Giants of the Rime there had been less than a dozen Lightcrafters.

His father the last one. Or so Cadmus had thought.

The people of the Realms knew of the Talent and the Curse.

They had little knowledge about the other sources of power that existed.

Some connected to the Talent or the Curse.

Some not.

Rarely seen.

Rarely used.

Though just as powerful.

Sometimes even more so.

Like the Light.

An older power. Almost primordial.

Similar to the Talent. Drawn from nature itself. Drawn from the sun.

Yet more intense. More demanding. More insistent. More mercurial.

And more worrisome when practiced by someone without the requisite skill and training.

The question was, would the Steelheart learn to master the skills demanded of a Lightcrafter?

Cadmus hoped so, and not just because Mikel was his friend. Also because he knew what would happen if he didn't.

Fate wouldn't have brought a Lightcrafter back to the Frozen Waste unless there was cause to do so.

Fate wouldn't have revealed the Blade of Light unless there was a need.

The Blade of Light was thousands of years old. One of the first weapons the Giants of the Rime crafted for the Order of the Magii.

More than just steel infused with immense power.

A test.

A lesson.

A trial.

And for the Giants, a source of hope.

An opportunity.

To ensure their safety and protection.

Prophesied to be used during their time of greatest need.

And perhaps the prophecy was right after what Cadmus and Mikel fought that afternoon.

Draugr were well known among the Giants of the Rime.

They were not just a story told to frighten children into their beds. Rather, they were fact. Dried flesh and bone rising from the grave. Bodies infused with the Curse. Controlled by a Dark Magus ... or something worse.

The Blade of Light would not have been revealed if not for a good and necessary reason. That's what worried Cadmus.

Did they have the time to prepare for what was coming?

And perhaps the better question was, what was it that they needed to prepare for?

What was the threat that had awakened the Blade?

What was the threat that had brought the dead back to life?

Staring at the weapons waiting to be taken up again,

Cadmus' mind drifting through the history of the Giants of the Rime, he understood that the common thread always was the Curse. Yet what form would it take now?

Cadmus sighed deeply, recalling once more his memories while looking into the fire.

There was one possibility that he preferred not to consider. Dreaded it, in fact.

But as the Frost Lord, Cadmus couldn't ignore it.

"Is Mikel all right?"

Cadmus smiled, expecting just that question. He turned, taking his daughter into his arms for a brief hug before she pulled back. She looked so like her mother, getting from him the blue eyes paler than a mountain lake and the curly hair that she kept under control with an intricate braid that ran down her back.

"I'm fine. Thank you for asking."

She ignored her father's sarcasm. "I know you're fine. I would have been told otherwise. That's why I asked about Mikel."

"He is well," Cadmus replied while wearing a bemused expression. "He wanted to say hello, but he needed to head back. He had business to attend to on the Crux."

"The new Queen?"

Cadmus shrugged, noting the tinge of jealousy in his daughter's voice yet saying nothing about it. "Perhaps. He did not say."

"Probably the Queen," Julia grumbled, not happy with her conclusion.

"How was the hunting?"

Her father's question brought Julia out of her cross musings. "Poor."

"No signs?" Cadmus had feared the worst. Perhaps they had time after all.

"No signs," Julia replied. She shook her head in puzzlement, not understanding why their efforts hadn't borne any fruit. "We began our sweep ten leagues to the north and then circled back in toward the Icehold. All appeared as it should."

Cadmus nodded. Pleased to hear that. Perhaps they did have time.

"Although we did find something that gave us pause."

"Explain," Cadmus ordered, realizing that his anxiety was coming out in his tone and that he needed to prevent that from happening. He was the Frost Lord. He had to remain calm. Under control. Always.

"The Barrows to the east of the city," Julia replied, sensing her father's unease. "The ones rarely checked. Five leagues distant."

"Several were disturbed?"

"How did you know?" Julia asked.

Cadmus frowned. He shouldn't have been surprised. He would begin making preparations as soon as he was done in the Great Hall. The evidence now too much to ignore.

"We will talk of that later," Cadmus promised. "And how is Jason? Have you spoken with him today?"

Julia blushed. "Not today, no. Not with me leading the patrol as you requested."

Cadmus was well aware of her daughter's feelings with respect to the Steelheart. Though he hoped that with time and maturity those feelings would be transferred to someone else. Like Jason. Because there was no future with the Steelheart. Not just because it was Giant and man. But because although Mikel didn't seem to know it yet himself, another already had staked a claim to Mikel's heart. Or if he did know, he was unwilling to admit it.

"He's been asking about you. He seemed very concerned, in an understated way, of course."

Julia's blush deepened, not certain that she wanted to have

this conversation with her father. "I will admit that he has ... caught my eye."

"And you his. Perhaps you should ..."

"I will think on it," she promised. Her tone commanding, much like her father's. Hoping to end the conversation then and there, she refused to say more.

Cadmus knew that he shouldn't push any farther. Though he could tease. "So did you really come here to check on me or the Steelheart?"

"You," Julia replied, her mischievous smile giving her away. "Who else?"

Cadmus nodded knowingly. His daughter spoke the truth. In part. She always had been sweet on Mikel. Almost protective of him, although he never required the protection and likely would refuse it even if he did.

"I need you to do a few things for me."

"Of course."

"Double the guard around the Icehold," Cadmus ordered. "Make sure as well that the signal towers in the surrounding mountains are manned and stocked. Also, I want all my captains here in the Great Hall at first light tomorrow morning."

"You believe we will come under attack?"

"We already are," Cadmus stated ominously, "and we need to be ready for the next one."

When her father was in a mood like this one, she never questioned him. Because at that moment she wasn't his daughter. Rather, she was his second in command. "Perhaps we should expand the range of our patrols from ten leagues to twenty."

"Excellent suggestion," Cadmus agreed. "See to it personally. And double the size of each patrol."

Julia nodded. About to leave, she had one more question,

although she already suspected the answer. "You don't believe that this was an isolated incident?"

"No."

Julia didn't reply. Instead she nodded and turned, leaving the Great Hall quickly so she could be about her work.

As soon as she exited, Scipio appeared. Despite his age, the Master Smith strode with a sure step into the Great Hall. One of the best armorers ever to serve the Rime, he had the muscles to prove it. "You called for me, Frost Lord?"

"I did, Scipio. I need you to make a saddle. As quickly as you can."

"For you?"

"No, the Steelheart."

"The Steelheart?"

Cadmus nodded. "It seems the Steelheart is more than just the Steelheart."

Scipio frowned at his king's cryptic comment, though he knew better than to pursue it. Not with the look that Cadmus was giving him. Saying that it was grim would have been an understatement.

"A saddle for a polar bear?" Scipio asked. He didn't know what to make of the request. Polar bears usually only accepted Giants of the Rime on their backs.

"No. For an ice dragon."

6

NASTY SURPRISE

It was quiet. Dawn still a few hours away when Lucius Hanover stepped toward the back of the small shop, only a couple of lamps lighting his way. It had once been an apothecary. One of the few serving the people of the Crux living on the First Ring.

The streets often flooded when the Churn surged over the seawall. That explained the damage to the shop. Much of the wood had rotted with mold growing along the walls and the ceiling. Sandbags that offered little protection sat piled along the outside of the shop.

The owner had closed after the last flood. Little thought was given to reopening because of the expense of restocking all the herbs, salves, and other items destroyed when the Churn flowed almost to the Third Ring.

Hanover had bought the space on the cheap recently. Quietly as well, through one of his many holding companies, so that it would be that much harder to follow the change in ownership.

He smiled thinking about that. Hanover did like coming out ahead. He couldn't think of anything in life more pleasurable than that. And that was saying quite a lot considering his many less than savory proclivities.

Yet his pleasure did little to assuage his anger.

Even after the passage of more than a month he was having a hard time keeping his temper under control. And with good reason he believed. His grievances legitimate.

He had been so close.

So close!

Yet that harpy had ripped his greatest dream right from his grasp just moments before it became a reality.

He still couldn't believe that his perfect plan hadn't been so perfect after all. Even more, he still couldn't believe that he wasn't sitting on the Crux throne.

Hanover growled softly, making a visible effort to focus on the present. He understood that no matter how much fun it might be, wallowing in the past did him little good.

It certainly didn't help him deal with the complications that arose after he failed to seize the throne.

The crushing debts were bad enough.

Hanover had spent a large part of his family's fortune to place himself in the position that he lusted after. Yet now the First Families had turned a deaf ear to his plight, having forgotten all that he had done for them along with the promises that they had made to him as a result of his largesse ... and the pressure that he applied. Subtly at times, and not so subtly when a more direct approach was called for.

Yet none of that mattered now.

He was overdrawn.

He had obligations to meet.

He didn't have the means to pay what he owed.

And since his silent ally had offered little material support, making his disappointment in Hanover's failure plain, the Lord of the Crux needed to expand his business operations in certain directions at a much faster pace to recoup his losses and pay his debts.

Directions that he wouldn't have considered if he didn't face such difficult circumstances.

Decisions made with such alacrity.

Desperate times and all that.

"It's all here?"

Marek nodded, the commander of Hanover's Guard stepping up next to him. He had worked for the Hanovers since he was a child. Beginning before Lucius was born and doing whatever was required of him, Marek's loyalty was unassailable. "Yes, it arrived last night. Right on time, in fact."

"You checked the shipment?"

Marek nodded. "The highest quality. Just as you were promised."

"All of it?"

"All of it. You have nothing to fear in that regard."

Lucius nodded. Good. He had sunk a good part of what little of his wealth he had left into this deal. Understanding the risk, he was willing to take it because the potential reward was too much for him to resist.

If it played out as he believed it would, from this one contract he would have the capacity to rebuild much of what he lost from his family's treasury. Although it would require more of his time and effort than he usually wished to devote to his business dealings, he was willing to do the work.

Because just a handful of these deals could put him back in a position where Celindria Dengannon would have no choice but to consider him as a consort, placing him right next to the throne. And then, after a few years passed ...

Well, he didn't want to get ahead of himself.

Regardless, what was required of him now was a small price to pay for the riches promised to him. Milk of the poppy was difficult to acquire on the Crux. Primarily because it was illegal in the Kingdom, its use restricted to the handful of physicks who worked in the capital city.

Nevertheless, there was a small market that went beyond the medicinal demand, and Hanover planned to grow that market.

He didn't believe that it would take much to do so.

The high cost of his product played to his advantage. As did the fact that he already had an in with the market.

Many of his friends in the First Families, along with the sons and daughters of the wealthier merchants and traders who had aspirations to live just below the Royal Ring, would be interested. In fact, if Hanover played his cards right, milk of the poppy would become a status symbol, an item exclusive to the rich, and that guaranteed that he would make a fortune. Because he would be the one to control the market.

"Let's see it," Hanover ordered.

Marek nodded then stepped past Hanover, stopping in front of the small fireplace behind the counter. He traced his fingers along the mantle until he felt the slight indentation. Pushing in, a segment of the paneled wall next to the fireplace swung open to reveal a storage space lit by several lamps.

Wary of thieves, the previous owner kept his more expensive products hidden before the last flood destroyed his inventory.

Hanover's milk of the poppy had been placed there when it was delivered only a few hours before.

There was a slight problem, however.

Hanover's eyes widened first in disbelief and then concern as he stared into the hidden room. "Did you move it?" Based on the quantity Hanover had purchased, the hideaway should have been packed to the rafters. Several thousand pounds of milk of the poppy should have been stacked in neat bundles one on top of the other.

But it wasn't there.

Nothing was there.

The room was empty.

"This isn't possible," Marek gasped. "No one has been here since last night. We locked up the shop. No one could have gotten in."

"How can you be sure?" Hanover demanded as he stepped into the storeroom. He didn't see anything that hinted at how his product could have been moved without any of his men knowing. Even so, he had been cleaned out.

"We had watchers on the outside just as you ordered. And we had men in the main part of the shop. Right there." Marek motioned back toward the way they had come. "There is no way anyone could have gotten in here without my knowledge."

Lucius didn't know what to say. What to do. His blood was boiling. Tempered only by his shock.

All of it stolen.

The last of his money in the form of a high-priced drug vanished with not a hint as to where it had gone or who had taken it.

How?

It just didn't make ...

Then he knew. The realization set his entire body shaking with anger and the desire for revenge.

Only one person could have done this to him.

Only one person had the means.

Only one person would dare.

That one person had been cutting at the edges of his business and his wealth ever since Celindria stole the throne from him.

Lucius growled in rage. That one person needed to die.

"Only a few more bundles," Samuel said, watching as Benji and Harold shoved a large crate over the sea wall. "Once we've finished making our offering to the gods of the Churn, we've been invited to a good meal and all the ale we can drink at The Fox's Lair."

Jensen and Micah handed their comrades another crate filled with sealed packages, ignoring the occasional splash of whitewater that surged up over the breakwater. A common occurrence along the rim of the Crux where four powerful rivers met, the resulting roil and boil often rising higher than the rogue waves that could be found in the Silent Sea. As a result, the small island only was accessible via gondolas connected by Giant-crafted chains that reached from the four harbors of the Crux to the small towns on the mainland.

"It seems like such a waste," grumbled Jensen.

"Like we're throwing away money," added Micah. Still, that didn't stop the pair from handing over the crate to Benji and Harold and then picking up one of the few remaining that were lined up neatly by Samuel's feet.

"You know the law," Samuel said. "Milk of the poppy is an illegal substance in the Crux."

"I'm not worried about the Queen and her soldiers," Jensen countered.

"Neither am I," Samuel replied. "But I am worried about the King of the Underworld. Remember, boys, his laws supersede all others. He's stated in no uncertain terms that there's no place for the drug on the Crux. And I can tell you from experience that you definitely don't want to get on his bad side."

7

ALWAYS LEARNING

"Don't ever do that again! Ever!" Finn pounded his fist on the table, spittle flying from his thin lips, his drawn face red with rage.

"Don't do what?" Nat demanded. She released her hold on the Talent reluctantly, not easily cowed by her instructor's angry display. She had dealt with far worse not too long before. "I was doing exactly as you said I should."

"Yes, but ..."

"Exactly as you said, Finn," Nat cut in, using a softer voice that helped to soothe her instructor's edge. "Exactly."

The Magus closed his eyes, listening to the soft roar of the Churn drifting up from below. It was getting harder for him now. He couldn't control the pain as he had in the beginning. That pain now a fiery agony in his bones, setting his blood to a sizzle.

What he was failing to manage affected his patience. His temper. It affected everything in his life.

It was only a matter of time. He couldn't deny that. And in some ways it would be a relief when it happened. His torture finally coming to an end.

Even so, it would have to wait a little longer. He wasn't ready. There were still several tasks that he needed to complete. And that list included training this difficult, obnoxious, studious, driven, supremely talented young lady.

"You're right, I'm sorry," Finn replied, nodding an apology to his student. His voice was softer as he forced himself to speak calmly. He pushed himself up from his seat, the exhaustion he held at bay by strength of will threatening to break through.

Working with Nat tired him out like nothing else had in quite some time. Still, it was a small price to pay for the chance to play a role as she came into her own. Besides, his daily lessons with her helped to distract him from his misery. Much of the time anyway.

"Then what is it?" demanded Nat, not easily assuaged. "Like I said, I did everything the way you told me to. And it was working just as it was supposed to."

Nat was in the right. She was sure of it. She hadn't made any mistakes.

Calling upon the Talent, she had been practicing how to manipulate water in its various forms, thereby gaining an understanding of its properties. The Churn roiling a few hundred feet below her the perfect playground.

Crafting large spheres of water that she brought level with her on the balcony before sending them blasting toward the far shore. Turning the water into mist. Transforming it into ice. Reconstructing the water into different shapes. Then manipulating those shapes. Learning how to attack with the shapes she created. Learning how to defend against those same shapes.

"What's the first lesson I taught you?" Finn asked, placing a hand on her slight shoulder as way of an apology.

"Never overextend myself. Never take in more of the Talent than I can hold safely."

"Correct, and that's what ..."

"I wasn't doing that," Nat argued. "You may not think that I listen to you, but I do. I was using a manageable amount of the Talent. I wasn't even close to my limit."

For just a heartbeat, Finn felt the urge to yell at Nat. To take her to task. But for what?

She was telling the truth. And if he gave in to his urge, he would be surrendering to his pain.

"You're right. As I said, I'm sorry."

"Then why were you so angry?" Nat refused to let go. She had been working with Finn for several months now, and she knew that he was many things. An excellent instructor in the Talent. Irascible. Grumpy. He told her what he really thought, never sugarcoating his words. But he was never angry with her without good cause.

"I'm not angry," Finn said. Though he could tell that Nat smelled the lie, he was grateful that she didn't challenge him further. Maybe it was because of the grimace of pain that flashed across his face right after he answered. "I'm just worried."

Nat nodded thoughtfully. "That I might overstep. That I might ..." She didn't feel the need to complete her thought.

"Yes," Finn sighed. "That is always my concern. I forget sometimes that you exercise a power that few can dream of. I worry that one misstep can take you down the road that needs to be avoided at all costs."

"You worry for nothing, Finn." Nat leaned up on her toes, giving him a light kiss on his whiskered cheek and earning a soft smile from her instructor. "I pay attention to everything you tell me. In part to keep the big lummox who keeps watch over me from getting on my back too much."

"I take exception to that description," Mikel said, stepping out of the shadows of the doorway. He had arrived on silent feet a half-hour before, watching the lesson. Impressed by Nat's display. Even more so how she stood up to the Magus. Though he worried about Finnelaus.

"I don't see how you can," Finn said. "You are a big lummox."

"Teaming up against me," Mikel said with a sad shake of his head. "Not very sporting."

"There's nothing sporting about using the Talent or a blade," Nat argued. "When you call upon either, you should have only one goal in mind."

"Impressive," Mikel said, placing an arm around Nat's shoulder and pulling her in close for a brief hug. "You were listening. It's so hard to tell sometimes."

"I'm just trying to keep you on your toes," Nat explained, giving Mikel a squeeze before letting go. She had led a difficult life before meeting him. He had given her something that she had never had before. Safety. And a sense of family.

"You're doing a very good job of it," Mikel confirmed. "You ready?"

"Just let me grab my books. Finn gave me several more to study." Nat trotted back into the apartment, packing into her satchel the latest pile of texts Finn selected for her.

"You spoil her," Mikel said.

"And you don't?" Finn countered.

"Fair point." Mikel turned his keen eyes toward the Magus. Studying him, he noticed the creases around his eyes and how his countenance was more a constant wince. "Is there anything I can do to help?"

Finn sighed again, closing his eyes for just a moment. Then he shook his head. "No."

"I'm sorry."

"So am I," Finn said. "But I have no one other than myself to blame. This is what I deserve."

"I don't know that anyone deserves this."

Finn smiled then. He had met Mikel more than a decade before. When he first came to the Crux. Seeking to start over, as he liked to tell himself. In reality, hiding from those who were after him. And he had proven successful thanks in large part to Mikel. "In this, my friend, trust me. I made a mistake. I deserve this. I have but one request."

"I'm afraid to ask."

"If the time comes when I can't do what needs to be done …"

Mikel's expression hardened, understanding exactly what Finn was asking of him. He nodded. "I'll do it."

"Thank you, my friend." Finn's relief was almost palpable.

"Although I won't take any pleasure in the task."

"I'm glad to hear it," Finn laughed softly. "Now get out of here. Your ward exhausts me. I need to take a nap."

"As you command," Mikel said as he clapped his friend warmly on the back, feeling how brittle Finn felt beneath his robes. Mikel strode into the apartment and took the full satchel of books out of Nat's hands. "I'll walk you back to The Fox's Lair then catch up with you later. There's somewhere I need to be."

"Visiting your sweetheart," Nat teased. Seconds before she had been a Magus in training. Now, her expression close to taunting, she had reverted to the teenage girl she truly was.

"She's not my sweetheart," Mikel protested as he led her out into the deserted streets of the First Ring. Keeping to the alleyways, he preferred the shadows to the broad main boulevard that was just a few streets over.

"Could have fooled me."

"I need to speak with her about something important." Mikel's eyes tracked everything around them. It would get much busier by the time they reached the Fifth Ring where his primary tavern was located. Here, on the bottom ring, the seawall at their backs, most of the activity occurred at the gondola berths, each one situated on a cardinal point of the compass. Even so, just because it seemed like they were alone didn't mean that they actually were.

"If you say so," Nat said, giving Mikel a lift of her eyebrows to suggest that she didn't quite believe him. Then she was all business. "You saw that?"

"The tail we picked up?" They were almost to where the main boulevard curled up to the Second Ring. "Yes. He was waiting for us. He knew we were down here. Just not where."

"Who is he?"

"You already know the answer to that," Mikel chided.

Nat growled in disappointment. At herself. Because Mikel was right. She did know. "One of Hanover's men." It only made sense after what happened to the Lord of the House earlier that morning.

"That would be my guess. It seems that it didn't take Hanover very long to determine who's been tweaking his nose."

"Do you want me to deal with him?"

Mikel heard the excitement lacing Nat's voice. She was probably thinking that she could try some of what she had been practicing with Finn on their shadow.

"Not yet," Mikel answered.

"You're taking all the fun out of this. You know that?"

"I didn't say that you couldn't have your fun," Mikel replied. "You just need to be patient."

Nat nodded. She knew that Mikel didn't do anything without a good reason. "You want to see if you can use our tail to your advantage."

"That's my hope, yes."

"And then when you're done with him?"

"As I said, then you can have your fun."

8

ILLUMINATING CONVERSATION

"If we keep spending time together like this people are going to talk," Drin murmured, giving her companion a smile that contained several potential meanings.

She sat by the large fireplace in her private apartment, enjoying the warmth that radiated out from the flames on what was a cool autumn night. She had been less than pleased to find Mikel waiting for her there, having slipped into her rooms uninvited. Her concern grew when her comment didn't even earn a lift of his eyebrow.

"Not my people." Legs crossed at the ankles and stretched out to the flames, Mikel appeared to be quite comfortable. As if he were just talking with a friend and not the Queen of the Crux.

Celindria Dengannon could take him to task for that. His overfamiliarity. Not giving her the respect that was her due.

But what was the point?

He would only find it amusing. Besides, she owed him a debt. Several in fact.

And, if she was being completely honest with herself, she

did enjoy his company. In large part because he didn't treat her like everyone else did.

"You're so certain of that?" she challenged.

"I am."

There wasn't a hint of arrogance in his voice. Just a deserved confidence. Which she could understand. Nevertheless ...

"That possibility doesn't bother you? That some may be speaking about what we might be doing privately?"

"Who is they?" Mikel shrugged, obviously unconcerned. "Besides, I'm certain that no one knows that I'm here, so your concern is for nothing."

"There are no secrets in the Citadel," Drin chided.

"There are always secrets," Mikel replied. Then he frowned. "What we're doing privately? You mean talking? Or did you have something else in mind?"

Drin didn't reply right away, realizing she fell into a trap of her own making. Mikel's brash grin confirmed that truth. "I mean some of the other things we could be doing privately other than talking." She refused to back down, wanting to learn how far she could push him. Also wanting to see if she could find a crack in the armor he wore around his emotions.

Mikel stared blankly at her for several seconds. Playing dumb. When her eyes tightened, he grinned again. That grin became a broad smile. Drin didn't know if she should be insulted that it took him that long to get there. As if he had never considered the possibility. Unlikely.

"If they want to talk about that, let them talk. There's worse that could be said about us."

Drin studied him, caught off guard by the seriousness of his reply, but then she glimpsed the twinkle in his eye. "You like the thought of them thinking that that's what we're up to."

"I doubt you have much to worry about, because no one knows that I'm here." Mikel shrugged again, his smile becoming devious. "But to your comment, I'm not that good-looking, and you're a beautiful woman and the Queen. So it works out quite well for my reputation if *they* are talking about us."

She leaned forward lightning fast and hit him in the arm. Hard. "I can't believe you're enjoying this." Drin tried to scowl, but it didn't last long. A smile soon graced her sharp features. She was enjoying this conversation much too much.

There was some quality to Mikel that she found intriguing.

It wasn't his size. He was almost hulking in appearance. And, as he admitted, he wasn't exactly handsome. Ruggedly ... rugged. That was as kind as she could be when trying to describe him.

Nevertheless, she felt drawn to him in a way that she had never felt drawn to anyone else. She planned on keeping that to herself, however. She didn't want his confidence to turn into arrogance.

"I'm not enjoying anything. I'm here to talk."

"Is that so?" Drin asked, her tone suggesting that she was less than pleased by his response.

Mikel didn't respond right away, not expecting such a reply from her. Not sure what to say, he felt distinctly uncomfortable because of what she might be insinuating. Recognizing that she expected a response, he offered one that was more a question. "Yes ..."

"Then let's talk," she ordered, grumbling softly as she straightened her skirts. Smoothing her face, Drin adopted the calm and composed countenance expected of the ruler of the Crux. Unwilling to reveal that what he said, or rather hadn't said, disappointed her. "You know what's happening later this evening. Why are we doing this? Shouldn't we be preparing?"

"Patience," Mikel requested. "This is something you need to know."

"Would you please just tell me instead of making me work for it? Just this once?"

"Where's the fun in that?"

"Mikel," Drin growled.

He held up his hands. "All right. All right." He pushed himself into a seated position and leaned forward, forearms resting on his knees. "Dragoran could not have gotten his soldiers onto the Crux without help from one of the First Families."

"Why the First Families?" Drin had asked Mikel to find out how so many raiders from the Tor had gotten across the Churn undetected, assuming that he already was investigating the matter. Her assumption proved accurate. "Why not some other smuggler?"

Mikel gave her a brash look, not feeling the need to say anything.

"Right, right," Drin nodded. It was her turn to raise her hands in apology. "All the smugglers work for you."

"There you go," Mikel confirmed. "As we know, the soldiers came over on freight gondolas usually used by House Hanover."

"That doesn't mean that Lucius Hanover had anything to do with the attempted kidnapping." Although a small voice in the back of her brain told her otherwise.

"Perhaps. Perhaps not. But often the most obvious answer …"

"Is the right answer," Drin sighed. "What did you discover?"

"Most of the people we wanted to talk to didn't have much to offer."

"You mean they're dead," Drin challenged, her eyes narrowing to reveal her displeasure.

Mikel shrugged. "An unfortunate occurrence, but necessary as well. At the time we were focused on saving your life. Not on collecting information."

"Are you going to hold that over me forever?" Drin meant

the question as a joke, hoping to add a little levity to what was a very serious conversation.

"No, that wasn't my intention," Mikel replied with a gravity that Drin rarely saw from him and hadn't expected. "I was simply stating a fact."

"Fair enough," Drin acknowledged. "Nevertheless, I'm assuming you did speak to the few survivors who there were."

"I did. Unfortunately, they didn't have much to give me. They were too low in rank to know all that was going on. They were following the orders of their king. They knew no more than that. Snatch you and get off the Crux as quickly as they could."

"You're sure?" Drin wondered. "You couldn't dig out any useful nuggets from them?"

Mikel's eyes hardened, his features tightening. He didn't like being challenged. Nevertheless, he could understand why she asked. She had only known him for a brief time, and she had yet to discover all that he was capable of. The lengths to which he would go when the circumstances demanded it.

"Quite sure," he replied. "If any of the Tor soldiers we took prisoner had anything useful to give us, we would have it."

Drin accepted that. She leaned closer to the fire, Mikel's expression sending a chill through her. There was a coldness to his features that reminded her of when they met for the first time in the Frozen Waste. "So you have no actionable intelligence that leads to Dragoran's ally on the Crux?"

"I didn't say that," Mikel replied, his lips curling into a dangerous smile.

"What do you mean?"

"If at first you don't succeed ..."

"Try, try again," Drin finished for him. "I'm familiar with the saying. Are you going to explain or must I continue to ask questions?"

Mikel didn't reply right away. Instead he took a few seconds to study the Queen of the Crux. She was tired. Under stress. That made sense. Claiming the throne upon her father's murder hadn't been easy. And, of course, you could prepare only so much for the responsibility, not really understanding what was required until you faced the difficulties of ruling the Crux firsthand.

Still, he didn't think that was the only cause for Drin's tartness. Something else was bothering her. He considered asking her what that might be, but then thought better of it.

Now wasn't the time.

Now was the time to deal with the business at hand.

The traitor.

"Just as is often the case, it comes down to the money."

Drin's eyes narrowed even more. Now almost a squint. "You have proof?"

"It's not incontrovertible, I'll give you that, but yes, I do. The evidence all points in one direction. Teddy and Nat did the dirty work for me."

"Teddy? Really?"

"Before his life took a sharp turn, Teddy was an accountant. He knows how to work the numbers to find what others are trying to keep hidden. And Nat has a knack for it as well. It didn't take them long."

"How long?"

"Less than a week," Mikel replied.

"And they found this out when?"

"Three weeks ago."

"Three weeks!" Drin exclaimed, hands squeezing the arm rests. About to launch out of her chair, she restrained herself, seeking to maintain some semblance of calm authority. "You've kept this from me for that long? You know how important this is to me."

Mikel smiled, though not warmly. He didn't like being pressed, even by the Queen of the Crux. "I did know."

"So you admit your error. You've known who's been trying to stab me in the back and you didn't come to me? If I was of a mind, I'd throw you in a cell beneath the Citadel."

"You won't though."

"Why are you so sure?"

"You really want me to say it?"

Drin growled just under her breath. He had her there. He'd be out of the cell as quickly as he wanted to be. After all, among Mikel's many talents, he was an accomplished thief. "Why did you wait?"

"I wanted to make sure so that once Teddy and Nat found the trail, we confirmed it against other sources," Mikel explained. "That took longer to do."

"You still should have told me sooner."

"That's a matter of opinion," Mikel said. "We've both been busy. This is the first chance I've had to get you alone."

Drin pursed her lips, deciding whether to accept Mikel's apology that really wasn't an apology. Acknowledging that continuing to take Mikel to task would be of little use, she motioned for him to explain. "Tell me."

"It all came down to the debt," Mikel began. "For gambling, whoring, several businesses failing, and, of course, most costly an attempt to garner support among the First Families so that he would be in a position to seize the throne. And, along with the power it would give him, it also would ..."

"Give him access to the Crux treasury."

Mikel nodded. He wasn't surprised that she beat him down the path. "Exactly."

Drin didn't say anything for quite some time. Mulling what Mikel told her. Lucius Hanover betrayed her? She didn't want to believe it. Still ...

"He wanted to marry me, and based on the politics of the succession, I doubt that I could have said no for much longer. He knew that. Why would he agree to aid Dragoran in kidnapping me when all he had to do was demonstrate a little more patience?"

"Maybe the kidnapping was a kidnapping. Maybe it wasn't."

"Meaning Lucius wanted to use the kidnapping to push me toward him that much faster?" Drin wondered.

"It's one possibility. Though not the only one."

"You know what it really comes down to," Drin said with a decisive nod.

"I do. Money and power. The two most important drivers when it comes to the First Families." Mikel leaned forward then, catching Drin's eyes with his own as he rested his forearms on his thighs. Waiting.

They were less than a foot apart. A heat built between them, and Mikel wasn't sure the cause was the fire. So he continued before his mind wandered down a path that it shouldn't.

"Dragoran gave him an offer that he couldn't refuse. Hanover's debts are massive. To the point where his House is close to bankruptcy. Did he want to marry you? Probably. That was the easiest solution. It gives him what he wants and puts him in a position to eliminate his problems. But there were other solutions that allowed him to get what he wanted faster. There were more games in play than just the obvious one."

Drin stared into Mikel's eyes, finding it hard to pull away. For a time not wanting to pull away. Also not wanting to believe all that Mikel was telling her. Not because of her connection to Lucius. Rather because it meant that she had failed to discern his true intentions.

If Mikel was correct, then Lucius had tricked her. That fact wasn't just galling. It was also concerning.

The Queen of the Crux couldn't afford to be deceived so easily by someone she knew so well. A failing such as that put not only her throne but also the entire Kingdom at risk.

"I know Lucius desperately wants the throne, but he wouldn't ..."

What Mikel was telling her couldn't be the truth. Could it?

She and Lucius had grown up together. Both a part of the same social circle. Friends. For a brief time something more.

Why would he stoop so low despite understanding that of all her potential suitors he was the most likely to sit by her side?

"Queen Dengannon, I know this is hard for you. It's never easy accepting that you were betrayed. That you missed the signs. That you didn't see it coming. I can tell you that from experience." Mikel sighed then leaned back in his chair, freeing Drin from his gaze as he fought to contain the memories that threatened to overwhelm him. Not wanting to relive the past. "You said it yourself just a moment ago. Hanover takes the throne and he gains not only power but also the ability to use the treasury for his own purposes. Dragoran is happy for a time, the Kingdom of the Crux essentially a vassal state until Malor decides to flex his muscles and make the new relationship official. Then he erases Hanover from the board and brings the two Kingdoms back together."

"But if Dragoran's plan was moving forward as he wanted, Lucius in his grasp, why would he send his soldiers here?"

Mikel shrugged. "As I said, perhaps trying to push you into Hanover's arms that much faster? Or just a general impatience? Lack of trust in Hanover's abilities? There are a host of possibilities. Once I get the chance to talk to the King of the Tor, I'll let you know what he had in mind."

"You're going to talk to Malor Dragoran? Just waltz into the Tor and ask him?"

Mikel offered Drin a mysterious smile. "I don't know how to waltz, so no, I'll employ a different approach. But yes, eventually I will get the truth from him."

"You say that with so much certainty I fear your innate arrogance is finally taking hold."

Mikel wasn't offended by Drin's comment, understanding from where it was coming. "I'm many things, Queen Dengannon. Arrogant isn't one of them."

Drin leaned back then. Once again she needed to revise her appraisal of Mikel. He was right. He wasn't arrogant. He was competent. Dangerously so. Because when he said he was going to do something, he did it. Without fail.

"You make a persuasive argument, Mikel. Still, I find all this difficult to accept."

"Why would I lie?" Mikel understood why Drin was struggling with Hanover's betrayal. He had, indeed, been in the same place that she was in now. The emotions visible on her face all too familiar. And he knew as well that all he could do was offer her the information she needed to make the right decision. Because he didn't doubt that she would and that she would learn from this harsh lesson, becoming that much stronger and capable.

"You're a thief," Drin replied without hesitation, needing to delay the reality of her circumstances for just a little while longer. "A smuggler. The King of the Underworld."

"All of that is true. But I never lie. I might not tell the whole truth, but I never lie."

"What's the difference?" Drin demanded.

"Good question, and perhaps there isn't a difference, but I like to think there is. Regardless, Teddy gave me the records." Mikel nodded toward the small leather knapsack he had placed on the table in the center of the living room before he took his seat by the fire. "You can go through it all and see for yourself."

"I'll take a look. But just because he has debts doesn't mean he's the one behind this. It could just mean that he has debts."

"You're right. I won't argue that."

"But ..."

"It doesn't matter your station in life. I've seen this happen before. When you're in arrears as he is, you do what's best for you. Always. No matter the cost. No matter the consequences."

"Wouldn't it just be best for him if he married me?" Drin needed to try to protect her dignity just one more time, finding it difficult to accept that someone she had grown up with and trusted had attempted to use her ... and she had almost allowed him to do it.

"It would from a political perspective."

Drin sighed, finally realizing that trying to deny the truth was a waste of time. "He would have power but he wouldn't be able to clear his debts. That would be the case so long as I was Queen of the Crux because he knows I would never permit the treasury to be used as a personal account. He'd need to get rid of me."

"Correct. As I said, it comes down to power and money. He needs both. Thus, his willingness to do whatever he must to ensure he achieves both."

"Still, that doesn't mean ..."

"There's something else you need to know." Mikel had little desire to beat what he viewed as a dead horse. Once Drin reviewed the materials he had brought, she would have no choice but to accept that she had made an error in judgment. From his perspective, the key was that she learn from it, because as Kaduna had taught him, you learned a great deal more from your mistakes than from your successes.

"Even more worrisome than this?"

"Yes, unfortunately so."

"Tell me," Drin sighed, more than just a little concerned by Mikel's flinty expression.

"As you know, I have business relationships with many different people in this and other cities."

"People of more nefarious means is what you're saying."

"People who make a living by applying a different definition of what's right and wrong, the argument being that someone is going to do what they shouldn't be doing so better they do it so it's done right."

Drin smiled. She appreciated Mikel's way with words. "That definition could apply to you."

"It could, yes." He said it with a smile, clearly not insulted. "In fact, I readily admit that it does."

"What did you learn?" She hoped that this was the last of his surprises for that evening.

"While Nat and Teddy were searching through Hanover's business dealings, they found a receipt of him owing several hundred pieces of gold to Alicia's Aromatherapy and Herbal Remedies."

"Why is that strange? It sounds like she's a physick of some sort."

"Alicia is, in fact, a physick. And a very good one."

"Now I'm worried. You say that like you know her quite well."

"I do know her. Quite well as you said. She's a lovely woman. And she's very good at what she does. I can tell you that from working with her."

A touch of trepidation ran through Drin. "Why am I worried that you know her so well?"

"Because though she runs a profitable business, she has an even more profitable side business. Poisons."

That touch of trepidation became more than a touch, Drin's entire body turning cold. "What did you find?"

"Amelia keeps meticulous records but they're in a code that only she can interpret. She was kind enough to decipher them for me so that I could match the bill of sale to Hanover's debt."

"Mikel, please just get to it."

"She makes a tea, though she won't tell me exactly what's in it, but it truly is ..."

"Mikel," Drin repeated, her tone commanding.

"Sorry. Amelia told me that she created an almost unde-tectable poison that she sold to House Hanover on credit."

Drin couldn't quite understand why she was experiencing so much angst in that moment. Perhaps it was because of the way Mikel was drawing the matter out rather than getting right to the heart of it. "What poison?"

"Whiteshade. The primary ingredient the poison's name-sake. And another interesting fact?"

"Do I really want to know?"

"You do. Amelia rarely makes this poison because it's so hard to obtain the primary ingredient. She didn't have to worry about that, however, because the ingredient was provided to her by the representative from House Hanover."

"Why is it so hard to obtain?"

"It only grows in one place and is jealously guarded by the man who rules there." Drin closed her eyes, shaking her head. "Let me guess. The Tor."

"Exactly so," Mikel confirmed, "and Malor Dragoran guards the release of Whiteshade jealously. In large part because it's often his preferred method for dealing with those who anger him."

"Why is this important to us now?"

"I had Amelia check your father's remains."

"You did what? He was interred beneath the Citadel." She could barely contain herself. Her anger white hot at Mikel's intrusion.

"I wanted to see ..."

"You did this without my permission? You're talking about my father! You had no right!"

Mikel could have been flippant. He could have attempted to deflect her anger. He didn't. "I'm sorry. I shouldn't have done it without your permission. But I thought we needed to know. Amelia and I did not disturb his remains in any way other than to look for the one sign that would confirm our suspicions."

"*We*? You make it sound like we're in this together."

"We," Mikel confirmed. "And are we not? Right now, it seems that our fortunes are linked together. I admit that might not always be the case. But until it is no longer so, it is."

There was a great deal that Drin wanted to say. Almost all of it dredged up by her anger. Instead she motioned for him to continue. "What did she find during her examination? Whiteshade?"

Mikel nodded. He didn't feel the need to say anything else.

They both knew what that meant. No one stood much of a chance against a Drude to begin with. That monster tearing her father apart confirmed that.

But just in case her father evaded the creature called forth by a practitioner of the Curse, he would have died anyway. Slowly. Painfully. His insides melting rather than a monster ripping out his guts.

"Amelia said as well that the amount of Whiteshade House Hanover ordered from her was enough for more than one person." The look he gave her was significant and unmistakable.

With all that Mikel had revealed to her, there was only one conclusion that Drin could reach.

Lucius Hanover and Malor Dragoran both wanted her father dead. Badly. And they wanted her as well. Because with her came the throne of the Crux.

Then, once they had the Crux, they'd get rid of her the way they got rid of her father without needing to call upon a Drude.

"This is all just a little much for this late in the evening," Drin sighed. She felt defeated, Mikel beating down her resistance. In as gentle a way as he could manage while still getting his point across.

"I understand it's not easy."

"It isn't." Drin laughed softly. "You know, there was a time when I thought that Lucius and I were made for one another."

"I can understand." And Mikel did, not feeling the need to reveal any more than that.

"I just can't believe ..." But thinking about it more from an objective perspective, Drin could believe. She couldn't deny the evidence Mikel presented to her. She couldn't ignore what her heart was telling her, even though she didn't want to listen to it.

"Perhaps Hanover did love you once. Perhaps he still does. But the need for money changes you. Sometimes for the good, more often for the bad. That and the promise of sitting on the throne on his own without anyone trying to hold him back was likely too much for him to resist."

Drin nodded. "Thank you for telling me that. I know it wasn't easy for you, taking the risk of coming here. Not sure how I would react."

"Yes, you do tend to fly off into wild rages."

Drin laughed then. A good laugh. The first time she had really laughed since she had claimed the throne. "I do, you're right. So I suggest that you do your best in the future not to set me off."

"As you command, my Queen." Mikel pushed himself out of his chair. His knee ached terribly, the damaged joint protesting during the lengthy conversation. The only thing to do for it was to get moving. And that he planned to do. Because he still had a great deal more to do before he called it a night, having a little more fun with Lucius Hanover at the top of his list.

"And how are Nat's lessons going?" Drin wasn't ready to let Mikel go just yet. For some reason she didn't quite understand, she took comfort from his presence. There was a calmness about him that seemed to wash off onto her, even when they were discussing matters such as a traitor and her father's murder.

"She's doing quite well," Mikel replied. "She's curious and she's driven. A potentially dangerous combination, but she's handling it well."

"You still won't tell me who's training her?"

Mikel chuckled before he took a few steps toward the hidden door at his back. "I made a promise."

"And you keep your promises," Drin finished for him. She didn't like the fact that there was a Magus in Innsbruck and she didn't know who it was.

"I do."

"Perhaps that is why I find you so exasperating yet don't throw you in the dungeon."

"Perhaps," Mikel agreed. Rather than walking through the doorway, he stepped up to the back wall of Drin's study. Twisting the very bottom of the oil lamp bolted to the wall, a small door slid open on silent hinges. He didn't mind revealing how he had gotten into Drin's chambers unseen. She already knew of this passageway. Though he doubted that she knew of the three other secret doors that were situated about her suite.

Before he could step into the darkness, Drin called to him. "I don't doubt what you have told me. And I thank you for doing so. But you are not to take any obvious action against Lucius Hanover."

Mikel turned back around. Half his body in shadow. Half his body in the light. "Obvious?"

"Obvious," Drin confirmed, finding Mikel's current positioning uniquely appropriate.

"Thank you, Queen Dengannon," Mikel said, nodding to her in respect. His smile, once warm, now devious. "I will use your words as my guide. Now I'll take my leave."

Yet before he could take two steps, she called him back one more time, certain that Mikel identified the loophole she had given him. "Why are you there to help me when I need you?"

"I couldn't really say."

"Probably just bad luck on my part," Drin said with a shrug.

"Funny." Mikel appreciated her humor, especially after all they had discussed.

"The best jokes have a pinch of truth to them. Wouldn't you agree, Broken Bear?"

"Broken Bear?" Mikel was surprised to hear that moniker. "Where did you learn that?"

"My sources might not be as many as yours, but they are still good at their work. One of your earlier calling cards, I believe. When you first started making a name for yourself in the shadows of the Crux. Something about an old injury," she said, nodding toward his knee, acknowledging that she had caught his limp, "that clearly still bothers you combined with your appearance ... well, the resemblance is uncanny."

He chose not to dispute her claim, allowing her the pleasure of her small victory. In part because he liked to see her smile. Even when she was seeking to get under his skin. "I haven't heard that name for so long that I've almost forgotten it."

Drin gave him a look that Mikel found difficult to decipher. "It fits you, and I kind of like it."

9

A DEBT TO PAY

"Showing off again, Malor?" Lucius Hanover leaned back in his chair, dropping the scroll he was reading atop the desk. He offered his conspirator a sly smile. "It might impress the ladies of your court, but it does very little for me."

The portal of spinning black mist had appeared without warning, then vanished once Malor Dragoran stepped through. He ignored Lucius' comment, not worthy of his notice since it came from an innate weakness. "Have you read all of these? Or are they just for show?"

The burly King of the Tor, black hair setting off the speckled grey of his beard, motioned to the shelves of books behind Hanover. All of the texts were classics, most of them centuries old. Yet he was certain that Hanover had never cracked the spine of a single volume.

He didn't perceive Lucius as a learned man. He did perceive Lucius as a man who wanted to maintain the fabrication of being learned, because it fit the image he sought to project.

"How dare you suggest otherwise," Lucius declared, his voice rising. His pique on further display when he leaned forward and pounded the top of his desk with an open palm. "Of course I have."

Malor's lips curled into a cruel smile. He heard the lie, confirmed by the young man's added histrionics to strengthen his pretense of taking offense.

"I find that hard to believe."

"I don't care what you believe, Malor," Lucius replied sharply. Not in the mood for his partner's often derogatory comments. Also made uncomfortable by the power Malor displayed so openly. A power that Lucius could scarcely comprehend. It was for those reasons that Lucius felt the need to demonstrate that he wasn't cowed, fearing what would happen if he showed any weakness. "Now tell me. Why are you here?"

Malor's eyes narrowed, his spiteful smile taking on the hint of a scowl. Though he disliked being talked to in such a manner, he allowed Hanover's disrespect to go unchallenged. This time.

Malor was consumed by other matters that were of greater importance than a whiny young lord, so he would put the head of House Hanover in his place another time. When he could take his time and enjoy it. Nevertheless, he would take him to task if only briefly because a lesson needed to be learned. "I would not be here if you demonstrated greater competence in the responsibilities assigned to you."

Lucius bristled at the insult, his anger blinding him as to who truly stood across from him. "I had everything under control."

"Did you really?" Malor's sarcasm dripped from his words.

"I did."

Malor smiled then, nodding his head slightly as he sat down uninvited on the edge of Lucius' desk, earning a glower that didn't faze him.

"You did not have Celindria Dengannon under control, did

you, Lucius? The most important piece of the puzzle slipped right through your fingers."

"Celindria didn't matter!" Lucius shouted, unable to control his rage. Still smarting from that failure, though he refused to acknowledge it openly as such.

He was going to protest more vigorously, but his words died in his throat when he caught the look that Malor gave him. That of a predator preparing to strike. A reminder that his partnership with the King of the Tor was not truly a partnership no matter how much he hated that fact.

"That didn't matter," he repeated much more quietly. "I was minutes away from the throne. Whether with or without Celindria Dengannon didn't matter. I was minutes away from achieving our objective when I was cut off at the knees."

"Why should I believe you, Lucius? I have received nothing except promises from you and not a hint of proof that you have done as charged." Malor lifted one hand up from Lucius' desk, a small swirl of black mist drifting out from his palm. He wanted to remind his compatriot exactly who he was and what he could do ... if he were provoked.

"I'm telling you the truth, Malor," Lucius explained, infusing his voice with an earnestness that was rarely there, unable to take his eyes from the tainted magic that now spun atop Malor's palm with the ferocity of a tornado. A warning that he needed to tread carefully with his ally.

"Then how did you fail?" Malor's voice was calm, not offering a hint of what he was thinking or feeling. Although his dark eyes were more revealing, his fury burning brightly in the center of his pitch-black orbs.

"I did not fail. I promise you. All was progressing as it should have. Exactly as we discussed. I did not fail." Lucius bit out his last few words, wanting to ensure that Malor understood that he was telling him the truth.

"You didn't?" Malor's tone suggested that he found Lucius'

claim difficult to swallow. "If you didn't fail, then what stopped you from claiming the throne you've lusted after almost as much as you've lusted after Celindria Dengannon?"

"A wildcard."

"Really," Malor mused. "Because knowing your history with the now Queen of the Crux, I can only assume that you let her slip from the trap we so painstakingly crafted for her because you still love her despite her not returning your affection."

"No, that's not true," Lucius protested, a slight wail seeping into his voice.

"Explain." Malor spoke in a conversational tone, though his flaring eyes demanded an answer.

"Celindria had unexpected help. The wildcard as I said."

"And who is this wildcard?"

"From what I've been able to piece together ... the King of the Underworld."

"The King of the Underworld," Malor snorted, both in amusement and disgust. The spinning tornado of black grew in size, matching its master's rising fury. "The King of the Under-world is no more than a myth."

"Apparently not."

The spinning black mist blinked out when Malor closed his fist then pushed himself off the desk and began to walk slowly around the study. "An interesting development if you speak the truth, Lucius. However, that does not change the fact that the Queen of the Crux is not in my thrall. That was your responsibility. That means the failure rests with you."

"Malor, there is no way that I could have known, any of us could have known, that she would receive such critical assistance when she did." Lucius started and stopped several times. Worried. Not sure how to convince his ally that he was speaking the truth. "There is no way that we could have prepared. This was the variable we could not have accounted for, because we didn't even know the variable existed until he revealed himself."

Malor did not reply right away, continuing to pace about the room, hands clasped behind his back. When he did, Lucius breathed a sigh of relief. "I will give you the benefit of the doubt this one time, Lucius."

Lucius nodded. More than grateful as he acknowledged his place with respect to the King of the Tor despite the pain of doing so.

"Nevertheless, I still need her. You will get her for me, Lucius. The charge remains in place."

"I have a debt to pay first, Malor. I have to kill the King of the Underworld. He has embarrassed me multiple times since I learned of his identity."

"Your embarrassment means nothing to me, Lucius," Malor scoffed, his contempt plain. "Forget him for now. Your debt to me takes precedence. And that debt won't be cleared until the Queen of the Crux is mine."

"Why? Why do you need her? She was supposed to be mine. She should still be mine."

"There is more at stake here than just the Splintered Empire, Lucius."

"What do you mean?"

"You need know no more than the fact that she has a role to play that I wasn't aware of until recently."

"And what if I still want her?" Lucius asked in a deflated tone, knowing how Malor was going to respond before he finished asking his question.

"What you want is of little concern to me, Lucius. I suggest that you accept what I give you before I take what little you have left away from you."

10

FALSE FLAG

"Is it supposed to work that way?" Henri Dengannon, Battle Lord of the Crux, nudged the wreckage at his feet with a steel-tipped boot. He had learned as a young soldier that you didn't need a blade in hand to kill an enemy. Blunt force worked just as well.

He and Leonardo stood over a kite larger than a wagon that had crashed almost in the exact middle of the Splintered Bridge, avoiding by no more than a few feet one of the many massive holes that pockmarked the span. Knowing what would emerge from those pits when night fell, they kept a wary eye. Ready to draw their blades. Sometimes the monsters' desire to eat was greater than their fear of the light.

They had spent so much time on the causeway that neither paid much attention to the massive stone spires that rose a mile and more in height from the canyon floor, white and purple heather growing along the sides contrasting with the smoky grey of the clouds that the upper third of the spikes pierced.

The murk hid what waited at the base of the Trench. Henri chose not to think of those perils, having enough challenges to deal with as it was with Malor Dragoran's soldiers massing for another attack from the eastern side of the only causeway that spanned the Trench.

The Splintered Bridge connected the Kingdom of the Crux to the Kingdom of the Tor, those two Kingdoms once forming what had been named the Splintered Empire, and what Malor Dragoran lusted to make the Splintered Empire once again.

"No, it's not." Leonardo stared down at the wood and cloth that had formed his latest creation. Three long spears were still fixed to the frame. That irritated him, because those spikes that more resembled harpoons should have been released before the kite crashed to the ground.

He could blame it on the gusty and unpredictable winds that swirled above the Trench and complicated his efforts to guide the kite to the Tor side of the causeway, but there was a simpler reason for his failure. He had gotten his math wrong.

"Why didn't it work?" Henri wasn't taking the young inventor to task. All of Leonardo's creations worked ... eventually.

Those that he had employed so far certainly had proven effective in keeping the Tor soldiers on their side of the Trench. The most effective at that moment the fire tubes that the Crux soldiers had snaked across the Splintered Bridge and fixed into place just a few yards behind them.

The Tor soldiers had yet to figure out a way to get past the streams of flame that made it seem like the dragons of old had taken up residence atop the bridge. Until they did, the stalemate between the opposing Kingdoms would remain, and that didn't bother the Battle Lord in the least.

"I'm not sure," Leonardo grumbled, not pleased, bending down and picking through the debris. "I designed these to work based on just a few very basic principles, so I don't know ..." He barked out a laugh as he swiped his long blonde hair out of his eyes. "It's always something simple."

"You know the cause?" Henri asked.

"I do," Leonardo confirmed. He moved a few pieces of crumpled cloth to reveal the undercarriage of his creation. "The kite is supposed to drift over the bridge and follow the guides that we chiseled into the stone rails. It was doing just as it should. But it didn't release the spears because the timing mechanism failed." Leonardo held up a bladder that was still half full of water. "This needs to be empty for that to happen."

"So a larger nail to increase the flow?" Henri couldn't say that he understood all the creations that Leonardo brought to him. The young man was full of ideas. Often speaking in the language of mathematics or physics or some other science that he didn't always follow as well as he would have liked.

But in this instance, the Battle Lord did comprehend what had gone wrong. The release mechanism worked according to a basic principle. When the kite left the last guide along the railing on the Crux side of the bridge, the nail sprung free and punctured the bladder. When the bladder was empty, the latch holding the spears in place unlocked. Those spears then dropped down out of the sky. When they struck true, they could cause a great deal of damage. And when they didn't, they sowed an undercurrent of fear among the Tor soldiers. At least that's how it was supposed to work.

"Precisely," Leonardo replied, his voice filled with excitement. "I'll modify the formula so we can try again tomorrow. And if this doesn't work, I still have three more kite prototypes to test."

"Then I'll let you get to it, Leonardo. Do you need anything from me?" Henri couldn't help but smile, the inventor's excitement contagious despite the bloody nature of his business.

"No, no, nothing at all." Leonardo trotted back toward the western side of the Splintered Bridge, holding the half-full water bladder in his hands. "This shouldn't take me more than a few hours to perfect."

Watching him go, Henri resolved to thank Mikel the next

time he met with him on the Crux. If the King of the Underworld had not suggested to Celindria that she employ Leonardo's talents to ensure the Tor soldiers were kept to their side of the causeway …

Well, Henri didn't want to think about where matters would stand.

He was simply grateful that the young inventor had jumped at the chance and proven his worth as soon as he arrived, viewing the constant skirmishing against Malor Dragoran's forces as the perfect testing ground for his creations.

"Battle Lord, we have visitors," Magnus said. The Sergeant who led the squad of soldiers who accompanied Henri out onto the Splintered Bridge motioned toward the eastern side.

An equal number of Tor soldiers approached, seeking to parley, one of them bearing the white flag.

"More threats, General Booruz?"

Henri squared up to the man who led the Tor soldiers charged with crossing the Splintered Bridge. A charge they had yet to meet. And so long as Henri drew breath, he meant to ensure that they didn't. Because if they did, the Kingdom of the Crux was doomed.

"Not threats, Battle Lord. Rather promises."

"There seems to be little difference between the two."

General Booruz shrugged apologetically. Motioning for the soldiers at his back to stay where they were, he continued forward to shake the Battle Lord's hand. Wanting to pay his respects and also engage in a private conversation without any curious ears close by. "I do what I must, Battle Lord. Just as you do."

They weren't friends. That wasn't possible. Not with them representing interests that were opposed to one another. But there was a mutual respect, having faced off for decades, the tension between the two Kingdoms separated by the Trench simmering, on occasion boiling over, just as it was then, ever since the Splintered Empire earned its name.

"So what shall we discuss today, General Booruz? The peaceful withdrawal of your soldiers?"

The barrel of a man, clean shaven to match his bald scalp, the only hair on his face his very prominent eyebrows, chuckled softly. "That's why I enjoy speaking with you, Battle Lord. Your sense of humor."

"I wasn't making a joke, General." Even so, Henri was smiling. They had engaged in this conversation many times before during the last few months. Booruz every so often made his way across the bridge to make his demands. Henri ignored them. The game they needed to play. Though both always ready to take advantage of the other's weakness when presented with the opportunity.

"You know that you cannot dislodge us, Battle Lord. We outnumber you at least three to one. We have no cause to leave."

"Not yet, perhaps."

Booruz snorted, shaking his head in annoyance. "More blasted contraptions coming our way. I must admit those dragons of yours are quite impressive and effective, but they cannot blow fire forever. We will find a way around them."

"And until you do we will continue to use them, while coming up with some new obstacles to place in your way."

"And right there is the very foundation of war." General Booruz's smile broadened. "Not just blood, steel, and death as most believe. But strategy. Identifying strengths and weaknesses. Looking for gaps and opportunities presented by your opponent. Trying to ensure your opponent doesn't find yours. Much like a game of chess."

"Except for the blood and death as you said," Henri clarified, "and the sorrow, anguish, and loss that inevitably follows."

"True," Booruz admitted. "Yet there is something to be said

for the mental aspect of the exercise. The matching of wits. That's what appealed to me when I first joined the Tor army." He nodded toward Henri. "And you, Battle Lord? What brought you to serve the Crux in your current capacity?"

"Duty, General Booruz. My brother was king. He required a Battle Lord."

"You didn't want to lead the Crux army?" Booruz wondered, his expression one of slight disbelief. He had striven for his current position as soon as he accepted his commission, working his way up the Tor ranks during the following decades.

"I had other interests, General Booruz. Yet it seems my brother recognized a talent I didn't know I had until I was placed in this position."

"Quite a talent, indeed, Battle Lord. I must admit that my liege, King Dragoran, is very impressed by your efforts. More than just a little irritated by them as well."

"Not just my efforts, General Booruz. My soldiers' efforts as well."

"Of course, Battle Lord. That goes without saying. A general can't be a general without the soldiers who fight for him. And that brings me to why I am here."

"It's not for us to cede the Splintered Bridge to you as you've been demanding since this stalemate began?"

General Booruz smiled again. "I admit that would make things easier for us. But no. King Dragoran has asked that I offer you a proposal."

"I can't wait to hear it."

"King Dragoran invites your niece, Queen Dengannon, to visit him on the Tor to discuss how they might bring this conflict to a close. She will be well guarded, I promise you that."

Henri didn't laugh as he wanted to. He heard the earnestness in his adversary's voice. He also believed that Booruz would keep his word. But his belief didn't extend to Malor

Dragoran. "I'm sorry, General Booruz, but you really expect me to share this invitation with the Queen? It's absurd. Why would she deign to accept such a proposal? Why would she willingly put herself in a cage crafted by a man seeking to take her Kingdom from her?"

"Because King Dragoran seeks her hand in marriage, Battle Lord. He seeks her, not just the Kingdom of the Crux."

Henri didn't reply right away. Booruz wasn't smiling now. He appeared to be completely serious.

"Bear with me, Battle Lord, for I must impart the message entrusted to me." Booruz sighed, not really believing his own words, yet having no choice except to say them. Because he understood the cost of disobeying his liege lord. "King Dragoran desires to end the conflict between us. Rather than blades, he desires to use the bonds of matrimony. Better an alliance in his opinion. He believes that he can offer to the Crux as much or more than the Crux can offer the Tor."

"King Dragoran expects Queen Dengannon to visit the Tor, essentially place herself in his custody, after Tor soldiers attempted to kidnap her just a month ago right before her coronation?" Henri couldn't quite believe what he was hearing. He didn't doubt Booruz's veracity, though he did doubt the veracity of the King of the Tor.

"An unfortunate occurrence I readily admit," General Booruz replied. "King Dragoran apologizes for that mishap, which occurred without his knowledge. Those responsible have been punished."

"Is that so?" Henri demanded.

"It is. King Dragoran promises that your niece has nothing to fear. She may come and go as she likes." Booruz shrugged again, offering a sly smile. "You know how it is, Battle Lord. There are many ways to wage war, the application of steel only one of them."

"Whether King Dragoran is or is not willing to accept the

blame, the attempted kidnapping of Queen Dengannon was more than just unfortunate, General Booruz," the Battle Lord said, his voice quiet but firm. "It was an act of war. Worse even than these games we play here above the Trench."

"I cannot speak more on that terrible event other than to reaffirm that your niece has nothing to fear and much to gain from the proposal King Dragoran offers her. Though I should note that there is more to this visit than just an opportunity to improve relations between our Kingdoms."

"I can't wait to hear what that might be," Henri prompted, although he already had a sense as to what was coming next. Dragoran had failed to gain what he wanted with the stick. Now he was going to try with the carrot.

"King Dragoran proposes a marriage with Queen Dengannon. Doing so would bring our two Kingdoms together just as they were before the events that led to the severing of the Splintered Empire. We would be whole once more and exercise a power and influence against which few other Realms could stand."

The Battle Lord nodded his head slowly. "This is nothing more than a farce, General. Queen Dengannon will never accede to such a request. King Dragoran thinking that she might demonstrates a lack of foresight that is truly stunning."

"Perhaps," Booruz admitted. "Then again, perhaps not. Your niece's ascension to the throne was not without its wobbles."

"Tor soldiers tried to kidnap her. Of course there were wobbles."

"Beyond that, however, there were other issues." Booruz shrugged. This is what he enjoyed the most. The strategy. Matching wits, not blades. "I believe that many of the First Families were not entirely enamored with a young, untried girl ruling the Crux. That and the fact that their business interests span both Kingdoms. So much so that another candidate was under consideration until your niece appeared at such a timely point in the proceedings to claim her place."

"Speak plainly, General. No more games."

"The First Families desire stability, because stability is good for business. And as I said, their business interests extend in both directions across the span upon which we stand now. We both know the First Families care only for themselves, desiring to expand their power, and that desire inevitably requires that they build their wealth. King Dragoran fears what might happen if Queen Dengannon does not meet the needs of the First Families as they expect and are accustomed. He assumes that she would like to rule without having to worry about the First Families looking at her every time there is a drop in their fortunes. King Dragoran is simply suggesting that to ameliorate that concern and accrue several other benefits that he will make plain to her upon her visiting with him on the Tor that she rule with him."

"The First Families desire a great deal, General Booruz, and in this they will be disappointed. Just as your liege will be. Queen Dengannon will never accept such a proposal. You know that just as well as I do." And Booruz did, Henri seeing it written on his face, which meant that he was making the proposal for another reason.

Not because of any belief that it would be accepted. Rather because he wanted to create the perception that Dragoran was willing to bend and demonstrate some flexibility.

Why? What benefit would that offer the King of the Tor?

To those questions, the answers were fairly obvious.

To curry more favor with the First Families. Because Booruz was right in one respect. Just as had happened when his brother, Charles Dengannon, was assassinated, the First Families would do what was best for the First Families. And they likely would be willing to ignore the rumors about Malor

Dragoran's predilections if they believed that his proposal helped to fill their coffers.

"Battle Lord, you are a worthy adversary, so I will speak out of turn, offering my perspective and not that of my lord." Booruz wasn't smiling now, his face descending into a frown. "You of all people must understand the position that you and your soldiers are in. Your numbers are nothing compared to ours. You may continue to offer us surprises here and there, you can continue to do all that you can to hold us back, but the truth is that you can only do so for so long. Eventually, we will cross the Splintered Bridge. And I suggest that it would be best for both our Kingdoms that we do so under the banner of peace rather than the banner of war."

"Clever, General Booruz, very clever indeed. Was this your idea?"

Henri had no doubt that word of the proposal would spread if it wasn't leaked already. With the appropriate rhetoric applied, the Dengannons would come across as warmongers.

Never a good thing in a Kingdom reliant on commerce, and that would weaken his niece's position even more, emboldening the First Families and increasing the pressure already being felt by the throne.

Because Booruz was correct in one respect. Many of the First Families were watching Celindria closely. Her youth and inexperience made them nervous. Several of the more powerful Families still had designs on her throne. One in particular just as had been the case prior to her coronation.

"The proposal ... no. This conversation, yes." Booruz smiled broadly then, clearly pleased with himself as he took the Battle Lord's question as a compliment. "For the success of both Kingdoms, Battle Lord, an alliance as proposed makes sense. This decision can't be personal. It must be political."

"And if my Queen chooses to make a personal decision rather than a political one?"

Booruz studied Henri for quite some time, then sighed apologetically. "The Queen of the Crux will marry the King of the Tor. It's only a matter of when and under what circumstances. The Splintered Empire will be whole again. I suggest that Queen Dengannon accept her fate willingly. As we both know, King Dragoran has little patience for those who defy him."

With that, General Booruz offered Henri a nod of respect before turning on his heel and heading back toward his camp. The sun was setting, which meant the creatures lurking beneath the bridge would be stirring soon.

The Wyverns that every so often broke through the clouds covering the Trench were bad enough. The nasties nesting on the span's underside were worse. Not only aggressive, but also cunning. And much more rapacious, which was saying something.

The Zaroi that came out when the sun went down ensured that there was little for Henri to worry about from the Tor soldiers until morning. Although now, after his conversation with Booruz, Henri had a great deal more to worry about than just holding the Splintered Bridge.

Still, he would keep to his routine and visit with the guards. Just to make sure they were ready for the evening. And he would visit with Leonardo after dinner. He wanted to check on the status of the young man's refinements to what he was calling his battle kite as well as what else might be spinning in the back of his devious mind.

He would decide as well how to forward to his niece Dragoran's proposal. She would refuse, just as he would counsel.

Nevertheless, there seemed to be more in play than just this proposal. For the life of him, however, he couldn't see what that might be. And that's what concerned him the most.

11

MAKING A NEW FRIEND

"Samuel seems to be in a good mood." Teddy sat across from Mikel, barely able to wiggle into the chair thanks to his great size.

Papers were strewn about the small circular table that separated them. They had spent the last few hours going through the previous month's balance sheets for Mikel's various businesses situated on the Crux and beyond. All of them doing quite well. Both those that were legitimate and those that were less so.

"You know him," Mikel replied. "He enjoys tweaking the nose of a First Family whenever he gets the chance. One in particular."

"That he does," Teddy agreed. "He stopped by right before we got started."

"He wanted his next job?"

"He did indeed."

Mikel nodded, not surprised. "I'm sure we can come up with something for him to do."

"I assumed as much. Before that, however, let me take you through the numbers for ..."

Teddy held onto his thought, hearing the commotion coming from the common room in The Fox's Lair. Pulling himself out of his seat, Teddy went to the door. He wasn't worried. Short of a company of soldiers, no one was coming back here without an invitation.

To prove Teddy's point, the noise died quickly. Then there was a quiet knock at the door.

Teddy opened it, speaking to the barkeep. He then shut the door and turned toward Mikel.

"An esteemed member of the Crux ruling class would like to speak with me I take it?" Mikel asked.

"Something like that, although esteemed might be too generous a term," Teddy confirmed with a sardonic smile. "He brought a squad of soldiers with him."

If nothing else, his visitor was quite predictable. Mikel assumed that this meeting would take place. It was just a matter of when. "They're being taken care of?"

"All disarmed. All enjoying a mug of ale on the house with a good number of the lads and lasses keeping an eye on them."

Mikel nodded. "Send him in then."

"You going to tweak his nose?"

Mikel sighed. "I don't know if I can. It's likely already quite bent out of shape."

Teddy smiled at that. "That it is. Wait until you see his face." He left then, leaving the door open so that Lucius Hanover, First of his House, could storm through. Reluctantly, Teddy closed the door behind him. He would have much preferred to stay in the room and listen to what he was certain was going to be an entertaining conversation.

"How dare you!" Hanover slammed a palm down on the table to underscore his point. "How dare you!"

Mikel didn't reply. Sitting there calmly, he studied the man who viewed him as his nemesis. Yet in Mikel's mind, the Lord of House Hanover was no more than a privileged pain in the ass not worthy of his attention if not for Hanover's intentions and his secret ally.

Then he smiled. Teddy was right. Hanover was apoplectic. His face redder than an overripe tomato. A vein on his forehead pulsed violently as a thin stream of spittle trickled down from his lower lip.

"I don't dare anything, Hanover. I do. That's the difference between you and me."

"You gutter-born upstart," Hanover hissed. "You would speak to me in such a way? I lead the most powerful House on the Crux. In all the Splintered Empire ..."

Fun though it might be to have Hanover continue with his tirade, Mikel was more interested in completing his discussion with Teddy so that he could move on to matters that actually made him money and didn't waste his time. So Mikel cut off Hanover, not bothering to suggest that there were in fact a few Houses that would take issue with his claim, particularly Dengannon and Dragoran since both sat on a throne.

"What used to be one of the most powerful Houses," Mikel corrected, enjoying how Hanover's face fell. Then how he spluttered for a few seconds as he tried to defend against Mikel's assertion and failed to get anything intelligible out of his craw.

"Not much you can say to that?" Mikel leaned forward, his eyes gleaming brightly. He didn't take a great deal of pleasure in putting someone in their place, unless it was someone like Lucius Hanover, who believed that the world revolved around him. "It only makes sense after all. You backed the wrong horse."

"The wrong horse?" Hanover's expression revealed that he didn't understand.

"Yes, the wrong horse. The losing horse." Mikel shook his head sadly. "You backed yourself for the throne, and that was just one of your many mistakes. Because now you're paying for it. Treasury depleted. Debts being called in. Business deals going bad. You've placed yourself in a very difficult position and I expect that it will only get worse."

"I had every right to move for the throne."

"Just because you had the right to do so didn't mean that it was the right thing to do." Mikel gave Hanover a wink. "Queen Dengannon certainly didn't appreciate your efforts."

"Queen Dengannon has her own difficulties," Hanover declared. "If she had accepted my proposal, then I have no doubt that much of the unpleasantness leading up to her Coronation could have been avoided."

Mikel's smile turned as cold as the frigid air of the Frozen Waste. Not an admission of guilt. Yet not a claim of innocence either. It really didn't matter. Celindria had taken a dim view of House Hanover once she assumed her father's place, and rightly so. "Queen Dengannon has a more discerning eye for horses."

"You, you mean?" snorted Hanover. "Really? The purported King of the Underworld?"

Mikel laughed with Hanover. "I wasn't suggesting as much. I was noting, though apparently not clearly enough, that she knows what you and House Hanover can offer her."

"And what would that be?" Hanover missed how he was being set up.

"Absolutely nothing ... other than misfortune and mishaps."

Hanover didn't respond right away. This interaction wasn't working out as he thought it would. Before he made his way to the tavern, he had envisioned the dialogue that would take place. And this was not it. "Queen Dengannon will be mine," he hissed, his fury threatening to get the better of him. "Have no fear of that."

"I have no fear indeed, Hanover. As I said, Queen Dengannon knows who she can trust ... and who she can't."

"I remind you, Caledonii, in this city as in most of the other

Realms, you are an outcast. With the pall of your heritage hanging over you, I suggest that you treat your betters with greater respect."

"I treat people how they treat me," Mikel replied. "Those who deserve respect are treated with respect. Those who don't … aren't."

"You think that because you are safe here in your tavern that you can say whatever you want to me?" Hanover shook his head from side to side, his smile threatening. "I can get to you whenever I want, Caledonii."

"And yet you haven't," Mikel challenged.

"I haven't tried yet, Caledonii." Hanover nodded then, gaze becoming a squint. "I will get to you when you are worth my time."

"And this is why you came here, Hanover? To threaten me?" Mikel wasn't worried. He was impatient. He wanted to finish the dialogue and get back to what was truly important.

"Down to business then," Hanover said. "Where is it?" He tried to maintain an expression of cold disinterest. It didn't work. The anger that he was feeling almost palpable in his voice.

"You'll need to enlighten me. Unlike you, I have a great many business interests, and it's difficult to keep track of them all. Where is what?"

Hanover's eyes flashed, his anger now burning brightly. Still, he managed to maintain control over his temper. And that only because he remembered his place in the world compared to that of this self-proclaimed King of the Underworld who was so far beneath him.

Looking down upon the Caledonii, he thought it was only appropriate that he stood above him. A reminder as to their true places in the world.

Even so, the Caledonii had a role to play even if he was the cause of Hanover's current predicament, so Lucius needed to manage him carefully. That in mind, he quashed his temper. All business now.

"My shipment."

"What shipment would that be?" Mikel's expression of innocence earned a growl from Hanover.

"You know exactly what shipment," Hanover pressed, forcing the words through gritted teeth.

Mikel chuckled softly. "As I said, I have a great many business interests, Hanover. I deal with a dozen or more shipments daily. And last I checked, we don't do business together. If your shipment has gone missing, I don't know why you believe I can help."

Hanover forced himself to remain calm. He kept his fingers away from the hilt of the sword hanging on his hip certain that if he touched the steel he would pull the blade free from its scabbard.

"From what I understand, you are aware of most of the shipments going to and from the Crux. Legitimate and less so."

"One of the requirements of my business, Hanover. What of it?"

"You just admitted your guilt."

Mikel offered Hanover a condescending smile. "I just admitted to knowing what's moving in and out of Innsbruck. It only makes sense, doesn't it? For me to be successful, I need to know what my competitors and business partners are doing."

"That is a flimsy excuse."

"I offer no excuse, Hanover. I speak the truth. Now what shipment have you lost?" Mikel laughed softly then, leaning back into his chair, crossing his arms. "You do seem to lose things on a much-too-frequent basis. Shipments. Thrones."

"You know what shipment, Caledonii," Lucius hissed, ignoring the latest insult though it was difficult to do. He promised himself that he would gain his revenge when the time was right. "Delivered last night to my shop on the First Ring. Stolen within hours."

"And you think I had something to do with that?" Mikel snorted in amusement. "You give me more credit than I deserve."

"Probably so," Hanover agreed, "but as you just confirmed, you know all that is going in and out of the Crux. You are best positioned to steal my shipment." Hanover tightened his fingers on his belt, his knuckles turning white. He hated having to play this game. With a Caledonii no less. Still, his product was more important than the aggravation he was experiencing. He had to get his shipment back. His future depended upon it.

"In that regard, Hanover, you're correct. I do know all that's going in and out of the Crux. And I must say that I am thoroughly disappointed in you." Mikel shook his head sadly, much as he would if a child had made a mistake, enjoying how the red of Hanover's face slowly turned white, fury becoming rage.

"You know just as I do that milk of the poppy is an illegal substance on the Crux," Mikel continued. "Dealing in it carries the death penalty. So says our good Queen Dengannon. The woman you believe will eventually raise you up to the throne. Though I find that highly unlikely what with your track record." Mikel enjoyed how Hanover's lips twisted into a scowl upon hearing the last part, clearly not ready to be reminded of his failure in the political realm.

"We both know that the laws do not apply to people like me," Hanover snorted, as if Mikel was a fool to think otherwise. "The First Families do as they wish when they wish. We always have. We always will."

"You mean the laws of the Crux?"

"I do," Hanover replied, confused by the question. "The First Families created the laws of the Crux. We follow them when they benefit us. We ignore them when they don't. One of the privileges of real power, Caledonii. Not the power that you like to play with down here in the lower rings of Innsbruck."

Mikel pushed himself up then, stepping around the table so that he and Hanover were almost nose to nose. Although now Mikel was looking down on the truculent lord. "There is another set of laws, Hanover. The laws of the City Below. Those laws apply to all. Low and high. Remember that."

"Really?" Hanover forced himself to stand straight, hating the fact that he needed to crook his neck because the Caledonii was taller than he was. He was going to say more, but he didn't, beginning to feel uncomfortable.

Mikel's eyes had taken on a hollow quality. As if all the emotion had drained away and that the Caledonii wasn't looking at the First of House Hanover, but rather just an object that was in his way.

Seeking to recover the momentum that he had lost, Hanover asked a question. "And what do these supposed laws of the City Below say about my stolen shipment?"

"That the one responsible for that shipment, which was confiscated, not stolen, pay the price demanded when bringing poison such as that onto the Crux."

"You would dare?" Hanover demanded, his face once more red with rage. He needed his anger, fearing that if he didn't bathe in his fury the rising fear within him would become visible.

"As I explained when this conversation began, Hanover, I don't dare. I do." Mikel smiled then, not a hint of humor in his expression. "The question now is whether to carry out the sentence here and now."

"You wouldn't ..." Hanover stopped himself, not wanting to give the Caledonii a chance to repeat again what seemed to be his mantra. "If you try to kill me here, now, you will regret it. I promise you that. The terrible wrath of the First Families will fall upon you."

Hanover's threat clearly had no impact on Mikel. "I don't plan on killing you. Not now anyway. The dance between us will continue for a little while longer."

Hanover studied the Caledonii rather than offering the reply on the tip of his tongue that likely would have made his already difficult circumstances completely untenable. He smiled thinly, a new perspective washing over him.

He was beginning to think that no matter how much it might grate, there was an approach that he hadn't tried that might improve relations between them. At least for a time. After all, the Caledonii did seem to care about making a profit.

"I have no doubt that you know where my shipment is, Caledonii. I'd be happy to pay you a finder's fee. That's what you're after, isn't it? That's all this is? Just a little business."

Mikel shook his head. Hanover didn't seem to understand exactly what was going on, and more was the pity. "I'm not here to do a deal with you, Hanover. If you want your product, I suggest you look in the Churn."

"You didn't!" Lucius was aghast.

"I was just looking out for you, Hanover," Mikel said, pulling his visitor out of his dark thoughts. "Next time I won't be so generous. Now back up before I knock you back."

Involuntarily, Hanover did as Mikel ordered, stepping closer to the door. Embarrassed. Infuriated. Yet he had no outlet to release the manic tension surging through him.

"You have made a terrible mistake, Caledonii. Involving yourself in my business."

"I make mistakes all the time, Hanover. It's the only way to learn."

"Be as flippant as you desire. Your humor will not help you when your reckoning comes."

"Promises, promises, Hanover. You know where to find me."

Unable to think of a clever reply, Hanover growled deeply,

then reached for the knob and pulled the door open, slamming it against the wall before storming out.

Mikel wasn't surprised when Teddy poked his head in a few seconds later. If he was guarding the door he probably heard most of what was said, at least when Hanover was yelling, which was quite often.

"You make another friend?"

"More like another enemy." He motioned for Teddy to come in. "Let's go through what we have planned next for Hanover. I want to see what it's going to take to push him over the edge."

12

OLD FRIEND

"Agnes, I'm very impressed." Mikel stepped out onto the front porch of the bordello. "I had no doubt that you would do well taking over The Cat's Claw. I just didn't know you would do so well so quickly."

"You're pleased?" The petite woman who followed him outside wore a long-sleeved shirt, a collar covering her throat. Much like any other respectable businesswoman. Although what many of her clients requested when they came to her establishment was anything but respectable.

"How could I not be?" She was nervous. Mikel understood why. Assuming responsibility for running one of his most profitable businesses after his previous manager of more than fifteen years retired was a daunting task. "In just the last two months you've increased net revenue by more than twenty percent."

Agnes sighed with relief, fearing that Mikel wouldn't be happy. That she hadn't met his standards. "That's good to hear. I was worried that I hadn't done enough."

"Agnes, you have nothing to worry about. I promoted you because I knew you could handle what's demanded of this position. I just wasn't aware that you would handle it so deftly." He smiled. "We've known each other for how long?"

"Nine years. Ten in just a few weeks." She would never forget when she first met Mikel. He had saved her life, and he had looked after her ever since.

"And during that time have I ever spoken falsely?"

"No, never," Agnes admitted.

"Then breathe a little easier and accept the credit you deserve for your success." He leaned in, as if they were sharing a secret. "Those new weekend events you started have certainly proven popular."

Agnes laughed softly at that. Finally relaxing. At least a little bit. Because whenever she was close to Mikel she felt a little uncomfortable. Usually in a good way, though. "I noticed it with some of our ladies' clients. They enjoyed spending time with them, but they wanted ... something a little ... different."

"An excellent catch. Keep your eyes open and keep thinking. Words that apply to most any situation." Mikel grasped Agnes' forearm, offering a warm squeeze before he stepped away. "And keep up the excellent work. Ten percent bonuses for everyone this Friday. Twenty percent for you."

Agnes beamed. She was pleased, though Mikel's generosity was only a part of it. It was more the freedom that Mikel granted her, how he trusted her, already having several other ideas in mind that she wanted to test based on what she knew about her clientele. "Are you sure you don't want to stay a little longer. Any of the ladies would be more than happy to spend time with you." She gave him a suggestive smile and a wink. "And me as well."

Mikel's smile broadened. He offered her a nod of respect. "Under other circumstances, I would accept your very kind offer. I can think of no better way to spend the afternoon than in your company. I apologize, however, because there are other matters that require my attention. Another time?"

"Another time," Agnes confirmed with a nod and a look that hinted she was already looking forward to their rendezvous.

Mikel watched the madame of The Cat's Claw more sway than walk back through the doors before he turned to the two grim gentlemen guarding the portico. Their expressions were at odds with their appearance, both dressed in the style and quality of any steward serving a First Family.

Bernie and Earnie.

Their eyes swept over him without sticking, focusing more of their attention on who passed by on the street. The Cat's Claw was located on the Seventh Ring. An upper-class establishment.

Bernie and Earnie did their best to ensure that only known, upper-class clients visited. Because no one entered The Cat's Claw without an invitation and without the two bouncers' express permission.

"All good, gentlemen?"

Mikel shook hands with each one, actually losing his hand in theirs for a time. They didn't say anything. They nodded.

Forced to serve as street fighters when they were boys, the slavers had cut out their tongues. When he came across them, Mikel remedied their misfortune through very decisive and final action. Then, he gave them an education and gainful employment, at the same time earning their trust. Particularly when he offered them the chance to go after the men who had taken their tongues.

"Excellent news. Steady hands, steady eyes, yes?"

Bernie and Earnie both frowned though their eyes never stopped moving.

Mikel offered more of an explanation. "Only a feeling. Nothing specific, just a sense that all isn't as it should be. You know how it is."

They did. The twin brothers were quite familiar with Mikel

picking up on some aspect of the world that seemed a bit off. They nodded in turn, promising with their hard gazes that they would do as he asked.

Mikel nodded as well before heading down the street on a route that would take him to the ring above.

Meandering along the avenues and alleys of Innsbruck, all the while he allowed his gaze to roam. He identified nothing that worried him, even as his sense of approaching danger kept getting stronger the closer he got to the Royal Ring.

He couldn't explain it. He could only heed his instincts.

Yet that growing concern wasn't his only worry.

What bothered him almost as much was the fact that he was thinking about the young woman who had confirmed her residence on the Royal Ring. His last conversation with her played through his mind. Again and again.

He couldn't seem to get the newly seated Queen of the Crux out of his mind for more than just a few minutes these days, and only then when he made a conscious effort to do so.

This was getting ridiculous.

She was getting in his way, and she wasn't even there.

Mikel shook his head, trying to clear it and knowing that it would do him little good. He didn't like how Celindria Dengannon was dominating his thoughts these days. He didn't like it all.

And he didn't like to waste his time on politics, yet that was dominating his thoughts as well.

Politics didn't matter to him. In almost any political climate, his many businesses would not only survive, but thrive. That's what he had worked so hard to ensure ever since he gained control over his first enterprise those many years before. A small tavern that had grown into The Fox's Lair.

The fighting at the Splintered Bridge wouldn't affect what he was doing.

Nor would the proposal from the King of the Tor.

He snorted in amusement. He probably learned of the proposal before Drin did. He had eyes and ears everywhere after all. It was only good for business.

So if the fighting at the Splintered Bridge had no impact on his business interests and Drin receiving a marriage proposal from Malor Dragoran meant little to his revenue streams, why did those two issues keep distracting him?

Why did he fear that raiders from the Kingdom of the Tor might make another play for the Queen of the Crux?

Why did he fear that they might succeed?

Why did he worry that any new incursion from the Tor might not be limited to an attempt on the Queen?

Probably because if he was Malor Dragoran, despite his initial failure he would send more raiders to cause unrest in the Crux. He would seek to weaken the Kingdom from within. Seizing the Queen was simply an added bonus.

Mikel stepped off the street and into an alley, leaning his shoulder against the rough stone. Glad to feel something solid at his back.

He needed to stop doing this.

He needed to stop thinking about Celindria Dengannon.

He needed to stop thinking about what Malor Dragoran wanted.

He needed to stop thinking about the dangers the Crux faced and how to solve them.

That wasn't his responsibility.

That was Drin's. And she had been quite clear that she was more than capable of managing the Crux's affairs. She appreciated his assistance and what he had done to help her gain the throne. But any additional assistance from him was neither desired nor appreciated unless he spoke with her beforehand.

He got the message loud and clear.

She didn't want him to get in her way.

Yet here she was getting in his way, because he couldn't get her out of his head!

Blast it!

Maybe he should have taken Agnes up on her offer. Maybe he should have permitted the distraction.

But he hadn't. Not because he wasn't interested. He and Agnes knew each other quite well.

Rather, hard though it was to believe, he felt guilty. As if he were betraying Drin's trust.

What was that about?

He and the Queen were no more than business associates, and she had been quite clear that their on-again, off-again partnership was based more on duress than desire.

He was about to mentally castigate himself a little more when he quashed the urge in a heartbeat.

He was being followed.

And not by his people. He knew that for a fact, because he had expressly ordered his people to leave him be.

Mikel stayed where he was, seemingly lost in thought while he surveyed the busy street to his front.

Two for certain. Likely a third off to the side. That shadow ducked into a shop before Mikel could catch more than a glimpse. Probably a few more who were staying out of sight. Ready to join the hunt when he started moving again.

None behind him. Yet. And he wanted to keep it that way.

Pushing off the wall he turned on his heel, heading farther down the alley and into the maze of side streets that were just as busy as the main boulevard that looped around the Crux from the seawall to the Citadel that looked down upon all of Innsbruck.

This is where he wanted to be. The tighter confines of the alleys would make it harder for Mikel's trackers to stay with him without being discovered.

For the next half hour, that was Mikel's goal. Confirming how many stalkers haunted his heels.

When he turned into the small courtyard he had been angling toward, he increased his count.

Six all told.

He could have evaded them. Giving them the slip wouldn't be too hard. But he chose not to, as he was holding a card up his sleeve. Besides, he was curious. He had glimpsed a familiar face.

Mikel turned when he reached the back wall. Scimitar in his hand, the dim glow from the steel burned away the shadows wrapped around the enclosed space.

"Something I can help you with?" Mikel didn't have long to wait before his hunters revealed themselves.

A lanky shape stepped out from the gloom of the alley. He was tall with the beginnings of a paunch along with long oily hair and an unkempt beard, which fit his ratlike face to perfection.

"Hello, Rodney." Mikel couldn't say that he was surprised. He had heard rumblings that some of his former crew were back in Innsbruck.

He had worked a few jobs with Rodney when he and Liria were together, and then only because Liria vouched for Rodney. Mikel hadn't liked his approach to their jobs. Rodney didn't take them as seriously as he thought should be the case. The thief was too arrogant for his tastes. Too prone to make mistakes. Several of Rodney's mistakes, in fact, almost cost Mikel his life.

But back then, Mikel had been a fool. He had been more taken with Liria than with what was going on around him. Not seeing the truth until it was almost too late.

Young love certainly had a way of blinding him to reality. A hard lesson to learn. Nevertheless, he was glad that he learned that lesson before it was too late.

"Mikel," Rodney replied. "Or should I bow down and offer my obeisance to the King of the Underworld?" He placed his left leg in front of his right, sweeping his cloak behind him as he made a great show of bending at the waist and giving Mikel a grin that revealed several broken teeth. When Rodney stood straight again, he gripped a short sword in his right hand.

"Very kind of you, Rodney, but it's not necessary."

"You certainly have come up in the world," Rodney mused. "I must give you credit for that. Credit as well for poisoning what was proving to be a good and profitable business arrangement." The thief's eyes flashed with a bitterness that had soured more with the passing of each year.

Mikel didn't bother to defend himself. He didn't have any desire to relive the past. What Rodney viewed as a good business arrangement had been anything but for the other members of the crew. "Where are the boys, Rodney?"

"The boys?"

Mikel saw right through the look of surprise Rodney gave him. "The boys, Rodney. You wouldn't take this job on your own."

Rodney stared at Mikel, the cold hate in his eyes difficult to miss. "I don't need the boys to take you on, Mikel. I don't need the boys to gain the blood you owe me."

"Actually, Rodney," Mikel replied, giving the thief a shrug and a sly look, "you do. So why don't you call them out so we can move this along. I've got other places to be this evening."

"You think you can talk to me as if ..."

"Rodney, please. You're wasting time," Mikel said, shaking his head and not having the patience for useless small talk. "You can act as offended as you want, but you know I'm better with a blade than you." He nodded toward the thief, Rodney's hand unconsciously reaching up and touching the scar across his forehead that was mostly hidden by his long scraggly hair. "That hasn't changed."

"You backstabbing son of a …"

Mikel stepped toward Rodney, who immediately stumbled backward, a boot getting caught on the rough cobblestones. The thief only prevented a fall because his hand found the courtyard wall.

"Come out, come out wherever you are," Mikel called. He could have made a play for Rodney while he was tottering about. He chose not to, certain that Rodney's boys were close by.

A good decision on his part, because just a few seconds later five men sauntered out of the alleyway, one of them helping Rodney back to his feet and earning a few curses from his father for his efforts.

Mikel called them the boys because they were all brothers. Quintuplets, in fact. Rodney's brood. All of them looking much like their father. The most obvious similarity their small, mean eyes.

"I'm going to take that blood you owe me," Rodney growled, less than pleased at being embarrassed in front of his children.

"I look forward to you trying, Rodney." Mikel offered the thief a wink that earned a deeper growl and a scowl.

"Liria wishes she could be here with us." Rodney stalked toward Mikel. His sons did the same as they spread out to the sides, wanting to make Mikel's task of defending himself more difficult while also ensuring that he didn't escape. There was a good bit of money riding on the King of the Underworld's scalp.

"It's too bad she isn't," Mikel replied with a shrug, earning another scowl from Rodney, who hoped he could throw Mikel off by mentioning his former partner who had been more than a partner. "We have some unfinished business as well."

"Sorry to disappoint, but she had a more pressing engagement. Apparently you weren't worth her time."

That comment got Mikel thinking, his mind traveling down

a worrisome road, although only for a heartbeat. Because he had a more immediate concern to address.

The steel cutting toward his gut.

Rodney lunged with his sword. Only a feint, he hoped to give one of his sons a chance to mark the man who had marked him.

It didn't work out as planned. Rodney reared back. Gasping in pain, he pulled his hand in close to his chest. The bloody slice across the top cutting to the bone, his thumb hung on by only a few thin strands of tendon and flesh.

Rodney's shriek of agony was lost in the ensuing fight. Mikel pivoted to avoid Rodney's son coming from his left – he had no idea what their names were, only that there were too many for his tastes -- then glided around the courtyard, gleaming blade streaking through the air as he slashed and sliced, ducked and dodged, just as much avoiding the attacks of Rodney's rat-faced progeny as matching blades with them.

Several times Mikel had the opportunity to deliver a killing blow.

He never took it.

He did mark each of Rodney's sons, some worse than others – usually those who were too aggressive paying a steeper price, all of them bloody and battered after just a few minutes of combat.

"Kill him!" Rodney roared from behind his sons. "Kill the traitor!"

Wishful thinking on Rodney's part, Mikel scoffed. Because their time had run out. Rodney was so consumed by his desire for revenge that he didn't realize the next act was about to begin.

Before continuing their attack as their father demanded, Rodney's five sons looked at one another for support. Seeking to rebuild their waning confidence as none of them had gained a mark on their adversary. All of them concerned not only by that fact but also the sword that their father's nemesis held. The sword whose keen edge, which they had all felt, glowed.

Mikel stepped back in the face of their indecision, creating a bit more space. His timing was perfect.

The first bolt of energy slammed into the cobblestones right in front of the quintet. Two were blown backward. The three still on their feet stumbled forward, reaching for the ground, their sense of balance stolen from them. Eardrums ruptured, black spots danced in front of their eyes.

The next blast of energy struck right in the middle of the staggering trio, strong enough to send two flying back against the courtyard walls with bone-crunching smacks. The third was blown backward into his father.

Mikel was impressed. In just a few seconds the combat was over. Rodney and his five sons down for the count. Broken. Battered. But not dead. At least he didn't think so.

"You didn't want to kill them all?" Finn had caught Mikel's signal when he and Nat approached through the alley.

He had found Mikel's request strange and slightly disappointing, but Finn had heeded it. He hadn't gotten into a good skirmish in quite some time, and he wanted to stretch his legs a bit. Mikel prevented it. Well, Mikel and the impressive skill demonstrated by his protege.

"Took you long enough." Mikel had seen Finn fall into step behind one of his hunters while he was working his way toward the courtyard. If he hadn't, he wouldn't have risked allowing himself to be cornered.

"By the looks of things we got here just in time," Finn replied. "Now answer my question."

"You already know the answer, Finn."

Mikel walked up to Nat. Running his eyes over her, he made sure that she was all right. And she was. She was also grinning from ear to ear, clearly pleased by her success with the Talent.

He reached out, wrapping an arm around her shoulder and

pulling her close for a few heartbeats before letting go. Nat didn't seem to mind, which made Mikel's look of concern shift into a warm smile.

"Enjoy your fun?" he asked.

"I did," Nat replied. "Friends of yours?"

Mikel chuckled. He should have assumed that she would make the connection. She was more perceptive than most. "From a previous life."

"That's why you didn't try to kill them? That's why you didn't want me to do more than I did?"

"Think it through," Finn instructed. He stepped up next to Mikel after checking the three men lying senseless on the shattered cobblestones. Concussions. After a few days they'd be no worse for wear. Although they wouldn't be waking up for the next few hours.

Nat did as Finn suggested, having learned that with the old Magus everything was a lesson. "You want to send a message, and you can do that more effectively with them alive rather than dead."

Mikel smiled proudly. "That I do. Well done." He didn't explain as well that he didn't want Nat using the Talent to kill anyone if it could be avoided. That was a burden he didn't want her to bear.

"To whom?"

"Another old friend."

"Now you're being evasive," Nat grouched.

Mikel sighed. She was right. And he should have assumed that she would push. "A woman named Liria. We used to work together."

"More than just an old friend," murmured Finn. The Magus offered a wink as well. He knew the history between the two, living through some of it.

"What do you mean?" Nat asked. In addition to being a fast learner and seeing everything going on around her, she heard everything and read into the pause that followed. She gave Mikel a raised eyebrow when she asked her question.

Mikel glared at Finn, which the Magus ignored, before turning his focus back to Nat. "Liria and I used to be partners. We used to work jobs together when I first came to the Crux. She and I ..." Mikel shrugged, not really feeling the need to offer more of an explanation.

"You were together," Nat said. The slight flush of red that crept onto Mikel's cheeks convinced Nat to push a little more. "You were lov ..."

"We don't need to talk about this any longer," Mikel cut in, refusing to allow a teenage girl to fluster him. "All that happened long ago."

"If it happened so long ago, then why is this Liria still such a forbidden topic?" Nat's eyes flashed. She believed that she had trapped Mikel with his own words.

"Have you ever heard the story about the curious cat?" Mikel asked.

"No," Nat admitted.

"That only makes sense," he continued. "Because unlike other cats, which have nine lives, the curious cat only had one."

Nat's eyes widened, understanding that she was treading on dangerous ground. "Touchy."

"Deservedly so," interjected Finn.

"Not you too," Mikel sighed in exasperation.

Finn raised his hands, offering Mikel a placating gesture. "I believe it's time to move off this topic."

"It is," Mikel confirmed. "What are you both doing here? Finding me wasn't happenstance."

"We sensed it," Nat replied.

"What do you mean you sensed it?"

"The Blade of Light," Finn explained. "At least we assumed it was the scimitar, although now I'm not so sure."

"Not so sure?" Mikel asked, his confusion deepening. He

studied the Blade, reading the inscription running along its length, the steel still glowing softly, before he sheathed it in the scabbard across his back.

"We can talk about that later," Finn said. "But to answer your question, while we were practicing the Talent, we sensed a surge of energy not too far away. And for whatever reason, we knew it was you."

Nat finished the story. "We were worried. We didn't think that we'd feel something like that unless there was good cause. So we came after you. It proved to be an easy thing."

"Easy?" Mikel wondered, thinking about the warren of streets he meandered through to get a better sense of his trackers' number.

"Easy," Nat confirmed. "We just followed the power we sensed that was so obviously you, and it led us right here."

"A good thing as well," Finn said with a nod.

"I won't argue that point," Mikel agreed.

"It could be a bad thing as well," Finn continued, earning a frown from both Nat and Mikel.

"What do you mean?"

"You need to be more careful, lad. If we can find you because of the power that is resident within the Blade, so can anyone with skill in the Talent ... or the Curse."

"You certainly know how to put a damper on what was a fine confrontation, Finn."

"I just want to make sure you understand the consequences of using the Blade."

"I don't know that it's fair to say I'm using the Blade. It seems more like the Blade is using me."

"That's something you're going to need to figure out, lad."

"And you can't help me?"

"We'll talk more about that later."

"It's strange, though," Nat interjected.

Mikel and Finn both looked at her. Nat had ignored their

private conversation as she considered an anomaly that had been bothering her.

"What do you mean?" Finn asked.

"It's not the only surge of power that I sensed."

"Really?" Finn was intrigued, in large part because he didn't sense another surge. Her ability to do so hinted that her skills were improving quickly and heading in a direction that was quite rare for Magii. "Another surge? Where?"

"The Citadel."

Mikel's frown deepened, his concern becoming plain.

"What are you worried about, lad?" Finn asked.

"That I'm just the first act."

13

TAKEN

"This is ridiculous!" Celindria Dengannon, Queen of the Crux, pushed herself up from behind her desk and strode toward the balcony at the other end of her office. Pulling her robe tighter around her, a cool breeze drifting through the open double doors, she reread the note from her uncle. Staring unnecessarily at the words, having memorized them, she crumpled it in her hand.

Her uncle was passing on the details of his meeting with his counterpart and referencing the proposal by the King of the Tor, advocating against consideration. Still, Dragoran wouldn't have put forward the idea unless ...

"Does he think I'm a fool?" Drin wondered. She let out a stream of curses that would have made any of her soldiers proud.

In part because of Dragoran's veiled attempt to steal her and her Kingdom through the bonds of matrimony, as if she would be deceived by such an obvious ploy.

In part because she kept talking to herself, a habit she couldn't seem to break and in truth had little desire to.

"No, not a fool," she murmured softly. "It's just a distraction." It made sense. Dragoran knew that she would never acquiesce. Not after what he had done to disrupt her Coronation. "But why?"

"To give me the chance to finally meet you."

Drin spun around, shocked to hear the husky voice that almost made her jump off the ground. Her anger at herself for being taken by surprise ameliorated by the fact that she had seized the Talent without even thinking.

A tall woman stood just a few feet away from her. A short sword sheathed on her hip, she was beautiful in a mysterious kind of way.

"How dare you enter my apartment without my permission," Drin growled.

"It was the only way to get in to see you, Queen Dengannon." The woman bowed her head slightly. What in most any other instance would be viewed as an apology, but now, with her slightly mocking grin, came across as more of a challenge. "My apologies for disturbing you."

"You are?" Drin's eyes narrowed. Something about this woman, other than the fact that she had snuck into her chambers without announcing herself, sent a bolt of concern through her.

"A friend of Mikel's."

"A friend of Mikel's?" Drin relaxed if only a little bit, still suspicious. "He never mentioned you. And he's never sent anyone in his place before."

"He tends to keep things close to the vest."

"On that we agree." Drin studied the woman a few seconds more, not sure what to make of her. "Your name?"

"Liria."

"What can I do for you Liria?" Drin assumed that Liria had made her way through one of the secret passageways that led into her suite. Mikel likely giving her the route. About that they would be having a conversation, and one that Mikel would not enjoy. These unscheduled visits had to stop. "Mikel needs something?"

Liria's eyes sparked, a wave of irritation running through her. There was a lilt in the Queen of the Crux's voice when she spoke of Mikel that suggested a close familiarity and put her nerves on edge.

"Yes, Queen Dengannon," Liria replied, bringing her focus back to the task at hand. "He has some information that he believes can't wait. He's asked that I escort you."

Drin tilted her head down toward the crumpled piece of paper on her carpet. "To his primary place of business?"

"Yes," Liria replied. "He couldn't break away, as he's trying to confirm some of what he learned. But he believed it couldn't wait, so he sent me in his stead."

"And it's so urgent that he couldn't come here to discuss it?" Drin noticed how Liria's eyes tightened at her words, as if the thought of Mikel sneaking into the Citadel, meeting with her in her private chamber, bothered her. "Which he has many times before. Usually at this hour. Prying eyes and all that."

"Unfortunately not, Queen Dengannon." Liria fought hard not to grind her teeth, her temper beginning to boil. "He offers his apologies. But I can take you to him."

Drin nodded, offering Liria a smile. "Of course. I take it that we'll be going to The Cat's Claw?" She had been doing some research on Mikel's many businesses on the Crux. She was certain that there were a great many more that her investigators had failed to uncover. The bordello the first that came to mind since it was the most salubrious of those revealed.

"Yes, that's the one," Liria replied, offering Drin a nod and a smile that seemed more a grimace.

Drin nodded as well. "Good. Let me just change my clothes."

"Queen Dengannon," Liria protested. "Mikel was quite

forceful with his request for your presence. He said time was of the essence."

"Of course he did," Drin replied. "As you are aware, that's just who he is. Everything always is urgent and needs to be done right away." She turned and started walking toward her bedchamber. "Give me just a few minutes. I can't walk around Innsbruck wearing nothing but my robe." Drin looked back over her shoulder, offering Liria a sly grin. "Although Mikel might like that." Drin turned back around after adding a suggestive wink.

Liria took a few steps toward Drin. "Queen Dengannon, I must insist that ..."

Having reached the chair by the door that led into her bedroom, Drin spun around. Her sword now in hand, she stood ready for a combat. One foot in front of the other. Knees bent. Balanced on her toes.

"You little minx!" Liria exclaimed. "I should have assumed that you weren't the fool everyone said you were."

"Far from it," Drin growled, refusing to be knocked off balance by the insult.

"I can see that now," Liria replied. She smiled then, glad that the need for deception was gone. She stepped closer to Drin, pulling her short sword free from its scabbard. "I had assumed that Mikel engineered you taking the throne. You just a pawn in a larger scheme. I can see now that you had a hand in it as well."

"We worked together." Drin offered Liria a knowing smile and another wink, having no doubt of the reaction her next few words would earn. "We do a lot together."

"You bit ..."

Drin was already moving, making use of the anger she infused within Liria. Twisting to the side, she avoided Liria's swipe with her sword.

The woman had tried to smack her in the head with the flat of her blade rather than kill her. Not an assassin, Drin realized.

A kidnapper instead.

Just as was the case when the Tor soldiers snuck into the Citadel a month before.

Regardless, killer or kidnapper, there was no confusion with respect to Drin's objective. She wasn't fighting to defeat her opponent. She was fighting to kill her.

That principle guiding her, Drin feinted to her left then spun back around to her right, her sword sweeping through the air and targeting her attacker's neck.

Liria ducked, chuckling when she stood straight again. "Clever girl. A trick Mikel taught you?"

Drin ignored the taunt, backing away then circling slowly around her attacker. "Mikel taught me many tricks. But not that one."

Liria cursed under her breath, catching the hidden meaning. Then she launched herself at Drin, short sword slicing through the air.

Drin smiled, already spinning back around in the other direction, pleased that she could poke at Liria and gain such a violent reaction so easily. Curious, as well as slightly concerned, regarding Liria's relationship with Mikel. But those worries would have to wait.

Drin didn't bother to defend against the blade streaking down toward her. Liria appeared to have lost interest in incapacitating her. Instead she kept moving, allowing the couch at her back to absorb the blow.

"You think you can escape me so easily?" Liria demanded. Tearing her sword free from the upholstery, she stalked after Drin.

"So far I have," Drin replied with a condescending smirk. "I don't know why you think that's going to change."

With another growl, Liria charged at Drin. A series of short, sharp blows followed. All designed to disable. Not kill. Not a single one connecting.

Drin glided about the room with an envious grace. She worked hard to maintain her smile. Liria's skill with a blade was obvious, and the pressure her kidnapper was placing on her was becoming more and more intense.

"You pretentious little ..."

Liria never spit out the rest of her insult, instead collapsing to the ground in a startled heap, Drin kicking a chair into her path that took out her legs.

Before Liria could push herself up, one foot still caught between the legs of the heavy piece of furniture, she froze.

The cold steel Drin pressed against her throat held her in place.

"This is something that Mikel taught me," Drin said. The Queen of the Crux stood above Liria with an absolute confidence.

"And did he teach you how to kill in cold blood?" Liria whispered, the steel cutting into her throat just enough to draw a slow trickle of blood.

Drin's smile darkened at the question. "That was something that he didn't need to teach me." Drin enjoyed how Liria's eyes widened at her response. Though she was disappointed more out of surprise than worry.

"Why not use your magic at the beginning?" demanded Liria. She acted as she usually did when she could feel death breathing down upon her. She got angry, refusing to buckle under the peril of her current circumstances. "Why draw this out?"

"I wanted to test myself against you," Drin replied, "and I wanted to take my measure of you."

"Because of Mikel," Liria nodded knowingly, though the steel at her neck hindered her movement.

"For that and other reasons. Now I think our time together

has come to an end. You've got a date with one of the cells at the bottom of the Citadel."

Rather than showing fear, Liria smiled instead. "You know what Mikel taught me? At least with respect to the blade?"

"I can't imagine," Drin replied, "and I can't say that I care."

Liria continued anyway. "He taught me that when you have someone under your blade, don't waste your time talking. Kill them quickly. Because you never know who might be coming at your back."

Drin's eyes sharpened, revealing her unease. She didn't want to do what Liria hinted at. Worried that it was just a trick. She breathed easier when she saw that Liria's leg was still caught beneath the chair. There was no way that she was going to get up quickly enough to make a play for her. So a momentary glance wouldn't cost her.

It was Drin's turn to freeze. Just for a heartbeat.

She reacted as swiftly as she could. Raising her free hand, the Talent flared from her palm.

But Drin wasn't fast enough.

A woman with threads of black dancing around her fingers stood poised at her back, a portal of spinning mist behind her.

As a spark of tainted power shot from the woman's hand, Drin realized much to her regret that it was too late. She'd never get her shield in place in time.

When the Curse struck her forehead an instant later, Drin collapsed, not even able to gasp in shock.

Awake.

Conscious.

Yet unable to move.

Unable to defend herself.

Before Drin hit the ground, Liria had disengaged herself from the chair and was ready to grab her.

"You know what to do," Assindra said to Liria.

Liria nodded, wiping the blood from her throat with one

hand, the other supporting the Queen of the Crux, who no longer could touch the Talent. Who no longer could do anything. Until her senses returned.

Assindra reached out, grasping Drin's hand and revealing her wrist. With her other hand she pulled out from her pocket a slim silver bracelet. Similar to a Protector's collar. Just a smaller version.

Locking it into place, Assindra smiled devilishly. "You're mine now, girl. Heart and soul. Get used to it."

Drin couldn't reply. She wasn't permitted to. All she could do was adhere to the compulsion centered on the magical artifact that forced her to obey the woman who obviously was a Dark Magus.

One slow step after another, she followed her captor through the portal of spinning black toward the fate that awaited her.

14

QUITE THE AUDIENCE

"What have you done to me?" Drin demanded in a harsh whisper, straining to break the magical hold the Dark Magus had upon her. All to no avail. Her effort wasted.

She didn't want to do as the woman required, but she couldn't help herself. It was like she was looking at the world through someone else's eyes. Moving through that same world in someone else's body. Her free will stripped from her. Her thoughts and her desires her own, yet she had no capacity to act upon them.

"Don't you know your history, girl?"

"Of course I know my history."

"Then you should know what it is that I affixed to your wrist."

"I've never seen one such as this," Drin admitted through gritted teeth. Growling softly in disgust, realizing that fighting the compulsion did her little good, she followed her captor through a shadowy doorway that opened into a large audience chamber.

If Drin had to describe it, she would call it more a vault

than a throne room. There was no ornamentation, the chamber bare except for the intricately carved chair set upon the dais that rose several feet above the floor. The back wall housed a series of stained glass windows, now no more than black and grey on a cloudless night.

An almost inhumanly handsome man with long black hair curling at his shoulders, face cleanshaven, lounged upon the throne.

Malor Dragoran.

King of the Tor.

Drin had little doubt as to why there was nothing else in the chamber except for his seat of power. He wanted all eyes drawn to him.

As she walked slowly toward the dais behind her captor, a shiver of fear streaked down her spine. She halted its progression in an instant, replacing her fear with steel.

Drin could do very little to help herself with the bracelet affixed to her wrist. But she could at least do that much. She could control her emotions and hunt for a way out of this mess.

She was the Queen of the Crux after all, and she would act as such. Moreover, even though she was a captive, she would demand to be treated with the respect she deserved.

"Just a smaller version that I discovered not so long ago," the Dark Magus explained, offering Malor Dragoran a slight nod as they approached. "A practice long forgotten, yet as you are experiencing still useful for my present purposes."

"I thought all the Protector collars were lost or destroyed. Bryen Keldragan made sure of it."

"You never know what you can find when you look hard enough," the Dark Magus replied in a soft chuckle. "Same material. Same magical properties. Simply in a different design."

"No problems, Assindra?" Malor Dragoran asked, not bothering to rise from his seat as he eyed Celindria Dengannon.

"Not a single one," Assindra replied with a supreme confidence.

"This is an act of war!" Drin growled. She may be under this Dark Magus' control, but still she would speak her mind.

"We are already at war, Queen Dengannon," Malor replied with a warm smile that was incongruous with his words. "Having you here with me actually will bring the war between our Kingdoms to an end before a great deal of bloodshed occurs."

"That's your excuse for doing this?" Drin wanted to say more. To take Malor Dragoran to task. But she found it difficult. Her eyes drawn to his otherworldly beauty, her thoughts became clouded, making it difficult for her to think. Not understanding why, yet not believing this new distress resulted from the bracelet locked around her wrist.

"I don't make excuses, my lovely Queen Dengannon. I get things done. Just as you've learned."

"And kidnapping me was on your list of things to do?" Drin's voice rose an octave. She found that if she didn't look directly at the King of the Tor, her mind functioned more effectively.

"Among other things," Malor admitted, his smile broadening. He was clearly quite pleased with himself.

"And now that you have me, what do you plan to do?" Drin demanded.

"Did you not receive my proposal, my dear Queen of the Crux?"

"You can't be serious?" Drin scoffed. "After this?"

"Quite serious, my dear. Deadly serious in fact." Malor's smile remained, though his eyes changed. A coldness settled within their depths that hinted at Dragoran's true nature.

"I will never agree to marry you."

Malor stared at Drin, then much to her chagrin he started to chuckle. That chuckle quickly became a full-throated laugh that turned Drin's face scarlet. When he was done, he leaned forward on his throne, resting his forearms on his legs.

"You don't seem to understand the situation that you're in, my dear Queen Dengannon. It's not a matter of needing your agreement. As I said just moments ago, I don't make excuses. I get things done. You will marry me, my dear."

"I will not!"

Malor pushed himself up from his throne in a flash, jumping down from the dais and closing the distance to Drin in two strides. He didn't seem angry by her outburst. Rather, he seemed intrigued. Almost ... excited.

"Assindra, I wasn't aware that my bride-to-be had such fire."

"From what I saw during her capture, she is quite feisty," the Dark Magus admitted.

Arms crossed, Malor nodded, brow coming together as he pursed his lips. "This will be more fun than I anticipated."

"I will not marry you," Drin repeated in a quieter, distinctly serious voice. "Now or ever."

Malor smiled then. Though not with humor. More in anticipation. He really was enjoying this encounter. "Celindria. Can I call you that? I feel like I can since we will soon be husband and wife."

"I will not ..."

Malor rode right over her. "Celindria, you do not have a choice in the matter. There is nothing with which you need agree. We will be married. That is a fact and nothing more. Better just to get used to the idea rather than fight it."

"You may force me to marry you, Malor. But you will not gain what you desire. Me or my Kingdom."

That statement led to a lift of Malor's right eyebrow. Not amused, he interpreted what she said as a challenge. "We shall see, my dear Celindria. We shall see."

"You should have entrusted this task to me at the very start rather than that fool Hanover." Assindra didn't like how Malor seemed to have forgotten her as he engaged with the Queen of the Crux, the young woman obviously captivating him. "It would have saved us both a great deal of time and effort."

"Hanover!" demanded Drin. "Lucius Hanover is in league with you?" She cursed silently. Mikel had been right, and she hadn't wanted to listen to him. Or rather she had been slow to listen to him.

"Yes, you're right, Assindra," Malor agreed. He ignored Drin's outburst. "A waste of time and resources. But lesson learned."

"I'll take his head from his neck," Drin hissed softly.

"Be my guest," Malor replied. "In fact, consider it a wedding present. With you here, I don't need him anymore. He's just a hindrance now. Besides, I could do without his constant whining."

"And I'll take ..."

"That's enough for now, Queen Dengannon," Assindra said, cutting off her words with a hard look. Drin started walking slowly back toward the entrance to the throne room, a contingent of Tor soldiers waiting for her. "We will speak more later."

"You quite enjoyed that," Malor accused, giving Assindra a cunning grin after Drin was gone, the soldiers pulling the doors closed behind them.

"She's going to be a handful," Assindra said, ignoring Malor's comment. "Even with her under our control, she will continue to push."

"I've broken many a stallion. I should have little trouble breaking a mare. And I have no doubt it will be fun for the both of us."

Assindra understood his true meaning. "Malor, don't believe for a second that ..."

Malor held up his hands, offering Assindra a broad smile meant to prevent her always simmering anger from reaching a boil. "Have no fear, Assindra. Nothing I do will interfere with your plans or our agreement. I promise you that."

"You promise, Malor?" Assindra chuckled softly. "I place little faith in your promises."

"Just as I place so little faith in yours," Malor countered quickly. "However, we both have the same objective, and so long as our interests are aligned, our partnership remains strong."

"Our partnership remains strong," Assindra repeated.

"And I assure you, Assindra, that Celindria Dengannon is no more than a piece to be played. Nothing but a temporary necessity. Once the Splintered Empire is whole again, her demise is assured. She will serve no purpose, and I do so hate dead weight."

Assindra stepped forward then. Right hand reaching up, she stroked his cheek softly. Her left hand moved lower, starting with his abdomen and then working her way lower. "Do not test me, Malor. Do not try to cheat me. You would not like to see me out of sorts."

"Testing and cheating you are the furthest things from my mind," Malor replied. "Have no fear of that. I know what I have standing right before me."

Feeling a squeeze, he groaned softly. Desire filling him, before he could reach out for her, Assindra released her hold then turned and walked away, a portal of spinning black appearing at the back of the throne room with the flick of her hand.

"Unfortunately, there is no time to play, Malor. Not yet. There is still more work to be done." She gave him a coy look over her shoulder and then a wink of her own. "Keep your promises, and I will keep mine. And I remind you that I am much, much more dangerous than the Queen of the Crux."

"What of the Blade?" Malor asked, his question bringing

Assindra to a halt before she stepped through the gateway crafted of the Curse. "I have waited too long for it."

Assindra promised him that she would retrieve the Blade of Light. That was the primary reason he had agreed to their arrangement. The ancient weapon was essential to the revenge he planned.

A revenge that he had been seeking for centuries.

A revenge that he believed was much deserved.

For a victory stolen from him at the very last second.

Betrayed by those he created.

Betrayed by those he trusted.

Betrayed by those who served him.

Yes, he would have his revenge.

The reemergence of the Splintered Empire first. Then, with the Blade that had been missing for centuries, he would exact the revenge that he so thoroughly deserved.

"It will soon be within your grasp."

"You have found it?" The spark of greed that shot through the back of his coal-black eyes was unmistakable.

"I have."

"Then where is it?"

"Patience, Malor," Assindra urged.

"I entrusted obtaining the Blade to you."

"And because you did, you will have it," Assindra assured him. "But there is no need to search for it. The Blade will come to you."

"Why do you believe that?"

"Because the Bearer of the Blade will come for the Queen of the Crux," Assindra said as she disappeared within the portal. "We just need to make sure that he has the necessary nudge."

15

FINDING THE WAY

"What was it, Finn?"

Mikel stood by the desk in Drin's private office. He and the Magus had slipped in through the hidden passageway set in the wall by the fireplace at their backs. They had spent the last quarter hour walking through her apartment before returning here.

There was no sign of her. Nothing was out of place. There wasn't a hint of a struggle. Yet ...

"You tell me, lad."

"Me tell you?" Mikel wasn't sure why the Magus believed that he could offer anything of use.

He knew what to look for to confirm that a theft had occurred. Breaking and entering was one of his specialties after all.

There was nothing here, however, that hinted that anything untoward had happened. Nothing other than this sense of ... he wasn't quite sure what.

"You tell me," Finn repeated, a bit more of a demand in his voice. "The weapon you have across your back isn't just good for fighting. It's good for other things as well."

"I am not as versed in magical artifacts as you are, Finn," Mikel growled, not in the mood for a lesson. "Making me work for the answer is a waste of time."

"It's not a waste," Finn replied. "The Blade of Light can tell you what you need to know."

"It can?" Mikel frowned, not quite understanding.

"I just said as much." Finn had no desire to engage in a circular conversation. "Yes, the Blade of Light, just like any other weapon crafted by the Giants of the Rime, was made specifically to serve as a repository of the Talent so that the Bearer would be on equal terms with those swayed by the Curse. But there is more to the Blade than just that. Within the craftsmanship there is a promise as well."

"A promise?" Mikel seemed less than certain of Finn's claim. "Enlighten me."

"You truly are aggravating, you know that?"

"I'm only aggravating because you're just as aggravating," Mikel countered, his frustration growing to match that of the Magus. That frustration goaded by the fear that he didn't want to acknowledge. "Maybe a little more guidance on your part would get us where we need to go that much faster."

"Fair enough," Finn replied after taking several deep breaths to calm his temper. The lad was right. He couldn't be expected to know what he didn't know. It seemed that he hadn't spent enough time in the Frozen Waste with the Frost Lord as would have been good for him. "As you know, a weapon crafted by the Giants of the Rime and infused with the Talent in many ways takes on a life of its own."

"A consciousness of a sort," Mikel suggested.

"Exactly lad. Exactly." Finn nodded, pleased that they were getting somewhere. Mikel had at least learned something during his visit with Cadmus. "Because of that consciousness, these unique weapons also have several unique qualities." He nodded to the scimitar sheathed on Mikel's back. "Read the inscription on the steel."

Mikel frowned again, already knowing the inscription by heart. Yet not wanting to antagonize his friend, he reached over his shoulder and pulled the scimitar free from its scabbard. "When the darkness surrounds, the Light will prevail."

Finn nodded. "Every weapon crafted by the Giants of the Rime for the Order of the Magii bears that inscription."

"Confirmation of a sort," Mikel suggested.

"Yes, and a reminder as well. Because each of these weapons is also a symbol. Not just a tool for confronting those touched by the Curse. And as I said, each has its own unique qualities."

"And what are those qualities with respect to the Blade of Light?" The scimitar felt right in Mikel's hands. As if the steel was crafted for his grip. Yet he found that hard to believe, because there were others who had come before him. Those Bearers spanned a thousand years or more. All of them Giants of the Rime.

Finn shrugged. "There often are similarities. Nevertheless, it depends on the weapon. It also depends on the need."

"You're being quite obtuse, you know that?"

"I do," Finn replied with a small smile. "Do you find that aggravating?"

Mikel thought about continuing the argument masquerading as a dialogue, actually enjoying the give and take. But he sensed that time was short.

Drin was supposed to be here. She wasn't. If she had slipped out as she liked to do on occasion, Mikel would have received word from his eyes and ears. So if she wasn't here in the Citadel, then where could she have gone?

"What do you mean by need?" Mikel asked, refusing to bite at Finn's bait.

"An artifact of this remarkable craftsmanship will sense

your need and provide you with what you need if it's within your power."

Mikel's frown deepened as he pulled his eyes away from the Magus and stared at the blade, which shone brightly in the lantern light. Every time he did, he marveled at the workmanship. He had some skill in the forge. Cadmus admitted as much. Though not of this quality.

Not wanting to ask Finn any more questions, because he didn't want to give his friend the chance to be even more difficult than he already was, he stared at the steel until it began to lose its shape. Until there was only the white glow that emanated from the steel.

He felt the connection with the Blade slowly take shape.

Two becoming one.

Mikel grew warm, the energy contained within the ancient weapon flowing through him.

But not just the Talent.

The Light as well that had been used to craft the blade. The bond gained strength as the steel flared with greater intensity.

"Listen to the Blade," Finn suggested, squinting as the brightness of the steel burned through the shadows around them.

Mikel didn't really hear what Finn said, instead losing himself within the artifact and strengthening the union between them. Connecting once again to the consciousnesses of the previous Bearers, all of whom still existed within the Blade. Building upon the steel's history. Augmenting the steel's strength.

Mikel recognized who they were. He observed what they had done. He saw all there was to see about them. And he learned all that they were willing to share with him, becoming one with those consciousnesses despite the doubt that surged through him.

Heroes all, many gave their lives to defend against the practitioners of the Curse. A truth that made him feel distinctly uncomfortable. Distinctly unworthy.

Because he wasn't a hero.

He was a thief at heart.

Still, he took in all that those distinct consciousnesses had to offer, because he never turned down knowledge freely given.

Marie Roucheau. Master swordswoman. Savior of the Bloody Steppe.

Jesai Katori. Captain of the Golden Brigade.

Knute Frost Lord. King of the Giants of the Rime and grandfather to Cadmus.

And then the rest.

Some remembered.

Some not.

All with the same fate.

The fate that Cadmus had hinted at was Mikel's as well, no matter how hard he might fight against it.

Not wanting to think about that potential inevitability, Mikel shifted his focus away from the Blade and to what was around him. The Light contained within the steel swept out in a wave to encompass Drin's apartment, Mikel viewing it in a way that shocked him. Also in a way that revealed what he needed to know. What he had missed, seeing both what was and what had been.

He had to give Finn credit. He was right. Mikel needed to learn how to listen to the Blade.

With a few brief words of thanks to the previous Bearers of the Blade for their assistance, Mikel broke the connection. The glow along the steel, blinding just a moment before, faded back to its usual dim glow.

Mikel walked out of Drin's office and into the living room. Coming to a stop in between two large couches, he saw it then.

The faint marks in the carpet that someone had tried to wipe out. The chair hadn't just been moved. It had been knocked over. And whoever put it back had missed its placement by a hair. He lifted a blanket set atop one of the couches. The damage was damningly conclusive.

That wasn't the most interesting thing that Mikel discovered, however.

More interesting – concerning as well – was the residue he felt. The energy that had been used right where he was standing. His skin prickled at its touch, the Blade pulsing brightly.

"What is it, lad?" Finn asked, following him into the living room.

"You can't sense it?"

Finn shook his head.

Mikel was surprised, particularly considering Finn's affliction. "The Curse."

Finn nodded. "That doesn't surprise me. Whoever took her used that insipid power against her."

Mikel nodded, agreeing with Finn's theory. "Yes, but there's more to it than that."

"Don't make me wait," Finn pushed.

"I'm not. I'm just trying to make sense of it." Mikel took a moment to think back to his lessons with Kaduna. The Magus showed him some of what she could do with the Talent. None of which Mikel could do himself despite being Caledonii. "A portal."

Finn's breath caught in his throat. "A Dark Magus took her through a portal?"

"That's what I believe."

"A worrisome discovery," Finn admitted.

"Why?"

"Because only the strongest Dark Magii can create portals. That suggests that our adversary is not only skilled but also quite powerful in the Curse."

"Skilled and powerful enough to call upon the services of a Drude?"

Finn opened his mouth to reply then closed it just as quickly. Thinking. They were already in dangerous territory. If Mikel was correct, then what he decided to do next could take him over the cliff. "Yes, I believe so. You know who it was?"

"I can't say for sure," Mikel replied, "but I've got a good idea as to who it might be." If he was right, and Mikel didn't think that we was wrong, then it could have been only one person who used the Curse to kidnap Drin. Based on that and what had happened on the Crux just a few short months ago, there was only one place that the Dark Magus would take her.

Finn wasn't pleased with Mikel's findings. He was pleased by his success, however. "Well done, lad. Are you certain enough? No doubt?"

"No doubt," Mikel confirmed.

"Why?"

"You told me to listen to the Blade."

"I did."

"I listened. Even better, I can follow the trail," Mikel explained. "Thanks to the Blade of Light I can follow the trail left by the Curse. Even though the Dark Magus used a portal, I can still sense where Drin is."

"I'm afraid to ask."

"There's no need. There's only one place where a Dark Magus would take the Queen of the Crux." Mikel sighed, not liking the situation in which he found himself, though he couldn't say that he was surprised. It seemed that ever since his initial chance encounter with Celindria Dengannon his life had been turned upside down. "Any suggestions?"

"You're going after her?" Finn asked, though it really wasn't a question.

Mikel shrugged.

Finn nodded. "Of course you are."

"I haven't decided," Mikel said, unwilling to commit. At least not yet. Several emotions rolled through him. Emotions he didn't want to deal with. Not liking how they were clouding his thinking.

"We need to talk."

Mikel turned around slowly. The Battle Lord stood behind him. Mikel had sensed Henri Dengannon as soon as he slipped in through the main door during his conversation with Finn. He assumed that the Battle Lord had heard the last part of that conversation.

"That's my cue." Finn nodded to the Battle Lord in respect then walked toward the open door set near the fireplace in the back of the Queen's private office, planning on using the same passageway that he and Mikel had used to enter the fortress unannounced to make his exit. "I'll wait for you outside the Citadel."

"Who was that?" the Battle Lord asked once Finn was gone.

"A friend."

Henri smiled thinly, not surprised that Mikel didn't offer more. It was a trait lacking among most of those living in the higher rings of the Crux. Discretion. "You have a lot of friends."

"Is that what we are now?"

"That depends," Henri replied, his hard eyes locking onto Mikel's. The man who had snuck into the Citadel and by all rights should be in a cell stared right back at him with a gaze just as hard.

"I didn't take her," Mikel said finally. He knew it was an unnecessary comment, but he wanted to get this encounter with the Battle Lord moving, Henri Dengannon seemingly not sure how to begin and Mikel attempting to assist him. Because he had a decision to make.

"I know you didn't."

"Then why are you here?"

"I could ask you the same question," Henri replied.

"You could."

The Battle Lord nodded. "I believe that once again we have a similar interest."

"How so?"

"We've had a partnership of sorts for a while," the Battle Lord began.

"We have."

"You have better sources of information than I do."

"I do." Mikel shrugged. It was only the truth.

"You know what happened to Celindria."

"I suspect. I can't say for sure. Not yet."

"Tell me what you suspect."

Mikel hesitated. He and the Battle Lord did have an agreement in place. But it was a very loose agreement. And Mikel wasn't sure that he wanted the agreement to become any more solid than it already was.

Yet recognizing the angst written all over Henri Dengannon's face, Mikel did something that he rarely did. He told the Battle Lord all of what he suspected, leaving out only why it was that he suspected it. The Battle Lord simply would assume that his information came from his eyes and ears, exactly how Mikel wanted it.

The Battle Lord didn't say anything for quite some time once Mikel was done, taking it all in and allowing it to run through his mind. "You wanted to know why I'm here. I was hoping that you would come and that I would catch you."

"Why?"

"I want you to go after Celindria. I want you to bring her back."

"I could be wrong."

"I don't think you are," the Battle Lord replied with a firm shake of his head.

"And what if she's dead?" Mikel hoped he was wrong about that, but still he needed to ask the question.

"Kill him." Then the Battle Lord offered additional clarification. "And if she's alive, kill him. Just kill the bastard. Kill anyone who dared to take my niece."

16

SWEET AND SOUR

"I want to be alone."

"No one wants to be alone, my dear. We may prefer it, but we never want it."

Drin turned reluctantly, pulling her eyes from a view that she had to admit was quite impressive. Far off in the distance the gleam of the Barbed Path that led up to the Tor flashed in the dying light of the day.

Drin strode back through the doors to the balcony and into the opulent, almost gaudily so, living quarters supplied to her in the Ring that lorded over the city of Graz. She stopped when she was just a chair away from her unwanted visitor, adopting her most regal pose. Hands clasped in front of her, her fingers touched the bracelet that shielded her from the Talent. Her efforts to break the hold of the ancient artifact had gained her nothing other than frustration so far.

"A stickler for language. I never thought that would be the case with you, King Dragoran," she stated in a haughty tone.

Drin tilted her head to the side, not looking at him directly. His features distracted her in a way that she couldn't quite understand.

He was handsome, she wouldn't deny that, and certainly quite better looking than the last King she had spoken with. Of course, that King hadn't kidnapped her. The worst that he had done was use her as bait.

Good looks notwithstanding, she believed that there was more to the spell that settled over her whenever she gazed upon the King of the Tor for too long. A natural magic that she would worry on later, once this encounter was over, curious if it came from him or the Dark Magus.

"There is much that you don't know about me, my dear Queen of the Crux," Malor Dragoran replied with a broad smile that revealed his polished white teeth. "Perhaps rather than pushing me away you should spend more time pulling me closer. There is much that I have to offer you." He gave her a wink and a less-than-respectful grin. "Much that I can do for you that you might ... enjoy."

Drin would have needed to be a fool to miss the intent contained within his words. "Is that why you chose to visit with me alone, King Dragoran? Fearful that your partner would be upset if we were having this conversation in her presence?"

"Of course not," he scoffed, laughing softly.

The King of the Tor was thoroughly unconcerned, which Drin found interesting since she assumed the Dark Magus exercised more power in their relationship than was obvious. Perhaps she was wrong. Perhaps there was more to the man posing before her than just what he chose to reveal.

"Though I will admit that Assindra can be difficult at times," he continued. "So there are certain pieces of business that are best conducted without her. It cuts down on any possible miscalculations or miscommunications and the prob-lems likely to result."

"And that's what I am to you?" Drin demanded, the heat in her voice rising. "Just another piece of business." She lifted her wrist, revealing the bracelet that had stolen her agency from her. The silver gleamed brightly, catching the light from the lanterns placed along the walls and hanging down from the ceiling. "Your Dark Magus kidnapped me because you failed the first time with your soldiers. Say what you want, but I am a prisoner here."

"Semantics only my dear."

"Semantics?" Drin snorted.

Malor interrupted before Drin could pick up a head of steam. "Semantics. As I explained before, the first attempt made those few months ago to bring you to the safety of the Tor was ill advised and conducted without my permission. That mission was underway before I could stop it."

"Bring me to the safety of the Tor? You can't be serious." Drin rolled her eyes, breaking character for just a moment as she found his claim to be less than credible.

"Quite serious, my dear," Malor confirmed with a nod. "After your father's unfortunate demise ..."

"Murder," Drin corrected.

Malor ignored the interruption, having no desire to fall into that rabbit hole. "Your position on the Crux was less than assured. I believe that my actions were necessary."

"Because of Hanover," Drin offered with a quiet grunt of disbelief.

"Hanover, yes, but you already know that. He was just one of many. The other First Families, all of whom also have business interests here in the Kingdom of the Tor, were less than certain about your rule. More than willing to consider Hanover before you to ensure the stability that they require for their own success."

"I was crowned the Queen of the Crux because I am the rightful heir and the rightful ruler. Hanover and anyone else believing otherwise is a traitor to the Crown."

Malor smiled more broadly. "In that I agree with you, my dear. And as I said when you first arrived yesterday, I am more than happy to aid you in that quest. There is no place in the world we are seeking to create for Hanover and anyone of the same mind-set and disposition."

Drin didn't miss how Malor attempted to include her in this world that he meant to build. Though she doubted her role was to be anything more than a pretty face for however long Dragoran required her services. "I will deal with Hanover."

"Of course you will, my dear. I was simply offering my aid."

"You were offering more than that."

"And should I not?" Malor asked. "It is only proper. We are to be married after all."

"We will not be married." Drin forced the words through clenched teeth.

"Celindria." Malor shook his head sadly, his smile suggesting that he was mildly amused and just a touch disappointed. "Best not to fight the inevitable. Best to focus on the future."

"The future? What future would that be? The one that you seek to create?"

"Exactly so," Malor confirmed with a clap of his hands and a warm smile. "I must warn you, however, that creating that future requires us to work together. To be of one mind."

"You can dream all you want, King Dragoran. That does not mean your dreams are mine. Further, that your dreams will become reality."

"I do dream, my dear. And many of my dreams include you." The look that Malor directed toward Drin sent a shiver down her spine, the magnetic pull of his gaze that so distressed her, that made her feel as if she was losing what little will she had left to resist the King of the Tor, too powerful. Her resistance replaced by a lechery that frightened her.

"I will not ..." she managed to push out, refusing to surrender.

"You will." Malor cut her off. His voice still quiet. His temperament calm.

Although Drin sensed that beneath the surface he was anything but. That he was losing patience with her. She interpreted that to be a good thing. A variable that she might be able to use to her advantage when the time was right.

"I will not ..."

"You will, my dear," Malor said with an absolute certainty that chilled Drin's blood. "Here on the Tor you have only me. You have no other allies to call upon." To emphasize his point, Malor began to walk around Drin as if he were examining a horse that he was interested in buying, not stopping until he blocked her view of the setting sun. "Tell me of this Broken Bear."

"Who?"

Malor studied Drin, hoping to catch her off guard, yet wondering if she offered an honest response to his order veiled as a request. "You don't know him?"

"I have no idea about whom you're talking."

Malor didn't respond right away. Eyes narrowing, he confirmed his initial instinct that she was telling the truth. "You may know him by another name. He is more commonly called the King of the Underworld. The man who most would agree ensured that you took the throne of the Crux rather than Hanover."

Drin didn't believe that lying now would do her any further damage or, in fact, give her any advantage so she didn't bother. "I know him. We have had several encounters. But I have never heard him called by that name before."

"It seems that this King of the Underworld has many names," Malor advised. "The Broken Bear one of his earlier appellations while he was building his hidden empire and gaining control of the City Below."

"And how did you learn of this name?"

"A woman who works for me. She seemed to know more about him than most anyone else. A very intimate knowledge if she's to be believed."

"A woman?" Drin repeated, her voice containing a calculated hint of disinterest. Although she was interested. More interested than she cared to be. And that surprised her. She didn't understand why this small pique of jealousy raised its head despite her immediate peril.

"How I obtained the information really is of little import. I understand you know this Broken Bear who rules the City Below quite well."

"I know him only because he assisted me when your soldiers tried to kidnap me."

"An unfortunate decision as I just admitted, and one that was beyond my means of correcting once it had been made. But that's beside the point." Malor leaned in then. "It seems that his aiding you prior to your Coronation is not the only reason you know him."

"I did not ask for his assistance. He simply provided it. I was not in a position to refuse him."

"Is that so?" Malor mused.

Drin didn't bother to reply.

"I don't believe you."

"I don't care what you believe, King Dragoran. I'm telling you the truth."

"Words, nothing more, my dear. In this respect, actions count. And from what I have heard, you have spent a good bit of time with this Broken Bear since you assumed the throne. Meeting with him privately more often than not."

"Are you jealous?" Drin offered Malor a lift of her eyebrows and a questioning glance, hoping to antagonize him just a little bit more. Watching his expression harden confirmed for her that she succeeded. Still, only a small victory because she needed some way to hide her worry.

Mikel was quite careful to ensure that his comings and goings to the Citadel went unnoticed. How could Dragoran have acquired this information?

"No, my dear. Not jealous. Concerned. I must question your decision making if you ally yourself with such a dangerous animal as the Broken Bear. I make my motives plain. He likely does not."

"Say what you mean, King Dragoran. I don't care for games such as these. And I don't care for you questioning my decisions."

"I believe that you and this King of the Underworld are more closely bound than you are letting on. I believe this King of the Underworld could present a threat to our future."

"Our future?" Drin snorted, shaking her head in amusement.

"Our future," Malor repeated with greater strength, not appreciating her continuing obstinance.

"I will decide my own future and that of my Kingdom," Drin replied in a very soft voice that demanded she be heard. "I am the Queen of the Crux. Me being here against my will does not change that."

"Of course you are," Malor agreed amiably, his guest's spark sending a not entirely unpleasant surge through him. His desire to break her was building. "And you should know that you are not a prisoner here in the Ring. As I said, you are here for your own protection. No other reason than that. You have free rein of the Tor and all that it has to offer."

"I do?" That surprised Drin. She assumed that with the guards at the door her apartment was to be a gilded cage.

"You do."

"Why?"

Malor chuckled at that. "So suspicious, although I can understand why what with all the challenges associated with your Coronation. Difficult circumstances that likely still weigh on you."

"Why?" Drin repeated, refusing to be put off.

"You don't need me to answer that question for you." Malor's expression made it clear that he was testing her.

"If the people of the Tor see me out and about, they'll see that our desire to unite our Kingdoms is mutual. Word will spread. Likely back to the Crux. The people of both Kingdoms will believe that you are not forcing our union. They will consider the benefits of such a joining."

"And thus one of the primary reasons for my proposal, my dear. Together we would make quite a formidable pair."

"I'm assuming a squad of your soldiers will be accompanying me?" Drin couldn't argue with Malor's reasoning, disturbed though not surprised by his political acuity. It did no more than solidify her belief that he was a much more daunting adversary than he let on.

But that was a problem for another time. Her most immediate concern was finding some way to escape the snare Malor Dragoran and the Dark Magus had placed around her. Her fingers once again touched the bracelet. The Talent right in front of her, the magic in the artifact prevented her from connecting to it.

"You assume correctly. But they are only there for your protection. They will not impede you in any way."

Malor turned to go, then spun back around, his dark eyes gleaming brightly with an emotion that Drin preferred not to interpret. "Although you should know that because of Assindra's gift," Malor nodding toward the bracelet that functioned just like a Protector's collar, "you cannot leave the Tor." He shrugged then. "Again, just for your protection."

"That's so very kind of you to be looking out for me."

Malor smiled thinly at Drin's sarcasm. Then he leaned in

close to her, reaching out and grasping her hand gently, his action pulling her eyes toward his.

Drin's breath caught, unable to break away from his gaze. His mesmerizing orbs -- black, green, blue, she couldn't tell for certain, the colors flashing with no discernible rhythm – froze her.

A significant part of her was more than willing to do nothing more than stare into those multicolored orbs. A smaller part of her fought against the pull Malor attempted to exert against her. That part gained strength slowly but surely, until finally, with a great effort of will, Drin pulled back her hand, breaking his hold upon her.

"I may be your prisoner, King Dragoran, but I am also the Queen of the Crux," she stated again with a rising heat. "You cannot treat me like one of your other conquests."

Malor laughed softly at that, clearly enjoying his quarry's fire. He walked around her slowly then, impressed by her demeanor, how she held herself despite the pressure he placed upon her, yet also relishing how she tensed when he was behind her. That was an emotion that he was quite familiar with. And one that he not only enjoyed but also thrived on.

When he was behind her right shoulder, he leaned forward and whispered into her ear. His breath warm on the back of her neck.

"And you could be so much more, my dear Celindria," Malor purred. "Why be satisfied with Queen of the Crux when you can rule the Splintered Empire?"

17

NOT LIKE OLD TIMES

"Another visit, Liria? I'm flattered."

The sun a dim glow in the east, Mikel stood atop The Fox's Lair. More often than not when he climbed to the crow's nest that gave him a view of the city in all directions, and just as he was doing now, he peered at the seawall and the Churn far below and the distant shores beyond.

Inevitably he focused on the west and the mountains that protected the Frozen Waste, thinking about what he had discovered while he was last with Cadmus. What else he needed to learn. Even more, what he expected would be required of him.

That last frustrating him, because he had no real sense as to what that might be, other than a vague feeling that there was a high price attached to the Blade of Light. A price that he would have no choice but to pay.

He was getting tired of not knowing what he didn't know.

He preferred to act. To do.

After careful calculation, of course.

Yet that was proving more difficult the more he discovered.

During the last few months, his decisions had pulled him in

directions that he usually tried to avoid. He was dealing with problems that he didn't want to deal with. He was engaging with people he didn't often associate with. And the resulting burdens of those decisions and interactions were growing heavier on his shoulders.

It wasn't a position he enjoyed being in.

He preferred to complete a task and move on.

Now, one task led to another. And then another. Followed by one more. A never-ending progression. Each task gained greater importance. Each task carried a weightier cost if he failed to pass the test.

Because that's how he viewed each of the tasks placed in his way, whether it was training with Cadmus in the Frozen Waste or assisting Celindria Dengannon from the shadows.

A test.

Just as the conversation about to take place was a test.

Potentially with lethal consequences if he failed to pass.

Turning around and giving his former partner a crooked grin, Mikel kept his hands down at his sides. Tired of deliberating. Ready to move. Ready to act. Savoring the rush of adrenaline that surged through him upon facing off against the woman who used to set his blood boiling with just a look.

Liria shook her head. Clearly amused. She should have assumed that Mikel would sense her there despite her sneaking into the tavern, slipping past Teddy with him none the wiser, then climbing the narrow stairs without making a sound. Demonstrating that her skills as a thief, skills she had once used while working with Mikel, were just as good as they ever were.

"Mikel. Still seeking to solve the world's problems from your roost?"

"Just my problems," he replied. He tilted his head to the side, studying her. Not really having a chance to do so the last time they met. She was little changed since their adventure beneath the Tor other than the crow's feet around her eyes and a few streaks of grey in her hair. "Here to kill me again?"

"Far from it," she replied with a soft snort of laughter. Her eyes sparked with delight. She always enjoyed sparring with Mikel, whether with blades, words, or in a more comfortable and seductive environment.

"Then why are you here?"

"More reasons than you can possibly imagine."

It was Mikel's turn to snort softly. "Don't tell me that you're here because you felt bad about how we left things."

"Not at all," Liria replied. "I did what I needed to do."

"Just as you always do," Mikel confirmed with a nod, expecting just such a response from her. "Doing what you need to do so long as it benefits you."

Liria sighed. She should have assumed that Mikel would raise this old argument again. "Don't we all, Mikel? Aren't you doing that now? Doing what you need to do because it benefits you?"

Mikel didn't respond at first, mulling her question. She was right. In part. It was only human, after all.

He liked to think, however, that what he did benefited others as well. Perhaps not as much as he hoped. Still, he preferred to believe that he had done some good for the people on the Crux and beyond who depended on him.

"I'm not really sure," Mikel sighed.

"I don't understand." Sensing Mikel's own uncertainty, Liria got caught up within it. An unusual occurrence for her.

Mikel smiled, enjoying how he flummoxed the woman who used to have his heart on a string. "Right now, I'm not really sure what I should do."

"So that's why you're up here," Liria nodded. "Another of your moments of reflection." She snorted again in laughter, this time more loudly. "Not a wise decision."

"How so?"

"Thinking too much never failed to get you into trouble."

"Actually, in my experience, my not thinking enough when we were together was exactly what got me into trouble."

Liria's look became mischievous, almost sultry. "What got you into trouble when we were together was that you were thinking with the wrong part of your body."

Mikel didn't bother to deny Liria's claim. Maybe she was correct, although he liked to think that there was more to it than that. "Maybe so."

"And what is it that you're thinking about now?" She took a few steps closer to him so that she was more than just a shadow, though she hesitated to get too close. She didn't want to be within his reach. For such a big man he was remarkably fast, and she still felt the need to be wary of him. They hadn't parted on the best of terms, of course, and she was having trouble reading him. He wasn't the same person she remembered. There was some aspect to him that was different, foreign to her, and she was certain it had to do with a great deal more than the scimitar sheathed across his back. "Your latest cause?"

"My latest cause?"

Liria laughed, clapping her hands softly. "Come now, Mikel. You always had a cause. Whether it was helping an orphanage, rebuilding the lower rings destroyed by the floods, or righting some wrong that no one else cared about. Even seeking to help a stray, one of your greatest weaknesses, in fact."

"I don't view my desire to help from time to time as a weakness."

"Of course you don't. I was simply hoping that you were thinking about that time we didn't leave your bedroom here at the Lair for almost a week."

"You mean when I was nursing you back from the wounds you suffered after that job on the Royal Ring went sour?"

Liria's lips curled into a suggestive smile, refusing to be put off. "Actually, I'm remembering when we went an entire week without wearing a single piece of clothing."

"That does bring back some very lucid memories," Mikel admitted.

"Very good memories," Liria gave Mikel a wink.

"On that we can agree."

"So if you're not thinking about that, what has caught your mind?"

Liria was a beautiful woman. And there had always been some quality to her personality that had drawn Mikel in like a fish to a baited line. He realized then that he still felt something for Liria, despite what she put him through.

Yet it was different now. No longer an attraction. More a ... sadness.

That was the only way that he could really describe it. A strange feeling and not one that he had anticipated.

He felt sad for her. But why? That's what he was struggling to put into words.

"Nothing worth sharing," Mikel replied, still studying Liria as the first rays of the sun illuminated the crow's nest. She was much the same, yet ... she wasn't. He could see it in the back of her eyes. What was it? Regret. No, definitely not that with Liria. Perhaps desperation?

"I doubt that very much." Liria took a step closer to him, eyes widening, feeling that familiar heat that she always experienced when she was close to Mikel rising within her. She didn't quite understand it, although she certainly enjoyed it.

Until Mikel, she had preferred a certain kind of man. And Mikel was far from that man. Not handsome, his face battered by too many fights and too many broken noses. Not slim of frame, though there wasn't an ounce of fat on him. Not silky long hair that played in the wind, instead a shorter cut. Not interested in the finer things in life. Not striving to become fabulously wealthy. Just ... not.

A contradiction for her. A man who was everything that she wasn't seeking.

Yet despite all that, despite how she left things with him, as soon as she set eyes on him, she felt the old attraction that remained even after all these years. And she wondered now whether she could rekindle the fires that had once flared between them.

She knew how it would end if she succeeded. But until then it would be more than worth getting burned again. "Tell me, Mikel. What are you thinking? When we were together, you used to share your thoughts when you needed an ear."

"On occasion," Mikel admitted, "because you so rarely cared to hear them."

"I've grown a great deal since we last saw one another," Liria replied.

"You mean from the time just a few weeks ago when you came after me with your Seekers?"

"Before then," Liria clarified, waving her hand as if she were wiping away that incident from both their memories. "And to be clear that was just a simple misunderstanding."

"Was it now?" Mikel wasn't convinced.

"It was. It was just for show." Liria took another step closer to Mikel, the heat within her growing in intensity. "No hard feelings, I hope."

She was about to take another step toward Mikel. Then she'd be able to reach out and touch his arm, and in the past he had never been able to resist her when her fingers played across his skin. What he said next stopped her cold.

"I know who you're working for, Liria." He was tired of the game they were playing. He was tired of the innuendo. He was tired of Liria attempting to turn back time. He was a different person back when they were together, and he had no desire to be that person again. "Why are you here?"

Liria had hoped to break through Mikel's defenses. Many if not all of those defenses constructed because of her.

No such luck this time, however.

Nevertheless, she held out hope for the future. Assuming she didn't have to kill him first. "Your latest cause has need of you."

"My latest cause?" Mikel wasn't certain to what Liria was referring.

"The girl you helped put on the throne. Remember her?"

"That I put on the throne? I didn't have anything to do with ..."

"Don't waste your breath, Mikel. Her ascension has your fingerprints all over it. I know it was you. That's the word in the City Above and the City Below."

"You're speaking about the Queen of the Crux? I know her in passing, though she took the throne of her own accord. What of her?"

"Of course she did," Liria agreed with a heavy dose of sarcasm that was as thick as molasses. Not wanting to get bogged down, she continued. "Your latest cause, Celindria Dengannon, needs you."

"You know this how?" Mikel kept his emotions in check, refusing to reveal anything to Liria and hoping that she didn't know all that he knew.

Her coming here now and raising this topic simply confirmed his suspicions. Initially, he had assumed that she worked for the Dark Magus who had hired him to steal the Blade on his back. Now, he understood who was really paying for her services. And what he wanted from him.

Liria's grin mimicked that of a cat about to pounce on a mouse. She knew him too well. "Come, come Mikel. Just as you admitted, you know who I work for."

"Is that why you stayed dead for so long?"

Liria didn't reply right away, unable to look at Mikel for a few breaths before forcing herself to lift her eyes. She never told him what she was really about when they were together, though she probably should have. Perhaps circumstances between them would have been different if she had.

What had started as a fling for her had become so much more than that. Liria had become absolutely and completely lost in Mikel. Finding something in him that she really couldn't define. That she didn't want to define. That she just wanted to savor. Which had surprised her at first. And then frightened her. Because based on the life that she had lived before she met Mikel, she had learned that she needed more than just love to survive in the world.

"It seemed like the best thing to do." She didn't offer any more than that. Not trusting herself to say more.

"For yourself," Mikel stated in a very quiet, very cold voice that sent a shiver through Liria for reasons that she didn't want to consider.

"I'm sure I'll see you again soon, Mikel. I'm glad this time it wasn't on the other end of a blade."

There was so much she wanted to say. And so much that she couldn't say. That instinct driving her, Liria slipped away then, giving Mikel a disappointed smile before stepping silently down the steps.

Mikel considered trying to stop her. But what was the point? Engaging with Liria only got in the way of what he really needed to do.

Besides, before he met her again – and he was certain that they would meet again -- Mikel wanted to gain a better sense of the environment that he was being pulled toward. He didn't understand all that was going on, and he didn't like that. The only certainty that he could identify was the fact that there was more going on here than just what he could see in that moment.

"You heard?"

"How did you know that I was here?" Nat released her hold on the Talent, having snuck up the steps not long after Liria and hiding herself with her natural magic to eavesdrop on the conversation. Ready to aid Mikel if there was a need. Not trusting the woman who had tried to kill him several times before.

"Why would I give away my secrets?" Mikel replied with a smile that irritated the young woman. "It takes the fun out of life."

"I did everything right. Everything Finn taught me to do. Yet still you knew I was there." Nat was less than pleased.

"Perhaps baths every day instead of once a week?" Mikel suggested in a helpful voice.

"Not funny," Nat replied, biting off her words and punching him lightly in the shoulder.

Mikel decided not to antagonize her any further, feeling the press of the day as the sun rose higher in the sky and the wonderful smells wafting up from his tavern's kitchen assaulted him. "What do you think?"

Nat frowned, then pursed her lips. "I wouldn't trust her."

"I don't."

"Good. I was worried."

"Why would you be worried?"

"Because I saw how you were looking at her." Nat's expression suggested that she was less than impressed with him.

"I was looking at her the way she wanted me to look at her," Mikel protested. "Not the way I wanted to look at her."

"You keep telling yourself that." Nat's frown turned into a broad smile. It was so easy to get under Mikel's skin. And so enjoyable. "You need to go after Drin."

"Drin? You're good friends now?"

Nat shrugged. "She said that's how she wanted me to address her."

"Why do I need to go after the Queen of the Crux? Politics don't concern me. It's not my problem to solve." Yet it was obvious that Nat didn't believe his protest, her expression hardening. Likely because he didn't believe his own words and she knew it.

"It's not about the politics," Nat said. Giving Mikel a disappointed shake of her head, she didn't understand why he wanted to delude himself to a truth that was quite obvious if he only chose to open his eyes and acknowledge it. "Drin is more than a cause for you, whether you like it or not."

Mikel growled. "Sometimes you're too smart for your own good." He had considered protesting further, but what was the point when dealing with a sharp teenage girl who could cut him into pieces with just a raised eyebrow. Wasted time and wasted effort, neither of which appealed to him.

"That's why you like me."

"One of the reasons," Mikel grumbled reluctantly.

"When do I need to be ready to go?"

"I'm sorry?"

"It's a simple question, Mikel. When do I need to be ready to go?"

"You're not going."

Nat stepped in close to Mikel. Hands on her hips. Expression angry. Neck craned because he was so much taller than she was, even as her presence made it seem like she was much bigger than she actually was. "I am. Don't waste your breath trying to argue."

"I'm not wasting my breath. I'm stating unequivocally that you're not going."

"You can say what you want. The truth is, you need me." Nat shrugged at the obviousness of her claim.

Mikel was prepared to continue with his argument. Instead, he thought about what she said. He thought about some of the challenges he would likely face. He thought about who had taken Drin. "We leave in an hour. I just need to talk to Teddy about a few things first."

18

UP IN THE AIR

"You've tested these, right?"

Leonardo offered Mikel a wide smile of gleaming white teeth, his long curly hair swirling around his scalp thanks to the gusty, unpredictable wind. Nat couldn't take her eyes off him, and she didn't want to. To say that he was handsome would be an understatement.

"Of course I have." What he added next caused Mikel to lift one of his eyebrows, a sign of his concern. "In certain conditions."

"What do you mean by certain conditions?" Nat frowned, no longer so taken by the inventor, not liking where this conversation was going.

Leonardo led them closer to the machine that offered enough space for a pilot and a navigator. What he had named a raptor. The wings were fixed to the long frame that was constructed of sailcloth and wood, the end result resembling a bird of prey right down to the nose.

"I've tested several smaller versions," Leonardo explained as he led Mikel and Nat around the craft, running his hand over the wood and cloth, clearly enthralled with his own work. "So there should be few if any concerns with this larger model."

"Wait a second." Mikel was impressed. The design suggested that the flying machine should work as Leonardo believed it would. He had been following his friend's work at the Splintered Bridge, of course. He knew that his assistance had proven invaluable to the Battle Lord in keeping the Tor soldiers on their side of the Trench because every new tool that Leonardo put into play worked ... eventually. So he was sold, just not entirely. He didn't want to be a part of the inventor's latest experiment without more assurance. "You haven't tested this version?"

Leonardo kicked one of the many rocks that littered the ground at the very rim of the Trench. Watching it sail over the edge and disappear in the clouds, he shrugged. "Not this version. Though I should stress that the principles are the same regardless of the size of the raptor. And I've taken into account the additional weight with this design, so you really should have little trouble crossing the Trench."

They were well south of the Splintered Bridge, the green blur of the Deep beckoning to them from the eastern side of the mile-wide canyon. The mile-long drop just a few steps away was hidden from them by a thick blanket of grey that masked what waited below. The billowing fog was broken only by the dozens of tors that soared up from the floor of the Trench and poked their heads out of the grey, hints of purple and white from the heather growing on the stone offering some color to an otherwise dreary scene.

"Not this version?" Nat asked. Arms crossed as she walked around the flying machine, she offered Leonardo a glare that almost made him flinch.

"I've been a little busy."

"That's no excuse," Nat replied, shaking her head. Living

near a beach when she was just a child, she had loved playing with kites. She assumed the raptor as Leonardo called it functioned according to the same principles. And it did resemble a bird, the wings fixed and long, the frame sleek and strong, the fuselage indeed having space for two people to strap themselves in with leather harnesses. So it should work.

An intriguing design, though slightly frightening as well. One mistake would be all it took to ensure a gruesome death.

"With what else I'm doing for the Battle Lord, I haven't had the chance to test the design as much as I would like."

Mikel frowned, studying the construction with just as much intensity as Nat. "This will fly?"

"I guarantee it," Leonardo confirmed with a sharp nod even as his face was obscured by his wild hair. "But ..."

"But what?" Mikel's voice became very soft, which clearly made Leonardo uncomfortable. This was a side of Mikel that the inventor preferred to avoid, having seen what could happen if the King of the Underworld became displeased ... or lost his temper.

"But I don't know for how long." He kicked another stone, once again with enough strength to send it over the edge to disappear in the fog.

"You don't know for how long?"

Leonardo offered Mikel an ingratiating smile, desperate to get out from under his friend's intense focus. "As I said, I haven't had a chance to test this latest prototype. However, if you catch the wind as it is now, you should have little trouble making it across."

"If?"

Leonardo kicked another stone, needing to release his nervous energy. "We've talked about it before, Mikel. With every new creation, there are a great many failures before success is achieved."

"I understand that. I just don't want Nat and me to be one of those failures."

Leonardo nodded soberly. "All the other prototypes, admittedly smaller than this one, have worked. So as I said, the same principles apply. What you'll be flying is simply a larger scale of a smaller, proven version. It's really just a matter of mastering the machine and navigating the wind. Do that and you both should be fine."

"You make it sound very easy," Nat said in a tone that did little to hide her irritation and doubt.

"It's not, young miss. I will give you that. But I promise you this can work." Leonardo shrugged again, looking for another rock to kick but not finding one. "If you're not comfortable, the only option other than the raptor is to sneak across the floor of the Trench."

Mikel considered Leonardo's suggestion for several minutes as he stared at the machine his friend had built. Then he looked at Nat, who stood across from him on the other side of the raptor, flicking a finger against the sailcloth. She had been pulling and tugging on where the cloth met the wood. She shrugged then nodded, essentially telling him that she was willing to take the risk if he was.

And that's what it came down to.

Risk.

Mikel trusted Leonardo's skill and ingenuity. Everything he imagined, designed, then constructed always worked.

Eventually.

Just as Leonardo had said.

Mikel just didn't want to be a part of the process to reach that point. Even more, he didn't want to place Nat in such a dangerous situation.

Yet what would be more dangerous?

Attempting to fly across the Trench or sneaking across the floor of the mile-wide canyon?

The former, if it proved successful, could take no more than a matter of minutes. The latter several days with a great many dangers to negotiate.

It was Mikel's trust in Leonardo and the sense of urgency that he was experiencing that decided it for him. The longer it took for them to reach the Tor, the more precarious Drin's position would become.

And the more perilous their position would become, the King of the Tor likely expecting a rescue attempt to be made.

Secrecy was essential. That was a given. Just as much, speed.

That was why Mikel had enlisted Leonardo's aid, believing that his friend offered him the best chance to get across the Trench without being discovered.

That was why they were opposite the Deep. The forest that was located south of the Tor was avoided by most anyone of sane mind.

The Trench was dangerous.

The Deep ... even more so.

Nevertheless, it was his best opportunity to reach the Tor covertly.

Mikel nodded then clapped his hands together. "Leonardo, why don't you take us through how we fly this raptor of yours. Then you can strap us in."

"ARE YOU READY?" Mikel sat in the front of the raptor, hands on a wooden stick centered between his legs that should allow him to adjust the positioning of the wings in relation to the demands of the wind.

He looked out over the glider's nose that resembled a beak. Nat was behind him.

Both were strapped in, sitting in wicker seats bolted into the wooden fuselage. Nat had a slightly better view since she sat a foot higher than Mikel did. She was able to scan all around them. Mikel's view was obstructed whenever he tried to look over either shoulder. A weakness that Leonardo readily acknowledged, the inventor promising to correct it when he built his next model.

Both were nervous. The wooden frame shook every time a powerful blast of wind struck, which was much too frequent for their tastes though not unexpected, the erratic bursts of air common along the rim of the Trench.

The flying machine only remained in place because Leonardo had strapped it down to a long wooden runner that extended out and over the billowing grey clouds that hid all but the very tops of the tors that lined the cavern floor. A thick band similar to a bowstring though a great deal larger was connected via hooks to the underside of the craft.

Leonardo had explained that once released the taut band, fastened to posts pounded into the ground at the very edge of the ledge, would shoot them out and over the Trench much like a slingshot. Or at least that's the way it was supposed to work. As he had explained, he hadn't yet had the opportunity to test his latest creation.

Neither Mikel nor Nat took much comfort from Leonardo's explanation. But it was too late now. They were committed to their decision.

"No," Nat replied forcefully, having second thoughts now that she was so close to the mile-high drop. Her stomach, queasy to begin with, worsened every time the wind buffeted the raptor, threatening to rip it free from its ramp.

"Just remember what I told you," Leonardo called from where he stood off to the side of the glider, a rope in hand. "The controls only require a gentle touch. Nature will do the rest."

"Right," Mikel nodded, choosing to not mention that in his

experience nature was a harsh master. "Now how do we get this raptor into the air?"

"Simple," Leonardo replied, a devilish smile brightening his features. "Have fun."

With a sharp yank on the rope, Leonardo disconnected the hooks holding the raptor in place.

The basic principles of force, acceleration, and momentum took over from there. The taut band freed, the raptor hurtled down the ramp at a bone-rattling speed.

"What the ..."

Mikel didn't get a chance to finish the curse he was desperate to utter. Hearing the snap of the band, seeing Leonardo's wide grin as he shot by, for the next few seconds everything around him was a blur. His heart lodged in his throat as the velocity pushed Mikel back into his chair and the raptor soared out over the Trench.

Caught by the blustery winds the instant it was free from the ramp, the raptor proved difficult to control as Mikel struggled to get a feel for the stick so essential to surviving their maiden flight. The glider dipping and diving, rising and falling, curling to the left or right at the whim of the wind, at first Mikel exerted very little discretion over the craft's movement.

He tried to be gentle with the yoke just as Leonardo had instructed, fearful that if he was too aggressive with his actions, he'd only hasten their deaths in a terrible crash. Yet it seemed that he had overcorrected.

Mikel needed to find a balance. Fast. Before the raptor cartwheeled through the fog or slammed against the top of a rocky spike.

Feeling a violent push against his right wing that forced the raptor down in that direction, the left wing rising higher until he and Nat were descending sideways toward the clouds, Mikel fought the yoke to correct the drop, pulling back hard and to the left, straining to return to a more even keel.

It didn't work.

The glider responded well to Mikel's ministrations. Too well.

The raptor rose too swiftly, revealing its belly to a mighty blast of air that struck the fuselage full on and threatened to flip the raptor backward and upside down.

"Mikel!" Nat screamed as she stared up at the sun for a brief, terrifying moment, the sun replaced by a clear blue sky as the nose tilted farther over.

"I know!"

Mikel strained at the yoke. Feeling helpless as he fought a battle that he knew he couldn't win.

He was well aware of the problem. He just didn't know how to fix it.

Understanding that attempting to battle the wind was a losing proposition, Mikel did something that he rarely did.

He gave in.

Easing up on the yoke, he allowed the wind to push the raptor backward, nose over the tail for just a second more before the craft dropped precipitously.

"Mikel!" Nat, feeling ill before they had even launched off the side of the Trench, released the contents of her stomach. The only good thing about their current predicament was that when it happened, she was facing the clouds hiding the Trench.

Mikel ignored Nat, concentrating on what he needed to do next. When the raptor was upside down, Mikel getting a good look at an inverted Leonardo on the cliff -- his face pale, terror in his eyes -- he pushed down on the yoke, which forced the front of the wings to rise up.

"Yes!" Mikel shouted, thrilled that what he did worked. Grateful that at that exact moment the wind died down, no longer pushing them back toward the cliff, which gave him a little more room for error.

Mikel eased off the yoke, the raptor curling down then back up and completing a circle. His luck holding, when the fuselage was level with the fog, Mikel evened out the wings, a strong burst of air at their backs propelling the raptor forward.

Taking Leonardo's advice to heart, Mikel applied just a few gentle touches on the yoke and the raptor shot forward on a fairly straight path. The machine still dipped to the left and the right, but no longer rose or fell, Mikel getting the hang of the subtle movements required to keep the raptor aloft with a better semblance of control.

"About time!" Nat shouted down to Mikel as she wiped her mouth with her sleeve, removing the last few strands of saliva and puke.

"Agreed!"

"Don't ever do that again!" Nat ordered.

"I'll try ..."

A sudden burst of air from above pushed the raptor down at a shocking speed, Mikel having no way to prevent it. As fast as the punch came, it stopped, the wind calmer.

Just in time as they had dropped several hundred feet in only a few heartbeats, the bottom of the fuselage skimming across the top of the clouds.

His immediate instinct was to pull up on the wooden yoke. He resisted that impulse, remembering what had happened just moments before when he was too aggressive at the controls.

Instead, he didn't do anything at all. He simply focused on maintaining an even keel, allowing the strong bluster at their backs to push them across the gap.

"Stop doing that! I have no desire to be sick again!"

"I didn't do anything!" Mikel shouted back over his shoulder.

"Likely story!"

Mikel didn't bother to reply. He smiled instead. Better that

Nat was angry. If she was angry, she didn't have time to be afraid.

Keeping his gaze to their front, the far side of the Trench drew steadily closer. Employing the rudder rarely and then with barely a touch, the raptor responded beautifully to Mikel's controlled and economical movements.

Mikel was impressed now that the surge of adrenaline that hit him as soon as he was in the air had subsided. Leonardo had done excellent work with this glider. Instead of feeling like their deaths were inevitable, he was beginning to believe that he and Nat might actually reach the far side in one piece.

His growing confidence fizzled when a large shadow swept over them.

What in blazes was …

"Mikel, behind us!"

"Nat, what are you …"

"Mikel, did you see that?"

"See what? I can't see behind me."

Another shadow swept over them. Mikel tried to catch sight of what it could be, but he lost it in the sun. All he knew for certain was that whatever it was, it had to be quite large to blot out the sun.

Then another shadow glided over them not long after the first.

"Did you see that?" Nat demanded again.

"I didn't …" Mikel's eyes widened, finally glimpsing what had caused the shadow. The creature drifted down and glided off their starboard side.

"Mikel!" Nat didn't bother to keep the note of fear from her voice. "What are they?"

"Wyverns."

"That can't be good."

"It's not," Mikel confirmed. The animal resembled a black dragon, the key difference besides its smaller size the fact that it had wings. Mikel judged the Wyvern keeping pace with them to be a quarter of the size of a black dragon. Even so, the Wyvern was still slightly larger than the raptor Mikel was flying. And with its sharp claws and foot-long teeth, the animal could rip them to shreds if it had a mind to do so.

"I thought Wyverns stayed beneath the clouds." Nat's voice rose an octave, her fear increasing. "You said that Wyverns stayed beneath the clouds!"

"I said they usually do. Sometimes they don't."

"Not very helpful right now," Nat growled. "What do we do?"

"Stay clear of them." Mikel was about to curl away from the Wyvern. He held back instead, avoiding the Wyvern that glided down next to them on the port side.

"Mikel, they look hungry."

He glanced to his left and then his right. Both Wyverns opened their maws and revealed their sharp teeth, snapping their jaws a few times as they communicated with one another in a series of grunts, hisses, and shrieks.

Nat was right. They did look hungry.

Mikel glanced toward their front. The eastern cliffs of the Trench were closer, but not close enough.

Not with the pair of Wyverns slowly angling in toward them from both sides.

He needed to act quickly. But what to do?

The Wyverns were faster than they were. More agile.

That limited his options.

Before he could decide, another shadow drifted over them ... and stayed there.

They were trapped.

"Can we make it to the far side before they attack?" Nat was just as aware as he was as to the deadly nature of their predicament.

Mikel glanced toward the far side of the Trench one more

time, judging the distance. Still a quarter mile away at the very least. There was no way the Wyverns would wait that long before attacking.

"No."

Sensing the change around them, Mikel pushed the yoke to the left, the right-side wing tilting up.

Excellent timing. The raptor on their starboard side cut in fast, snapping at that same wing.

Mikel's quick thinking kept the sailcloth free of the Wyvern's teeth.

But evading that strike brought them closer to the Wyvern on their port side. Not wanting to draw any nearer, he pushed down on the yoke sharply, the raptor dropping precipitously before he pulled up on the stick to even out again.

The Wyvern on their left swiped at the wing and missed by no more than the length of one of its daggerlike talons.

Close. Much too close.

"They won't leave us alone!" Nat proclaimed. The three Wyverns adjusted their positioning in relation to the raptor, keeping them hemmed in on both sides, the animal above them gliding down even closer. "What do we do?"

Excellent question, Mikel thought. He was worried most about the Wyvern flying above them. The animals on each side had drifted farther away from them. The shadow above growing in size suggested that this Wyvern was larger than the other two, which meant that the beast was exerting its dominance and preparing to go for the kill as it glided down.

"We do the unexpected," Mikel declared, refusing to be easy meat.

Pushing down sharply on the yoke, the raptor shot into the clouds.

~

PUNCHING THROUGH THE GREY, Mikel pushing the stick down, the glider plunged toward the ground.

Mikel gripped the yoke with both hands, fighting to pull back on the stick. It wouldn't budge. The natural forces working against him were too strong.

"Mikel!"

The fear and consternation in Nat's voice struck Mikel like a physical blow. No other ideas coming to mind to arrest their descent, he redoubled his efforts. Placing his feet against the wooden frame, he set himself and once more pulled back on the yoke with everything he had, every muscle in his body straining, his frame taut with tension.

The blasted stick still wouldn't budge!

"Nat, I can't get us out of this! You need to do something!"

He hoped she heard him. He couldn't be certain. Not with the wind shrieking in his ears.

Then he felt a tingle along his skin.

Nat was reaching for the Talent.

But what could she possibly do now?

A few hundred feet was all that they had to work with.

The rocky floor of the Trench was rising up to meet them much too swiftly.

He felt a slight jolt. Then another. And one more. A force punched against the frame, though Mikel knew it was more than that. Creases around his eyes tightening, he prepared himself for the opportunity the young Magus perched behind him was trying to give them.

Nat used the Talent in a way that she never had before, seeking to balance the power that she could call upon against the need for a delicacy that ensured she didn't destroy the raptor's fuselage. Sending gentle bursts of energy curling out from her fingertips, she attempted to punch them out of their vertical dive. Focusing on the nose of the flying machine, she was afraid that if she hit the frame too hard the raptor would break apart.

Was she doing enough?

They were no longer in a vertical dive. However, she had scarcely shifted the angle of their tongue-swallowing descent. And they were almost out of time.

Having no choice, she sent a stronger blast of power curling out from her hand to strike the underside of the nose.

She heard the crack when her magical punch hit the frame, sending a spike of terror down her spine.

Nat sighed with relief.

Somehow the raptor held together.

Just as important, their dive was no longer a dive.

Finally, the raptor responded to Mikel pulling back on the yoke.

Growling, calling upon every ounce of strength remaining to him, Mikel pulled the yoke all the way back to his chest. The farthest it would go.

It was working!

The nose was pulling up.

The raptor began to curl away from the ground.

Slowly.

Too slowly!

They had fallen too far.

They had fallen too fast.

The ground was too close.

They weren't going to make it.

Yet they did.

Their fate decided by an errant gust of wind that swirled around the base of the tor at their backs and struck the raptor at exactly the right moment and exactly the right place.

The glider, responding to Mikel's ministrations and caught within the burst of air, shot back up into the sky. Missing the ground by no more than a few feet, the raptor streaked away from certain destruction.

Mikel maintained a strong grip on the stick, happy to use the blast of air for as long as he could to gain the safety of the grey swirls that hemmed them in from above.

Averting disaster by no more than a heartbeat, he didn't have the chance to breathe any more easily.

"Mikel, left side!"

He didn't bother to look, focused on the tor that was growing larger right before his eyes. His decision to stay within the gust coming off the cavern floor had taken the raptor away from one rocky spire and sent them right toward another that was only a few hundred yards away.

Relying on his instincts, he waited two breaths before he pushed the stick to the left and then pulled up. Just a slight touch as he began to get a feel for how responsive the glider was.

That was all that was required.

The Wyvern diving down toward them, certain of its kill, failed to turn in time. Soaring above them, a single sharp talon sliced through their tipping right wing rather than crunching into the fuselage.

Mikel curled the raptor around the outside of the tor. Still caught in the gust of air that saved them from certain death, they looped around the rocky spire and toward the clouds far above.

Catching a hint of movement out of the corner of his eye, Mikel pushed down hard on the stick again. The raptor responded instantly, diving away from the tor and toward the ground.

Nat didn't bother to complain this time. Ready to use the Talent again if there was need, she held on to the grip in front of her as Mikel tried to evade the next attack.

His quick maneuvering saved them again.

Another Wyvern passed right over them. Snapping with its jaws, the small dragon bit into the very tip of the tail, taking off a few feet from the top rather than the entire assembly.

"Are we good?" Mikel asked over his shoulder.

Nat examined the damage. It wasn't as bad as it could have been. Maybe two feet ripped away, but it didn't seem to be affecting Mikel's efforts to keep them aloft.

"We are so long as you keep us away from any more of those beasts. Another bite and we're done."

"I'll do my best."

"Do better than that," Nat ordered.

Mikel smiled. Still snarky with death knocking at the door. He had to give her credit for that. He had to give credit to Leonardo as well, grateful that the inventor was as fastidious with this creation as he was with all his others. What could have been a devastating bite only made his ability to maneuver through the air a touch more difficult.

For the next few minutes Mikel didn't spend much time thinking. Instead he listened to his gut much as he did when he was in the midst of a difficult combat. Having no choice but to master the raptor as he twisted and turned in the air, ducking and dodging around the stone spires that punched through the clouds, he evaded what seemed like an endless number of Wyverns seeking to make a meal of them. The smaller dragons eager to leap from their nests along the sides of the tors Mikel curled around and join the hunt.

Several times Mikel escaped certain doom because the Wyverns, all hungry to make the kill, got in one another's way. Fights broke out between the dragons. And when that occurred, Mikel was more than happy to use the discord to his advantage.

"Mikel, on our tail!" Nat had been keeping an eye on their rear, remembering that Mikel's vision was limited and wanting to avoid any more surprises.

Mikel didn't see the Wyvern at their back. He didn't need to. He could feel the malevolent presence shooting down toward them. Much like when he was in the Frozen Waste and he could sense a predator hunting him.

Then he heard the sound that set his teeth on edge. The Wyvern's jaws snapping at the raptor's damaged tail.

Mikel pushed the yoke hard to the left. Then to the right.

The Wyvern stayed with them. Tracking them, the dragon continued to bite at their damaged tail as Mikel curled this way and that.

Desperate to evade their hunter, Mikel put the raptor through a series of maneuvers that he never would have dared to try if the circumstances weren't so dire. Dipping and diving. Corkscrewing. Seeking to catch one of the many gusts of air that whipped around the stone spires and gave them some much-needed additional speed, he preferred to be caught within the maelstrom so that they could stay clear of their hunter.

Yet even then, the determined Wyvern refused to be put off. Never falling too far behind no matter what Mikel did.

Frustrated by their hunter's persistence, Mikel realized that a more drastic tactic was necessary.

He pushed down on the yoke. Sending the raptor into another dive, the floor of the Trench rushed up toward them.

However, Mikel was less concerned about their imminent crash than the Wyvern that kept close to their tail, biting at the damaged wood and cloth and hissing each time it failed to grab hold.

"Mikel!" Nat screamed. She didn't know if she was more afraid of their impending crash or the Wyvern about to take them out of the air. Reaching for the Talent, she prepared to do as she had done before. And for just a moment, she considered sending a bolt of energy back toward the Wyvern, wiping that idea from her mind as quickly as it came to her, certain that she had little chance of hitting her target while in their dive. "Mikelllll!"

"Don't worry, I've got it," Mikel called back, hoping that Nat trusted him.

She didn't see it. He did.

A black dragon, bursting out from its nest in the base of the tor right to their front, was racing across the canyon floor, its huge claws digging into the dirt and the rock as it propelled itself toward them at a breath-taking speed. The animal that was bigger than a gatehouse had eyes only for them.

Mikel sensed a chance.

A slim one.

But still a chance to escape their terrifying dilemma.

If he was willing to take the risk.

And he was. Mikel ensured that the raptor remained in an angled dive rather than a vertical one, understanding now the limitations of their craft. He breathed easier when the glider responded to his pulling back slightly on the yoke and they turned directly toward the black dragon.

Nat, so focused on the Wyvern snapping at them from behind, was slow to see what was rushing toward them on the ground. When she did, she didn't even have time to scream.

"Mike ..."

Staring into the gaping maw of the black dragon, at the last possible second Mikel pushed the yoke hard to the right then pulled up. The raptor responded beautifully to his touch, soaring up and away.

There was a brief shudder, the black dragon's claw slicing through the tip of their portside wing. But it wasn't enough to slow down the raptor.

It was enough to end the Wyvern's pursuit. The dragon's claw cut through wood and cloth and then right into the Wyvern's gut, impaling the smaller creature that was so intent on its prey that it ignored the danger presented by the larger predator.

Mikel closed his eyes for just a moment, finally taking a breath that didn't include a shudder of fear. Excellent timing with a lot of luck mixed in. Nevertheless, he would take it.

The black dragon shrieked in triumph at its kill as Mikel kept close to the tor from which the animal had emerged. Using the warm current rising from the base of the canyon, he gained the height to escape the Trench. In a matter of minutes they were through the cloud cover, Mikel curling the raptor toward the eastern cliffs. Best of all, there wasn't a Wyvern in sight.

"Don't ever do that again!" Nat ordered. "Ever!"

"Is it really that much more dangerous to cross the bottom of the Trench?" Nat asked.

Nat still felt queasy, as if the world continued to spin, not yet recovered from Mikel's acrobatics that got them free of the Wyverns. She glanced one more time at what was left of their raptor, the sick feeling in her stomach forcing her to clench her teeth together. The black dragon's claw mark, just a few hands to the right, would have struck the fuselage and taken them out of the air.

It had been a hard landing with the damaged wing and tail. Thankfully, the frame held together. Although the raptor wouldn't be soaring through the air again anytime soon. If ever. The once elegant glider more resembled a pile of scrap lumber held together by torn cloth.

"It can be. As you saw, the Wyverns are quite frisky."

"Frisky?" Nat took issue with his description. "That's how you would describe them?" The Wyverns were more than frisky. They were starving. Rapacious. Vicious.

"The black dragons are worse. Very territorial. Incredibly aggressive. I'm just glad that worked in our favor at the end."

"I'll give you that," Nat relented.

"Finally," Mikel replied in a soft chuckle.

"What was that road on the canyon floor?"

"A creation of the Magii," Mikel explained. He had seen it as well, a broad path -- one hundred yards wide, its border marked by large boulders set along both sides – that wound its way around the tors and through the canyon, though he paid little attention to it. He was more concerned about the Wyverns shooting toward them from every direction. "Or at least that's what Finn told me."

"The Wyverns avoided it when you were making me sick to my stomach."

"I was trying to get us to safety," Mikel protested. "I thought the effort was worth an upset stomach."

"While making me sick," Nat repeated before returning to the anomaly that had caught her interest, "I sensed that the Wyverns couldn't get too close to that road."

"I'm not surprised."

"Why do you say that?"

"The Talent," Mikel replied. "Finn said the Order of the Magii constructed that route centuries ago so that they could build the Sanctuary. They needed safe passage. Not wanting to deal with the threat presented by the black dragons and Wyverns, they created that road. A protected passageway."

"So it still works?"

"It does. The Wyverns and black dragons continue to steer clear of it."

"And the Sanctuary?" Nat asked, never lacking for questions on matters that interested her. Even when Mikel wanted to turn his attention to more pressing concerns.

"The Sanctuary was built atop a tor hundreds of leagues to the south. It was there that the Magii crafted the Weir." Before

Natalie could ask the question that was on the tip of her tongue, Mikel continued. "The Weir is a magical barrier that prevents the Ghoules of the Lost Land from invading Caledonia. Based on what you've seen, it's safe to say that the natural magic the Magii employed to construct the path has held up over the centuries, so I assume the same holds true for the Weir. If not, we likely would have heard about it."

"Good to know."

"It could be," Mikel agreed. He didn't offer anything more than that. He wanted to touch on another topic before they headed deeper into the Kingdom of the Tor, their ultimate goal Graz, the capital city. "I want to discuss what happens once we're through the Deep."

"What do you mean?" Nat asked, the hint of concern in her voice mirroring her expression.

"Once we're through the Deep we'll be just south of the Tor."

Nat frowned, already knowing where Mikel was headed. "You don't want me to go with you." Her voice rose as her anger did. "We went over this. You know that I can help you. I just did, in fact. Without me, there was no way that you were going to pull us out of that first dive."

"You're right, I'm not fighting you on that." Mikel held up his hands, seeking to head off an argument that he didn't view as necessary. "You can help me. You did help. You saved our lives. I agree. You're here with me now because I can't do this without you."

"Then why would you not want me to continue with you after we get through the Deep?"

"It's easier for me to make my way onto the Tor if I'm on my own."

"That's not good enough. I'm sure that I can ..."

"And a feeling."

Nat frowned. "What do you mean by a feeling?" She had never taken Mikel to be the superstitious sort.

Mikel shrugged, not really in a position to explain it. "Feeling. Instinct. Call it what you want. They come to me on occasion, and I never ignore them when they do."

"Why not?"

"Because they've never been wrong before."

"And this is why you won't let me come with you to the Tor?"

"In part," Mikel nodded.

"What's the other part?" Drin pursed her lips, gaze narrowing in suspicion.

"I didn't want to leave you on your own in Innsbruck. I figured that if I did, you'd take over all my businesses in just a few days and then I'd be out on the street."

Nat fought the smile that wanted to break free and failed. "You're right about that."

"Finally no pushback," Mikel murmured. "Will wonders never cease?"

"And what is this feeling of yours telling you?"

"That if you go to the Tor with me you're going to die."

"Ominous," Nat admitted.

"But not something I want to ignore."

"And if I don't, I live?" Nat asked, a slight shiver working its way through her. Mikel's premonition was more frightening than the black dragon that had almost gobbled them up.

Mikel nodded. "Yes, and I live as well. Because if you go to the Tor, I die too. Neither of us make it back to the Crux."

"So what you're saying is that you're really more concerned about yourself rather than me."

"Always," Mikel replied with a straight face, although Nat heard the lie in his voice. "Besides, I need you to do something for me."

"What would that be?" She was smiling again, unable to

help herself. Mikel was frustrating. Enigmatic. Challenging. Aggravating. And also endearing.

Nat knew that he cared about her. That he would do everything he could to keep her safe … without restricting her unnecessarily. Their just-completed death-defying flight evidence of that.

"Be ready for when I come off the Tor. I expect you to save me from whatever is chasing me just like you did in the Trench."

"Fine," Nat grumbled, shaking her head. Not happy with what Mikel was asking of her, still she would adhere to his request. And she did appreciate his speaking to her about it rather than just telling her what he expected her to do. "Of course you're assuming that we'll survive our journey through the Deep."

"You've heard the stories?"

"A few. Finn likes to talk before and after our lessons, regaling me with some of his adventures."

"I wouldn't take all that he tells you as fact."

"I don't, no worries there. Although when he talks about some of your adventures, I have to wonder."

"Wonder what?"

"Whether you're of sound mind," Nat teased.

"A valid concern," Mikel agreed. "We are about to enter the Deep, after all, a decision that most sane people would question. What did Finn say?" He nodded over his shoulder toward the towering heart trees that rose at his back just a hundred yards away from the lip of the Trench.

"He said not to go into the forest."

"Good advice, but advice we need to ignore," Mikel replied. "What else did he say?"

"That the trees are so tall, so big, that they touch the sky. That the canopy is so thick that you walk in a never-ending gloom. And the roots are an indecipherable maze and much like an obstacle course running across the forest floor."

"Heart trees," Mikel confirmed. "The largest a hundred or more feet around at the base. Some reaching a height of four hundred feet if not more. Their leaves larger than a soldier's scutum."

"They're imposing," Nat said as she examined those growing at the edge of the wood.

"Very. Did he mention any of the hazards we need to avoid?"

"Sinkholes that will swallow you whole. Monsters that will emerge from the gloom before you even know they're there. Spirits and shadows and other nasties lost to time just waiting for some hapless fool to enter their domain." Nat shrugged. "It sounded more like a fairy tale to keep people out."

"Finn does spin a good story."

"Was he speaking the truth?"

"About the monsters and the sinkholes and the other perils?"

Nat nodded.

Mikel smiled. She was a tough one. She had to be after what she endured during the last few years. Right at that moment, however, he was beginning to see the cracks in her armor. Just because she was tough didn't mean she couldn't be frightened as well.

"Yes, Finn was speaking the truth. For the most part." He placed a hand on her shoulder and squeezed warmly, hoping to infuse her with some of his confidence and thereby ease her concern. "But don't worry. I've traveled through the Deep several times and I've come out the other end with little difficulty."

"You have?" The tone of her voice suggested that she didn't believe him.

"I have," Mikel confirmed with a nod. "The Deep is just like any other place. Stay wary. Stay sharp. Stay ready. And, most important of all, stay with me, and we'll make it to the other side."

"Comforting, I guess," Nat replied in her preferred snarky tone.

Mikel smiled, glad to see that her natural spark hadn't dimmed too much. "Just a word of warning."

"I'm afraid to ask."

"The dangers of the Deep are much like Innsbruck."

"How so?"

"The dangers above don't come close to the dangers below."

19

A LITTLE SPARRING

"You couldn't go for your stroll along the battlements?" Liria complained. "You had to leave the Ring?"

Drin smiled thinly, pleased that she had irritated the woman charged with keeping an eye on her. "I could have, but where's the fun in that? Better to see all that Graz has to offer."

Liria snorted. Mostly in disgust, only a little amusement mixed in. "You're used to doing whatever you want, aren't you?" There was a clear accusation in her question.

"I'm used to doing what I need to do," Drin replied, adopting the hard tone she had learned at a young age while sitting next to her father in the Crux throne room. Despite her protestations, Malor had put the woman who had played a role in her kidnapping by Drin's side when she announced that she would be taking a closer look at the city. "Just as you are."

"Yes, I've always wanted to be a Queen's nursemaid." Sarcasm dripped off Liria's reply, the leader of the squad of soldiers responsible for protecting the Queen of the Crux – and ensuring that she didn't get into or cause any trouble – not missing her charge's real meaning.

"Then I'm glad I was able to give you that chance." Drin's sarcasm was just as thick.

Liria pursed her lips then locked them together, holding back several sharp replies. She had learned that it was best to be cautious these days.

She was beholden to no one. That's what she prided herself on. Free to go where she wanted. Free to do what she wanted.

Or she had been when she was with Mikel. That had all changed when she began working for Assindra, not perceiving the invisible bindings the Magus had wrapped around her until it was too late.

"You're really quite arrogant." Liria was unable to restrain all her barbs, letting loose with the least offensive that had come to mind. "I guess that's what happens when you're born into wealth and power."

Drin chuckled at that, which surprised Liria. Irritated her as well. She was seeking to get a rise from her charge, yet it seemed instead that she was entertaining her.

"What you view as arrogance, I view as certainty. Confidence."

"And that just makes you sound even more arrogant," Liria concluded.

"It's no more than a matter of perception," Drin replied as she led the small troop down the steep steps that led away from Dragoran's fortress, which was perched atop the highest bluff on the Tor. Her goal was the main market square, which was located midway down the steep slope.

Graz was a city of terraces. One built on top of the other. The largest and widest on the bottom of the Tor. The smallest and most highly sought after just below Dragoran's Ring, his massive fortress built in the shape of seven concentric circles, each with a wall fifty feet in height.

It was little different in Innsbruck, Drin realized. The primary distinction the means of getting from the upper to the lower levels. A long, winding boulevard that ran from the seawall to the Citadel on the Crux and here a series of wide steps with culverts lining both sides that allowed people and goods to be pulled up from the base of the scarp to the very top on wheeled funiculars.

"Now you're just avoiding the truth," Liria snorted.

"I'm speaking the truth," Drin corrected with an undeniable authority that set Liria's teeth on edge. "Yes, I was born to power and privilege. I won't deny it. But with that comes responsibility."

"Responsibility to yourself, you mean. To do whatever you can to improve your position in life."

Drin offered Liria a sly look as she stopped in the plaza filled with stalls and shops that wrapped itself around the monstrous spike of stone. Just like on the Crux there were nine levels to Graz. Here, on the fifth, the merchants and traders ruled.

"And is that how you approach life?" Drin asked. Her raised eyebrow carried more bite than her words. "Looking out solely for yourself? Seeking to improve your position no matter the cost?"

"That's the way of the world, isn't it?" asked Liria, clearly not bothered by Drin's accusation. "If you're not looking out for yourself, then no one is."

"In your world perhaps. Not mine."

"Really?" Liria snorted again. "I find that hard to believe."

"I don't care what you believe," Drin replied in a disinterested tone. "True, there are many born to power and privilege who care only to improve their own fortunes. However, there are just as many if not more who seek to use their power and privilege to improve the fortunes of those less fortunate than they are."

"And you're one of those? The do-gooder? Looking out for

others before you look out for yourself? All while looking down from your gilded perch atop the Crux?"

"I try to be," Drin replied, ignoring Liria's barbs. Winding her way through the stalls at the edge of the plaza and then working her way deeper into the crowded mix, the soldiers clearing a path for them as she strode along one of the many side streets, she was drawn to a small shop that had caught her eye.

The Steelheart Foundry.

Drin had planned on using the afternoon to wander the city and get a better feel for the sprawling capital of the Kingdom of the Tor. She wanted to gain a sense of its layout in case an opportunity presented itself. All the while knowing that it was likely wasted effort. The silver bracelet on her wrist not only prevented her from using the Talent, but also ensured that she couldn't leave the Tor, the magic contained within the artifact only permitting her to go as far as the Barbed Path.

Still, she had to make some effort to change her circumstances. She couldn't wallow in her cage and wait for her fate to crush her. She needed to look for some way to nudge her fate in a more favorable direction.

And now she wondered if she had stumbled onto an unforeseen opportunity.

Steelheart.

Could it be fortuitous happenstance? Or was she hoping for something that wasn't there?

There was only one way to find out.

"You try to be?" Liria asked. "That's not saying much."

"Perhaps if you served someone other than yourself you would understand," Drin replied in a disinterested though sharp tone. "We cannot always help everyone though we may try. And the decisions that need to be made are never easy. They are always more confusing than they appear to be. Having consequences, both good and bad, that are unanticipated."

"Spoken like a true queen," Liria spat as she stayed by Drin's side. Irritated. Primarily with herself. Because rather than getting under Celindria Dengannon's skin, the Queen of the Crux was getting under hers.

"Yes, you're right," Drin replied, not embarrassed to admit it. "Because I am the Queen of the Crux."

Liria growled softly under her breath. She felt like she was in a knife fight, words her weapon rather than steel, and she was losing. Not one to give in easily, Liria decided to take a different tack and perhaps learn something that might be of use to her. "Strange isn't it, though, how the high-minded Queen of the Crux associates with the King of the Underworld."

Drin smiled, eyes narrowing. She wondered when Liria would get to this topic. She didn't know all of the history between her captor and Mikel, but she had picked up a few useful pieces. "Our interests were aligned for a time. As I said, I will do what is necessary if it serves the Crux."

"Our interests?" Liria offered a knowing nod. Drin didn't bite.

"Our interests."

"What would those interests be?"

"Why do you care?"

Liria bit her lip, her hand going to the hilt of her dagger. To say that the Queen of the Crux was difficult would be an understatement. She'd like nothing more than to slice her throat and be done with her.

But she couldn't do that. Not yet anyway. Hopefully when Assindra's plans were more mature. With a sigh, she released her hold on her weapon, offering Drin a too-sweet smile.

"The King of the Underworld does nothing unless it benefits him. So I wonder why he decided to back an untried girl and put her on the throne of the Crux."

Drin didn't respond right away. Recognizing the slight, she chose to ignore it. Beginning to wonder herself.

She disliked Liria. With a passion. Yet the woman raised a legitimate point.

Why did Mikel help her?

She had never really considered that question.

Once she assumed the throne, she tried to learn more about the workings of Mikel's hidden empire. She had discovered very little except for one simple truth.

He had insulated himself and his businesses from the vagaries of politics. Who sat the throne on either the Crux or the Tor mattered little to his success and the success of those who depended on him.

So why did he help her take the throne?

He could have stayed out of the succession fight and risked nothing. In fact, he probably could have gained more by allowing Hanover to claim the throne.

"Perhaps there are some things this untried girl could do for him that you could not?" Drin mused, offering Liria an evocative smile before she pushed open the door to The Steelheart Foundry.

Liria didn't follow her. Feet glued to the cobblestones. Shocked. Infuriated. Fuming that once again the Queen of the Crux had given just as good as she got. If not better.

With a grunt of satisfaction, Drin stepped up to the counter. Drin placed her hands on the polished wood, pressing her palms into it. Closing her eyes for a few seconds, she took several deep breaths. For the first time since she had been taken to the Tor, other than when she slept, she was alone.

Then she smiled. She had won that brief skirmish with Liria, but she didn't doubt that the battle would continue. So better not to be smug about her victory. Better to be prepared for the next clash.

She opened her eyes then. The advice that she had just given herself was something that Mikel would say.

"Can I help you, my Lady?"

Drin's gaze was pulled to the deep voice that resembled the rumble of thunder. A man with thick arms covered in soot and ash was wiping his hands on a white cloth as he stepped through the door that separated the smithy from the shop.

"Are you the maker of these masterpieces?"

"I am," the man replied proudly. "Arturo. Can I help you with something?"

"Perhaps." Drin let her gaze wander over some of the examples of Arturo's work. They were all exceptional. All of the highest quality. Swords. Daggers. Spears. Fixtures for the home. It seemed that if steel was required for a particular piece, Arturo could shape it with an immaculate skill. Then her breath caught. Just over the doorway that led to the foundry was a small carving in the wood. A mark that she had seen before, back in Innsbruck.

For the next several minutes, Drin asked to see several of the pieces behind the counter. Examining the workmanship closely, she was impressed by each one. Yet still wary. Not sure how to raise the topic that was top of mind because Liria, growing tired of waiting, had pushed her way into the shop. Leaning back against the wall, arms crossed, seemingly bored, yet watching Drin like a hawk.

"Anything to your liking?" Arturo asked.

Handing back the sword she had slashed through the air a few times, marveling at the weapon's balance, Drin sighed. "All of it is to my liking. Unfortunately, I'm not in a position currently to acquire any of your wonderful pieces. I'm sorry."

"No need to be sorry," Arturo replied. "There's a moment for everything. Now just isn't that moment."

Drin's gaze narrowed. Arturo stared right back at her, a small smile gracing his chiseled face. Then he winked at her.

"I couldn't agree more."

"Though it's important to be prepared for that moment," Arturo said with an eloquent nod. "Thank you, my Lady, for your business. You're very kind. And a small gift if you'd be willing to accept it. Word of the Queen of the Crux visiting my shop will increase my business tenfold, if not more."

Drin marveled at the throwing dagger Arturo held out to her. A true work of art. The steel gleamed at the faintest touch of the light. The hilt plain except for the mark on the knob.

A tiny fox's head.

"I made it for another customer, but he's been delayed," Arturo explained. "I doubt that he'd mind that I gave it to you. Besides, you might have need of it before he arrives."

20

WORD OF WARNING

"A word of advice?" Liria offered.

Assindra's lips curled into a small smile that held more menace than pleasure, surprised by the audacity of the woman reporting to her. "Advice?" Her tone was quiet but sharp.

Liria didn't pay much heed to it, barely tempering what she wanted to say. Clearly not intimidated by Assindra despite the power she wielded. "Then a word of warning if that makes you feel better."

Assindra didn't reply for quite some time, eyes narrowing as she took in Liria. The woman had started working for her because her skills as a thief were beyond exceptional, those skills easily translating to other areas that benefited her.

Liria's competence and willingness to do whatever was required to complete an assignment had convinced Assindra to send more work her way. Now the woman functioned as her lieutenant.

Yet Assindra sensed that despite all that she had done for Liria, there was little loyalty there. At least not to her.

Liria was only loyal to herself. Thus, Assindra decided to conduct a test.

Giving the job of claiming the Blade of Light to the King of the Underworld, who demonstrated a skill and patience that exceeded Liria's -- an unwelcome intransigence as well, had forced Assindra to rethink her commitment to the woman who offered her a slightly contemptuous grin. Of course, the King of the Underworld had not completed the assignment as he was supposed to, keeping the artifact for himself. A problem she hadn't anticipated. Yet also a problem that she believed could be turned to her advantage.

Assindra nodded slightly, giving Liria permission to continue.

"You seem more intrigued with him than worried about him."

"Intrigued?" Assindra pondered. "Perhaps. He appears to be a better thief than you." She said the last to judge Liria's reaction.

Liria didn't disappoint, hissing, "No one is a better thief than I am."

Assindra's lips curled ever so slightly into a knowing smile. Just as she anticipated. "Worried? Why would I be worried?"

Liria frowned. Then a smile finally broke free that was quickly replaced by a soft chuckle.

"I have some sense of the power you wield, Magus," Liria responded when she saw Assindra's expression sour.

"And yet you seek to antagonize me."

"No, Magus, not antagonize. As I said, warn."

"Then give me your warning, Liria, so that we can move on to more important matters. There is still a great deal more to do even with the Queen of the Crux a reluctant guest here on the Tor."

Liria nodded, though she didn't respond right away as she thought about what to share. "I have told you all that I know about Mikel. I have told you as well all that I learned from our reluctant guest."

"No need to remind me of your most recent success, Liria. It does not balance out your most recent failure."

"And that's my point, Magus. Mikel is …" She struggled for words. "Mikel is more than just unpredictable."

"I could say the same of you."

"Perhaps," Liria agreed tepidly. "But there is a difference. With Mikel, you have not just unpredictability. What you see with him isn't what you get. What you see is what he wants you to see."

"Not uncommon," Assindra challenged.

"On that we agree, but with him there is more to it."

"You're suggesting that he's hiding something?" Assindra wouldn't be surprised if he was. He couldn't have risen to his current station otherwise. He couldn't have stolen the artifact for her and then stolen it from her if he wasn't concealing some aspect of who he was.

"We're all hiding something, Magus," Liria explained with absolute confidence. "With Mikel … I've always had the feeling that there's some aspect to who he is that he's repressed for so long that he doesn't even know that he's doing it."

"And I should be concerned about that?"

"You should, because when he finally frees whatever it is he's holding back, I get the feeling that we're not just going to dislike that unveiling. I get the feeling that whatever it might be is going to take a bite out of us, possibly with devastating conse-quences for all that we're trying to accomplish."

"You give your former lover too much credit."

"No," Liria replied with a sharp shake of her head. "I give him too little. And that's exactly how he wants it."

∾

After Liria revealed her concern, Assindra had been able to think of little else.

And she still didn't know what to make of Mikel Stahlherz, King of the Underworld. She had come to realize that he was many things, the information Liria gave her helping to confirm that. Still, first and foremost, he was a thief. All else second to that truth.

She had been trying to convince herself of that as she struggled to find sleep. All to no avail.

The King of the Underworld was a thief. But he was a great deal more. She readily admitted that. After all, he had the Blade of Light.

Yet, she refused to admit to Liria that Mikel intrigued her.

She had yet to figure out why, feeling as if the answer was just beyond her grasp. Certain only that his possessing the Blade of Light was but one part of the answer.

True, she was angry about his betrayal. There was no point in carrying that anger with her, however. She would ensure that he paid for that poor decision at the appropriate time.

Maybe some of what Liria had said contained some truth. Yet there was another aspect to her intrigue that she couldn't ignore.

Assindra had only met with Mikel briefly. Yet there was some feature to him that made her feel not only uncomfortable, but also as if his very presence, his very existence, opened a wound within her that she thought she had stitched closed years before.

Perhaps that was it.

He reminded her of her weakness.

Then, to add insult to injury, she had failed because of him. She had misjudged him. And she rarely made that mistake.

Because by all rights, the King of the Underworld should be dead.

Yet he wasn't.

And, more galling, Mikel still held what she wanted.

His betrayal was bad enough. The fact that she had to devote even more time and effort to acquire the artifact from him worse. It had made a mess of her plans. Much of what she needed to do next depended on her acquiring the Blade of Light.

Punching both fists into the mattress, she pushed herself out of Malor's bed. She threw on her robe even as her anger kept her warm against the chill breeze drifting through the open balcony doors.

Malor had left her more than an hour ago, believing that he could slip out without waking her.

Assindra snorted softly. She didn't need to be with him to know what he was doing. He sought to keep a veil between them. That was fine so long as nothing he did negatively affected her interests. So far, that had been the case. When it no longer was ...

Well, she would deal with it then.

Strolling slowly through Malor's apartment, she spent more time in his private office than anywhere else before heading toward the source of the chill. She had yet to find anything of interest, having searched every chance she got with means mundane and mystical.

Either Malor had removed any article or detail that might be of use to her or somehow he had found a way to hide or protect what she could use against him. She thought the former more likely than the latter.

Malor was many things.

Conniving.

Scheming.

Greedy.

Vindictive

Yet he was not as smart as he believed he was. Nor as powerful.

All failings that she had used against him in the past for her own benefit. All failings that she would continue to use against him until Malor was no longer a part of her larger plan.

Stepping out onto the balcony of the tallest tower of the Ring, thin robe billowing in rhythm to the gusty wind, she enjoyed the cool touch of the air on her skin. Still struggling to let go of the anger that swept through her every time she thought of Mikel.

Malor was simply a tool she needed to use to get what she wanted. Assindra knew exactly how to play him.

Mikel?

Mikel remained an enigma. And she didn't like enigmas.

She believed there was a place for everything in life, and everything should be in place – just as she decided.

But the King of the Underworld?

He disturbed her in a way that nothing and no one else had in quite some time, because so far every effort she made to put him in his place had failed.

Shaking her head to clear it of her sour thoughts, she decided on her next move.

Assindra would send one of her servants to find the King of the Underworld and give him a little push. She would make sure he did as she wanted.

And what did she want beyond the return of the Blade of Light?

That was easy. Her desire hadn't changed despite the passing of the centuries.

She wanted it all.

21

FOOLISH CONCEIT

"Blast it!"

Drin pulled the throwing dagger hidden in the sheath just below her wrist, her movement sure and swift. Flinging it underhanded, the steel struck the manlike dummy fifteen yards distant.

She grunted, her primary objective still eluding her.

She took some satisfaction in seeing her throw hit exactly where she aimed it. Right between the eyes.

Her success only lessened her anger, however.

Despite her best efforts, Drin had failed to free herself from the restrictive power of the silver bracelet locked around her wrist and destroy the target with the Talent.

Growing frustrated with her lack of success, feeling as if she were doing nothing more than banging her head against an invisible wall, she had given in to her anger and substituted steel for the Talent.

When her father had learned that she had some skill in the natural magic, he had ensured that she received the best instruction that she could by sending her to Haven, home of the Order of the Magii. While there she had excelled, mastering the power of nature and learning skills and knowledge that she would never have come across otherwise.

Yet despite all that, the slim piece of jewelry prevented her from touching the Talent.

It was there.

Just a fingertip beyond her grasp.

Yet she couldn't reach it.

The power of nature shielded from her.

It was more than just frustrating. It was painful.

The Talent was a part of her. In every real way it made her who she was. It largely defined her.

Not being able to touch it …

It was as if she had lost a part of herself.

"I'd hate to think where you'd aim if I was standing in place of that target."

Drin spun swiftly, so caught up in her own misery that she hadn't heard Lucius Hanover approach. Every time she saw him, her heart skipped a beat. He was handsome, even dashing at times. His gentle laugh a cool salve.

Yet all that was balanced by his oversized ego and greed.

"You know exactly where I would aim, Lucius," Drin replied. Voice cold, matching her eyes.

"You're still angry about the mishap over the Succession?" Lucius offered Drin his best smile, hoping to overcome her open animosity.

"How could I not be?" Drin demanded. She took three fast steps toward him, stopping when she was no more than a foot away. "You betrayed me."

Lucius looked down. Another dagger had appeared in her hand. It wouldn't take much for her to punch that blade right between his ribs.

"It was simply a misunderstanding," Lucius explained,

raising his hands in mock supplication. "No more than that. I swear it. I was trying to save you. That's all that I've been trying to do. Save you and save your throne."

"You had all the First Families in your back pocket, Lucius. You were about to be crowned until I crashed your party."

"That wasn't my choice, Celindria, I was pushed into that," Lucius replied with a shrug, as if he had nothing to do with the events that had led to that fateful day. He had been seconds away from taking the throne of the Crux. Instead, Celindria assumed the throne previously occupied by her father thanks to the aid of a man who deserved nothing less than a noose around his neck.

"By whom?" Drin demanded, Lucius' words meaning nothing to her.

That question caught him out, Lucius needing a few seconds to think before he responded. "The First Families, of course. No one knew where you were. We feared that you were dead. And we needed stability with the increasing frequency and intensity of the clashes occurring on the Splintered Bridge."

"Because of the threat presented by Malor Dragoran and his army?"

"Exactly so," Lucius agreed.

"And yet here you are now. On the Tor. Walking freely in Malor Dragoran's fortress. Seemingly without a care in the world."

Lucius smiled at that, though not for long, recognizing that he was failing miserably with his attempt to ingratiate himself with Drin. "Just like all the First Families of the Crux, I have business interests in the Kingdom of the Tor as well. The result of the empire being sundered as you well know. There is no way to get around that. We must all do on occasion what we might dislike if we wish to maintain strong streams of revenue. Even more to maintain our power."

Drin didn't miss his very obvious hint. "Your excuse holds little water, Lucius. Mikel warned me about you. I should have spent more time listening to him rather than arguing with him."

"Mikel?" There was a hint of jealousy in his voice even though he wasn't sure who she was speaking about.

"Mikel," Drin repeated.

She didn't offer anything more than that, but it didn't take Lucius long to figure it out. He smiled again, this time more an arrogant leer. "Your hidden benefactor. The reason you're on the throne."

"I am on the throne because I deserve to be on the throne," Drin replied, seeing no need to keep the heat from her voice.

"I can tell that you don't believe your own words." Lucius' voice was filled with spite. He had grown tired of playing this game. Of having to step carefully around the young woman who had prevented him from taking the throne of the Crux when it was within his grasp. "I am not here to relive the past. I am here to discuss business."

"Business?" Drin snorted. "You should be in a cell beneath the Crux. Locked away and forgotten. Why would I belittle myself and discuss business with you?"

"How could you not?" He motioned with his hands toward the training ground around them. "You're not really in a position to say no, now are you?"

"I'm not in a position?" Drin demanded. "What of your position?"

"What do you mean?" Lucius asked, trying to appear surprised by her question. Trying and failing.

"How could you be a part of this? We were friends. Since we were children. We were to be more than that, and I might have even agreed to your proposal. But you had to have it all for yourself. And now you serve Dragoran."

"I don't serve ..."

"You allowed the Tor soldiers that came for me onto the Crux."

"I did no such ..."

"They were hidden in gondolas owned by you," Drin cut in, eyes flinty. Her fury gained substance now that she had a real target standing before her. "That's treason."

"I had nothing to do with ..."

"You had everything to do with it," Drin growled. "If not for Mikel I already would be wed to Dragoran if not dead."

"That was never ..."

"Nothing is ever your intention, Lucius. That's been your excuse since we were children."

"It's not an excuse ..."

"Always trying to avoid the consequences of your decisions and actions," Drin scoffed. "Always trying to get what you want through others. That's why you bought off the First Families. That's why you're kissing Dragoran's ring."

"I am not kissing his ring," Lucius hissed, his face red with fury. In part because he wasn't used to being taken to task in such a way. In part because Drin's words were much too close to the truth.

"So you say. Yet I have learned that your words are no more than a smokescreen." Drin stepped back, flipping the dagger in her hand. Always three rotations before she caught the tip of the blade between her fingers and flipped it back into the air. "You couldn't take the Crux from me and now you're Dragoran's toady. What do you want, Lucius? I have little time for traitors."

"Such a harsh perspective." Lucius shook his head sadly. He hoped that by controlling his emotions and not allowing his fury to rage he could gain the upper hand in this conversation.

"A realistic perspective," Drin countered.

"And that's the reason I'm here," Lucius explained. "You look at the world in a very limited way."

"I look at the world the way it is."

"If that were the case, Drin, you wouldn't be here."

Drin's expression, already severe, tightened. She had little interest in engaging in a philosophical debate with someone she had once considered a friend and possible partner. "What do you want, Lucius?"

"Just because you face difficult circumstances at this very moment doesn't mean that we still can't have what we want."

"What we want?" Drin wondered, not understanding. "Speak plainly, Lucius. Otherwise, just as you fear, I might make use of you as a target."

"My lovely Celindria," Lucius tsked, adding a light tone to his voice even as his insides churned at the many insults she had offered him. "Always making strong proclamations when you're not in a position to carry through."

Drin caught the tip of her dagger between her fingers, then kept it there. Her gaze harsh, Lucius realized that he had pushed her as far as he could. He didn't think she'd throw at him. But he couldn't be sure. So he moved quickly to the reason he was there.

"As I said, we can still both get what we want."

"What would that be, Lucius?"

It was his turn to snort. Usually she was quite astute. Yet now it seemed her emotions were preventing her from seeing what was quite obvious to him. "Our ruling the Crux wasn't just a political arrangement."

Drin offered Lucius a confused look, trying to make sense of what he was saying. When it finally hit her, she almost laughed. "You believe that after what you've done you still have a chance with me? That I'd actually ally myself with you?"

"I can think of no better match than you and me," Lucius said with a broad smile.

"I can think of quite a few better matches than you," Drin snorted, unable to comprehend Lucius' arrogance or hide her disdain.

"You need to let this anger of yours go," Lucius urged in a pedantic tone that set Drin's teeth on edge.

"Let go ..." Drin couldn't quite believe her ears.

"Yes, let go. It's holding you back. It's holding us back."

"Us? There is no us."

"But there was," Lucius prodded, "and there can be again."

Drin pursed her lips, eyes narrowing, trying to make sense of what Lucius was telling her. Was he delusional? Or did he just not want to accept the truth? "You believe that after what happened on the Crux I would consider sharing the throne with you?"

"I do," Lucius replied with complete confidence. "Because you look at the world the same way I do. For what it is, not for what you want it to be."

"Have you been taking your own product, Lucius? Is this you talking or the milk of the poppy?"

"How did you ..." Lucius cut himself off quickly. He couldn't afford to give free rein to the anger that surged up within him, forcing himself to stay under control.

"I'm the Queen of the Crux, Lucius. I know all that occurs in Innsbruck."

"You have the throne, Celindria," Lucius agreed. At the same time trying to figure out how she might have learned about what he had been doing to add to his badly depleted coffers. The shipment that he had lost. All because of that blasted ...

He took a deep breath. Now wasn't the time to release his rage so he started again. "You have the throne, Celindria. That's true. But your grasp on the throne isn't as strong as it needs to be."

Drin caught the dagger she had been flipping. This time by the hilt. Her eyes sparked with a challenge. "Speak plainly, Lucius."

"I will if you promise not to throw at me." He laughed softly, hoping that Drin would be caught up in his feigned good humor. It didn't work. The expression she gave him was colder than the Frozen Waste. So he continued quickly. "We can argue about many things, Drin. About desires and decisions. About our motivations. About why we do what we do. But there are certain truths with respect to ruling the Crux that we can't deny or ignore. To do so would not only be folly, but also ensure our downfall."

"I can't wait to hear what wisdom you mean to offer."

Lucius ignored the sarcasm that dripped from her words. "You can't rule the Crux without the support of the First Families."

"I'm well aware of that, Lucius, and I have the support of the First Families. That's why I'm on the throne."

"You *think* you have the support of the First Families."

"Meaning what, Lucius? You plan to take the throne from me?" Her voice was deathly cold, hinting that she would enjoy that confrontation. "You tried to do so once before. I will not give you a second chance."

"No, I won't need to. Because right now the First Families are likely meeting to discuss what to do about the fact that you're a prisoner of Malor Dragoran. And after ruling the Crux for only a few months. Truly terrible circumstances and, though it pains me to say it, truly poor judgment on your part. Definitely not the best way to begin your reign."

Drin's hard stare prompted Lucius to continue.

"In truth, you've put them in a difficult position. As I said before, they seek stability. You know it just as well as I do. It's good for business. And, just as I do, they have businesses both on the Tor and the Crux."

Drin's eyes widened, unable to hide her shock. "You can't be serious! They wouldn't dare."

"The First Families are aware of Dragoran's proposal. If they believe that your marriage to him ensures a good climate for their businesses, they won't stand in the way." Lucius' voice carried a trace of authority that was rarely there. On this, at least, he knew about what he was talking.

"They wouldn't ..."

"They would and you know it."

And she did. There was one absolute truth with respect to the First Families. There was little in the way of loyalty. There was only business. "I will not marry Dragoran."

"And perhaps you won't have to."

Drin closed her eyes. Already knowing what was coming next. Hating that she was even considering it. She nodded for him to proceed. "Tell me."

"As I said when we began this delightful conversation, the succession was no more than a mishap that resulted from miscommunication. It wasn't supposed to play out that way."

He took a step toward her, but no more than that. Stopping when she lifted her dagger. Not wanting to tempt fate ... or the emotions rolling across her face. "I was simply trying to prepare for all the possible options. And with good reason, considering how things turned out."

"You mean my claiming the throne that belonged to me in the first place?" Drin said in a deflated tone.

"Yes. Well no." He growled softly, losing patience. Then with a force of will he held himself back. The conversation was at a delicate point. "The fact is that I should be there with you. But I'm not."

"You don't deserve to be there, Lucius. You're a traitor to the Crux."

"Perspective, remember? Yours is quite narrow. Mine quite a bit broader. I don't see the Crux or the Tor, Drin." His eyes flashed with an unmistakable greed. Then he explained in a very quiet voice. "I see the Splintered Empire."

Drin opened her mouth to respond, but she couldn't. Astounded. It was then that she finally began to understand the extent of Lucius' true ambition. What he truly desired. Drin didn't know if she should be impressed or frightened by how warped his perspective was. "You can't be serious?"

"Why not?" Lucius challenged. "You're the key, Drin. Someone must sit by your side. Who would you prefer? Dragoran? Or me?"

22

INTO THE WOOD

"What are your intentions toward Drin?"

Nat asked Mikel that question after they settled in by the fire, catching him off guard. At first not sure where she was coming from, Mikel responded with his own question. "My intentions?"

"Yes, your intentions," Nat repeated. She stared at him through the flames, head tilted slightly to the right just as she usually did when seeking to judge the value of what someone had to say. And he had learned that she was a very good judge. Several of his business partners would testify to that.

"Why are you asking about my intentions?" Mikel gave her an appraising look, though he didn't push too hard.

"Just curious," she said as she cocooned herself in her bedroll.

"Right," Mikel nodded sagely. He leaned forward then, enjoying the warmth coming off the flames. Not so much the topic Nat had raised. "Why are you worried about my intentions?"

Nat shrugged, her blankets moving with her, trying to make

him think that it wasn't important to her. Though clearly it was. "You've been spending a lot of time with Drin."

"I have not."

"You have."

"Have not." Mikel understood how childish he sounded. He couldn't help himself, however.

"Have," Nat stated with greater force. She spoke in a softer tone, her exhaustion getting the better of her. "You're visiting the Citadel almost every evening now. And don't tell me it's to see the Battle Lord. He's at the Splintered Bridge."

It was Mikel's turn to shrug. "There are matters that I need to discuss with her, and she's not in a position to come down to The Fox's Lair as she was before she took the throne."

"Matters to discuss?" Nat asked, offering Mikel a raised eyebrow, the only feature he could see now that she was hidden within her blankets. It was her way of challenging him. She had hoped that allowing the silence to stretch between them, he would say more than he wanted to.

Mikel had to give her credit for that. A good move on her part. Of course, it didn't work.

"Matters," he confirmed, saying no more than that. Then he gave her a smile designed to get under her skin.

"So that's what we're calling it now?" she challenged.

"Calling what?"

"You tell me?"

"I just did."

"You're being difficult," Nat charged.

"Guilty."

"This conversation isn't over."

"I didn't think it was."

"We'll speak more in the morning," Nat promised.

"Can't wait." Although he really could. And he was glad when Nat fell asleep just seconds later, Mikel watching over her.

That circular conversation between them brought a smile to Mikel's usually grim expression. Nat was being protective of him. Of them both, actually. He knew that, and he understood why. Because he was just as protective of her.

But he understood as well that she was torn. Nat liked Drin. The Queen of the Crux had befriended her, taking the time to instruct her in the use of the Talent when she could. Nat appreciated that.

Yet Mikel realized as well that Nat faced a unique dilemma.

She was worried, and she hadn't wanted to reveal it to him.

It had only been a few months since Mikel had rescued her. Given her a home. A safe place to live. To learn. To be the teenager that she couldn't be before she met him.

Once Nat had gotten to know him, she had settled in quickly. Enjoying her new life. Valuing the stability that had been lacking previously. A stability that she didn't want to lose.

Mikel pushed himself up from his bedroll, ignoring the aches and pains that were a constant reminder of his mistakes and failures, as well as the fact that he was getting older. Not even the soft loam of the Deep offered him much comfort.

After walking away from what Nat was describing as a crash landing, they had hiked a few miles into the forest before stopping for the night. Mikel didn't want to be caught out by any of Dragoran's patrols that regularly scouted along the eastern side of the Trench, and setting fire to what was left of the raptor might grab the attention of any Tor soldiers who were close by.

Walking in the dim shadows of the towering heart trees, the forest floor a maze of twisting roots that curled and corkscrewed in every conceivable direction, it seemed a completely different world from the one they had left just hours before.

Forbidding to most.

For Mikel, an opportunity.

A way to approach the Tor from the south without being

discovered. So long as he and Nat stayed clear of the many dangers lurking within the Deep.

It was early morning. The sky just beginning to brighten.

With the heavy overlay of branches above him, the shift from night to day was barely noticeable. The ever-present grey only a little brighter than when they had chosen their campsite.

Mikel wanted to get moving. Time was of the essence.

Looking over at the bundle of blankets in which Nat had buried herself, he didn't have the heart to wake her just yet. Instead he decided to give her a few more minutes.

He smiled. Just like back at home on the Crux, rousing Nat out of bed at a reasonable hour was a daily challenge. The stress of her previous life replaced by the desire to enjoy the little things that she had missed while growing up, such as sleeping without having to keep one eye open.

Of course, their hours-long conversation – or interrogation as Mikel viewed it -- from the night before likely didn't help. There was no end to her questions until she finally nodded off when the adrenaline that had gotten her through their harrowing flight across the Trench finally drained out of her.

Mikel really could have used a few hours of sleep himself. But there was little point in trying to force it.

His struggle didn't result from the regular challenge he faced. His brain never turning off.

No, it was because the Deep didn't feel as it should. He had sensed the discord as soon as he walked among the heart trees.

He had traveled through the wood several dozen times. He was used to the gloom. The shadow. The uneasy feeling that there was someone right behind him, about to whisper in his ear. That he was being watched. Always.

Yet this ...

Mikel spun slowly as he tried to penetrate the shadows that

draped their camp. The heart trees stood silent sentinel. Imposing. Revealing nothing that should make him feel so edgy.

What was bothering him?

What was making him feel as if he was being hunted?

Mikel started to walk slowly around the small clearing. A rare space to find among the twisting tree roots that were often as thick as he was tall.

He didn't identify any tracks. Nothing had disturbed the soft loam during the night other than him and Nat.

Mikel turned briefly back toward their campsite. The pot of porridge he had placed on the fire for breakfast was bubbling softly and making his stomach growl.

Then he realized what it was.

It was too quiet.

The sun was rising.

The day beginning.

And there wasn't an animal to be seen or heard.

Not a single black squirrel scampered about on the branches or roots in search of a nut.

Not a song was to be heard from the jays, finches, warblers, and many other birds that called the heart trees their homes.

He reached over his shoulder, pulling the Blade of Light from its scabbard.

The steel glowed dimly, Mikel taking comfort in the streak of energy that lit the Blade. The flame licking across its surface.

Listening to his instincts, he spun, sensing the evil presence coming at him from behind.

Raising his Blade, he deflected the claw that was a hair away from ripping out his throat.

Mikel stepped back quickly, placing himself in front of Nat. Understanding just how dangerous his attacker was, he only took a small amount of pleasure from the growl that erupted from the Drude freeing itself from the shadows.

He wanted to take himself to task for not recognizing the threat sooner, but he didn't have the time.

He should have recognized it, having come up against monsters bound to a Dark Magus before. And he promised himself that he would remember this feeling in the future ... assuming that he had a future.

"What? Don't like it when your opponent has some bite?" Mikel smiled, though it was a bit forced. He understood the danger that he and Nat were in. A malevolent spirit given substance with the Curse, a Drude was almost impossible to destroy.

Unless you had a sword infused with a unique natural magic.

Just like Mikel did.

Reaching out with his consciousness to connect with that of the blindingly bright steel, he smiled, welcoming the link that formed with the previous Bearers of the Blade.

Growing in confidence as a result, he decided to take the fight to the monster gliding toward him across the soft dirt.

Stepping forward swiftly, Mikel slashed with the Blade of Light, the blazing steel singing through the air. Every one of his movements was controlled. Economical. He lacked emotion in the decisions he made. Only cold, clinical calculation.

As he forced the Drude back toward the edge of the small glade, Mikel wasn't certain that he was fighting the creature raised by a Dark Magus alone. It felt more like he was part of a larger collective, the warriors of the past sharing their knowledge with him in a way that made his actions swifter. His decisions faster. Better. And his skills with the sword devastatingly lethal.

The Drude, so used to making an easy kill, had no choice but to evade Mikel's assault. Taken by surprise. Hissing and spitting every time the glowing blade struck, which was more often than not.

Each time it did, the Drude's very essence was cut away. The severed piece faded, vanishing into obscurity. The strength of the malevolent spirit diminishing as it was literally cut down in size.

Several times the Drude sought to steal the tempo of the combat. Each time it failed.

Mikel maintained the intensity of his assault. Driving the spirit back until the Drude butted up against the rough bark of a heart tree.

Having nowhere to go, nowhere to hide, the Drude launched itself at Mikel. And then again. And again. Never stopping. Yet always forced to retreat after each failed attack. Still trapped.

Mikel reveled in the power he exercised. More confident with the Blade and the Blade more confident in him, the light from the steel burned away the surrounding gloom just as it did the Drude every time the ancient weapon struck true.

Sensing that now was the time, Mikel prepared to lunge, having no doubt that he was about to dispatch the Drude with a great deal more ease than the last time he had faced one of these monsters.

Yet before he could shift forward, he turned away, a bolt of blazingly hot energy streaking right over his shoulder and slamming into the Drude.

The creature shrieked in agony, its very essence consumed by the Talent. Its shadowy substance flaking away, the ash dissolved into nothing before it could settle on the forest floor.

When Mikel was back to his full height, he frowned. Nat stood by the fire, not too far behind him.

"Drude?"

Mikel nodded. "Unfortunately, yes." He offered a silent word of thanks to his scimitar before sheathing it, nonplused that he was talking in his own mind to his weapon and the spirits linked to it, then pursed his lips. "You do realize that I was about to destroy it, right?"

Nat smiled then. Pleased to get a rise out of Mikel so early in the morning. One of her favorite pastimes. "Of course you were."

Nat's snarkiness rubbed him the wrong way. Nevertheless, he chose not to pursue it. Instead, he decided to be gracious. "Thank you for your help."

Nat hadn't been expecting that reply. She was anticipating irritation. Hoping for it actually. Not getting the response she wanted, she turned her attention to the topic that was now top of mind. "I'll leave you to finish making breakfast since I did the hard work. I'm starving."

Mikel didn't say anything, watching her as she began to pack up her bedroll. Cool as a cat. Impressive.

Then he shrugged, smiling. He was no longer tired, the combat and the connection he felt with those who had the privilege of wielding the Blade of Light invigorating him.

He was hungry. He could think about why a Drude would be hunting for them while they were eating. And also why it seemed as if the combat with the Drude was easier than it should have been.

True, he was becoming more proficient with the Blade of Light. In that he was only acknowledging a truth.

Still, he had expected a harder fight.

The way the Drude acted, not attacking with its usual vigor until the very end, that didn't make sense. Unless ...

PLANS WITHIN PLANS

"I am simply saying that we need to consider all our possible options." Lucius Hanover pushed out of his chair, strode away from the table, and then came back swiftly, slapping his hands on the table and leaning toward Malor Dragoran. He was trying to infuse some dramatic urgency into the conversation, believing that his intensity would give him an advantage in the negotiation. Not sure what to do when the King of the Tor appeared more amused than concerned other than to press forward. "There is always more than one path that will get us both what we want."

"You have been saying that for quite a while, Lucius." Malor sighed, clasping his hands as he leaned back into his chair. Unaffected by the Lord of House Hanover's theatrics. "And for longer than is necessary. I see no cause to adjust our strategy."

"I know her better than you do, Malor. I know the Crux better than you do."

"And that's important why, Lucius?" Malor surged forward faster than a striking serpent, hands on the table, eyes gleaming with a dangerous darkness. Lucius stumbled back a few feet from the table. "I hold all the cards. The most important being

Celindria Dengannon. I will do as I must to gain what I deserve."

Lucius started and stopped several times, struggling to find some new avenue that would persuade Malor of his perspective, thereby better meeting his own needs. Yet he was struggling to think, finding it difficult to keep his eyes on Malor. The man radiated a palpable menace that Lucius had never experienced before.

"This needs to stop, Lucius. You had your chance. Now you need to ..." Malor straightened, clasping his hands behind his back, a pleasant smile now gracing what just a heartbeat before had been a flinty expression as he offered a slight bow of his head. "Magus. I didn't hear you come in."

Assindra stepped into Malor's private office, giving him a smile that could be interpreted in multiple ways. She had been listening from the other side of the double doors, masking her entry into his apartment with natural magic. Malor could tell she was not quite sure how he'd known she was there.

"I didn't want to disturb you," she explained.

"Of course you didn't," Malor agreed, the glint in his eyes revealing his disbelief.

Assindra ignored Malor. "What are you two scheming about?"

"Just talking, my dear," Malor replied.

"I find that hard to believe. Our young friend here seems quite agitated."

"Not in the least," Lucius replied quickly. Perhaps too quickly. But it was too late now. He had never been comfortable with Malor, though he believed that he could work with him. Assindra, on the other hand, made him more than nervous. When they were together, he always viewed himself as the deer and she the wolf, though he'd never admit to that truth. "As Malor said, we were just talking. No more than that."

"Since Lucius has shifted his allegiance, there is much that we need to discuss," Malor explained with a shrug of his shoulders, cutting off Hanover before he could say more. Not trusting what the younger man might reveal.

Assindra didn't respond. Nodding instead, he waited. She was curious to see if the silence she permitted would lead either of the conspirators to divulge more. A tactic that had worked well for her in the past. And if not now, she would pull what she wanted to know out of Malor later.

Of course, she really wasn't surprised that Hanover was attempting to craft a better deal for himself. He was drowning in debt and was more vulnerable on the Crux than on the Tor because of his very expensive and failed attempt at claiming the throne on his own.

Making matters even worse, his businesses were bleeding money and his coffers were almost empty. Primarily because ever since Celindria Dengannon's Coronation, the King of the Underworld had been cutting into him. Hard. Every chance he got.

"Yes, exactly so, Assindra," Lucius agreed nervously, feeling the need to fill the quiet. "We were just discussing ..."

"The next steps in our plan to guarantee that all that we've discussed with respect to the Queen of the Crux occurs as it should."

Assindra offered Malor a knowing smile, the King of the Tor quick to interrupt Hanover before he spoke out of turn. She would definitely take the time when they were alone that evening to pull everything she needed to know from Malor.

"Correct," Lucius agreed again, nodding more than he needed to and looking anywhere else but at Assindra.

Understanding that continuing to press would yield her little, Assindra let it go. "I'll leave you to it then." She walked to the doorway before stopping and offering one more comment, her back still turned. "Though I don't need to tell either of you that our success will depend most of all on ensuring that we are not betrayed." She looked over her shoulder then, locking eyes with both men before walking away and having no doubt they understood her veiled warning.

She could have been angry that Lucius sought to go around her and change the terms of the agreement. But there was little point. She would get rid of him soon enough. Once he outlived his usefulness.

Besides, she had heard enough before the two conspirators held their tongues.

Assindra had been meaning to have a conversation with Celindria Dengannon. Now she had no doubt that some of what she had learned would help her achieve the objective she had set for herself.

It was time to break the Queen of the Crux.

24

ACROSS THE BRIDGE

"Are we ready, Chekin?"

"We are, Battle Lord."

Henri Dengannon, commander of the Crux army, gripped the steel bars bolted into the side of the Splintered Bridge, his feet resting on rails his engineers had fixed in place just a few days before. Below him the wispy grey of the clouds draped over the Trench danced to the tune of the breeze, every so often kissing the soles of his boots.

He tried not to give any thought to what waited for him beneath the grey. Even so, he took a few seconds to tug on the cord linked to his harness that was connected to the bar to make certain that if he slipped he would only fall so far.

Clipped next to him was his second in command. Soldiers were arrayed on both sides of him and also on the southern edge of the Splintered Bridge. All of them were wearing the harnesses that pinched in all the wrong places.

There was nothing for it, however. Better that than risk a fall through the grey and the guarantee of a gruesome death.

Henri closed his eyes for a few breaths. Listening.

It was quiet. Just as it usually was at this time in the morning. The sun only just beginning to announce itself in the east.

The Zaroi were back in their nests beneath the bridge.

Henri hoped that they stayed there. So long as they weren't disturbed or provoked, all should be well. Only the hungriest of the creatures were willing to risk the scorching touch of the sun.

Henri had given a great deal of thought to clearing the bridge of these monsters. Not as tall as a man though stronger, the goblin-like Zaroi had bulbous eyes that allowed them to see in the dark as if it were clear as day and their daggerlike nails gave them the capacity to climb almost any surface with little difficulty.

The Zaroi usually kept to the walls of the Trench. Except here. Where they claimed the Splintered Bridge as their own when the moon rose, nesting beneath the bridge to avoid the sun.

In the end, he decided to leave the Zaroi be. His men knew how to deal with the creatures. And, perhaps more importantly, they served as an effective deterrent for any nighttime actions by their enemy. General Booruz, commander of the Tor forces, had learned the hard way that when the night fell the Zaroi were more a threat to his men than the Crux soldiers.

Which was why Henri kept a wary eye. If the Zaroi emerged from their warrens, he and his soldiers would be at a distinct disadvantage. Worse, it would ruin the surprise Henri had planned.

Though he doubted that he needed to concern himself with the Zaroi as a reddish orange began to color the horizon.

He just needed to wait a few minutes more.

He used that time to clear his mind.

His focus centered on how he wanted the upcoming engagement to play out.

To do that, he tamped down his anger.

He hated that his niece had been taken.

He hated even more that he wasn't in a position to aid her.

He didn't like needing to trust Mikel to do as he promised. Although, in truth, the King of the Underworld was likely the only one who could accomplish what was required.

It was because of his anxiety over Celindria's fate that he had concocted his latest strategy.

He refused to stay on the defensive, every fiber in his being demanding that he act. And if he couldn't aid his niece while she was imprisoned on the Tor, he could act here and perhaps help her in a more indirect manner.

Charging across the bridge, however, to engage the Tor soldiers would only waste lives. That held no appeal for him.

He decided instead to put to use one of Leonardo's latest creations. One yet to be revealed to their enemies.

Mikel introducing Henri to the inventor had been a stroke of good fortune. The young man had more ideas spinning around in his head than he could ever hope to give substance and he was proving indispensable to the Crux's effort to keep the Tor soldiers on the eastern side of the Trench.

The only limitation with the sun rising being that they couldn't use Leonardo's raptors. Henri had been thinking a great deal about how to incorporate the gliders into a battle, but he remained wary of the Wyverns. The flying dragons had a habit of diving in and out of the fog when the sun first appeared in the sky.

Henri glanced to his left and right. His men looked right back at him. Expectant. Grim. Eager for a fight. He nodded. "Then let's begin."

Chekin whistled, the sound mimicking the call of a Nachtkrapp, one of the massive ravens that roosted in the Deep and often ventured out in search of an easy kill along the rim of the Trench.

The response was immediate and well-coordinated.

Crux soldiers released the tension on the modified trebuchets placed just behind the barricades on the western side of the span, steel balls as large as wagons swinging in high arcs across the bridge.

Connected to pliant cords, the spheres not only crushed unlucky Tor soldiers and widened the already significant holes that marred the surface of the bridge, but also when retracted just seconds later caused even more devastation, injuring and killing soldiers and sweeping away large segments of the Tor barricades.

It was into that destruction that Henri and his soldiers leapt, more than happy to make use of the chaos and confusion.

Dropping off the bridge, the Crux soldiers trusted in the pliant ropes Leonardo had made from a plant that he had discovered growing at the base of the Dragon's Tail Mountains. The material stretched then returned to its original length when pulled and didn't snap, aiding the soldiers as they swept along the side of the bridge and then up and over the stone balustrade, landing right in the midst of the scrambling Tor soldiers. A few, not yet having mastered the flight through the air, chose to use their bodies, barreling into shocked Tor soldiers and taking them to the broken cobblestones or knocking them over the side to fall screaming through the clouds.

Two minutes.

That's all the time that Henri permitted.

Chekin and the rest of his men made good use of the seconds gifted to them.

The Crux soldiers fought in teams of five.

Fists.

Advancing in a wedge formation, the soldier at the point, assisted by the men on each shoulder, stabbed into the disorganized Tor soldiers. The men behind those three prevented any of their enemies from sweeping around a flank and attacking from the rear.

Henri was pleased to see that his strategy was working so well. His soldiers were cutting deep into the Tor ranks, sustaining few casualties themselves. Enhancing the confusion around them. Sending many of the Tor soldiers fleeing to the east and the safety of the far side of the Splintered Bridge.

"Time!" Henri roared.

None of the Crux soldiers hesitated. The fists, maintaining their formation, cut through the Tor soldiers on either side of the bridge then jumped off. Swinging back to the western approach and landing safely well behind the barricades manned by the Crux soldiers who operated the trebuchets.

Cheers echoed through the Trench as they delighted in their swift and quite decisive victory.

Glad to see so many of his men whole and healthy, the Battle Lord patted Chekin on the shoulder once he regained his feet. Missing his landing by a step, he ended up on his ass. A small embarrassment he was more than happy to suffer through.

Then he smiled.

A rare action on his part.

He was pleased.

Henri would need to congratulate Leonardo on another success as he unfastened the harness around his waist and upper body. More than happy to live with the chafing if he could enjoy a victory like this one every time he employed a new tool against the soldiers of the Tor.

He would be even more pleased when his niece was back on the Crux. And in that he would need to trust the King of the Underworld.

25

GIVE AND TAKE, TAKE, TAKE

"Why so reticent, child?"

"I am not a child, Magus." Drin kept her irritation from her voice, speaking forcefully. As if she were issuing a ruling from the throne of the Crux.

"To me, you are." Assindra offered her response with the calm that she had perfected when speaking with Malor and others who saw more in themselves than was really there. Nevertheless, the intensity of her gaze betrayed her interest.

Drin's eyes narrowed, expression hardening. "How you see me does not change the fact that I am the Queen of the Crux."

"Yes, and for how much longer that remains the case ..." Assindra didn't feel the need to say anything more, enjoying how her unfinished comment wormed its way past Celindria Dengannon's poised outward demeanor. The young woman put on a brave face, though the slight slouch to her shoulders, along with her right hand playing with the bracelet locked around her left wrist, revealed that she understood all too well the perilous nature of her position.

"What is it that you want, Assindra?" Drin had grown tired of the Magus seeking to dig out whatever nuggets she was seeking, she in turn doing her best to answer in a way that wasn't much of an answer. A skill she had mastered at a young age while sitting next to her father while engaging with trade delegations and representatives from other Realms.

"I did not expect such directness from you, child."

Drin didn't fall for the bait, maintaining control over her temper despite the slight. And she chose not to respond with the barb on the tip of her tongue, wanting to see if her delay irritated the Magus.

To strengthen her grip on the conversation that Assindra sought to turn into an interrogation, Drin gazed out over the city of Graz. In truth, there was little difference when compared to Innsbruck on the Crux other than staircases versus a curling road. After all, in the histories, they were known as the sister cities. Until the Empire splintered and one Realm became two.

"Are you well, child? You seem lost."

The left side of Drin's mouth curled ever so slightly. Pleased that her ploy worked upon hearing the first hint of pique in the Magus' voice.

"Quite well, Assindra. Thank you for asking. I was simply enjoying the view ... and our conversation, of course."

Assindra's lips came together as if she bit into a grapefruit. Unable to ignore the bitterness with which the Queen of the Crux soaked her words.

Under other circumstances, Assindra's immediate reaction would have been to act more forcefully. To demonstrate that she was the predator, her subject the prey. That to play games and waste her time came with a cost. Painful and long-lasting.

Yet she couldn't. Not yet. Not until the pieces on the gameboard moved as she required. Until then she needed to manage Celindria Dengannon delicately.

In other circumstances that limitation would have bothered Assindra. Not now, however. Because the Queen of the Crux intrigued Assindra. There was some aspect to the young woman – many aspects, actually – that pulled at her.

The girl was quite strong in the Talent, so initially Assindra had thought that might have been the catalyst. She was certain now that wasn't it. At least not entirely.

It was a pull that had nothing to do with the Talent.

A connection of some type. But to what? Or who?

Acknowledging that she could only push so hard – for now – Assindra decided to take a different tack. "I would think that you would want to talk with me."

"Why is that?" Drin asked, her gaze still focused on the city below, the gleaming spikes and curls of the Barbed Path visible several leagues off in the distance.

"Your childhood friend."

"My childhood friend?" It took Drin a moment to figure out to whom the Magus was referring, her thoughts on someone else at that moment. Wondering what he might be doing. Wondering where he was. Wondering if he knew what had happened to her. Wondering if he cared. "You mean Lucius." Her flat tone held a clear note of disinterest.

"The young Lord of House Hanover, yes."

"Dare I ask what scheme he has in play now?"

"You know him well, don't you?"

"Too well," Drin grimaced.

"That's quite understandable," Assindra offered in commiseration. "He trying to usurp your place on the throne. Quite the betrayal on his part."

"Much of it Malor's doing," Drin stated in a clinical tone, "and much the same that Malor seeks to do now all on his own."

Assindra smiled, eyebrows arched. She was impressed. The Queen of the Crux controlled her emotions exceedingly well, though not so well as to prevent her from sensing the rage emanating from the young woman. "There is a difference between what Lucius Hanover tried to do and what Malor Dragoran is trying to do for you."

"For me?" Drin snorted, chuckling softly. Glad to see how her laughter aggravated the Magus. "That's rich."

"Indeed, for you," Assindra continued, not put off by Drin's dismissiveness, though it took some effort. "Lucius Hanover seeks only to take. For himself. Malor Dragoran seeks to give you a gift."

"Himself, you mean? That's what he's giving me?" Drin snorted again, this time more softly as she shook her head in disbelief. "While he takes my Kingdom from me." She finally turned toward the Magus, eyes flashing with resistance. "Please, Magus, I am not Lucius Hanover who hasn't met a dream he hasn't liked. I see the world for what it is. I see Malor Dragoran for who he truly is."

"I would never think to place you in the same category as Lucius Hanover, my dear. However, I do suggest that you consider moving more quickly toward your alliance with Malor Dragoran."

"And I assume that you will tell me why?" Drin needed to fight hard to keep the scorn that consumed her from seeping into her voice.

"If you wish," Assindra replied gracefully, even offering a slight nod of her head as if she were deigning to perform a task for the Queen of the Crux. "Your childhood friend seeks to insinuate himself between you and Malor. To once again claim what he most desires. I suggest you admit the reality of your circumstance and move quickly to solidify your position. Better that you decide rather than having someone else decide for you."

Drin stared at Assindra, the Magus not quite understanding her expression. Until she broke out in soft laughter. "Lucius can play whatever games he wants. He's more than welcome to join with Malor. In fact, I would surely like to see that union."

Assindra's eyes narrowed, her patience waning and not appreciating Drin's humor. "You mistake me, Celindria. If you are not quick to complete your union with the King of the Tor, the King of the Tor will look in another direction. He will use Lucius Hanover as a shill and claim the Crux through him. Leaving you high and dry. Not a position that I believe you want to be in." She stepped toward Drin then, catching her eyes and wanting to make sure Celindria understood what she was telling her. "You have a choice. You can be the Queen of the Crux ..."

"But only if I partner with Malor Dragoran." Drin's eyes burned with a fury that started her body shaking. "I understand, yes. Only Lucius Hanover would miss the point you were making."

"And still you hesitate? I would think that such a union would benefit you."

"Benefit me," Drin nodded sagely. "That's where I hesitate."

"Because of Malor Dragoran?"

"No. He is much like Lucius Hanover in many ways. Older, though. Likely more grasping as well. Ambitious. Cutthroat. Therefore quite obvious in what he wants."

"Then what is the cause of your concern?" Assindra was pleased that they finally had hit the heart of the matter.

"It is obvious, isn't it?" Drin smiled then, pleased to finally feel as if she had the upper hand, at least for a time.

"Speak openly, dear, I have little patience for games."

"The problem isn't Lucius Hanover or Malor Dragoran, Magus. The problem is ... you."

"Me?" Assindra replied, genuinely surprised. Not so much at the assertion, but rather that the Queen of the Crux had worked out the truth. "Quite a claim to make. And one that Malor Dragoran would not ..."

"Malor Dragoran has ruled the Tor for decades. Yes, I know. Yet does he rule now? Has he ruled since you joined him as a ...

partner?" Drin left her full insinuation unsaid, not needing to make plain the obvious. "That's the question that's been playing through my mind."

Drin didn't say anything more, waiting, studying the Magus. Wondering if Assindra would defend herself and perhaps let loose a critical fact. It wasn't to be, however. Assindra offered her a glare worthy of any Magus in the Realms. So Drin continued, not wanting to lose the momentum she believed that she had earned.

"You're the real power here on the Tor." Drin sensed it then. She couldn't touch the Talent because of the bracelet, yet she could still feel it. Another essence mixed in with the natural magic of the world. An essence that carried the taint of corruption.

Then she saw it. Assindra's eyes narrowed. And, in the very back, if only for a brief moment, for less time than it took for a heart to beat, a spark of black. Undeniable proof if the portal the Magus created to bring her here wasn't enough already.

"It's the only conclusion that any reasonable person could make, in particular one who has been forced to spend so much time here in the Ring," Drin continued. There was a great deal more that she could say. Claims and accusations that she could make. She chose not to, realizing then that she needed to be very careful. With the bracelet, she wasn't in a position to defend herself against a Dark Magus.

"Just as sharp as I was told. I'm glad that my sources have proven accurate." Assindra's gaze sharpened even more. She recognized not just a challenge in the Queen of the Crux, but also a potential threat.

Drin smiled then, appearing amused, though she recognized the change that occurred within Assindra. She reminded herself to tread even more carefully, understanding just how important this conversation was. Sensing that if she said too much or the wrong thing the complexion of their engagement would change in an instant ... and not in her favor. Still, she couldn't help herself, believing that she had a little leeway with which to work.

"Does Malor know that he's not the real ruler of the Tor?"

It was Assindra's turn to smile. A nasty crease. Her predatory gaze revealed an innate meanness that she didn't bother to hide. "He might suspect. But I doubt he cares."

"Because you have him wrapped around your finger?"

"I have many things wrapped around him."

Drin didn't miss her meaning, unable to prevent a slight blush from touching her cheeks. She hated how the Magus so enjoyed making her uncomfortable. "You're very confident. Perhaps too confident."

Assindra was impressed by the young woman. Despite her pushing and provocations, the Queen of the Crux never lost her composure. "I am confident, and I deserve to be."

"Because you never fail."

"I never do."

"Which is why you're here now." Drin nodded. She had met many people like Assindra before. Along the way she had learned that confidence could be a good thing, unless it exploded into arrogance. And it was that all-too common failing that Drin hoped to use to her benefit.

"Correct."

"You believe that you can get whatever you want from me."

"I don't just believe. I know."

"Why?" Drin was looking for that one opportunity, that one mistake, that Assindra might offer her.

"Because I've never failed before."

"There's always a first time," Drin suggested.

"There is," Assindra acknowledged. "Though not now."

"Why so sure?"

Assindra leaned forward, locking eyes with Drin. Her smile no longer welcoming. Now sinister. "You are strong. Not just in the Talent. I'll give you that. You're not strong enough, however."

"There's only one way to confirm it." Drin wondered if she could goad the Dark Magus into removing the bracelet. Likely a losing proposition even if she did. Nevertheless, better to act like a knight rather than serve as another's pawn.

"There is."

"Though I sense that now isn't that time," Drin murmured, evaluating Assindra's smug countenance.

"It's not."

That disappointed Drin, though she wasn't surprised. "Then why are you here, Assindra. Lucius and Malor were just opening moves, and you don't seem the type of person who enjoys wasting her time."

"I'm not," Assindra confirmed. "I'm here for another reason."

"I can't wait to hear why."

"I want to know more about the Broken Bear."

Drin leaned back against the railing, crossing her arms as a cunning look graced her previously placid expression. She should have assumed as much.

Assindra had more in mind for her than just the role of hostage. Yet until she deemed it necessary for her role to change, there were other pieces to Drin's world that she wanted to explore. Understanding now where she stood, Drin chose to start aggressively.

"My Bear, you mean."

"Your Bear?" Drin's response caught Assindra by surprise.

"Yes, I've heard others call him the Broken Bear. And I must admit it's a worthy appellation." She leaned forward then, mimicking Assindra's previous action. Her expression as well. "Though I haven't decided what name I like best. Celindria's Bear or the Broken Bear. Or just My Bear. All appeal to me."

"You think quite a lot of yourself."

"Likely no more than you think of yourself."

"Tell me about him." Assindra's order was veiled in a light-hearted tone, ignoring the challenge the young woman offered her.

"Why?"

"Why?" Drin's response more than aggravated Assindra, not used to such open defiance.

"Why?" Drin repeated.

"Because he interests me," Assindra consented to reply, struggling hard to control her rising temper. "Because I know who he is."

"Then you know as well what he's capable of."

Assindra leaned back then, eyes narrowing as she considered Drin's reply. The Queen of the Crux could be talking about almost anything. "Such as?"

"If you know who My Bear is, then you know what he's done. What he's willing to do when circumstances demand it."

Assindra chuckled then. Softly at first before she let loose a full-throated laugh. The Queen of the Crux was quite good at deception and deflection. Of saying quite a lot without saying anything at all. Yet she had made a mistake. She had revealed a weakness.

"Your Bear will not be coming here to rescue you, girl. To believe that would mean that you believe in fairy tales."

"In every tale there is a hint of truth," Drin murmured before replying. "I doubt there is much that I can tell you that you don't already know."

Assindra graced Drin a crafty smile then. Yes, the Queen of the Crux was a sly one. But that only stood to reason having sat and learned at her father's knee for so long.

Under other circumstances, Assindra would hesitate to ask the question that had been at the top of her mind when she raised the matter of the Broken Bear. But now, with the Queen of the Crux firmly under her control, she decided to take the risk, not believing that it was much of a risk at all.

"I understand that you enjoy a very close connection to the Broken Bear."

"Why would you say that?" Drin challenged.

"Because I have it on good authority that he's visited you many times in your private quarters since you ascended the throne."

Drin froze for just a moment. Not upset by the insinuation, rather wondering how it was that Assindra could learn such a thing. She was absolutely certain that Mikel would be shocked to hear that the Dark Magus had knowledge of his comings and goings. To hide her concern, she adopted a more suggestive tone. "And does that bother you?"

Assindra hmphed, appreciating her captive's attempt to deflect. "It doesn't bother me in the least. Rather it suggests to me that you may know more about the Broken Bear than anyone else."

"I doubt that very much. When he visits, we rarely spend much time talking."

Assindra stood in silence for a few seconds, then clapped her hands together just once as she offered the Queen of the Crux a nod of respect. "Well done, girl. Well done, indeed. You certainly have mastered the art of deception. But it won't work on me."

"You don't believe so?"

"I know so, because I created the art of deception. You can deflect, obfuscate, ignore, delay, lie … it doesn't matter. Eventually I will get what I want from you."

"Again so sure of yourself."

"I am indeed. And with good reason, as I said earlier in this conversation. Now answer me this. What do you know of the Broken Bear's connection to the Giants of the Rime?"

"I wouldn't be able to tell you," Drin said with as much

disinterest as she could infuse into her voice, finally understanding what it was that Assindra wanted from her. "He has connections everywhere. And as I said, when we are together, we rarely talk of such things. We rarely talk at all."

With the speed of a viper, Assindra lunged. Grasping Drin's forearms with her hands, squeezing tightly, her eyes flashed, the threat contained there unmistakable.

"You will tell me, girl," Assindra hissed. "That I promise you. Whether in reasonable conversation or in a conversation that is much less pleasant for you, though certainly quite a bit more fun for me. Do you understand?"

Drin's eyes hardened, her own anger rising. Hating how she was being treated. Though fearful as well. The promise in the back of Assindra's eyes was one that she couldn't ignore. She nodded. Still, despite the threat offered by the Dark Magus, she felt the need to push. "Why do you want to know so much about My Bear?"

"So I can figure out how to put him down."

26

INTO THE DEEP

"Why are we doing this?"

"Doing what?" Mikel asked, although he was only listening to Nat with half an ear. His focus was on the shadows and brief flashes of light that broke through the gloom when a stray ray of sunlight managed to work its way past the shield-sized leaves above.

He stopped abruptly, holding out a hand so that Nat halted as well.

Watching.

Listening.

He frowned, seeing nothing but a smothering dusk leaning toward darkness. And all was quiet. Just as he liked it when he dared to journey through this ancient forest.

Yet there was some aspect to the whole experience that felt ... off.

That bothered him, because they were several leagues into the Deep, hiking toward the east before they turned to the north and the Tor. And once in the Deep, there were few options other than to keep moving forward until they were out of the wood.

"Moving as we are."

Mikel nodded once they started walking again. Nat found it interesting that whenever possible Mikel kept them atop the roots of the heart trees, the gnarly wood twisting, corkscrewing, and curling along the forest floor. In some places it created an almost indecipherable maze. In others, it was an easy path to follow, though those sections were few and far between.

"Stopping and starting?" Mikel shrugged. "You know why."

"The Drude?"

"In part. In a place like the Deep, our hearing is more important than our sight. Although we're listening for more than just the Drude."

"What else do we need to worry about?" Nat regretted asking the question as soon as the words left her lips. She had just given Mikel another chance to offer a brief lesson, of which he always had several ready as the occasion demanded.

"Nachtkrapp. Huge ravens that perch in the trees. Some aren't much smaller than the Wyverns we dealt with while crossing the Trench."

"They don't sound very pleasant."

"That would be an understatement. Nachtkrapp are synonymous with their names. Thankfully, they usually stay in their roosts during the day. They're a threat when they come out at night."

"I understand they might be big, but a single Nachtkrapp?" Nat was having a difficult time wrapping her mind around Mikel's concern. "Could we not deal with one with little difficulty?"

"Not just a single Nachtkrapp. An unkindness."

"An unkindness?" Nat frowned, having no idea what Mikel was talking about. "What do you mean by unkindness?"

Mikel didn't bother to stop while explaining. Continuing along the path he had selected, he walked almost seven feet above the ground and allowed the roots to lead him where they would so long as they went in the general direction he desired. "An unkindness is a flock of ravens, just like a flock of crows is a murder. Nachtkrapp hunt in an unkindness. So it's not one bird as large as a Wyvern. It's twenty or more."

"That makes more sense," Nat murmured, glancing up at the few branches above her that she could see. Most hidden in the gloom.

"I'm glad you agree."

"So that's it in terms of threats we need to worry about?"

"That isn't enough for you?"

Nat shrugged. "We've dealt with Wyverns, more than one, so I'd like to think we can deal with Nachtkrapp if we need to."

Mikel smiled, although it never reached his eyes. "I appreciate your confidence." He stopped again, Nat standing right next to him. "What do you hear?"

Nat didn't say anything for several seconds. Listening. Trying to pierce the gloom that surrounded them. "Nothing. Nothing at all."

"That's what worries me."

"Why?"

"There's always more to worry about in the Deep." Mikel started walking again. Nat kept close to his shoulder as she began to feel the oppressiveness of the surrounding wooden giants that extended more than three hundred feet into the sky.

"I'm afraid to even ask," Nat said in a voice barely above a whisper, not wanting her words to travel very far. "What else besides the Nachtkrapp?"

"The Nachtkrapp rarely emerge from their roosts until full dark," Mikel explained, "so we have a few hours yet before we need to worry about them. My primary concern are the Grim. No matter the hour of the day, they are always on the hunt."

"I'm not sure I want to know."

"You probably don't. Because the Grim are quite grim."

"Funny," Nat muttered, clearly not amused by Mikel's play on words.

"I try." Mikel offered Nat a small smile. The feeling that was bothering him was only getting stronger. The silence within the Deep didn't help, because he knew what it could mean. He just hoped that he was wrong. "The Grim are wild dogs that are bigger than wolves. More vicious as well. Wolves kill to eat. Grim kill because they like to. They were bred for it."

"Who bred them?"

"No one knows for sure but most stories point to the Magus known as the Dread. The Grim picked the Deep as their preferred hunting ground and enjoyed their newfound freedom when their master disappeared."

"The Dread?"

"You don't know about the Dread?"

Nat shook her head, not embarrassed in the least. "You know where I came from. Why would I know about the Dread?"

"Fair enough," Mikel agreed, not making a judgment. "We'll need to remedy that gap in your education. Just not now."

"Are there many Grim in the Deep?"

"No one knows how many," Mikel shrugged. He began to walk faster. Nat kept pace with him. His instincts were telling him that they weren't alone anymore. "A dozen packs. Maybe more."

"How big is a pack?"

"Twenty or thirty Grim."

"That doesn't sound good."

"It's not," Mikel confirmed. "That's why I want to avoid them. That's why I'm stopping to listen so often. They'll know we're here before we know they're here. So the sooner I can hear them the better. I expect that we won't see them until they attack."

"Now I'm really beginning to wonder why I came with you."

"I was wondering the same thing before we even started this journey."

Nat punched him in the arm. "You know why I'm here."

"I do," Mikel said, wrapping an arm around her shoulders from the side and giving her a hug, "and I appreciate it."

"Is that also why you're walking on the tree limbs? It cuts down on the sounds we make? It makes it harder for the Grim and whatever other monstrosities that might be living in the Deep to track us?"

"A good thought but no. If I really wanted to stay quiet, it would be best to walk on the forest floor. The several feet of dirt and rotting leaves make for a very springy and quiet surface."

"Then why walk on the limbs?"

"So I can see the other threat we need to be aware of."

"I can't wait to hear," Nat sighed. "An animal worse than the Grim or the Nachtkrapp?"

"You just like to say Nachtkrapp," Mikel accused.

Nat grinned. She did enjoy saying the word, biting off the last syllable. "You caught me. Now tell me about the other danger."

"The hollows."

"What's a hollow?"

"A sinkhole."

"Where are they?"

"All around us."

"All around us?" Nat repeated. She peered over the edge of the arching branch that took them ten feet above the ground, scanning the black dirt littered with the fallen leaves of the heart trees. In doing so she almost missed a step, grabbing Mikel by the arm before she fell.

"All around us. The heart trees have a root system that reaches several hundred feet into the earth. It's necessary because these trees are so monstrously tall. In fact, if you can believe it, there are more roots belowground than above.

Because of all those roots, there are spaces – thousands of spaces, hundreds of thousands, I don't know how many – some large, some not, but it's created an environment where the ground can give way beneath you without a hint of warning."

"That sounds worse than coming up against Grim or Nachtkrapp."

Mikel stopped again, fighting to keep a smile from breaking free because of Nat's smile. Clearly, she was trying to gain a crack in the severe mask that had covered his face during the last few minutes. Hoping her wordplay would do it.

"It can be," he said, pleased that he kept a sober countenance.

Nat grunted, disappointed that she failed to get at least a grin but vowing to try again. "How do you identify these hollows?"

"More often than not you can't. But, when you stand atop a root, you can sometimes see the few signs that warn you to stay clear."

"Such as?"

"An indentation in the ground several inches deep, the dirt almost perfectly smooth, suggests the earth isn't as strong there as it should be. Almost like it's been sifted. Or a space between the roots that's clean of markings. The squirrels and other animals that make the Deep their home know not to step there. So if they don't, you don't. And sometimes ..."

Mikel turned his head to the left, believing he caught a flash of movement a dozen yards deeper within the wood. He couldn't tell for certain. And he hadn't seen the tell-tale twin flecks of gold that would confirm his suspicion that was quickly turning to fear.

"Sometimes?" Nat prodded.

Mikel continued his explanation a few seconds later, still frowning, and still staring where he thought he saw a shadow move in a way that it shouldn't have. Turning in a slow circle, he frustrated himself as he failed to identify any movement that might give some substance to the ephemeral feeling of concern that teased him. "Sometimes you just don't know until you've fallen through one."

"Have you fallen through?"

"I have. A few times in fact." He was about to start walking again, but then decided against it. His instincts told him to stay where they were atop another arched root that had taken them almost fifteen feet off the ground. The surface was wide enough for them both to walk along the natural bridge side by side.

"When did that happen? What did you see? How did ..."

Mikel held up his hand, pleading for quiet with his eyes. He thought that he had heard something just a second before. A whisper of movement off to their left, just over his shoulder, grabbed his attention. And it certainly wasn't a squirrel or a badger, because all the smaller animals of the Deep had taken refuge in their dens.

"Mikel, what's the ..."

Nat didn't get the chance to finish asking her question. Mikel turned toward his left. In the same motion he pulled the Blade of Light from the scabbard across his back. As soon as he did, the steel of the scimitar blazed to life. Responding to Mikel's call, a dome of light illuminated the space around them for several dozen yards.

Mikel feared that it might come to this.

Even with the brilliance offered by his Blade, it was difficult to pick out the shapes of the four Grim that hid among the roots.

They were watching him.

Their golden eyes sparking in the light.

"To your right!"

Mikel appreciated Nat's attempt to help, but it was all he could do to keep at bay the Grim to his front. He had hoped that the arch taking them fifteen feet above the ground would offer them some protection from the animals.

It didn't.

The Grim, almost as large as ponies, were dangerously agile. The beast he had wounded three times still snapped at him, trying to dig its front claws into the root upon which he and Nat stood.

Once that happened ...

Mikel didn't want to think about that.

Taking a half-step back, he pivoted. The Grim's paw, nails several inches long, missed him by only a hair. Before the beast fell back to the ground, he offered the Grim a fourth gift, this one a painful slash across its right shoulder.

Even better, the Grim Nat warned him about, which leapt for the root from his right, got tangled with the animal he had just sent tumbling back to the ground. The two beasts snapped at one another until they disentangled themselves.

Believing that he had earned a few seconds of peace on that flank, he turned. Ready to go to Nat's aid.

He snorted softly. Not in disbelief. More in wonder.

Nat was more than holding her own against the pair of Grim on the other side of the arched root, sending spheres of energy shooting this way and that.

The Grim danced out of the way most of the time, though not all of the time. The scorches along their backs testified to Nat's success.

Yet even the pain of their wounds didn't prevent the beasts from stalking toward their tormentor and seeking a way to knock her from her perch.

"What's that?" Nat asked, a hint of worry in her voice.

Mikel heard the howls now, coming from perhaps a mile away. He couldn't be sure because sound traveled strangely within the Deep. Yet he was certain that the pack was close. Much too close.

"We've been fighting off the scouts. The rest of the beasts are coming this way. We need to go."

"The scouts?"

"Yes, three or four of the Grim leading the pack toward their next kill."

"You mean us."

"Not if I can help it. Or rather if you can."

"Me? What do you mean me?" Nat didn't quite understand.

"We need a distraction."

Nat stared at him for just a second more. Then she nodded, an evil smile gracing her young features.

Reaching for more of the Talent, she began to turn slowly, spheres of energy blasting out from her hands.

She wasn't aiming for the Grim, the beasts too nimble, although she wouldn't have been upset if she got lucky. Rather, she wanted to change the landscape of the battlefield.

And she did. Quickly and decisively.

The ground around them was torn apart by her use of the Talent, millions of splinters blasted into the air. Clouds of deadly projectiles shooting this way and that.

The Grim scampered about, seeking to avoid the worst of it, benefiting from their agility and their tough hides. Though they still suffered. Blood marred their fur and larger shards of wood pierced their flesh.

"Well done. Now come on!" Mikel sprinted down the bridge and along the root, Nat right behind him.

The four Grim were still alive, one barely able to stand because of the many wounds it sustained. All of them disoriented.

"They're gaining on us."

"I'm aware," Mikel replied, running shoulder to shoulder next to Nat.

"What do we do?"

"I'm working on it."

"Work faster!" Nat ordered.

He would have laughed if he didn't note the shadow racing toward him from the side.

Mikel skidded to a stop and spun, slicing with the Blade of Light. The blazing steel cut deep into the beast's shoulder through muscle and bone then slid free when the badly wounded monster dropped to the ground with a whimper.

"Down!" Nat ordered.

Mikel didn't hesitate, crouching right before a ball of fire shot just over his shoulder and struck a second Grim full in the chest, another of the scouts that had taken up the hunt again.

The frothing animal, soaring through the air, unable to change its trajectory, grunted more in surprise than pain when the Talent sizzled across its body. Falling to the ground, the Grim lay still. It's body charred and smoldering.

"Thank you," Mikel murmured.

"This isn't working."

Mikel nodded. Nat was right. They had no chance of escaping the pack. Even with the Blade of Light in his hand, the steel illuminating the forest for a dozen yards around them, and Nat's skill with the Talent, eventually the Grim would take them down. There were just too many of them.

"No argument there."

"Then what do we do?" Nat was gasping for air, not used to exerting herself with such intensity. Desperate for her second wind, she prepared to set off once more along the web of roots, wanting to stay ahead of the baying Grim.

Mikel didn't reply right away. Instead he focused on the movement he sensed just at the edge of the light. There but not seen. There was something lurking just beyond the radiance of the scimitar.

He assumed that this was going to happen. It was just a matter of when. And he didn't have to wait much longer.

Silence descended within the Deep as the growls, barks, and howls came to an end.

First one pair of golden eyes appeared at the very border of the light, reflecting the brilliance of the Blade of Light. Then another pair. And another.

Mikel spun around slowly.

Just as he suspected.

Just as he dreaded.

They were surrounded.

"What do we do?" Nat repeated. Fear in her voice. She knew just as well as Mikel did what it meant to have so many of the Grim around them.

A painful and gruesome death.

A result that Mikel really wanted to avoid. And he believed that there might just be one more option available to them that would keep them alive. At least for a little while longer.

"Take a chance."

Reaching out, Mikel grabbed Nat's hand and jumped.

Pulling her from her perch on the root, he took her down toward the soft loam of the forest floor and right through the slight depression he had noticed just below them.

They slid into the hollow that was their only means of escape.

For a time.

MIKEL CLENCHED his teeth so hard that his jaw ached. He had no choice, however. Fearing that if he didn't he'd bite through his tongue because of the bone-jarring ride.

This was definitely not what he wanted to do. Yet there were few options from which to select, so he did the best with what he had.

He and Nat had been out of time, and there was only one place for them to go to avoid a fatal clash with the Grim.

And despite the precariousness of their position, he was grateful. Their current plight could have been a great deal worse.

Nat's quick thinking – crafting a sled out of the Talent – made their teeth-rattling escape a little more bearable as they hurtled deeper beneath the earth.

What really helped as they sought to survive their reckless run was that Mikel had done this before – twice – though not while riding a magical creation. Instead using a steel shield as his conveyance.

This was a definite improvement. As was the fact that because of his previous experiences, he had learned how the root system grew beneath the heart trees.

There actually was some order to the maze if you knew how to read it.

And he did.

Although this latest adventure clearly was more difficult than the previous two. Rather than just him, he needed to worry about Nat as well, who was crowded right behind him.

Their combined weight added to their velocity, which meant that the gentlest of touches, the slightest overcompensation, to either side would take them flying off the twisting root to land in a broken heap far below.

A great many worries weighed Mikel down as a result. Thankfully seeing where they were going wasn't one of them.

Nat had used the Talent to light their way, sending spheres of energy all around them. Just as important, her cleverness allowed him to sheathe his sword and use both hands on the rudder to his front, needing all his strength to stick to the path and navigate the route that he had chosen.

Their wild ride began the instant they passed through the hollow, the loose dirt giving way beneath them. He and Nat slid into the darkness and down a steep embankment made of the same soft loam that covered the forest floor.

As soon as Nat put the sled beneath them, Mikel tilted them at what he judged to be a forty-five-degree angle. Having learned that it was best to let the roots take them where they would, his primary objective was ensuring that they stayed alive until their rapid descent came to an end.

"This was your plan?" Nat demanded. Not enjoying how much dirt she was eating, Nat watched as Mikel pressed the front of the sled into the track to slow them down, though not so much as to flip them, the rudder in the center of her construction mitigating that risk.

"It was," he confirmed, shouting over his shoulder. He was afraid to take his eyes from the system of roots to their front, understanding that just a split-second of distraction could spell their doom.

Observing how the root curled to the left just up ahead, Mikel bent his left knee and brought his foot close to his right leg, tilting his body toward the left as he pulled up ever so slightly on the right side of their sled. Nat, seated behind him, arms gripping him tightly around the waist, moved with him, dreading the possibility of being thrown clear.

Perfect timing. Rather than hurtling off their chosen path, they turned with it and kept to the rough track of dirt-covered root.

Yet now they faced a new challenge. They were on a straightaway.

Their speed increased at an alarming rate despite Mikel's efforts to slow them down. Straining with every muscle, pushing down on the sled and the rudder in an attempt to slow them down, it became harder and harder for Mikel to keep them on what was a swiftly narrowing pathway.

More worrisome, just a few dozen yards ahead, the straight-away ended, their route corkscrewing.

Eyes widening in alarm and glad that Nat couldn't see what they faced, he did the only thing that he could right before the first curl of the corkscrew.

"Hold on!"

Nat didn't question Mikel's order, her arms around his waist tightening and crushing the air out of him.

Straightening his left leg and then bending his right leg, he leaned hard in that direction. The sled crafted of the Talent obeyed, taking them off the root in a flash.

Hurtling through the air, neither Mikel nor Nat had the time to scream, smacking back down on another track just a heartbeat later, the maze of roots growing thicker in this section of web.

"Duck!" Mikel roared.

Nat obeyed, pushing her head between his shoulder blades and scrunching down behind Mikel as far as she could go.

And just in time as Mikel steered them into a hollow root that was scarcely wide enough for their passage.

They were still going too fast. But here within the chute he could exercise more control now that he didn't have to worry about being shot off the track.

Instead, he just needed to worry about how to stop.

That decision was made for him only a few seconds later.

Their ride was coming to an end, the chute about to deposit them on the ground much like a rock released from a slingshot.

"Nat! Be ready!"

They were out of the root before Mikel could finish his warning. The ground rose up to meet them, the whiplash speed of their descent ensuring a back-breaking landing.

Mikel chuckled softly. "Well done, lass. Well done indeed."

He floated just a few feet above the ground, body splayed out, Nat right next to him in the same position.

If they had struck the ground, neither likely would have walked away.

But once again, thanks to Nat's quick thinking, they didn't have to worry about that. She didn't release her hold on the Talent until they were both standing safely in the thick loam, neither much the worse for wear other than for the physical reminders of their bone-jarring ride.

"I'm glad I decided to bring you along for this," Mikel murmured, offering Nat a warm smile and a hug around her shoulders. "Truly impressive."

Rather than receiving the snarky response that Mikel anticipated and was the norm for his young ward, Nat didn't have anything to say. A true rarity for her.

She was shaky. Hands on her knees, she was reluctant to push her lanky frame to its full height. The ride along the system of roots upset her stomach. The urge to release all that she had eaten that day threatening to get the better of her.

"This doesn't look right," Nat finally grouched when her stomach no longer roiled like the Churn.

"How did you expect it to look?" Mikel asked.

"I assumed that we would be in complete darkness," Nat replied. She had anticipated the roots and the dirt, but not what was growing on them.

A thick moss and strange tubers that glowed with a bright luminescence similar in color to the light of the day after a summer thunderstorm. So bright, in fact, that she released her hold on the Talent, no longer needing the natural magic to light their way.

"A welcome change, isn't it?" Mikel looked around in wonder. Just as amazed now as he had been the two other times he had come down here. Once by choice. Once because it was the only way to stay alive, just as it was now with Nat. "And us being a quarter mile or more beneath the surface. Truly remarkable."

"It is," Nat agreed. She spun in a slow circle, taking in their new surroundings. She felt as if she should be frightened of where they had ended up. Yet she wasn't. Rather, she couldn't escape the surge of wonder that raced through her. "What is this place?"

"This is the real Deep," Mikel replied in a quiet voice, almost afraid to break the silence that hung heavily around them.

27

A NEW HUNT

"Do you know where we're going?"

"You seem concerned." Mikel spoke just above a whisper as he crouched and crawled through the dense undergrowth, navigating around the taproots of the heart trees that reached down from the surface much like stalactites from a cavern ceiling. Those roots often interwoven with tubers and vines created an almost indecipherable maze.

Mikel sought the best path, having no desire to hack his way through the undergrowth. It was too much work and, more important, too noisy in a place where the faintest sound could be heard for a mile or more.

This underground warren was much like the one aboveground. Although Mikel preferred the roots that curled and cut along the forest floor to this jungle. Because here the difficult passage was playing havoc on his back and his bad leg. Not so much of a challenge for Nat, however. She didn't need to duck down as frequently, benefiting as well from the trail he blazed for her.

"I am concerned." Nat followed right behind Mikel's right shoulder. What she saw astounded her. Never believing that such a strange and compelling environment was possible, she was captivated by the uniqueness of all that was around her. The light radiated from the luminescent lichen and moss that grew everywhere. On the roots. The vines. Even on the ground. Eliminating the need to use the Talent to illuminate the path Mikel forged.

She was unsettled as well.

They had entered a world unto itself. A world where she didn't believe they belonged.

She was used to the constant noise of the Crux -- the people, the markets, the Churn. But here there was silence and an undercurrent that made the hair on her arms and on the back of her neck stick up.

There was nothing close to them that gave her any cause to worry. She knew that for a fact, checking regularly with the Talent. Still, she felt like she was being watched, and she didn't like it.

"As soon as we got down here I felt as if we didn't belong," she tried to explain. "There's something about this place that feels ... wrong."

"I won't argue with you about that," Mikel grunted. Ducking lower to get past the tip of a taproot that almost touched the ground, he pushed a wall of effulgent vines out of the way so that they could pass through to a large open space that extended for several hundred yards that was clear of the many obstructions they had been battling for the past hour.

However, instead of taking the easy path and continuing through the hollow, Mikel cut to his right, pushing past another wall of glowing vines and then curling around several taproots that blocked his way.

"So you feel it too?"

"Of course I do," Mikel murmured in a soft voice. Nat passed by him before he dropped the vines back into place. He didn't follow her right away. Staying in place, he listened for several seconds. Hearing only the quiet touch of her boots on the soft loam. Then he stalked past her, a frown creasing his already sharp features. "Where we are now ... wasn't made for us. You're right. That's in large part why we've been on the move the entire time. The sooner we get out of here, the better."

"I don't like it when you're nervous."

"I'm not nervous," Mikel said in a gentle tone, trying to put Nat at ease.

"Then what are you? You can pretend to be calm all you want. But you're not fooling me."

"You're way too sharp for someone so young."

"Thank you."

"How do you know I meant that as a compliment?"

"I don't care if you didn't mean it as a compliment," Nat countered, smiling for the first time since she entered the Deep. "That's how I chose to take it."

Mikel snorted softly, barely a huff. "Sometimes I wonder about whether I should have taken you in."

"And I wonder all the time whether I should have accepted."

Mikel's smile broadened. He understood that Nat's nerves were talking. It only made sense. There was an oppressiveness down here that not only rivaled the forest above, but surpassed it.

"I am calm," Mikel explained as they worked their way through another shroud of vines. "But I'm also wary."

"Not worried?"

"No, not worried." Yet even as he said it, he stopped again for a few seconds. Nat stopped with him as he listened, hearing only their breaths. Mikel was pleased. The silence was a good thing, though he feared that silence would not last while they were down in the Deep. Because based on his previous experience, it rarely did.

"You're not lost?" Nat didn't have any idea how to navigate

this underground warren, feeling turned around ever since they began their trek.

"Not lost, no. No fears in that regard." He started walking again. A step more slowly now. Nat almost walking into his back before she adjusted her pace to his.

"How could you possibly know where to go?" Nat sighed, believing they were lost and that Mikel was simply attempting to hide the truth of their dilemma. She had absolutely no idea where they were in relation to where they dropped through the hollow. "This maze is disorienting. Yet you've led us through the Deep without blinking ever since we survived our plunge down here."

"It is disorienting down here. But I am following a path." Mikel continued past the vines and tubers, avoiding the roots that reached down from above to block their way, before getting right back on course. He never doubted that he was headed in the right direction.

"How could you be following a path? There is no path. It's just a convoluted mess."

"I've been down here before." He said it a bit distractedly right before he scrambled below several roots that had joined together and formed a narrow arch just above the ground.

He stayed on his knees for a moment longer than necessary. Studying the ground, running his fingers through the soft loam, he identified the faint indentations that confirmed they weren't alone in this section of the Deep.

He had been hoping they could steer clear of what had made the impression in the dirt. He knew just how much hope was worth, however.

The shock in Nat's voice brought him back from his dark musings. "You're serious? You've been down here before? I thought you were just telling me that to make me feel better." Despite her surprise, she kept her voice low as the silence squeezed the breath from her. She had no desire to disturb it any more than she already was.

"I have, yes." He pushed himself back to his feet and continued between two taproots that bracketed him on both sides.

"Two times you said? Why? Because of the Grim? How did you get out? Are there ladders of some sort? How do you even know where we're going? How can you be certain that you can even get us out of here? Why were you even down here in the first place? Were you by yourself or with a group? Who was with you?"

Mikel stopped and turned to face her. He held up his hands, his severe glance requesting a brief moment of silence.

Nat granted it to him, even though she found it difficult to make that concession. She had a dozen more questions to ask.

"Right now, we don't have time for all of your questions," Mikel explained in a whisper. "So let me just answer the one that is most important."

"How you know where we're going."

"Correct. I didn't figure out how to navigate through the Deep on my own. I had help."

"From whom?" Nat couldn't control herself. Her curiosity, a seemingly endless ocean as Mikel liked to say, heightened all the more by her concern regarding their surroundings, led to another constant stream of queries. "They came down here with you? Why would they ..."

Nat cut herself off. She nodded an apology when Mikel raised his hands again.

"I will answer all your questions later," he promised. "Right now, let's focus on getting out of here."

He started walking again, Nat falling into step beside him. The way ahead was relatively clear, particularly when compared to the path they had already trod. Only a few roots reached down from above and none that required Mikel to dip his head. Even better, their flanks were shielded by thick vines that offered the impression of an underground corridor that he was content to follow for now.

"I know which way I'm going because of this." Mikel pulled out a medallion hanging from a leather strap around his neck.

"Why is that so special?" Nat had never seen it before, though she really couldn't say that she was surprised. She had learned quickly upon taking up residence in Mikel's home that he had secrets upon secrets and that it would take her a great deal more time than just a few months to unearth all of them.

Mikel held up the silver necklace so that she could make out the etching in the dim light. The head of a fox. She had seen the design before. Many times, in fact.

"It was a gift from a good friend and someone quite knowledgeable in the use of the Talent."

"More knowledgeable than Finn?" Nat asked, finding Mikel's claim hard to believe.

"More knowledgeable than Finn," Mikel confirmed with a nod. Despite the openness of their path, Mikel slowed their pace. The tracks that he had discovered were still top of mind. As a result, he was spending more of his time examining the dirt to their front rather than keeping his eyes up and on a swivel, having learned that down in the Deep usually you didn't know you were in danger until you were fighting for your life.

"My friend explained that with this, I would never lose my way. I need only think about where I want to go, and the amulet will lead me there. It doesn't matter where I am. It doesn't matter how far away I am. I can never get lost." Mikel smiled, then placed the medallion back beneath his shirt. "So far, so good."

"How does the medallion work?" Nat was intensely curious, wondering if the Magus had used the Talent. Because she didn't sense the world's natural magic at work. Rather, she sensed an older power. One that she had never come across before. Not all that unlikely considering she had only been training with Finn for a brief time.

Before she could ask her next question, Nat felt Mikel grasp her elbow. Gently. Though strongly enough to guide her away from a rock formation that rose up on their right and sliced through the wall of vines that ran along that side.

"Why are you ..."

"Perhaps a little more patience and you wouldn't have to ask so many questions," Mikel suggested. He guided them farther down the vine-shrouded corridor at a faster clip, then nodded toward a crevice in the base of the stone outcropping. "Stay away from slits like that one."

"Why should I ..."

Nat lifted her hands again at the sharp look he gave her. Her way of offering an apology as Mikel took them past the crevice and back within the vines.

Mikel didn't explain until they were a hundred yards farther along and had slipped through the glowing vines on their left, entering what appeared to be a large cavern. One side was shrouded in vines and tubers, the undergrowth hanging from the tips of the taproots that stopped a few hundred feet above their heads. The other side a rocky crag that disappeared in the darkness.

He could breathe easier now. Though not completely. Every slit in the stone behind them potentially hid a deadly threat. "Spiders."

Nat frowned. "Seriously? You're afraid of spiders?"

Mikel smiled. Not saying anything for several steps, he wanted more space from the crag before he pointed up above them. The dim light revealed the massive construction that extended across the top of the hollow and connected the rock-face to the roots.

Nat didn't see anything at first. Not knowing what she was

looking for. Not until she stepped to the side and the green luminescence struck in just the right way.

Strands of silk. More than just a web. Many webs. A network with a mesmerizing intricacy that extended for hundreds of feet in every direction. "How many spiders are there?" She couldn't quite comprehend the number that might be required to create such an extensive masterpiece, and that concern brought her voice down to a whisper.

"One."

"One?" Nat scoffed. "You've got to be joking."

Mikel shook his head. "One."

"How big is this spider?"

"Bigger than a horse. That's why we want to avoid it."

"And it could be in any of these crevices?" She realized upon closer inspection that these crevices were more caves, the size of the crag distorting her perspective.

"It could," Mikel confirmed. He was spending just as much time as they hiked through the underground cavern studying the slits in the stone as he was the web above. Having learned from hard experience that often the only way to locate one of these monsters was to catch the gleam of the cavern's dim light off one of its many eyes.

"Where is it now?" Nat scanned the web above them, marveling at the design even as her voice threatened to crack, all the while seeing nothing that hinted the creature lurked among the strands. Not satisfied with what she could see, she searched with the Talent. Still nothing. A positive result she believed. Maybe Mikel had little cause for being so on edge.

"Probably in that first crevice we passed. There were scrapes in the dirt that suggested the beast had made its way into its nest."

"You're certain?"

Mikel smiled. Nat was a doubter. That was a good thing. It would help her going forward. Not being easily swayed or convinced. Though it did require him to exercise a level of patience that wasn't always there.

"I'm certain. I believe the master of the web was in the first crevice. I can't say for certain. Unless you want to go back and check. Just to make sure."

"That's all right," Nat replied, not feeling the need to take him up on his offer. Feeling magnanimous, she grinned, which earned a smile from Mikel in return.

"Why didn't it come out when we passed?"

"It was probably already eating. Cave spiders catch their prey in their webs then bring them down to their lairs. They like to take their time. And they don't like to be disturbed."

"What could possibly be down here that's large enough to feed a cave spider?"

Mikel reached out a hand, grasping her elbow again and stopping her. He nodded to the left. "Do you see the ground over there? How it looks different?"

Nat studied the surface. The same dark earth, but not like what she was standing on. It didn't look as solid. The surface wrinkled every so often. "A swamp? Down here?"

"It is," Mikel nodded. "Swamp. Quicksand. A deadly combination. Often you don't know what until you're about to suffocate. But that's where the cave spider's primary prey prowls. They get hungry as well. And on occasion they make the mistake of hunting a cave spider, then getting caught in that monster's web."

Nat wasn't pleased to hear that there was a second threat so close to them, perhaps just yards to her left, lurking in the muck. "I'm afraid to even ask."

"Finally," Mikel chuckled.

"What?" Nat didn't understand his humor.

"Finally some peace. No more questions."

Nat hit him in the arm. Playfully though. He accepted it.

The stress he was feeling, that he knew Nat was experiencing as well, relieved if only for a brief moment.

They took a few more steps before Mikel bent down, coming to a stop not too far from where the swamp began. Nat crouched down next to him.

"You see that?" he pointed. He had observed what happened to someone who got too close to the swamp's border, and he refused to make that same mistake.

Nat picked out large tracks, each with four toes. The deep indentations in the dirt at the end of each clawlike toe hinted at a very sharp claw. "The cave spider's meal?"

"Probably not," Mikel said, shaking his head as if he were disappointed. "Thus the need to remain wary."

"You want me to search around us with the Talent?"

"That would help. Thank you."

She did. Extending her senses for several hundred yards, including out over the swamp.

She didn't find anything that worried her. Feeling better, she asked another question. "Can you go through a swamp like this one?"

"Better that we avoid the muck if we can. I don't like the idea of getting sucked down in quicksand. Much less making it easy for the predators beneath the surface."

"You'd rather deal with a cave spider?"

"I'd rather not deal with any of the dangers of the Deep. But if I need to pick, I'll take the cave spider."

"Why?"

"Because cave spiders are territorial. Usually there's only one." Mikel nodded to a point about twenty yards out in the swamp. The mucky water rippled there. "In the swamp you never know how many Creepers there might be."

Nat's eyes widened as she watched the monster emerge from the muck, berating herself for her failure. She searched all around the cavern, but not below the surface of the swamp.

The Creeper took its time, allowing the water and mud to drip free from its scaled and muscular body, having eyes only for Mikel and Nat. Its black orbs were shielded by a clear lid, allowing it to see when hiding within the muck.

Tall, slim, the claws on its hands larger than those on its feet, the Creeper was a clear deterrent to crossing through the swamp.

"These monsters are fast on two feet," Mikel explained, stepping farther away from the swamp and bringing Nat with him. His sword, gleaming brightly, was already in hand. "Even faster when they're running on all fours."

"They look like walking crocodiles," Nat murmured, having seen such creatures before. Those animals, sometimes twenty feet or more from snout to tail, were a constant threat along the banks of the river where she grew up before she was enslaved.

Mikel nodded, acknowledging the resemblance. The monster's maw was long and tapered, resembling a snout. Its razor-sharp teeth were on display as the Creeper snapped at them a few times. It approached them slowly, clearly not worried about its prey trying to escape. Because there was nowhere for them to go. "You're right. They hunt like crocodiles as well."

"What do you mean?"

"Rather than trying to cut you open with those claws of theirs, they prefer to latch onto a meaty part – leg, arm, midsection, it really doesn't matter to them -- then take you back into the swamp. They'll drown you if they can."

"How do you know this?"

"Because I've seen it happen."

Nat bit her lip, not wanting to waste what little time they had on the questions running through her mind. The Creeper was almost out of the swamp now, approaching at a slow but steady pace. At least eight feet tall, the monster would have little trouble ripping her head from her shoulders if it wrapped its jaws around her skull.

Still, there was one query that she couldn't hold back. "Why would they bother to drown you? Why not slice you open?"

"Because as you've already guessed, there isn't a lot of prey down here. The Creepers aren't just feeding themselves. They're feeding their nest. Twenty. Thirty. Maybe more. No one really knows how many to a nest and how many nests. They can get more food from a drowned corpse rather than one that's ripped apart. That and the fact that the cave spiders can't steal it from them when they're feasting in the swamp."

"This is not the conversation I wanted to have right now."

"You asked."

"I did," Nat grunted, beginning to think that perhaps Mikel was right. Perhaps it would be better if she started to put more effort into answering her own questions instead of just blurting them out. Especially now that the Creeper was only ten yards away. "Are there more of these beasts close by?"

"Most likely," Mikel admitted. He set himself on the ground, left foot in front of the right. He held his scimitar in both hands, off to the side and level with his hip. "Right now, however, I believe that we're only dealing with a scout."

"And what do we do?" The Creeper hissed at them. It was no more than a handful of yards away from them now. "Can we escape? Do we run?"

"We fight."

That wasn't what Nat wanted to hear. She was hoping that since Mikel had some experience down in the Deep that he might have a card up his sleeve for getting them out of this latest challenge without having to risk their lives.

"Where do you want me?" Nat asked, resigned to their circumstances. She was behind Mikel's right shoulder, caught in the gleam of the Blade of Light as they stepped farther back from the edge of the swamp. Mikel preferred harder ground to cut down on the possibility of an ill-timed slip.

"Exactly where you are. Be ready."

Nat nodded, though she knew Mikel missed it. His focus was solely on the approaching Creeper. She did take three quick strides back, not wanting to get in Mikel's way.

Her timing was perfect. The instant she created space between her and Mikel, the Creeper hissed a final time and charged. Its claws dug into the muck and dirt as it scrambled across the ground on all fours. Maw gaping wide, the beast sought to clamp down with its serrated teeth on one of Mikel's limbs.

Someone caught unprepared would be snatched back into the swamp before they knew what was going on.

Not Mikel. He was ready. Having observed these creatures at work before, he understood that it was best to seize the initiative right from the start.

And he did.

Surging forward in a burst of speed surprising for such a large man, Mikel rushed toward the Creeper.

The beast skidded in the dirt, trying to slow itself down, not expecting its prey to charge.

His adversary's hesitation worked to Mikel's advantage. Caught off guard, the Creeper lifted itself to two feet, claws raised to protect itself from Mikel's blazing sword. Not knowing that Mikel had no intention of challenging the creature with steel. Not yet.

Instead, just a few yards away from the Creeper, Mikel slid feet first through the soft loam.

The Creeper flipped head over heels when Mikel slammed into the creature's legs. Before its back even hit the ground, Mikel was on top of the Creeper's chest, crushing the air from its lungs with his knees.

The Creeper tried to push itself up. It tried to raise its claws and rip into Mikel's flesh. It tried to snap at Mikel with its elongated jaw.

It failed.

With the speed of a scorpion's strike, Mikel slid the Blade of Light through the Creeper's throat.

The beast emitted a soft gurgle before it fell back into the dirt.

"I'm glad you've been down here before," Nat said, watching the combat while waiting for her chance. Realizing that she wouldn't be called upon for this clash, she was amazed at how quickly Mikel dispatched the monster.

"In this case, so am I." He pushed himself off the Creeper and stepped back. Standing next to Nat, his eyes never left the swamp to their front. "Now it's your turn."

"My turn?" She didn't understand.

Mikel nodded toward the muck. "This Creeper was a scout just as I thought. That last hiss was the Creeper's call to its nest mates."

"Wonderful."

"Sarcasm at a time like this," Mikel murmured. "Why am I not surprised?"

Nat ignored Mikel's dry humor. Her eyes were fixed on the many ripples running through the swamp that gained speed as they rushed toward them through the underground bog. Several of the creatures already were pushing themselves out of the slimy water.

Two. Four. Three more. And there were more ripples heading their way.

Too many for them to fight.

"What do we do?" Nat was proud of herself for keeping the fear that she was experiencing from her voice.

"It's not what we do. It's what you do."

"What I do?"

Mikel nodded, then placed a large hand on her shoulder

and squeezed warmly. "You learn anything from Finn that can give us a head start?"

Rather than freezing as more of the Creepers slipped free from the swamp, the creatures spreading out with the goal of moving around their flanks to surround them, Nat considered Mikel's question. She put her answer into play in a flash.

Literally.

Reaching for the Talent, Nat released a stream of fire from her hand. The flames curled from left to right and halted the Creepers in their tracks.

The monsters turned away from the scorching flames and the searing heat, scrambling back toward the bog.

"Come on," Mikel urged as he took off in a run. "We don't have much time."

Nat didn't chase after Mikel for long. They went about thirty yards before stopping, Mikel motioning above them.

The roots from the heart trees grew more thickly here, forming a latticework that they could make use of.

"Up you go," Mikel said as he gave Nat a boost so that she could climb up the roots that resembled a rough-hewn ladder.

"How far do I need to go?" she called over her shoulder.

"As far as you can." Mikel pulled himself up onto the natural ladder and was soon right behind her. "The flames won't last for long. As soon as they die out, the Creepers will be after us."

"How far should I go?" Nat was climbing the roots and vines as fast as she could, Mikel often giving her a nudge from behind. He was also there when she lost her grip, making sure that she didn't fall.

Yet that was only one of his worries. The Creepers were closing on them. Of that he was certain. The creatures could make use of their claws and dexterity during what had become a vertical hunt. His primary concern was their razor-sharp teeth biting into his ankle.

"As far as you can until I tell you to stop. It doesn't matter what direction you select now so long as it's up."

Nat grunted then picked up her pace. She shifted to a root system on her right that was freer of the vines and tubers that grasped at her and slowed her down.

Her thoughts had narrowed since she began her climb, concerned only about the next handhold. The next foothold. Where she could find a sure grip.

She wasn't even thinking about escaping the Deep. She simply wanted to escape the monsters chasing them, the Creepers' constant hissing depositing a cold ball of fear in her belly while making her teeth hurt.

Mikel glanced quickly over his shoulder. No visible sign yet. He had no doubt, however, that the kings of the bog were not far behind. He could feel them coming, the latticework shaking ever so slightly from the Creepers' passage.

He was grateful for the network of ladders -- some crafted of roots, others from the vines, often of both -- that allowed them to stay ahead of their pursuers. But he knew that their good fortune would last for only so long. And based on the sensation running down his spine, he believed that good fortune would soon run out.

It did fifty yards higher up.

The vibrations intensifying on the natural trellis, Mikel turned. Pulling the Blade of Light free, in the same motion he slashed with a tight, economical motion. The blazing steel took three razor-sharp digits from the claw reaching for his leg. For his efforts he earned a sharp bark of pain and a rattling hiss of anger.

He slashed again, this time targeting the Creeper's other claw. The beast, focused on its bloody wound, was too slow to react to Mikel's second attack. The Creeper fell away from the latticework and toward the dirt far below, its claw, severed at the wrist, still gripping the root.

Mikel was pleased. One less challenge to face.

Unfortunately dozens more remained. The hisses of the Creepers only yards below him now mixed with snarls of hate and hunger. It looked like the entire nest of bog dwellers had joined the hunt.

"Nat, a little help!"

She responded in an instant. Short bursts of energy shot from her free palm, her other hand wrapped tightly around a root so that she could keep her position.

Her aim was poor. She would be the first to admit that. Nonetheless, she achieved her objective.

The Creepers were so closely packed together as they climbed after them that so long as she wasn't too off target she couldn't miss.

And she didn't.

Four of the Creepers fell from their places among the vines and roots to join their dead brethren far below. The others scattered the best they could. Some injured, black slashes of burning and charred flesh on their backs and shoulders. Some avoided the streaks of energy that threatened to dislodge them and sought a safer path up. The rungs and vines they had been using destroyed, the flames licked up and down the living web, devouring the taproots and vines.

"Remind me to stay on your good side." With just a glance, Mikel surveyed the chaos and damage Nat caused. His thoughts not on what was but rather on what needed to be.

Focused on his desire to exit the true Deep, he was away again. Right behind Nat. Urging her on, he helped her when she required it. Trying to milk as much speed from their efforts as he could. Believing that every second counted.

"I will," she promised. "Frequently. Have no fear of that."

Despite the increasingly dire nature of their current engagement, she smiled. Pleased by Mikel's compliment.

They gained almost a hundred yards on the Creepers before the beasts resumed the hunt. Peeking over his shoulder every other second to gauge the rate of pursuit, Mikel spat out several curses. He and Nat were engaged in a losing race.

If they were going to have any chance of winning, they needed to change the rules. Scanning above them, he found what he was looking for twenty yards further up.

"The taproot just up ahead that branches to the right. The single stalk that resembles a ledge."

"What about it?" Nat was almost there. Just a few more feet.

"That's where we get off."

"Why here?" she demanded when Mikel joined her on the root that extended away from them for fifty yards. The far edge offered a peek at a fall that ensured a painful death for any misstep.

"You'll find out soon enough." He pulled the Blade of Light from the scabbard across his back, placing himself in front of Nat.

"What do you want me to do?"

"Same as you did before. Slow them down if you can. Make them think twice."

Nat nodded. "And after that?"

"After that you take a leap of faith." He motioned to the tip of the root.

She didn't see it at first. Not until she took a few steps closer to the end of the root. The beginning of another massive web. Was he insane? "You want me to climb right into a cave spider's trap?"

"It's just like climbing the roots and vines," Mikel explained. Not turning to face her, he had eyes only for the Creepers that would be joining them in just a few seconds. "So long as you keep moving."

"What does that even mean?" Nat had no clue what he was talking about.

"You'll see. Just don't stop moving. Now a little help please."

The Creeper in the lead was just about to dig its claw into the root upon which they were standing. A handful of its brethren were right behind.

The creature never made it to the ledge.

Struck by a spike of energy, its chest a charred and smoking ruin, the monster slipped from its perch. Dropping back toward the ground far below, it took several of its ilk with it.

Those Creepers that avoided that unlucky fate scrabbled in every direction, seeking what cover they could find among the vines and roots as Nat sent several more bursts of energy their way.

Her goal?

Giving her and Mikel the few seconds they needed to take what she viewed as an even greater risk than jumping through a hollow.

"Go!" Mikel yelled, judging the time to be right.

Nat didn't hesitate despite her apprehension. She sprinted toward the tip of the root and leapt off into the abyss ...

Grunting with pleasure when she landed among the silky strands that extended high above the cavern floor, she heeded his advice and began climbing immediately. She didn't look back or down. She understood that if she did stop it wouldn't take long for the glue covering the strands to grasp hold of her and never let go. She would be locked in place, the bond as strong as stone. Then she would become just another offering for the animal that crafted the web.

Sighing with relief that Nat had heeded his advice and was already well away from the root, Mikel was about to follow her.

He just wanted to try one thing first.

One more attempt to slow down their hunters.

He didn't really know what he was doing.

He did know why.

The Blade of Light.

As soon as his fingers wrapped around the hilt, he heard the voices tickling the back of his mind. The spirits and memories of those several others who had once been privileged to wield the ancient Blade whispered once again.

And now, with the Creepers closing in on them after Nat's latest effort, he decided to listen to them. To use the knowledge they willingly gifted to him.

The voices desired that he become worthy of the Blade that served him and that he served. He was to carry on the tradition that they themselves had lived.

He understood that now. He and the artifact were joined together in a symbiotic relationship. Both achieved their goals while working together. Both became greater together rather than alone.

The sense of selflessness associated with that concept slightly unnerved Mikel. It was not an arrangement he was used to. Not after what he had experienced in his homeland. Not after what he was forced to do in order to survive.

He had learned that there were times in life when a man or woman exercised a choice that would take him or her in a new direction. The choice would affect their lives so profoundly that breaking away from the old required an almost otherworldly courage. It meant taking a new path along the web of options laid before them, much as he and Nat were doing just then.

Mikel was absolutely certain that one of those few, unique, absolutely crucial choices was now upon him. And strangely, he wasn't afraid. He wasn't worried. He was actually slightly ... excited. An uncommon emotion for him.

When the darkness surrounds, the Light will prevail.

He read the phrase carved into both sides of the steel one more time, nodding to himself as he did so. Taking in the expertise offered by the previous Bearers of the Blade, he understood what would be required of him in the future, and he was comfortable in that knowledge and responsibility.

He waited as a pair of Creepers climbed toward the ledge. Demonstrating the calm so essential to the role he played on the Crux, both in the City Above and in the City Below, he didn't move, wanting as many of the creatures as possible close to him when he acted.

"Mikel!" Nat didn't stop on the web, keeping his advice top of mind and knowing if she hesitated too long the glue would bind her to the strands. She did look over her shoulder, not understanding why he wasn't right behind her as he had been since they began their climb.

Mikel didn't hear her cry. The world around him was growing smaller. He only saw and heard the Creepers that were a few yards away from him and the blindingly brilliant light cascading out from the steel with an even greater potency.

In a swift motion, both hands on the hilt of the Blade of Light, Mikel drove the fiery steel into the root.

The result?

A catastrophic wave of energy blasted out in all directions.

Sweeping the Creepers away from him, the energy surged down into the roots and the vines, electrifying them as if they were metal struck by a lightning bolt.

Those Creepers not caught in the blast were flung clear from where they clung to the latticework when struck by the sizzling energy.

Whispering a few brief words of thanks to the Bearers of the Blade, Mikel pulled the ancient steel free then sheathed it in a single motion.

Sprinting down the root, he leapt for the web.

28

COMBAT ON THE WEB

"We're not safe, are we?"

"Not yet," Mikel grunted, working hard to catch up to Nat on the web.

He was still slightly in shock at what had just happened.

What he had done.

What he had decided and committed himself to.

How he had used the Blade to earn them some additional time.

But he understood it wouldn't last.

Because in the Deep there were always more Creepers.

And he knew that he had done more than just use the Blade of Light. He had bound himself to the ancient artifact, accepting the duty demanded of a Bearer of the Blade.

That was a concern for a later time, however, when he could reflect more on the ramifications of his decision.

He was certain that those few Creepers that avoided the magic contained within the Blade of Light were still hunting them. Would continue to hunt them. The kings of the bog refused to give up the chase when prey was in sight.

Mikel could feel the monsters already seeking to close the

gap. The strands he was climbing shook with greater vigor, and not because of him or Nat.

"Have I told you that I'm getting a little tired of this?"

"No need. I'm already tired of this. I do not like the thought of being some monster's dinner."

Nat snorted out a laugh. Grateful for Mikel's joke. Her nerves frayed, close to breaking. His dark humor helped to ease the strain that was pressing down on both of them.

About to offer a rejoinder, she stopped abruptly. She felt a new sensation. One unique to their peculiar conveyance. A heavier and more rhythmic vibration on the web.

It wasn't the Creepers chasing them. She was sure of it. Because it came from above her.

"You need to keep moving," Mikel urged. Right next to her now, he had a clear sense of exactly where the Creepers were without having to look. The essence of the Blade of Light, now a part of him, shared itself with him and gave him an ability much like the one Nat exercised when extending her senses with the Talent.

She didn't reply, instead extending her senses ahead of them. She searched for what she was absolutely certain was there. Not seeing anything and unable to shake the truth of her conviction, Nat reached for the Talent.

That's when she found it.

The monster waited for them just above.

Twenty yards away. Perhaps a bit less.

Hidden in large part because the color of its body matched the color of the silk strands.

"Mikel ..."

He looked to where she was pointing. He didn't see anything ... except for a very brief shift. Then several sparks.

Relying on his new skill, his senses reaching out, he identified what waited for them in all its terrible glory, not needing to see the creature with his own eyes.

The master of this web.

"Keep moving!" Mikel ordered, giving her a push. "Don't stop!"

"But you can't …"

"Let me worry about the spider," Mikel growled. They were so close to exiting the Deep, yet still so far. The threat above them was even more dangerous than the Creepers below. "I know what I'm doing."

Mikel surged above Nat, taking the lead despite the sharp spikes of pain in his damaged knee. Having eyes only for the monster that waited for him, he planned on making use of the hard knowledge he earned the last time he traveled within the true Deep.

For just a second he feared that she wouldn't move as he instructed. Hesitating for just a few seconds on a cave spider's web ensured that you never left it alive. Mikel breathed easier when he felt Nat following him.

Once again his world narrowed. His objective gained a precision that he valued.

Ensure that Nat got away safely.

That's all that mattered to him in that moment. And he would do everything in his power to make that happen.

As he drew closer, Mikel observed the beast with a frightening clarity. The cave spider was larger than he believed possible. Not just bigger than a horse. Bigger than a wagon.

This monster obviously ruled its domain.

And it didn't like being challenged.

The loud hiss that assaulted Mikel's ears confirmed that truth.

That and the cave spider scrambling forward. Its eight eyes sparkling. Its hairy hide bristling. Its eight legs with tips as sharp as lances propelling itself across the silken strands with a frightening grace.

"Mikel, what are you …"

"Be ready! Get ahead of me as soon as you see the chance."

He hoped that Nat understood what he was trying to do. He had fought a cave spider before. Reluctantly as he had little choice. And he had survived, though that combat hadn't occurred on a spider's web.

None of his companions who had joined him in the true Deep had deigned to do so. None of them had any desire to assume such a risk. All of them convinced that accepting such a challenge meant certain death.

Mikel couldn't argue with their sensible perspective. But he had another advantage besides previous combat experience.

He had watched a cave spider in battle. Two, in fact. Both fighting for dominance of a single web.

Mikel was amazed and terrified both at the same time while observing that encounter. Locking away that information for a time just like this one.

He might not survive this combat on the web. Nevertheless, he believed that he could do enough to ensure that Nat did.

The cave spider almost upon him, Mikel held his ground. The glue of the strands less of a concern than the monstrosity charging toward him.

Pulling free the Blade of Light and calling to the spirits that were a part of the artifact, he sighed with relief when they answered.

Eager to be of service.

Eager to engage once more in a combat.

The steel flashed with such brilliance that the spider was forced to duck away, unused to the blazingly bright light.

That's when Mikel struck.

During the cave spider's brief moment of hesitation.

No more than a heartbeat. Perhaps two.

But that's all the time that Mikel required.

Steel had little effect on the cave spider's armored hide.

That was a truth that could not be denied. Nevertheless, that hide could not stand against steel infused with the Light.

A power similar to the Talent, yet distinct.

Older.

More aware.

More severe.

More demanding.

More selective.

Based not only on the natural magic of the world but also on the spirit of the one gifted with its use.

Mikel started with the spider's front legs. In a single swipe he took three feet off of the spike to his right that streaked toward his chest. On his backswing he managed to cut off more than a foot from the leg on his left that was aimed for his neck.

The cave spider reared back. Shrieking angrily, it hissed and spit. The wounds Mikel caused sizzled. The flesh charred. The power of the Light released into the spider much like the flame of a fire.

Alive.

Ravenous.

Scorching.

Burning.

Turning flesh to ash.

Mikel didn't spend any time admiring his handiwork. Already on the move, he climbed up the web to the left with one hand, seeking to get above the spider.

Thankfully Nat was already ahead of him and well away from the animal. Seeing her chance, she had taken it just as Mikel wanted her to.

He was almost past the spider as well before he realized that he wasn't moving fast enough.

The cave spider already faced him. Two of its uninjured legs reaching for him.

Understanding that this was the kind of battle he had little chance of winning, Mikel took a risk. Hoping that it would pay off though prepared for the worst.

He leapt forward. Directly toward the monstrous animal. Scrambling across the web, Mikel got past the spider's legs before they could pierce his flesh.

Unable to halt its attack, the spider paid a heavy price.

Mikel punched up with his blade, the gleaming steel sliding easily into the monster's abdomen and then slicing through flesh and muscle as the cave spider slipped by him.

Avoiding the splash of blood that threatened to drown him, Mikel started climbing once again after getting out from beneath the sagging and badly wounded monster.

Once he was free of the beast, he looked back over his shoulder. The cave spider hadn't turned toward him yet, and he wasn't sure if the monster would.

The creature was struggling. Screeching in pain, the beast found it difficult to keep its heavy body atop its own creation.

Mikel did identify the last of the Creepers climbing toward him. Only a handful were left just as he suspected. Still more than enough to make his life difficult, however.

So he decided to try to make their lives more difficult than his.

Ignoring the spider that had lost interest in him, Mikel concentrated on the web. The silk strands were as strong as steel. Even so, they were no match for the Blade of Light.

All it took was a slash at three key junctures.

The strands snapped and floated away, and with those strands went the cave spider.

The beast, though badly wounded, still had some fight left in it, scrambling for a better hold as its web began to collapse around it.

The spider's effort proved to be too little too late.

With more of the strands snapping and slipping away, the

cave spider tumbled from its position on the web. Screeching its angry displeasure as it fell.

The jarring noise made Mikel's ears hurt, but he didn't mind in the least.

Because as the spider spilled down its swiftly disintegrating web, it slammed into the Creepers that remained in the hunt and took the creatures of the bog with it.

Mikel turned and started climbing again, seeking to catch up to Nat. Pleased with his work, though not entirely satisfied.

Much of the web was gone, but not all of it.

A small portion of the cave spider's creation was still fixed in place.

And a new battle had erupted upon it.

This one pitted a wounded cave spider against the Creepers still clinging to the strands. More than one of the bog dwellers tried to tear free and fight the master of the web, yet had no capacity to do so. The glue streaking the strands was too sticky, catching the Creepers, who were now just offerings if they failed to free themselves with their claws.

Not certain how the melee would conclude, though hoping that none of the combatants survived, Mikel sheathed his blade so that he could increase the speed of his ascent. Nat was just a few feet above him and still climbing.

He could sense it now. They were close. They did not have much farther to go.

The medallion on his chest was growing steadily warmer as they approached the surface.

The roots were denser here. Thicker. In some places a solid barrier because of how they curled and twisted, preventing them from slinking through.

"Here," Mikel said, directing Nat toward a root with its tip broken off. The inside was hollow and large enough for both of them to enter one after the other.

Nat didn't have the energy to question Mikel's choice,

smiling when she found smaller roots within the larger that allowed her to continue her climb within the chute.

Mikel was right behind her. "Just a little farther. We're almost there. You can do this."

Nat didn't say anything. Gasping for breath, she was covered in sweat, the muscles in her arms, shoulders, and thighs aching.

She did her best to block out her worsening exhaustion, concentrating on where she put her hands and feet while hoping with all her heart that this part of their adventure was almost over.

"Twenty more yards and then we're free. Just up ahead ..."

Mikel turned swiftly, hanging from a smaller root with just one hand, his boots each to a side to prop himself up within the hollow root.

He didn't hear what was coming after them. He felt it. The inside of the root moved differently now that there were three rather than two climbing through it.

He didn't need the power of the Light to confirm what was just below him.

A Creeper.

He hoped the last one.

The monster hissed, reaching with its free claw and seeking to dig its needlelike fingers into Mikel's flesh.

Unable to draw the Blade of Light because of his narrow confines, worried that he didn't have the space to use the mace that he always carried on the back of his belt, Mikel relied on a skill that he had learned when he was much younger. A skill that kept him alive in the meaner streets of Innsbruck.

With a quick snap of his wrist, Mikel felt the small dagger sheathed on the inside of his left forearm slip free. Grasping the tip between his thumb and forefinger, he flicked it straight down.

His instincts guided the throw.

Mikel got lucky. He wouldn't deny that. And he would certainly take it.

At exactly the wrong moment, the Creeper tilted its head up, the point of the blade punching through one of its eyes and piercing its brain.

There was no scream of pain. No violent death throes. Just a sad sigh as the dead Creeper collapsed within itself, crumpling against the walls of the chute.

Mikel breathed a sigh of relief, then hurried to catch up to Nat. She was climbing more slowly now, the strain of her efforts finally catching up to her.

They were both grateful that they didn't have much farther to go.

"Right here," Mikel said, reaching around an exhausted Nat. He pushed several vines out of the way that because of the gloom of the chute wouldn't have been noticeable if not for Mikel's fox head medallion telling him that he was in the right place.

Nat slipped between the vines, Mikel right behind her. Both were breathing heavily from their efforts. Both were exceedingly glad to be free from the true Deep.

"How did you know about that exit?" Nat no longer gasped, finally breathing easier after several minutes passed, drinking from the canteen Mikel offered her.

"I've had cause to use a similar chute before. It's just a matter of knowing what to look for and listening to my guide."

"Right now, I don't have the patience for the mystery you seem to enjoy so much," Nat murmured. "I don't want to know."

"Really?" Mikel offered her a grin. "That's uncommon. Usually you want to know everything. Right away. Angry when I'm too slow to provide you with the information you can't live without."

"You can tell me later. I can wait. At least until ..."

The howls of the Grim tore through the silence of the

forest. Before the haunting cry died, Mikel pushed himself off the root he was leaning against.

"Later it is." He pulled himself up and onto the root that rose to his shoulders then offered Nat his hand and hauled her up. "Come on. We're not done yet."

Mikel trotted down the root, Nat doing her best to stay with him despite her fatigue.

Another hunt had begun in the Deep.

And once again they were the prey.

29

LIFE FROM STONE

"I'm really getting tired of this, Mikel."

"You told me that before." Mikel grinned. He was leading Nat on a winding route across the top of the roots that snaked along the forest floor. Although there was no direct path that would take them where he wanted to go, it was faster than testing themselves against the obstacle course below them.

And at that moment speed was all that mattered.

The calls of the Grim were growing louder.

The pack was a mile away, perhaps less.

It was difficult to be precise since noises traveled differently through the Deep. Echoing. Dying in some places. Gaining new life in others.

Regardless, it was only a matter of when the fearsome beasts appeared. And when they did, Mikel wanted to be in a stronger position where they stood a better chance of defending themselves.

He only hoped that what he was seeking was still there.

If it wasn't …

Well, he didn't need to worry about that … yet.

"Do you have any idea where we're going?"

"I do," Mikel confirmed as he picked up the pace just a little, understanding that he could push Nat only so hard, the latest howls of the Grim hinting that their hunters were closing their trap.

"Because of the amulet you wear?" Nat cursed under her breath. Her tiredness caused her to trip on a knob that stuck up on the root. She was more stumbling than trotting at this point. She would have fallen if Mikel hadn't stopped and turned, catching her before she slipped off the elevated path.

"No, although the medallion doesn't hurt. As I said, I've been here before. Many times, in fact. Come on. It's just a hundred yards further on. No more than that."

Taking heart from Mikel's confidence, Nat stayed with him. Her exhaustion drained away as her second wind hit. She hoped that it lasted long enough for her to challenge the beasts baying for their blood.

Mikel was no stranger to the Deep. Nor a stranger to the Grim.

The primary predators of the wood preferred to hunt in the evening and at night, which in the Deep was simply a shift in the light from a dark grey to a suffocating black.

Unless the beasts had the scent of their prey.

Then, the Grim hunted until they earned their kill.

Just as they were doing now.

The Grim had picked up their scent again when Mikel and Nat emerged from the real Deep.

Mikel's goal was to reach the northern border of the wood. And, after traveling beneath the surface, they were close. A league. No more than that.

That knowledge lifted Mikel's spirits.

Because it was here near the edge of the great forest that he had set up a series of fortified huts. Waystations when there was need. Storage facilities he used as he moved goods to and from the Tor. And, with their hunters at their heels, strongholds.

"You've got to be kidding me!"

Mikel let fly a string of curses when he and Nat raced into the small clearing. The roots of the heart trees not so thick here near the forest border.

Up against the base of a towering heart tree that rose more than four hundred feet into the air one of Mikel's huts waited for them.

Unfortunately, its heavy door sat askew with the upper section off its hinge.

He would need to talk to Teddy about that and make sure it was repaired. Assuming, of course, that he and Nat escaped the peril that fast approached.

"This is what you're looking for?"

"It is," Mikel confirmed. It was too late now to change his plan. They would need to make do with what they had. "Into the doorway. You know what to do."

"And what are you going to do?"

Mikel pulled the Blade of Light from the scabbard across his back. The steel blazed to life.

"Feed the flames."

NAT GROWLED, allowing her anger to drive her and keep her exhaustion from consuming her.

She stood in the doorway of the stronghold. Not thinking. Just doing. Responding to all that occurred around her and adding to the chaos of the small clearing Mikel had selected as a battlefield.

She sent spikes and bursts of energy sizzling between the heart trees. Seeking a clear hit on the beasts, Nat grew more and more frustrated. The Grim never stood in place long enough for her to earn an accurate strike.

She was grateful for the heart tree at her back. The width of its base prevented their hunters from coming at them from behind.

The roots that snaked around the clearing were the problem. The Grim could stalk in and out of the obstructed space, allowing the roots to bear the brunt of the energy Nat sent their way.

And that, she realized, was the solution to her problem.

The Grim were using the natural obstacles to their advantage. Leaping over the roots and lunging or feinting at Mikel then jumping right back before she could bring the Talent to bear.

Why couldn't she use the roots as well?

A second later a Grim leapt over a root. The massive beast snapped at Mikel. Then it tensed. About to jump back rather than face the gleaming steel already arcing toward its neck.

That's when Nat struck.

She didn't aim for the Grim, knowing that she had little chance of harming the beast.

Instead she targeted the root over which it planned to jump back to safety.

The Grim were fast, but this beast was not fast enough to escape the millions of sharp slivers that exploded into the air when the Talent blasted into the root.

The Grim dropped onto the root and slid over the far side. Its body shredded in hundreds of places.

An inexact approach Nat would be the first to admit, and Finn would likely be disappointed in her accuracy.

But she was tired. More tired than she ever had been before. And she would take whatever success she could achieve.

She shifted her approach in an instant.

The rest of the Grim were wary now, having witnessed the power employed against their dying brethren.

Uncommonly hesitant as well.

They were unable to make a clear run at Nat because of Mikel, who stood in front of her, gleaming Blade streaking through the air like a comet across the sky.

~

MIKEL WAS IMPRESSED. Nat's new strategy had changed the tenor of the clash.

In their favor?

He couldn't say so with any certainty. Not yet. But at least their odds had improved, and that's all that he could ask for.

Holding the Blade of Light with both hands, Mikel was a whirlwind of movement and death. Never failing to strike the Grim he targeted and always with a devastating result, the power contained within the sword surged out and sizzled through the beasts, burning until there was nothing left to burn.

Yet even though they had removed ten of the Grim from the fight, most of those permanently, still a score of the pack remained and none of the beasts had any intention of withdrawing until they clamped their jaws around their prey, ripping into flesh and crushing bone.

Mikel understood the reality of what they faced. He believed that Nat did as well. That this was a battle to the ...

"Mikel, what's going on?" Nat shouted to be heard above the deep growls of the Grim that darted around the clearing before taking refuge on the other side of the roots.

Mikel smiled. It seemed that the Grim's window of opportunity was about to close.

The ground had begun to shake. Softly at first. Barely a tremor. Then just seconds later with a greater fervor, the soft loam between the roots jumping a foot or more into the air. A rush of wind blasted into the clearing, disturbing the usual stillness of the Deep.

Nat continued to fight, firing burst after burst of the Talent at the Grim. More often she aimed at their points of ingress and egress, the devastating splinters and shards she created working to her advantage.

"My friends are almost here!" he yelled. "Keep fighting! Just a little longer!"

Twisting to the side, Mikel allowed the Grim that sought to take him from the right to pass him by. Not bothering to take a swipe at the beast, he was certain that the Grim was just a diversion for its partner charging toward him from the other side. The second Grim soared through the air, claws outstretched, eager to take a bite out of its prey.

Mikel held his ground for just a breath longer, wanting to ensure the creature was committed and couldn't change course, before doing as he had done with the cave spider. He stepped forward and then slid through the soft loam, getting beneath his attacker and trailing his blade along the creature's soft belly.

The dying Grim crumpled at his feet. Its guts spilling out.

Mikel's focus swiftly shifted to the first Grim. The one that tried to distract him. The one that was right behind him and preparing to spring.

Spinning as swiftly as he could, Mikel feared that he would be too late as he caught out of the corner of his eye the Grim already launching itself toward him ...

And then disappearing.

Swiped away with a bone-crunching yelp.

For the first time since he and Nat entered the Deep, he breathed a sigh of relief.

His friends had arrived.

While the Giants of the Rime called the Frozen Waste their home, here in the Deep the Peikkos ruled.

Related to the Frost Giants, they were just as large. Just as fast. Just as determined and resolute.

The primary difference being how they adapted to their environment, dressing in green, brown, grey, and black to blend into the landscape. Their brown hair tinted with green also helped. Their weapons of choice scythes crafted from stones that were just as sharp as steel.

Several more yelps sounded throughout the clearing as massive shadows detached themselves from the gloom.

The Giants of the Deep swatted away the Grim as if they were no more than flies.

Though aid arrived, the battle was not yet over.

Mikel pivoted, sensing the Grim that had just leapt over the root to his right.

The beast's sharp claws ripped into the dirt as it charged him.

Then just as fast the beast disappeared. Sent back the way it had come. Tumbling back over the root.

A large scythe had swept along the Grim's path and connected with a crushing force.

30

A NEW DIRECTION

"This is the only way?"

Mikel frowned as he stared into the gloom blanketing the heart trees. It was darker here. The murk more substantial. More sinister.

He could tell that Nat was feeling it as well. That's why she was standing so close to him. Her shoulder brushed his as she sought strength and comfort for a threat that neither could identify with their senses.

Even the fist of Peikkos who accompanied them from the clearing littered with the bodies of the Grim were acting strangely, affected by the change in the forest's mood. The Giants who feared little in the Deep were uneasy. Hesitant. Rather than standing ramrod straight as was their practice, stone scythes resting on their shoulders, imperturbable, they were on edge. Shuffling from one foot to the other, their eyes shifted from side to side. Looking over their shoulders every so often as if they had heard a whisper in an ear.

Not a good sign in Mikel's opinion.

"Not the only way," rumbled Rusan Rulebreaker, King of the Peikkos. The giant was a head taller than his hunters.

Though his beard was flecked with grey, his dark green eyes flashed with life.

"But the best way," Mikel completed for him.

"The best way, Steelheart," Rusan confirmed with a sigh. He had already explained the danger of crossing the grasslands that separated the Deep from the Tor. The regular patrols by Dragoran's soldiers weren't the cause of his worry. Both Rusan and Mikel were certain that he could avoid them.

It was an unexpected development that concerned the Peikkos in a way that Mikel had never encountered before.

"Do you have any idea why this is happening?"

"We don't," Rusan grumbled. Reluctant to admit the truth. "We can only assume."

Mikel thought again about what Rusan had told him. Packs of the Grim were ranging out from the Deep. Sometimes to the very base of the Tor.

Why?

Hunting?

Was there a lack of game in the Deep?

Rusan didn't believe so. His Peikkos had no trouble filling their stewpots. And ever since the Peikkos had claimed the ancient wood as their own, the Grim had hunted within the heart trees. They never emerged onto the grasslands. But now it seemed that those beasts were expanding their territory.

Or perhaps hunting for something ... or someone.

An intriguing possibility. A potentially dangerous one as well for Mikel and Nat.

Mikel preferred not to think about that. It raised a host of questions for which he didn't have answers.

His hand drifted down, fingers grasping the hilt of the Blade of Light and taking some comfort from the warmth that surged through him. It wasn't the first time he wondered if the risk he planned on taking was worth it. Whether he was doing more harm than good.

He sought to enter the lion's den.

Was the lion waiting for him? Hoping that he would come?

"If you choose to brave the grasslands, we cannot go with you. I'm sorry. You understand why."

"Why?" Nat asked before thinking about whether she should ask that question.

Rusan tilted his head down toward her. His expression grave, though his eyes glowed with mirth. "The Little Magus prefers to speak rather than listen."

"It's one of her more endearing, and often difficult, traits," Mikel explained.

"I'm not being difficult," Nat countered. Even though the King of the Peikkos towered above her, his scythe taller than she was, she refused to back down. "I'm just being curious." She nudged Mikel's shoulder with her own. "Asking questions is the only way to learn. You've told me that many times."

"I have," Mikel admitted.

"Then why?" Nat repeated, doing her best to hold Rusan's hard glance even as every nerve in her body was telling her to put some space between them.

Rusan glared at Nat for a few seconds more, then broke into a laugh that earned several smiles from the Peikkos standing around them. "Fiery. I like that." He crouched down so that he was almost eye to eye with the Little Magus, only forcing her to bend her neck slightly. "I will answer your question."

"Thank you."

"Respectful," Rusan nodded. "I like that even more." He crossed his arms over his knees as he crouched. "We seek to protect your guardian. And you, of course."

"What are you talking about, Rusan?" Mikel's gaze sharpened, pulling it free from the gloom to lock eyes with the King of the Peikkos before turning away and continuing his search for ... he didn't know what. Not even a shadow flitted through the gloom that could help explain the trepidation he was experiencing.

"There is much to be said, but it will not be said here."

"You're dissembling," Nat accused.

"Am I, Little Magus? Perhaps I am just being circumspect."

"Speak what must be spoken," Mikel urged. "Best that we know all before we take this new direction you're suggesting."

"Then I will speak plainly," Rusan grumbled, acceding to Mikel's request because of their friendship. "You are important to us, Steelheart. We would not see you risk your life any more than necessary."

"What are you worried about, Rusan?" Mikel ignored the whisper of the soft voices that played past his ears. Not knowing where the sound came from. Not wanting to know. Yet certain that he would soon find out.

"Let me begin by stepping back," Rusan started. "For our history plays a role in the present. The Peikkos did not always rule the Deep. Before that, we ruled the Tor. It was our home. For centuries. A terrible loss."

"What happened?" Nat asked.

"You came."

"Me?" Nat didn't understand how she could be responsible for the Peikkos' loss.

"Not you specifically, Little Magus. But rather your kind. Men. Soldiers. Those loyal to the ruler of the Splintered Empire. Although back then the Empire was whole. The Steel Empire it was called, because it was built on the steel blades of the Emperor's Legions."

"What happened? How did you lose the Tor?"

"When the Steel Empire first came into being, the Peikkos were left alone." Rusan shrugged. "That is how it usually begins. A peace of sorts until the betrayal."

"The Steel Empire betrayed you?"

"No, the Splintered Empire did. The men who used to rule

this land from the Frozen Waste in the west to the sea far to the east in the name of the last Emperor had no interest in us. The treaty we agreed to governed our relations for centuries. The people of the Steel Empire were pleased to trade with us. We paid well for what we needed, and there was great demand for the stone crafts and ceramics that only we could provide. It was a beneficial relationship for all."

"That came to an end?"

Rusan nodded sadly. "When the Empire splintered it did. The change wasn't fast. It was gradual. The civil war not coming to this part of the Empire until the fighting exceeded a score of years. But when it did the combatants wanted the Tor. Our Tor. It didn't matter what side they fought on. They viewed the Tor as the fortress it was, wanting to make use of it for themselves because from its walls they could rule the surrounding lands."

"You didn't give it to them." Nat said that with absolute confidence, her expression hard.

Rusan liked that. Fiery and tough. He chuckled softly. Not because of the Little Magus, but rather thinking about how the Little Magus would make his friend's life more challenging in the years ahead. If there were more years to be had.

"We did not," Rusan confirmed. "It was stolen from us."

"Stolen? How?"

"By our allies at the time. We gave them sanctuary as they requested. They turned on us." Rusan's eyes were colored with sadness, as if he were remembering a terrible time that had occurred just the other day rather than one that was centuries old. "Breaking our customs. Breaking the treaty."

"Men loyal to Malor Dragoran?"

Rusan chuckled again. "Close, but no. Malor Dragoran was not yet alive. This was well in the past. No, it was the ancestors of Malor Dragoran. I remember him even to this day. In fact he's the spitting image of Malor though many generations removed. Rickard Dragoran. The beginning of the current line of Tor kings."

Rusan shook his head, memories returning to him that he had not dredged up in quite some time. "The Peikkos were neutral during the wars for the Empire. We had little interest in the machinations of men. Yet we could not stay out of the conflict. The Tor was too important to whatever side could grasp hold of it."

"This Rickard did?" Nat frowned, not quite understanding how men could defeat such formidable opponents as Peikkos, these Giants handling the Grim with a terrifying ease.

"He did. Under the pretense of a neutral flag. We granted him sanctuary, believing that the treaty still held. Yet we were foolish to trust him." Rusan began to bite out his words, clearly still upset over the betrayal. "We fought. We did not relinquish the Tor easily. We battled both steel and magic. But the Peikkos are few in number compared to men. It was like swatting at ants, yet the ants kept coming. Biting at our legs."

"You escaped."

"We did," Rusan nodded. "Barely. Rickard Dragoran was a crafty adversary, setting several traps for us. Using his magic against us."

"How did you do it?"

Rusan offered Nat a sly look then. "We knew all the secrets of the Tor. He did not."

"And that's why you won't go back to the Tor?"

"Since then, our relations with the rulers of the Tor have not been good."

"Nonexistent you mean," Mikel corrected.

"That is perhaps a better way to describe it, Steelheart," Rusan admitted. "We Peikkos remain at war with the Kingdom of the Tor. An open conflict that has cooled during the last few hundred years because we have chosen to stay within the Deep. We have also employed some unique means to keep the soldiers of the Tor away from our home. I have no desire for the conflict with the Kingdom of the Tor to burst into flames once more. It does us little good to rekindle the fires of war."

Nat considered all that Rusan shared with her. Understanding his logic, she agreed with it. Yet just as always she had more questions.

"How do you keep the soldiers of the Tor out of the Deep?"

Rusan laughed again, thoroughly enjoying his engagement with the Little Magus. "There is little in the Deep of interest to them. On occasion Malor Dragoran sends woodcutters this way, seeking to use the heart trees as his own. Just as much curious as to whether we still remain."

"He doesn't know?"

"He doesn't know though he might suspect. We have done what we can to make him believe that the Deep is free of us."

"You dissuade them? How without revealing yourselves?"

Rusan smiled. "No, not us. True, we are always there when Malor's men enter the Deep. Watching them. Though keeping our distance. Believing that what Malor Dragoran doesn't know is more powerful than what he does." He pushed himself back to his feet. Stretching his back to remove the kink when he attained his full height, Rusan almost knocked his head on the lowest branch of the heart tree that soared above them. "Instead we rely on the tools our friend here gifted to us."

"Your friend?"

"That would be me," Mikel said quietly. The whispers in his ears had increased in intensity, so he was more than happy to partake in a real conversation.

"What did you do?"

Rusan reached into a pocket and pulled out what appeared to be a reed. Although in the Giant's hand, as he turned it this way and that, its use became obvious. A whistle. He lifted the carved wood to his lips and blew.

The ear-splitting shriek echoed all around them, traveling

back toward the center of the Deep. Several seconds passed before it finally died away.

"The call of a basilisk," Rusan explained. "Every Peikko hunter carries one. When Tor soldiers appear, this usually keeps them away if they get too curious."

"They're afraid of that noise?"

"They're afraid of what they believe is making that noise. No one has seen a basilisk in these parts for centuries. That doesn't mean, however, that the belief in these monstrous serpents doesn't remain. Because they did once roam in the Deep. We use these," Rusan grinned as he lifted the whistle supplied by Mikel, "against the Tor soldiers. Playing off their fears. Fears that the Steelheart continues to stoke atop the crag that used to be our home. His campaign of whispering just as strong a defense as our stone." He lifted his scythe to emphasize his point.

"Is there anywhere in the Splintered Empire where you don't have a finger on the harp?"

Mikel shrugged. "Probably. Though thinking on it now I can't really recall where I'm not plucking at a chord."

"Full of yourself much?"

Rusan laughed again. He enjoyed the Little Magus' bite. And all credit to his friend for keeping his temper in check when he replied.

"Not full of myself. Just speaking truthfully."

"And we are glad that he does," Rusan explained. "The Steelheart plays an important role for us. Without him, our surviving in the Deep would be a great deal more challenging. In addition to giving us a bloodless defense, he acquires for us special goods that we need. Healing herbs and other necessaries that can't be found in our forest home. In turn, he sells our goods in markets in the Splintered Empire and beyond. But I must point out that our friendship with the Steelheart isn't based solely on trade. Or because he gives us the connection we need to our brothers and sisters, the Giants of the Rime. No, the Steelheart is appropriately named. He is true to his word. He keeps his promises. He is not like Malor Dragoran and his forebears."

"He would not betray you," Nat murmured quietly, although her soft words traveled to the ears of the Peikkos standing with her. The Giants of the Deep nodded, acknowledging the truth of her statement.

"He would not. He would die first. And for us, he almost has. Several times. Which is why I worry now."

"These Grim extending their range," Mikel prompted, not liking where his thoughts were taking him. "Do you think it's possible that they're doing so at someone's instigation?"

He was all too aware of Malor Dragoran's interest in the Blade of Light. That coupled with rumors circulating around the King of the Tor ever since he took the throne gave Mikel pause. Those rumors hinted at Malor demonstrating unique abilities that had been thought lost to history. Mikel couldn't discount the fact that the Dark Magus who had hired him to steal the Blade was likely working with Malor.

"You mean as if they are obeying a master?"

Mikel shrugged. Not really certain that his theory had legs. "Why not? There are dark forces at play in this business. Why couldn't those dark forces be directed in such a way?"

"A Dark Magus you mean?"

Mikel nodded, not feeling the need to elaborate.

Rusan pursed his lips, frowning at Mikel's suggestion, though not disregarding it. "I do not know if such a thing is possible with the Grim. But I will not say it is impossible. We have heard rumors just as you have, Steelheart. We will not believe these rumors until we see the truth in them. But we will not ignore them either. To do so would be unwise."

"A good strategy," Mikel agreed. He offered Nat a smile as he placed a hand on her shoulder, squeezing warmly, having no desire to put her in front of a pack of hungry Grim again. "If the grasslands are barred to us, you have another way for us to reach the Tor. That's why you brought us here to this part of the Deep that you prefer to avoid."

"You know us too well, Steelheart," Rusan rumbled, giving Mikel a gentle clap on the back, careful not to knock his friend from his perch. "And it is because you are so familiar with us that you are aware of the Bloody Gates."

"I am," Mikel replied, a cold settling in the pit of his stomach. He knew what Rusan was going to say next and was dreading it.

He had never been to the Bloody Gates. And he had never had the desire to go there.

In large part because the Peikkos avoided the Bloody Gates like the plague. The stories they told about the battlefield froze his blood worse than the cold of the Frozen Waste.

"We will lead you closer to where the Bloody Gates lie. From there, you can seek the hidden passage into the Tor."

Before Nat could ask the dozens of questions that popped into her mind, Mikel raised a hand and asked her to wait. A request that proved difficult for her, yet still she acquiesced, but only by clamping her lips together and biting her tongue.

"This is the only way?"

"It is, Steelheart. I am sorry."

Mikel sighed. It seemed that this journey was only getting more demanding. For the hundredth time he wondered if the effort he was expending to assist the Queen of the Crux was worth it. Thinking of that crooked smile of hers almost made him believe that it was. Almost.

"There is nothing to be sorry about, Rusan. Thank you for your assistance."

"We do what we can, Steelheart." Rusan began walking along the root they had been standing on, turning toward the right and allowing the maze that snaked out before him to guide him in an easterly direction. "We will take you to the path that leads to the Bloody Gates."

"From there, what do I do?"

"Reveal the Blade you carry, Steelheart. Call to the Light within. Our ancestors who have passed through the Bloody Gates will answer."

31

CHARM OFFENSIVE

"This seems to be your favorite place in the Ring." Malor Dragoran strode confidently across the battlements, stopping where a graceful tower that mimicked the flames of a torch rose. It was one of eight that formed the original wall to the keep. The fortress long since expanded in all directions atop the highest crag of the Tor.

The Queen of the Crux gazed out upon Graz, the gleam of the Barbed Path just at the edge of her vision. The city covered almost every inch of free space atop the three-mile-wide plateau that loomed above the Plains. The Spike, jagged mountains cut off from the Bitter Heights, a snow-capped vista to the north. The Deep, a hazy smudge at the very edge of the horizon, to the south.

"It is a place where few come," Drin replied evenly, not feeling the need to explain more.

Although understanding that she couldn't be rude to the King of the Tor no matter how much she might want to be, needing to bide her time. She held fast to the hope that the opportunity to escape would come to her. If she was smart and disciplined. All the while the silver bracelet around her wrist that restricted her use of the Talent a constant reminder that her hope may be no more than just that.

"You seek privacy?"

"I prefer it," Drin replied. She was certain that he wouldn't take the hint.

"Then why leave your chambers?"

"Because even there I'm not alone, am I?" She offered Dragoran a meaningful look, referencing the soldiers that were always posted on the inside of her door even when she slept just a room beyond. Those same soldiers there with them now, standing at attention on the backside of the turret.

"Precautions must be taken," Malor shrugged, as if what she noted was no more than a slight inconvenience. "For your protection, of course. I can't have anything happen to you while you're in my care."

"Precautions? Where am I to go with this on my wrist, King Dragoran?" Drin demanded, her tone calm yet accusatory. She lifted her arm to accentuate her point, the bright sunlight shining off the silver.

"You may go where you will," he replied with a forced patience, "within reason, of course. I simply desire to keep you safe. There are some who seek to claim your throne in a way that involves removing you. I can't bear the thought of that happening."

Drin's eyes tightened. "Not you, King Dragoran?"

Malor smiled, his white teeth gleaming brightly. "I have made my desires clear, Celindria. Those desires have not changed."

"Forgive me if I don't demonstrate the same desire, King Dragoran," Drin replied, turning her gaze back toward the Barbed Path and hoping to end the conversation.

"Yes, I can understand why you seek some time to yourself," Malor stated after a period of silence.

He had hoped that the Queen of the Crux would come to

her senses after a few days passed. The reality of her circumstances taking root within her moving her to accept his proposal.

He hadn't expected such obstinance from her. Yet rather than angering him, it made her that much more appealing. He was never one to back down from a challenge. Especially one with such a sweet prize awaiting him.

"Is that so?" Drin mused. "I find that hard to believe."

"You are not the only one who faces challenging circumstances. Someone always seeking your time and attention. Wanting something from you. Seeking to use your position to their benefit. Thinking of themselves rather than about the good of all."

"Just as you are, King Dragoran?" Drin didn't hesitate to call out Malor on his claim. She might be at a disadvantage with the bracelet on her wrist. But she didn't require the Talent to fight this battle.

Malor smiled. He had walked right into that. "An unfortunate occurrence, Celindria, but as you know as the Queen of the Crux, those of us with power are often placed in uncomfortable and undesired positions that require us to make decisions that we don't like. As I said, decisions made in the best interests of the many, not the few."

"And that's what this is, King Dragoran? You kidnapping me not out of choice but rather out of necessity? You make a peculiar argument."

Malor frowned, seeking a new path of attack. "As I said, Celindria, as leaders of our Kingdoms, there are times when we must do what we might not want to do."

"So you're saying that you don't want to marry me?"

"I'm not saying that at all."

"Then what are you saying?" Drin lifted an eyebrow, her challenge obvious. She wanted to push him and learn just how far she could go. A moment later she wondered if she pushed too hard and too fast.

"That I don't want to marry you in this way," Malor explained. With the speed of a stinging scorpion, his hand shot out. Locking Drin's wrists in his grip, he pulled her closer so that they were no more than a foot apart. Drin had nowhere to look other than Malor's arresting eyes. "You are a beautiful woman, Celindria. The fact that you are a Magus, the power that you can control continuing to mature as you come into your potency, means little to me. The power that you exercise as the Queen of the Crux means little to me. The woman ... you ... is what interests me."

She forced herself not to pull away. She was acting a role now and she needed to stay in character. "You contradict your-self, King Dragoran." She cared little for how he played with words. The truth revealed in his voice.

"I explain myself, Queen Dengannon."

He gripped her wrists with greater strength, pulling her even closer. Drin watched as his eyes changed from one breath to the next. Spinning. Changing color as if on a whim. An enchantment seeping into her very being, Drin found that she didn't have the strength to resist. More alarming, she didn't want to resist.

His dancing orbs made it difficult for her to think much less challenge what he said or did as he stepped even closer. His presence shifted from menacing to comforting, then to warm and beguiling.

Drin began to wonder if perhaps Malor was right. That perhaps what he proposed was what she should ...

Drin shook her head ever so slightly. Refusing to be led down a path she did not want to follow, she sought to clear the fog that made it so hard for her to think. "Then please do so with greater clarity, King Dragoran, so that there will be no confusion between us."

"It is quite simple, Queen Dengannon," Malor replied with a dazzling smile that made Drin smile and then blush. "Think of the tower we stand upon as a precipice. Together, you and I, if we were to jump, we would not fall. Instead we would rise. We would rise together. There is so much that I can offer you. Just as there is so much you can offer to me. Yes, the proposal I gave you, upon first glance, appears political in nature."

He shook his head sadly, as if acknowledging that fact disappointed him deeply. "That is undeniable. But I will not hide the truth from you in that regard. Once we are together, I will never hide the truth from you. Because we will be of the same mind."

"Bold words," Drin murmured. Still smiling. A gentle heat rising within her along with a hint of warning that broke through the haze affecting her mind and making it so hard for her to think.

In a brief moment of clarity, Drin realized that Malor was so much more than he appeared to be and likely a greater threat than the Dark Magus.

"True words," Malor continued. "The proposal I make to you now does not have to be one of politics. Because I believe that if we were to join ourselves to one another, we could build a future for ourselves, for our people, that is not based on politics. We can build a future that allows us to experience the joys and pleasures of one another. The joys and pleasures that make the difficult and lonely times that we experience alone a thing of the past. Because we would be together. Always together. Of the same mind ... and the same body."

Malor's words snared Drin, her smile widening in delight as her hard-earned clarity faded. The warmth within her became a slow burn. His swirling eyes, more hypnotic than the Churn, impressed his argument upon her. Beginning to sway her.

Until the joys and pleasures that Malor referenced poked her, awakening a small voice in the back of her brain. Yet still a strong voice. The voice of a Queen not to be challenged. A Queen who did not need a man for her to live and rule as she deemed fit. The dignity and self-possession so ingrained within her by her father and uncle swept through her and burned away the haze that clouded her mind.

It was then that she realized the game she was playing was much more complex than she imagined. That the adversary standing before her had chosen to keep his true self, his true power, hidden. Until then.

Yet rather than that new knowledge causing a cold ball of fear to form in her stomach, instead she felt empowered and strangely free. Malor's enchantment no more than a memory. And Drin certain that she could use his belief in himself as a lever for her own purposes.

"And what about Assindra?" Drin purred. A hint of worry now colored her voice as, despite her distaste, she leaned into Malor, bringing her lips very close to his. "Would she not be disturbed by your interest in me? By your ... desire ... for me?" She took a step forward. Pushing up against him. Making her point just as he was trying to make his.

Malor's smile deepened as he perceived that first crack in the Queen of the Crux's armor splitting farther apart. His opportunity to shatter her defenses close at hand. "We have an understanding, my dear. For she and I are connected by nothing more than politics. A baser foundation for a relationship I cannot imagine. But with you, my dear, it could be different."

He leaned down. His whiskered cheek slid against hers. His breath tickled the curve of her neck. "There is nothing to fear from her. I promise you that. Besides, we both have a realistic perspective on the world. We understand how it really works."

"That eases my fears," Drin sighed, her expression one of pleasure even as she fought the urge to cringe at his touch.

"And there is so much more that I can ease for you, my dear. You can be sure about that."

His desire becoming painfully obvious, Drin smiled devilishly. "And how does the world work?" She leaned up so that her lips came closer to his.

Malor smiled then laughed softly. "The way we want it to, my dear. I was doing a poor job of explaining that to you. Together, we can do whatever we wish if we bind ourselves one to the other. Not just in politics. But in the matters of the heart. The matters of the flesh." He leaned down again, bringing his lips closer to hers. Just a hair separating them. Malor wanted Celindria to make the next move. If she did, she would be his forever. "Think on that. Think of what we could do, you and me, if we were to bare ourselves of the shackles holding us back."

"And what is it that you really want to do, King Dragoran? What is it that you truly desire?" Her tone was seductive, hinting that she might want exactly what he did. "Other than me, of course."

Malor couldn't stop his smile from shifting into a smirk. More than just a few cracks in his prey's armor now. She was ripe for the taking. "By binding ourselves to one another, the Splintered Empire becomes whole. And we, my Celindria ... we become one. In spirit. In heart. In body. Will you accept, my dear? Will you grace me with what only you can give me?"

Drin didn't respond right away, though she didn't say no. In part because he was being so obvious. In part because she was once again having such a difficult time retaining her thoughts.

Drin was losing her battle for clear thinking. Just a glimpse of Dragoran's swirling eyes was enough to pull her into a fog that clouded her mind.

The strain of standing against his enchantment was becoming too much for her to resist.

"More than just intriguing, King Dragoran," she replied. Then she bit her tongue so that she didn't say even more.

"You remain unconvinced by my proposal."

"I remain wary," Drin corrected, still fighting his spell.

"Why wary when I offer you so much?" Malor's expression darkened. Just for a heartbeat. His doubt and irritation finally visible. Not sure how to proceed, sensing that the cracks in her armor were knitting themselves back together, he took a risk. "Do you love someone else? A sad turn of events if true."

Drin kept her expression as it had been, pushing back against his enchantment, a cold sweat starting to work its way through her as she fought to pull her eyes from his.

"No, there is no one else," she replied in a quiet voice. Then she smiled, freeing herself from Malor's gaze as an unexpected face flashed right in front of her eyes.

A battered face.

A face that for some unknowable reason she found intriguing. Heartening.

A face that sent a surge of warmth through her.

Although startled, she kept her feet. Standing strong. Feeling like herself once more. Absolutely certain that Malor Dragoran was much more than what he appeared to be.

Malor chuckled, then laughed. "Of course there isn't." He leaned closer. His lips just a breath away from touching hers. "There is no one else my dear. Not one else but me."

Drin's first instinct when he pressed his lips against hers was to use the Talent. To teach him a lesson that he would never forget. She couldn't. The bracelet prevented her from touching the magic that flowed within her.

Her next thought was to reach for the dagger she kept on the inside of her wrist, realizing as well that she couldn't. Based on how she was positioned, his hands on her wrists, he prevented her from using the only real defense she had against him.

However, there was another reason she didn't struggle. No matter how unpleasant it might be. She gained more by surrendering than fighting. At least right then. Even as her insides churned and a hot bile scalded the back of her throat.

He kissed her just a few seconds more before releasing his grip and stepping back. Drin sighed softly, grateful for the distance between them. The fog that played at the edges of her mind gone. The immense strain of holding it back relieved. She was certain she could defend against his enchantment now, knowing exactly what to do.

"We shall continue this discussion later, my Celindria. Perhaps in a more private setting when we can get to know one another ... better."

Watching the King of the Tor exit the tower, Drin leaned back against the parapet. Her mind was racing, understanding now what she truly faced. Wondering if she had the skill and, more importantly, the strength to do what was required of her.

32

DRUDE INTERRUPTION

"I can't take much more of this. Isn't there something that we can do?" Nat asked.

The voices that had been plaguing Mikel and Nat as they worked their way through the Deep toward what the Peikkos named the Bloody Gates were growing not just louder, but also more excited. Worse, more insistent. The deafening clamor made their heads ache.

And, in Nat's opinion, more than annoying.

The cacophony of whisperings echoed incessantly in their ears, pleading, demanding, coaxing.

The voices were desperate to turn the only warm bodies to enter that part of the wood in centuries to their designs.

At first, Nat found the entire experience more than just unsettling. It was unnerving.

Then, heeding Mikel's advice as the voices didn't appear to be bothering him as much as they were her, she searched around them with the Talent.

And she discovered that there was nothing there.

Nothing but the Deep.

It started to become clear that the voices, though aggravating, couldn't do anything to her or Mikel unless they allowed them to.

A welcome revelation, which helped her to breathe a little easier and shift her attention more toward where they were going.

"All you can do is try to ignore them," Mikel explained, though the squint of his eyes suggested that was no easy task. "Think of it as having to ignore the constant barbs of a teenage girl."

Nat snorted out a laugh, unable to catch it in time. She didn't want Mikel to think that he was anything other than a clueless adult. Disappointed in herself, she did her best to recover. "Not very funny." A weak attempt, but she blamed their current circumstances for her lack of creativity.

"You laughed." Mikel's grin widened, obviously pleased to have drawn such a reaction.

"I still take exception to it."

"And that doesn't bother me in the least. Because now the voices are softer, are they not?"

Nat frowned, not realizing until he said it that indeed the voices had quieted. She confirmed her agreement with a nod. "That's how you do it? Poor attempts at sarcastic humor?" She smiled. Pleased with herself. A better response than the last one.

It was Mikel's turn to snort out a laugh. She certainly kept him on his toes. "More turning your mind away from them and focusing on what's before us. If you don't pay attention to the voices, they won't pay attention to you."

"Where are the voices coming from?" She took a step closer to Mikel, eyes widening, when her initial supposition came to mind. "Are they the voices of the dead? If we agree to what they want can they claim our bodies and consign us to their fate? Taking our places in the Natural World?"

Mikel gave Nat a quizzical expression. Less than impressed with her reasoning. "Where'd you get that idea?"

She shrugged. "Last time I trained with Finn he was talking about how there were more powers in the world than just the Talent and the Curse."

"And he didn't know if all the different types of magic that he was talking about came from the same source."

"How did you know that?" Nat demanded.

"I had the same conversation with Finn. But he didn't like my answer. So he keeps wondering about it."

"What did you tell him?"

"Something I learned from Kaduna." He scrambled up the tree root they were traveling across where it lifted into an arch that rose almost ten feet off the ground. Mikel offered Nat a hand to help her up the steep slope. "She said that where the power came from didn't matter. What mattered was how that power was used. Our intent took precedence over all else."

"That makes sense to me." She followed Mikel as he led her across the arch and then back down to a more reasonable height. Glancing ahead, she saw that the root they were walking across snaked off into the distance. "Finn didn't like that?"

"He did not," Mikel confirmed with a nod.

"I can understand why."

"You can?" For a moment, Mikel worried that Nat might have some knowledge regarding Finn's affliction, which was a closely guarded secret.

"I can. He never likes it when you don't give him an answer he doesn't agree with."

"That he doesn't," Mikel agreed with a soft chuckle. Apparently, Nat wasn't yet aware of the true crisis Finn faced. Though if she continued to work with him she would discover it. In time. It was inevitable.

"Kaduna seemed quite clever."

"More than clever." He smiled warmly as he thought about the woman who raised him. The woman who saw him for who he was. Not as the Caledonii who was not a true Caledonii.

"You said we needed to focus on what's before us."

"I did," Mikel replied, having little doubt that she would get back to that comment eventually.

"You weren't just speaking about the voices," Nat said with absolute certainty. The voices were still there, though little more than a buzz now as she blocked them out. And it seemed that the less attention paid to them, the less strength they could exert. They were now no louder than a soft whisper of the wind through long grass. Or in this case the leaves that were the size of shields that littered the ground below them.

"You really are much too clever."

"Thank you."

"How do you know I meant that as a compliment?"

"How could you not have?" Nat asked with her usual assured confidence.

Mikel bit his lip so that he wouldn't laugh. "Have you ever heard the phrase getting too big for your britches?"

"It doesn't matter if I have or not."

"Why not?" Mikel asked, curious, expecting a different reply from her.

"Because I don't wear britches." Nat gave him a grin designed to irritate. "I wear leggings."

Mikel didn't give her the pleasure of a response, not feeling the need to egg her on. Instead he enjoyed a few seconds of silence. The voices that had followed them now no more than a memory. That could mean only one thing based on what Rusan had told him. They were getting close.

"And what is really before us?" Nat asked, disappointed that her poke at Mikel failed.

"The Bloody Gates."

"Are they the gates to the afterworld as the Peikkos believe?"

"No one knows for sure, though I doubt it." He was pleased that she had been listening to his conversation with Rusan even though she had appeared to be disinterested the entire time.

"Why not?"

"Something else I learned from Kaduna. There are many places in the world like the Bloody Gates where the dead can touch the living."

"There are?"

"There are. And they are almost always associated with a place where a great many people, or Peikkos, died."

"A battlefield, you mean?"

"I do," Mikel confirmed with a nod. "When Kaduna helped me escape my homeland, we traveled through several places similar to the Bloody Gates. She actually talked to some of the spirits there. All of them soldiers killed on the battlefield. All those soldiers seeking ... I don't know what. All I know is that they never found the peace they desired when they died. Lost hopes. Lost dreams. Lost loves."

"So what happened at the Bloody Gates?"

"Not too far ahead of us is where the Peikkos fought the soldiers of Rickard Dragoran. The ruler of the Tor more than five centuries ago sought to subjugate the Peikkos after he conquered the fortress. Instead, the Peikkos took advantage of Dragoran's hubris."

"His hubris?"

"Yes, Rickard Dragoran was so certain of his victory over the Peikkos that he failed to take certain precautions. He did not send scouting missions into the Deep. He did not use the Talent to get a real sense of the battlefield. The Peikkos were able to make use of those errors."

Nat thought about that for a moment, knowing from experience that Mikel wasn't going to give her the answer. She would need to work it out for herself. It didn't take her long. "The real Deep."

"Correct," Mikel replied with a broad smile, pleased by her success. "The King of the Peikkos, Rusan's forebear, Regulus, sent dozens of small bands through the real Deep. The Peikkos traveled beneath Dragoran and his army as they advanced through the wood. Once past the attacking force, they emerged behind Dragoran."

"A classic pincer movement. The Peikkos caught Dragoran and his army in a vise."

"I'm glad that you pay attention to at least some of what I teach you."

"When it's interesting." Nat didn't want to give him full credit. And she felt the need to insert a barb as well.

Mikel didn't miss it, but he didn't say anything. He simply continued with his explanation. "Caught completely by surprise, the Peikkos drove Dragoran from the wood and claimed the Deep as their own. Nevertheless, it was not an easy fight for them. Because Dragoran employed a power that most Magii avoid."

"The Curse." Just the thought of that unnatural energy made Nat cringe. A natural reaction based on her lessons with Finn.

"Indeed. The Peikkos won, but at a great cost."

"Why wouldn't the Peikkos go with us? I would think they would want to honor those who gave their lives to ensure the freedom of their kind."

"They do that. Every year. I've had the privilege of attending the ceremony and festivities several times."

"You have? What's it like?"

Mikel raised a hand before Nat could ask any more questions. "A conversation for another time."

Nat reluctantly agreed with a disappointed grumble.

"The Peikkos believe that the battlefield is a portal to their Hall of the Dead."

"Is it?"

"The Peikkos *believe* that the Bloody Gates, where we are going, is where the veil between the living and the dead has been weakened. Irreparably so. And that if they get too close they may be pulled through the veil against their will. Though I emphasized that word for a reason. Belief is often all that matters. A belief doesn't need to be right. It just needs to be ... believed."

"Very philosophical of you," Nat said, her bored tone suggesting that she clearly was not impressed.

Mikel didn't care. "I thought so."

"The spirits of the dead remain there? We can speak to them?"

"That's the claim that's been made. Whether there's any truth to it ..." Mikel shrugged. "We'll have to see. Although what we're dealing with now, the voices, suggests that we might not be on a wild goose chase."

Nat stopped before Mikel could offer any more details on what they might be walking into. Tensing.

Noticing her reaction, Mikel halted a step later. "What's the matter?"

"You didn't see it?"

"See what?"

Nat nodded to the left. "It was right at the edge of my vision. A shadow."

That discovery normally wouldn't have bothered Mikel. After all, they were hiking through the gloom of the Deep. There were always strange shadows flitting about that shouldn't move the way they did.

Rather it was the cold of the silver amulet against his skin that put him into motion. The Blade of Light already in his hand and blazing to life at his touch.

Mikel slashed from left to right, the Blade no more than a streak of light targeting the shadow surging toward him.

Wary of the fiery steel, the Drude hissed, gliding backward.

Nat and Mikel watched as several folds of its whispery essence were cut free and flaked away. Dissolving into nothing. The creature from the Spirit World becoming less.

Before the monster could decide whether it should fight or flee, Nat struck. She enjoyed her lessons with Mikel and Teddy, although she would never admit that to either of them. However, she loved her lessons with Finn. The Magus unveiled a brand-new perspective on the world and a feeling of empowerment of which just months before she could never have conceived.

A white-hot bolt of energy shot from her palm, cutting right through the Drude whose attention was still on the glowing steel, unaware of the strike until it was too late.

With a shriek louder than a banshee's wail, the Drude shriveled in on itself, the folds of black becoming a cloud of ash that slowly drifted down to the forest floor.

"Very impressive." Mikel stood just a few feet in front of Nat and to her left. Not wanting to get in her way if she decided to use the Talent again.

"I thought so."

"And there's the humility I was expecting."

Mikel's dry humor wasn't lost on Nat. But she didn't have time to come up with an appropriate snarky reply.

Three more Druden appeared. Separating themselves from the gloom, they positioned themselves so they blocked the path Nat and Mikel had taken to reach that point in the Deep.

"Why aren't they attacking?" Wisps of the Talent slinked around her fingers, Nat ready for what she assumed would be the next attack.

Mikel believed that was an excellent question. Three Druden. Yet not one made a move toward them. Instead, they held their places. Not in a rush.

Why not?

The Druden could have been sent by only one person.

Assindra.

Yet why would she send the Druden when he was heading toward the Tor and bringing what she wanted to her?

He had little doubt that there would be a confrontation between them before this was all over. Mikel understood from the very beginning that he'd have little chance of entering Dragoran's fortress without being noticed by the Dark Magus.

The Blade so effective against the Druden also put a target on his back. One of the key reasons Nat only would be accompanying him so far. Assuming they got themselves out of this mess.

Could Assindra be hurrying him along? Herding him? Anxious to claim the item he had stolen for her. Or ...

Perhaps there was more in play.

Perhaps Assindra was playing a double game. Because if she could claim the Blade of Light for her own, she'd have little need for a partner.

What purpose would Malor Dragoran serve if she could claim the power of the artifact as her own?

She might believe that she could do that through the assistance of the Druden. That stood to reason, since she had tried much the same on the Crux. Claim the Blade. Cut loose her ally at the same time. Perhaps permanently.

Rather than wait to see which of his theories proved to be the most accurate -- the Druden herding them or seeking to kill him and take the Blade to their master – Mikel preferred to act.

"This isn't the best place for a fight," Mikel murmured.

Nat looked around, understanding his concern. They were caught out on a labyrinthine network of roots with nothing at their backs.

They could fight one Drude quite effectively, just as they demonstrated. They could probably fight two and come out of the clash alive and well, though perhaps a bit worse for wear. Three would be asking too much. The third Drude would need only wait to strike, gliding through the shadows until one of its ilk created the opportunity that it needed.

"Where then?"

"Fifty yards behind us. There are two heart trees growing on top of one another."

Nat glanced over her shoulder. Mikel was right. There seemed to be an arch connecting the two. And behind the arch was a tangle of roots that would prevent the Druden from coming at them from behind.

"Be ready."

"Try not to have too much fun," Mikel warned. He wanted to get out of this clash in one piece. Three Druden were bad enough, but he was more worried about the overeager Magus in training standing behind him who clearly was quite pleased with herself after her latest success.

"What's the point of being a Magus if you can't have any fun?"

Mikel didn't bother to reply, showing his back to Assindra's servants and sprinting toward Nat. Urging her down the curling root that would take them to the battleground he had selected.

The spikes of energy Nat sent blasting into the roots and dirt engulfed the Druden in a gritty cloud filled with razor-sharp shards, surprising the monsters and forcing them to turn away for the split-second Mikel and Nat needed to shift the battleground.

Skidding to a stop beneath the arch, Mikel caught Nat before she fell. The young Magus tripped on an item that looked like metal and stuck up out of the soft earth.

Once she had her feet under her again, together they turned.

It was as Mikel anticipated.

The trio glided out of the swirl of dirt and splinters with a deadly anticipation.

Mikel and Nat hadn't gained much time. But they had gained enough to choose the ground for the clash.

"Mikel, what is this place?"

"Not now, Nat."

"Mikel, this is important," she repeated, her voice demanding that he pay attention. "Look around us. What is this place? There's more to it than meets the eye."

Nat was right. He was so focused on the Druden that were advancing at a cautious pace, wary of his glowing scimitar and Nat's ability, that he hadn't been paying attention to all that was around them.

He could sense it. The Deep never felt comfortable. Even for him. And he had journeyed through the wood, both above and below, more than anyone else in the Splintered Empire. Yet here …

He frowned. Was that what had caused Nat to stumble? A helmet? If so, it was much too large for him. Made for a …

Understanding came to him. Just to his left, the hilt of a sword stuck up out of the ground. And in the deep loam to his right, he glimpsed the outline of a spear as large as a harpoon.

All of the martial items were too big for a man and made specifically for a Giant.

If he was right, then the ground he had picked for the clash could be …

Mikel glanced over his shoulder. Roots twisted above them, forming an arch.

And the roots behind the arch were twisted into a design unlike anything he had ever seen in the Deep.

Those twisting roots appeared to be a gate.

Having a few more seconds before the Druden were upon them, he studied the ground with a closer eye. The layer of dirt wasn't very deep here. Glancing to either side he picked out more items that confirmed his suspicions.

Another spear was lying in the loam.

A helmet with twisted horns sat atop it.

A shield that was twice as large as the scuta the Blood Company were famed for using lay partially buried in the ground.

Finally, the skeleton of a Giant was propped up against the heart tree to his right, the roots growing around the bones obscuring Mikel's perspective until he knew what he was looking for.

Rusan's directions had proven accurate.

Not just a gate.

The Bloody Gates.

"Mikel!"

He picked up his gaze at Nat's call. They were out of time. The Druden were almost upon them, the fight about to begin again. And this a fight that he and Nat stood little chance of surviving much less winning.

"Reveal the Blade you carry, Steelheart," Rusan had said before he and Nat left the Giants of the Deep. *"Call to the Light within and our ancestors who have passed through the Bloody Gates will answer."*

The Blade of Light was revealed. He held it in his hand. The steel blazed just as brightly as it usually did.

But how was he supposed to call to the Light?

What did that even mean?

Was there more to the power contained within the scimitar?

Or was it more that the Blade of Light was a tool? A catalyst? A way for the Bearer to harness the Light?

Mikel didn't know for sure. And although his theory made sense to him, he had no time to explore it further.

The Druden were no more than ten yards away. Drawing inexorably closer, Nat prepared to unleash another blast of the Talent.

"Call to the Light."

He knew that he needed to shift his focus to the creatures

from the Spirit World, but that comment by Rusan was stuck in his brain. Running on a continuous loop.

"Call to the Light."

Surrendering to his instincts, Mikel did the only thing that came to mind.

The shield of a fallen Peikko right at his feet, he knelt, slamming the hilt of the Blade of Light against the rusted steel with a bone-jarring force that sent an uncomfortable tingle up his arm.

The blast of light that erupted turned dusk into day.

The gloom pushed back.

And then farther back still.

The Druden with it.

The glow grew stronger with each breath Mikel took. The energy coming from the Blade of Light and from him burned brighter than the rising sun.

He felt the change in the Blade then. The power that he had unleashed intensified. The Light blinding. Yet for some reason he didn't need to turn away. He didn't need to shield his eyes.

He was one with the Blade.

He was one with the Light.

He stared across at the Druden, the creatures of the Spirit World now deeper within the heart trees, unwilling to step into the brilliance crafted by the scimitar.

That's when Mikel felt the change that was occurring.

What he had done.

How he had untethered the natural laws.

The worlds of the living and the dead drew closer.

Joining.

Becoming one.

Right there at the Bloody Gates.

Right where he was standing.

A gust of air swept through the Deep, the branches above shaking, the leaves rattling. And then all was still. A bone-chilling cold settled within the space illuminated by Mikel's ancient Blade.

He sensed it then.

He and Nat were no longer alone.

He watched in amazement as misty essences drifted up and out of the soft loam of the Deep.

Those essences took shape.

They stood next to Mikel.

They stood taller than Mikel.

Bigger.

Broader.

Having a heavy weight despite lacking in substance.

The spirits of the dead Peikkos who gave their lives to ensure their brethren's freedom took shape around him.

Warriors from the battle past.

Hearing Mikel's call, they answered the Blade of Light.

And they were prepared for a new clash.

Because here, at the Bloody Gates, the spirits of the Peikkos ruled.

33

GUIDED BY THE SPIRIT

"What did you do, Mikel?" Nat's gaze was fixed on the Druden, the monsters staying at the edge of the light. She wasn't certain if she should provoke them with a few blasts of the Talent.

"What Rusan told me to do."

"And that's keeping the Druden away from us?"

"In part perhaps. I think the larger reason is behind us."

Nat glanced over her shoulder, almost losing her grasp on the Talent when she saw what greeted her.

Spirits.

Peikkos.

The Giants of the Deep stood right at their backs.

Hundreds of them if not thousands.

They looked as they did in life except for the haziness of their forms. Flickering in and out. There than not. The link between the Natural World and the Spirit World a fragile and tenuous one. The balance in a continuous tension.

"The Army of the Peikkos," she whispered, not certain if she should be afraid or pleased.

"That we are," a spirit said, gliding to the front of the long-dead warriors aligned before the Bloody Gates. "All hail two unafraid of the Ancient One's servants."

"Maximus," Mikel murmured in quiet awe.

"You know your history, lad." The spirit chuckled and offered Mikel a warm smile. Or as warm as could be when you were centuries dead.

"Enough," Mikel admitted. Grateful once again for Kaduna taking such a strong interest in his education. "Rusan Rule-breaker sends his greetings. The Giants of the Deep stand as strong as the trees."

"I expect no less, lad." Maximus nodded in approval, pleased to hear that his ancestor remained true to his heritage. "We died here. We must stay here. But still we watch. Rusan has done well, just as I knew he would, though the real test is not yet upon us."

"The real test?" Nat asked, her confusion deepening. She never anticipated that they'd actually engage with the spirits of the dead.

"More on that later, Magus," Maximus promised, offering Nat a nod of respect that made her blush. He then turned his attention to Mikel. "You're worried about the Druden."

Mikel nodded. The monsters obviously desired to attack, likely compelled to do just that. Yet they were unable to do so, keeping to the edge of the light and refusing to engage with the spirits.

"Have no fear, lad. We will hold them. And if they decide to get frisky, well, we haven't had a good fight in quite some time." Maximus' dead eyes sparked with delight at the thought of a ruckus. "My Peikkos would be happy to set straight these abominations that have no place in the Natural World."

At that proclamation, the spirits standing behind Mikel surged forward until they were at the very edge of the illumination provided by the Blade of Light. Going no farther. Not needing to.

The Druden faded back into the gloom, demonstrating a caution that Mikel doubted their master would appreciate.

"That's what I thought," Maximus snorted in disgust. "The Ancient One and his servants rule the Spirit World. They do not rule here."

A rumble of agreement from the Peikkos army followed Maximus' pronouncement.

"Who is Maximus?" Nat asked Mikel in a whisper.

He smiled. Another item he would need to add to her lessons when there was time. Before he could explain, Maximus did.

"I might be dead, Magus, but I'm not deaf. I am Maximus Rulebreaker, a many times removed forebear of Rusan, and the leader of these spirits, these brave Peikkos who gave their lives in the fight against Rickard Dragoran."

"You honor us, Maximus." Mikel offered the spirit general a slight tilt of his head in respect. "We were ready to fight, but it wasn't a fight that we were looking forward to."

"Understandable," Maximus muttered, "although by the looks of you, you've gotten yourself into a great many scrapes and gotten out of them as well, so you know your way around a blade."

"I have more experience with steel than I care to."

"Spoken like a true warrior." The Peikkos spirits murmured their agreement once again at their general's comment. "Accompanied by a humility that is to be valued."

"My thanks, Maximus. But you give me too much credit."

"Perhaps. Perhaps not. We shall see." Maximus stared in the direction the Druden had gone. "You've stirred up quite the hornet's nest."

"Not by choice."

"Once more, spoken like a true warrior." Maximus motioned toward Mikel's Blade. "I have not seen that scimitar since I was a boy, and then it was in the hand of a Giant."

"I'm honored to carry it," Mikel said with an honest modesty.

"As you should be," Maximus murmured. "Very few are chosen to bear the Blade. None until you not of the Giants, either of the Deep or the Rime."

"Which is why I am so honored."

"You don't know why you were selected?"

Mikel frowned, then shook his head ruefully. "If I did, I would tell you. I only know that the Blade and I are now ..."

"Linked," Maximus finished for Mikel. "Yes, that is the start. And you will learn more if you continue to draw breath, because the Blade is more than a weapon. It offers a great deal and demands even more in return."

"So I've discovered."

Maximus nodded. "You are learning about what comes with the Blade?"

"I am."

Maximus didn't know what to make of the fact that Mikel carried a weapon with a long history tied to the Giants of the Rime and the Deep. Yet, in what he saw from the young man, both his skill with the magicked steel and his steely determination, he couldn't fault the decision made by the ancient weapon. Because the weapon had never proven wrong before. "Who wants the Blade of Light?"

"Assindra, ally to Malor Dragoran."

"A Dark Magus?"

"Unfortunately, yes."

Mikel referencing the King of the Tor led to a murmur of disgust running through the assembled spirits that didn't quiet until Maximus gave a sharp command for silence. "Malor Dragoran? There's another one?"

Mikel didn't respond right away, mulling Maximus' question. A flicker of doubt followed closely by a potential insight passed through his mind. "Why do you ask?"

"When my nephew killed Rickard Dragoran, the line ended. At least that's what we believed."

"You're certain of that?"

"Why do you ask, lad? You've got a look about you that's making me nervous."

"Just thinking about something I haven't thought about before." Mikel would need to talk with Finn. The Magus might be in a position to aid him in his search. If what he was thinking was correct, all that was occurring in the Splintered Empire was beginning to make a terrible kind of sense. "The histories show an unbroken line of Dragorans ruling the Tor. But those histories …"

"Were written by the Dragorans," Maximus concluded, pursuing the same track of thought as Mikel was.

"Correct. I'll need to look into that."

"You should, because if this Dark Magus is after the Blade of Light along with this Malor Dragoran, then based on what I know …"

"I understand."

"I hope you do, lad. Because if I'm right, three Druden and a Dark Magus are the least of your worries." Maximus sighed then. "Now what would you have of us, Lightcrafter?"

"Lightcrafter?" Nat voiced Mikel's confusion.

Maximus frowned at Mikel, then slowly nodded as understanding dawned. "You don't know yet, do you?" The spirit general shook his head, almost amused. "Enjoy your ignorance for a little while longer, for you will find out soon enough. Now what would you have of us, Bladebearer?"

"HAVE NO FEAR, LITTLE MAGUS," Maximus intoned. "They will not bother you and the Lightcrafter so long as my brothers and sisters are with you."

Nat nodded, not saying a word. Still, her eyes never strayed from the black bog off to their left. Their trackers hadn't revealed themselves, but she knew that they were there. She could see them gliding just beneath the surface, leaving wakes and ripples in the muck.

Creepers.

Just like the Druden, the kings of the bog were wary of the ghostly Peikkos who led her and Mikel toward the base of the Tor. The crag rose more than a mile into the sky, blocking the sun and putting them into an early dusk. It was a league wide and much like the Crux on the other side of the Splintered Bridge. The key distinction was the lack of four rivers meeting around its base. A dense wood mixed with swamp that came to a stop at the foundation of the promontory served that function.

Upon leaving the Bloody Gates, Maximus and his troop led Nat and Mikel back down into the real Deep, traveling beneath the heart trees and then the grasslands that separated that dark forest from the flat-topped mountain that was their goal. Although not to the very bottom. Instead, the Peikkos took them across a system of roots closer to the surface that resembled bridges and ladders before it gave way to a single tunnel from which they had emerged only moments before.

The entire time they were hidden from the many patrols that guarded the Tor. Malor Dragoran was certain in his power, yet not so arrogant as to believe that no one would dare to challenge him if he displayed even the slightest hint of weakness.

"How do you know of this path, Maximus?" Nat needed to talk about something besides what lurked near them. Her last encounter with the Creepers was too fresh in her mind.

"The dead do not reveal the secrets of the dead."

Nat couldn't argue with that. The natural tunnel of vines, roots, and dirt leading below the plain had been dry and musty, a strong breeze gusting through every so often. The smell and the cold made her think of a crypt.

"Very mysterious," Nat replied. Lips pursed. Her snarkiness thick.

Maximus enjoyed her response, laughing softly. "I must have what fun I can. I'm a spirit after all. Tied to the Deep and the Bloody Gates."

"That I can understand."

"Thank you for your forbearance," he said with all seriousness. "In truth, the Splintered Empire was built on the backs of the dead. The Tor especially so. We know the paths that the living do not."

"And for that we are grateful." Mikel strode next to Maximus on his other side.

"And we are grateful to serve. It has been too long." The spirit's eyes flashed when he glanced to his right. "A request, Lightcrafter."

"If it's in my power."

"It is. Or it will be."

Mikel didn't know how to respond to that, so he simply nodded.

"The time will come when the living will battle the dead. Call to us in your time of need. We may be dead, but still we fight for the living."

"Of course," Mikel replied in a solemn tone. Not quite understanding what Maximus meant, not sure that he wanted to understand because of what the spirit implied, still he didn't want to deny his request just because of his lack of comprehension.

Maximus grunted with pleasure, then halted. The Peikko escort stopped with him.

"We go no farther."

"Why not?" Nat asked.

"Because Little Magus though you cannot sense it yet, we

can," Maximus explained. "There is a dark power set around the Tor. Consuming it. Hunting within it. If we were to enter, we would reveal ourselves. And in so doing we would reveal you."

"Something I would like to avoid," Mikel admitted. "Although in all truth I wish that I could have you and your fighters with me, Maximus. I doubt any in the Tor could stand against you."

Maximus stood a bit taller at the praise. "As would we. But it cannot be."

"My thanks then, Maximus."

"There is no need for thanks. We do what we must. Not what is beyond us."

"And you will take Nat to the place you referenced? Where she'll be safe until I exit the Tor?"

"You have my word, Lightcrafter."

"Thank you, Maximus." Mikel really wished that he had the time to talk more with Maximus about the title the Giant had bestowed upon him. Not understanding the reference and wanting to. But he didn't. With the Druden still in play, he needed to keep moving. "All honor to the Peikkos."

"All honor to the Lightcrafter," Maximus intoned, treating the leave-taking with the solemnity of a sacred ceremony. He then glided backward, giving Nat the space to talk privately with Mikel.

"I still don't like this."

"You've made your position quite clear." Mikel understood that Nat wasn't arguing with him. She simply needed to say what she needed to say.

"I could prove useful while you're going after Drin."

"I can't argue with you about that."

"But you're still going to make me miss out on the fun."

Mikel smiled at Nat's characterization. What she described as fun was going to be anything but.

"We talked about this," he said quietly in a tone that brooked no argument, "and Maximus agreed."

"I know, I know. I'd just put more of a target on your back. Assindra and Malor would get a fix on us as soon as we entered the Tor because I can use the Talent." She hmphed, clearly not happy. "I just don't like leaving you ..." She had more to say, but she didn't know that she could.

Mikel smiled then pulled her in for a hug. "I know," he said, talking to her hair. "I don't like leaving you either. You've grown on me."

"I've grown on you?" Nat released her hold on Mikel as he stepped back from her and made his way toward the last of the trees and the Tor beyond.

"Yes ... kind of like a fungus." He offered a smile and a bark of a laugh before he disappeared within the gloom of the wood.

"Funny," Nat grumbled, although she said it with a smile. She of all people appreciated sarcastic humor. "Maximus, why do you call Mikel the Lightcrafter?"

The Peikko general glided up to her, his soldiers forming around them again. They did not have far to go, but it required traversing more of the swamp. He had promised the Lightcrafter that he would keep the Little Magus safe, and he would. "Because he has earned the title even if he doesn't understand why."

"Because he carries the Blade of Light now?" She was already worried about Mikel. She understood why he needed to do this on his own. Still, she wasn't happy about it.

"In part, yes. But there is more to it than that." He looked down at the Little Magus, liking her fierce countenance. A true warrior, just like the one who had claimed her. "The Steelheart bears the Blade of Light. That is true. But the artifact is only a tool. The real power of the Lightcrafter comes from within. When the Steelheart unlocks that secret, he will be a sight to behold, because the power within him was meant for more than just destroying."

"You can't help Mikel unlock this secret?"

"No," Maximus replied with a sad shake of his head. "He must do it on his own." He sighed then. "He must do it on his own or die trying."

MIKEL FROWNED as he stared at the rock that blocked his way. A hint of anxiety warmed his chest.

Craning his neck, he saw nothing other than the slate grey stone of the Tor and the rapidly dwindling daylight far above him. He was losing what little time he had earned thanks to the Peikkos.

He needed to be inside the Tor before full dark.

But how to do that?

He was certain that he was in the right place based on the description Maximus gave him. But the Peikko general hadn't given him much more instruction beyond that.

"Trust in the Blade," the Giant of the Deep had said with a strange reverence.

What was that supposed to mean?

He did trust in the Blade, the steel unbreakable. A keen edge that never needed to be sharpened. The weapon had proven its worth the instant Mikel took it in hand.

Yet none of that mattered with respect to his current challenge.

"Trust in the Blade," he murmured to himself quietly.

Thinking back on what little Finn was able to tell him about the Blade of Light, and not knowing what else to do, he pulled the scimitar from the scabbard across his back. The ancient steel glowed with an ethereal brilliance as soon as his fingers touched the hilt.

A small smile cracked Mikel's grim visage.

The stone blocking his path responded in an entirely unexpected way. Lines of power and runic symbols sprang to life on the rockface, outlining a doorway large enough for three Peikkos to walk through standing shoulder to shoulder.

Mikel was more than pleased. He was thrilled. A rare occurrence for him.

A good first step.

Yet there was more to do and he wasn't sure how to do it.

"Trust in the Blade," he repeated.

Maximus had been quite succinct yet explicit with that instruction. And perhaps that was it. Perhaps he needed to do something he rarely did.

He needed to place his trust in someone else.

Or in this case something else.

A power he didn't fully understand.

A knowledge that made him distinctly uncomfortable.

Closing his eyes, Mikel brought the gleaming steel to his forehead, enjoying the cool touch of the metal as a spark of energy surged through his body.

When he opened his eyes, he wasn't surprised to see who stood before him.

Knute Frost Lord.

King of the Giants of the Rime a few generations before Cadmus.

A former Bearer of the Blade.

Now tied to the Blade just like every other Bearer.

His essence part of the artifact's collective consciousness.

"You are learning, Steelheart." A broad smile broke the towering figure's craggy features.

Mikel snorted softly at the praise. "Slowly, Frost Lord, but that's kind of you to say." His expression became more discerning. "Maximus didn't want to come too close to the Tor. He was concerned that Malor Dragoran would spy him out."

"Malor Dragoran!" scoffed Knute, his anger and distaste for the ruler of the Tor making his wispy body shimmer for several seconds before he regained control over his temper and, as a result, his form. "The Dragorans are a curse upon what was once the Frozen Waste. How they could still rule I do not understand. They should have died out long ago, and for a time I thought they had. In fact, when I ruled the Giants of the Rime, I took a unique pleasure in doing all that I could to remove as many Dragorans from the Natural World as possible."

Knute's comments caught Mikel's ear, bringing to the forefront his conversation with Maximus and his own suspicions. Unfortunately, now was not the time to pursue what was percolating in his mind.

"Have no fear, Steelheart. Dragoran will not be aware of my presence nor yours so long as we desire that to be the case."

"You're to be my guide?"

The spirit of the long-dead Frost Lord nodded. "I am. I used to rule here when the ice and snow covered what is now called the Splintered Empire. I know the Tor better than any other. I will get you where you need to go."

Mikel certainly wouldn't turn down the offered assistance, even though he already had a good sense as to how to navigate the bastion. Much like the Citadel atop the Tor, he was quite familiar with the hidden passageways that cut through the Ring like worms through the soft earth of the Deep. Although a problem remained.

"I appreciate your help, Frost Lord. But before we begin, perhaps you could offer a hint as to how I'm supposed to get past this door?"

"So much to learn in so little time," Knute murmured, his quiet tone still a deep rumble. "You need only will it, Steelheart, and your will be done. Such is the way of the Lightcrafter."

There it was again.

Lightcrafter.

Mikel was getting tired of receiving vague references from those more knowledgeable than he was as to what might come his way in the future. Most of which he didn't understand. All of which offered an indication of risk and danger that he would have preferred to avoid.

But, again, a topic for another time. The sun was sinking quickly in the west with the darkness only held at bay by the gleaming carvings that revealed the door.

Having no real sense of what to do, that failure pushing Mikel to listen to his instincts, he did much as Cadmus and Knute instructed.

Placing his hand on the glowing stone, he willed the doorway to open. The already bright light sparked in response. Its radiance blinding.

~

"CAN YOU SENSE THEM, STEELHEART?" The spirit whispered in the back of Mikel's brain, taking up residence in the Bearer of the Blade's head after he faded away.

Mikel nodded, not saying anything. Their hunters were close, and he didn't want to reveal where he was.

Knute had proven his worth as soon as they entered the Tor. He guided Mikel unerringly through the warren of caverns and hollows that formed the base of the crag. They didn't stop until they reached the deepest cellar.

It was here, on the lowest floor, in what had once been used as a jail -- and something worse based on what Mikel had seen in the room he had just exited -- that Mikel came to a halt.

The air had shifted around him in a way that didn't feel right.

He and Knute were no longer alone.

Some other creatures lurked just beyond his perception.

Drawing closer, they were getting ready to strike.

"I cannot aid you in this. If I do, Dragoran will be made aware of our presence."

"I'll handle it," Mikel confirmed, speaking to the former Bearer of the Blade as if he knelt right next to him.

"Be careful, Steelheart. What approaches is not what it seems."

Another obscure warning. *"Speak plainly, Knute."*

"Only the Blade of Light can aid you against what comes."

Before Mikel could take issue with his guide's latest piece of incomplete advice, he was moving.

The attack came from his right. No more than a whisper of movement.

Mikel rolled out of the way. A claw with nails several inches long scraped against the large rock that Mikel had been hiding behind rather than across his back.

Mikel kept moving, aware that more than one hunter was in the corridor with him.

Another claw streaked by his face. Sparks flashed when the keen nails struck the wall right where his head had been just a heartbeat before.

Seeking more room to maneuver, Mikel darted into the open doorway that he felt more than saw. Turning quickly, he placed the far wall at his back, having no doubt that his hunters would come to him.

He didn't have long to wait.

Sensing the space around him becoming more crowded, Mikel called to the Light, his scimitar blazing to life. His attackers were still no more than shadows at the very edge of the brilliance, but that was all that he required.

For the next several minutes, Mikel pushed everything else out of his mind except for what he needed to do to stay alive. Gliding about the chamber with a grace that mirrored that of his hunters, he sliced and slashed, lunged and parried.

Blocking claw with steel.

Earning not a single hit on his adversaries yet just as important his adversaries not earning a hit on him.

His attackers were big. Bigger than him. Though not as big as Knute.

They were animals of some type.

Mikel couldn't tell what.

The gloom hid them too well.

Only the claws that sought his flesh were visible, and even then just for the few breaths when they crossed the boundary from dark to light.

"Only the Blade of Light can aid you against what comes," Knute whispered again in the back of Mikel's mind. *"But not the steel itself."*

"You didn't mention that last part," Mikel grumbled as he continued the dangerous dance that was keeping him alive.

"I didn't have the time."

Mikel ducked and rocked backward, a claw slashing through the air just above his head, then stepped forward. Avoiding another claw that was scarcely more than a shadow, he offered a counterstroke. His steel sang through the space behind him.

All the while Mikel understood that he would gain nothing for his effort other than the chance to try again as the creature glided backward with little difficulty.

Cursing in frustration, Mikel raised his steel just in time to catch the slash from the other hunter that sought to take him in the hip while he was occupied.

"I can trust you in this?" Mikel understood the precariousness of his circumstances. That he was engaged in a losing battle. *"If I do as you ask I won't die a gruesome death?"*

"Not if you do it correctly."

Mikel almost laughed at the Frost Lord's response. That was asking quite a lot since he had little idea as to what he was doing to begin with. *"And it won't alert Dragoran?"*

The Frost Lord did not reply right away, apparently unconcerned by the threat posed by Mikel's hunters as he took his time considering Mikel's question.

The two creatures now drifting in and out of the light were getting bolder. They were less concerned about Mikel's efforts to defend himself.

One looked like a wolf, though twice as large. The other resembled a panther and was jet black in color. Hence their ability to hide in the darkness.

Mikel found his discovery disconcerting. A wolf in this part of the world made sense. But a panther?

No, those animals lived far to the south. Why would one be here of all places? And why were the two beasts so unnaturally large?

"I don't believe it would. The power you exercise is one that he desires but one that he does not understand. He should not sense it."

Mikel growled. He had hoped for a more definitive response all the while knowing that he wasn't going to get one, not with his two attackers about to come at him again. *"So be it."*

Mikel then went against his instincts and did something that made him more nervous than swimming in the Churn. He stepped back and held his sword next to his leg, allowing the power coursing along the steel to wink out.

The chamber was now in complete darkness.

Mikel couldn't see his hunters.

His hunters couldn't see him.

Their snarls gave the creatures away.

Mikel certain that they were about to attack.

He stood ready, confident, despite being at a distinct disadvantage.

As soon as he felt the air to his front shift, Mikel did as Knute commanded. He used the Blade of Light, but not the steel itself.

He called to the power hidden within the weapon, the

power that was within him, a discovery that unsettled him and that he was not in a position to explore despite his desperate desire to do so. A blinding light erupted within the chamber that revealed the wolf and panther.

The creatures stalking toward him staggered back, blinded momentarily by the stunning brightness.

The light radiated out from Mikel, bathing everything around him in a crackling brilliance.

He felt like he stood in the center of a lightning storm. The electricity surged through him. Around him. On him.

And though this was all new to him, it felt strangely familiar. As if a door within himself that had been locked for longer than he could remember had been unlocked and all he needed to do now was push it open.

The beasts on the verge of finding their footing, Mikel gave that door just a slight nudge. That was all that it took.

As he savored a power that made him feel more alive than he ever had before, he wondered if this was what it was like to truly be Caledonii. He felt a sense of completeness that had evaded him for so long.

He pushed his thoughts away in an instant. It was time for the here and now, not the what was or could be.

Having lost the comfort of the darkness but having regained their senses, the beasts launched themselves at Mikel. Certain of their victory. Unafraid of the one who stood against them.

Mikel was more than ready to test the power unleashed within him.

Scimitar still held against his thigh, he raised his hand before the beasts' paws left the ground.

Two streaks of energy shot from his palm. One right after the other.

The first struck the wolf. The second the panther. The result the same.

The creatures shrieked in shocked agony, crashing back against the far wall and sliding down the stone. Silent. No more than corpses now, charred and smoking.

Yet it wasn't the smell of burnt meat that threatened to unnerve Mikel.

It was the realization that he had killed his hunters with the Light.

Kaduna came to mind as he relished the energy flowing through him. Concluding that the woman who raised him, who had spent so much time teaching him control, had done so to ensure that he could control the power within him without even needing to think about it.

Only now did Mikel realize what that meant. And he was not yet certain if what she had done was a betrayal or a gift.

He never comprehended that the energy was dormant within him. Released thanks to Knute's instruction. Finn correct in his initial estimation.

What Mikel viewed as a hole within himself, a lacking, was not that at all. Rather, it was a pressure point just waiting to be released.

Shutting down his emotions for now, Mikel concentrated on what was in front of him.

Werebeasts.

Creatures of legend.

Crafted centuries before for a specific purpose.

Created by an evil long thought eradicated from the Natural World.

Knute appeared once more in his ethereal form as Mikel stared down at what remained of his hunters. The beasts were caught mid-change when they died. Some characteristics human. Others animal. Taken together an unnatural hatching.

Mikel had assumed that the greatest peril he would face during his attempt to rescue Drin would come from Assindra.

The Dark Magus was the obvious threat, notwithstanding the Druden she so liked to employ.

Yet now he realized that Assindra was but one threat. And the lesser of the two, in fact.

"Do you understand what you truly face now, Steelheart? Who Malor Dragoran truly is?"

"I do." Mikel had suspected. Gaining confirmation in this way didn't make him feel any better.

He didn't think he could be surprised by much of anything after all that he had seen and experienced, but clearly he was mistaken. More worrisome, the task that he had set for himself had just gotten a great deal harder. The potential for a fatal conclusion, for him, much more real.

"Then I leave you for now, Steelheart." Knute offered Mikel a nod of respect. "Good luck and be wary, for Dragoran's minions are nothing compared to Dragoran himself."

34

HELLO AGAIN

"This is not the position I want to be in," Drin murmured.

She was speaking to herself. Again. Common for her when she was feeling stressed or worried.

Her father's disapproving look flashed in her mind, a reminder of what he viewed as a bad habit.

She, on the other hand, believed that engaging in a dialogue with herself helped to get her to a solution faster.

Especially in difficult circumstances when even more difficult decisions needed to be made. Like now.

Drin stalked around her chamber like a caged beast. She was more than worried about her last encounter with Malor. She was frightened.

Worse, she believed that she had few if any options left to extricate herself from her current situation.

She was free to wander through much of the Tor, but she was a prisoner all the same. All thanks to the slim piece of silver encircling her wrist.

She growled in frustration. Nothing had worked. She could sense the Talent but couldn't touch it. A form of torture in and of itself. And she couldn't cut through the silver. She had tried.

All she had succeeded in doing was snapping her dagger and almost slicing her wrist.

So nowhere to go.

And no way to cancel out the magic that prevented her from touching the Talent.

Rather than giving into her frustration, Drin calmed herself. Thinking. Considering. Her way of addressing challenges wasn't working. Perhaps another perspective would prove more useful.

"What would Mikel do?" she grumbled.

From her vantage point standing in front of the doors that led out to the balcony, Graz spread out below her. However, she saw little of the grand view.

Instead, she saw the rough-and-tumble face with the crooked nose that revealed a keen intelligence that tended toward cunning.

"Why would you care about what Mikel would do?" Liria glided into the room on silent feet unannounced and uninvited, the thick carpet masking her entrance.

Drin's gaze narrowed, eyes flashing with anger. Liria was a dangerous adversary. Just as lethal as Malor Dragoran in her own way.

Yet that didn't concern Drin so much as the tension that crackled between them. Therefore, she forced herself to adopt a neutral expression, all the while believing that despite the risk involved she might be able to use that tension against the woman.

"Why wouldn't you?" Drin replied, cursing herself under her breath for what she perceived was a lame reply. She should have done better than that. She knew there was a connection between this woman and Mikel. She didn't know the details, though she could guess.

"You believe that he's on his way to rescue you?" Liria chuckled, shaking her head in scorn as if she were lecturing a dreamy young girl on the realities of the world. She circled Drin like a lioness eyeing up a challenger to her place in the pride before smiling thinly and sitting down on one of the many couches set around the spacious living room. "How very sad."

"And you think that I require Mikel's assistance to escape from you?" Drin shook her head, incorporating a heavy dose of dismay in her expression. "Such a limiting and archaic view."

Liria stared at Drin, eyes narrowing, lips curling from a grin to a smirk. Then she nodded toward the silver bracelet around the Queen of the Crux's wrist, reminding her captive of her fate. "Without being able to touch the Talent, you have no choice but to make your play with a dagger. You wouldn't get very far. And unlike Assindra or Malor, I have no compunction about marking you. In fact, I would welcome the chance. It would be a good reminder that you are not all that you believe yourself to be."

Drin didn't reply right away. Instead, she studied the woman sitting so casually in front of her. A woman who clearly had little respect for rank or title, and little to no respect for her. "Give me a dagger and we can find out."

Liria's smirk deepened, tempted by the veiled threat. She laughed softly upon seeing the broken blade on the table to the side.

She had come here because Liria felt the need to better understand why Mikel would do so much for the woman sitting on the Crux throne. And she was beginning to believe that the catalyst involved more than just business between them. She saw some of herself in the young woman standing in front of her. The defiance. The strength of will. The impulse to push back when pushed back against a wall.

Liria pulled a dagger from the sheath on her belt. Not a fancy weapon, though well made. After examining how the light from the lamps played off the steel, Liria looked up. A challenge in her voice and gaze. "You believe that you can best me with this?" She extended the dagger as if she were offering it to the Queen of the Crux.

Drin's smile mirrored Liria's. "There's only one way to find out."

Liria nodded her head several times as she examined Drin. Then with a flourish she slammed the dagger back into its sheath. "Perhaps another time."

"You're afraid to face me?" Drin asked in a contemptuous tone. "How ... unsurprising."

"Afraid to face you?" Liria laughed. "No. I'd be more than happy to give you the spanking you deserve."

"I'm right here. Why not try?" Drin offered Liria a challenging glare.

"Because if I gave in to my desires and gave you that spanking, there are those who would be less than pleased."

"You're afraid of Assindra?" It was Drin's turn to chuckle softly. "That doesn't say much for the strength of your spine."

"Her? No, not afraid, though I am cautious," Liria explained with surprising honesty, her eyes clouding with a concern that swiftly drifted away, the insolent spark that was usually there returning in a flash. "Malor Dragoran as well. I may not work for him directly, but there is something about Malor Dragoran that burns away my natural desire to challenge him."

"An assassin and kidnapper afraid of the King of the Tor?" Drin tsked. She shook her head in disappointment, trying to work her way beneath her captor's skin even though she couldn't fault the woman's perspective.

Malor Dragoran troubled her in a way that she couldn't explain either. It was much like coming to the realization that in some parts of the Realms, the wilds and wilderness, man was still the prey and not the predator. With Malor, though she didn't like to admit the truth, she felt no better than the quarry.

Liria ignored the attempted insult. Unconcerned with the

truth her captive offered. Even willing to offer some advice. Not because she cared about the Queen of the Crux's fate. Rather because Celindria Dengannon might prove to be a useful tool for a little while longer. "I would advise that you step cautiously around him. He is not what he seems."

"Why would you warn me? You're one of the reasons I'm here."

Her forearms on her thighs, Liria leaned forward. Pleased that the Queen of the Crux took a step back from her. She hadn't lost the sense of menace she had worked so diligently to cultivate. "You're just a business deal, Queenie. No more than that. The sooner you understand that the better."

Drin thought about what Liria said. Allowing the woman's disrespect to wash off her, she identified an opportunity hidden within her words. "Are you seeking to conduct some private business between us?" Drin's gaze sharpened. Assindra had bought Liria. Why couldn't Drin do the same?

"Don't get your hopes up. I won't betray those two. If you're seeking some way to get yourself out of this mess, you'll have to find some other way."

"Then why are you here?" Drin demanded, aggravated that she couldn't seem to acquire the pieces she needed to play a proper game.

"Because of the knight in shining armor you so desperately hope will risk his life to save you, overcoming the many challenges placed in his way to take you away from here so that he can recite poems of his undying devotion and love," Liria snorted scornfully. "A fairy tale come to life."

It was Drin's turn to smile thinly, finally understanding what was driving Liria's interest in her. "Mikel? That's why you're here? You seek to get to him through me?"

Liria leaned back into the couch, trying to adopt the cool composure with which she usually glided through the world. "A long time ago Mikel was important to me." She paused, wanting to make sure the Queen of the Crux understood just how important. "He is becoming important to me again."

Drin nodded. Not really surprised by that admittance, and not betraying what she was feeling. At least now the larger picture was beginning to take shape. "And you don't understand his ... attraction ... to someone like me." Drin believed that she had found Liria's pressure point.

"You give yourself too much credit, Queenie. Attraction? I would suggest instead passing interest."

"You think Mikel has an issue with commitment?"

"He did," Liria confirmed. "Except with me."

"Strange then."

"What is strange?" Liria found Drin's expression, one of confidence and certainty, more than just off putting. The veiled taunt burrowed within her in a bad way.

"Well, you note that Mikel has an issue with commitment. Yet every time I have had need of him, he has been there for me. No matter where I might be. No matter the challenge or danger." Drin offered a lift of her eyebrows, her expression shifting to a question. One hand on her hip, she placed her left foot slightly forward then leaned back, her left foot slowly tapping. Her pose obviously setting Liria's teeth on edge. "Very strange indeed."

Drin smiled then. A smile that demonstrated a knowledge and experience well beyond her years. "In fact, I doubt if I could get rid of him if I wanted to. Always there by my side. Always there to ... help ... with whatever I might require. Day ... or ... night."

"You think too much of yourself, Queenie." Liria was on her feet. Her hand moved to the hilt of her dagger. Her most common response when angry or challenged.

For just a second, Drin considered making a play for that dagger. She was only a few feet away. One quick lunge to lock the dagger in place with her hand then a sweep of her foot behind Liria's legs. Once she had the woman down on the carpet, she should be able to claim the weapon.

But what then?

Even if she succeeded in taking the steel from Liria, killing or disabling her, Drin would still be stuck exactly where she was with no good opportunity to escape the Tor.

Wasted effort on her part. The only satisfaction to be earned that of besting the only woman who perhaps knew Mikel better than she did.

"Do I?" Drin wondered, realizing reluctantly that the only real play she had was to water the seed of doubt she had placed within Liria and hope that it might prove fruitful for her later. "Frankly, I don't agree."

"Why would that be?"

"It's the reason that you're here, after all. Whatever you once had with Mikel is gone. Yet you don't want that. You want to rekindle whatever there was between you." Drin ignored the murderous look Liria gave her. "And you're curious, anxious as well based on that glimmer of fear in the back of your eye, as to whether you're wrong and I'm right."

"You're far off the mark, Queenie."

"Am I?" Drin asked, more and more certain that she was right on target.

"You are," Liria growled through gritted teeth, hating how easily Celindria Dengannon had cracked the façade she presented.

"Say what you want, but we both know the truth."

"What truth would that be?" Liria couldn't stop herself from asking even though she didn't want to give the Queen of the Crux even more to work with.

"That I've taken your place. That I have Mikel now and you don't. You won't. Ever again." Drin's smile was more a smirk as she relished how each of her words was like a dagger strike right in Liria's gut.

"What Mikel and I had can be rekindled easily," Liria spat. "All it requires is a little effort on my part. He's never been able to say no to what only I can offer him."

"And yet you're here, speaking with me now, because you're not sure about that. Are you? You're worried. You see me as a competitor. One who could knock you from your perch for good. But you missed a key point."

"What would that be?" Liria demanded.

"That I already knocked you from your perch."

"Again, you give yourself too much credit, Queenie. When last I was with Mikel I had him wrapped around my finger. It won't take much to do so again."

"You may believe whatever you like," Drin countered. "But there's something you're forgetting."

"What would that be?"

"You're not with Mikel any longer," Drin stated with a contained heat, hoping to tilt Liria off balance. "Your history with him mitigates any attraction he might have had for you."

"You have the nerve to talk about attraction. You who are seeking to steal ..."

"You tried to kill him," Drin cut in, her voice as keen as the knife she wished she held in her hand. "You failed. You say you know Mikel." Drin stepped back then as if she needed to take a better look at Liria, lifting her head, tilting it slightly, as she gazed down on her. "Well, if that's the case, then you know that he's not one to just forgive and forget no matter what you two might have had in the past. He has a rather long memory for those who tried to kill him. A long memory for anyone who has tried to slight him."

"Are you suggesting that I can't charm him any longer?" Liria popped up from where she was sitting, shaking slightly, fingers gripped tightly into fists, offended by Celindria Dengannon's lack of belief in her prowess. "He was mine the moment I saw him. You're just a passing fancy. Someone new.

Someone different. Not what he needs. You will never be what he needs."

"I'm not suggesting anything to you, Liria," Drin stated with the quiet confidence she used so frequently while sitting on the Crux throne and negotiating with haughty lords and ladies more than twice her age. "I'm telling you. You are dead to him."

"Why so certain?" Liria hissed, willing herself to keep her shaking hands at her side. She understood what would happen if she reached for her dagger with her anger about to explode. She didn't want to deal with the repercussions of an intemperate decision.

Drin stepped right up to Liria, crushing the tremor of worry that attempted to sweep through her. Unafraid, she relished the confrontation. Pleased by her success. Proud of herself. All the while prepared to defend herself if her adversary lost control, which she believed was a distinct possibility. She just needed to give the woman one more nudge.

"Because I've seen how he looks at me." Drin infused her voice with as much arrogance as she could so that it matched her contemptuous expression. "Because I know what he's thinking, what he wants, when he looks at me. What only I can give him."

"Are you certain about that?" Liria sought to challenge Celindria Dengannon's claims even as her doubts increased, burrowing into her heart, soul, and mind. "How do you know that when I see him next his feelings for me won't return? How do you know he won't desire me as he once did?"

Drin snorted softly, shaking her head as if she were sadly disappointed with Liria. All the while trying to hold back a laugh, but giving up upon realizing what effect releasing her scorn would have on the stone-faced woman who was so close to cracking. When Liria's face turned red with rage, Drin laughed that much harder.

"You tried to kill him, almost succeeded in fact, and you

think he will have you back? Add to that the fact that I'm sure he hasn't forgotten how you left him for dead." Drin clapped her hands together slowly and softly, offering Liria a contemptuous nod of respect. "Quite the ego you have. Although not much of a grasp on reality."

"A much-deserved ego," Liria growled, no other words coming to her. Her anger neared the boiling point. "Even after all that has happened between us, he will not be able to say no to me. He was never able to in the past. He cannot now. Only I can give him what he wants and needs."

"You certainly do like to look at the world from a unique perspective, although deluded might be the better way to describe it," Drin murmured. Seemingly intrigued. In reality, doing all that she could to keep Liria on edge as she felt the air shift in her private quarters, a spark of hope taking shape within her.

"More power to you, but in the end it will only increase the pain you feel. Because I am absolutely certain," Drin said, offering Liria a sharp, emphatic nod as she spoke the last, "that Mikel has much better taste now than when he was with you. And how could he not?"

She stepped back a few feet then, using that space to lift her arms and offer a slight curtsey that turned Liria's cheeks splotched with the red of rage to a cold, pale fury.

"You made the cardinal mistake," Drin continued. "You've forgotten that in Mikel's world, there is only one thing that truly matters. Trust. You lost his trust. I've gained it."

"You dare to insult me?" Liria hissed.

"I simply speak the truth," Drin tsked, "and as I've discovered, the truth is often quite difficult to hear."

"You don't speak the truth," Liria growled, once again failing to come up with the response she desired as her fury colored her thoughts.

"Unfortunately for you, I do speak the truth. Because the

truth is that Mikel has been spending almost all of his time with me, and he wouldn't do that if I couldn't offer him something that you ... couldn't."

Drin smiled then and went for the final blow. "Then again, it could be that he doesn't want what you could offer him. He doesn't want you."

Liria had visited Celindria Dengannon with the goal of obtaining information. Also desiring to put her in her place. She had failed miserably on both counts.

Not liking what she had learned, she hated how easily the Queen of the Crux had turned the tables on her as she taunted her with the haughtiness that could only be expected from a royal.

Liria was livid, barely able to contain herself. Moreover, she was desperate to strike at the source of her rage.

The Queen of the Crux's sharp comments cutting almost as deeply as a knife between her ribs awakened Liria's deep-seated fears and insecurities. She would have liked nothing more than to wipe the arrogant smirk from her antagonist's face with a quick swipe of her dagger.

But she couldn't.

Not yet.

Not until Assindra and Malor were done with her.

"You delude yourself, Queenie," Liria replied, having no other argument to make other than to steal from her competitor. The seeds of doubt still worked their way through her, making her wonder if her statement was true, yet having nothing else with which to contend her opponents' claims. "Mikel always will be mine."

"It's that overconfidence of yours that will be your downfall, Liria," Mikel whispered into her ear. Sliding up behind her, he placed his dagger at her throat. The sharp gasp of shock that he elicited strangely appealed to him.

"How did you get in here?" Liria demanded in a hoarse

whisper, fearful of the cool steel just a flick away from slicing into her flesh. Angry that the man who dominated her thoughts had taken her by surprise.

"The fact that you even need to ask that question suggests that you don't really know me at all," Mikel replied, having listened to the last few minutes of the conversation between Liria and Drin. "And what I heard was quite enlightening. Though not surprising. Still playing the games you so enjoy, or at least trying to. Because it seems that in the Queen of the Crux you have met your match."

"There is no way that Queenie ..." Liria began to protest.

"Enough," Drin stated harshly, cutting her off. "You can explore these issues of yours another time."

If Liria wasn't there, Drin would have surrendered to her urge to pull Mikel into a hug, never expecting him to appear as he did. Grateful to have him there with her and hopeful that he had some way to get them free of her prison, though worried that he was risking his life for nothing.

"Another time then," Mikel agreed. He gave Liria a slight nudge in the small of her back, directing her out toward the balcony. "Or perhaps not at all. The Queen played her role quite well, and you fell for it. But in one matter she spoke the truth. Trust. There is no trust between us, Liria, and there never will be again."

"You're going to kill me after all that we did together? All that we meant to one another?"

"It's only fair," Mikel replied in an exceedingly calm tone. "You almost killed me, so I view it as fair play."

"That was only business, Mikel," Liria argued as she grudgingly stepped across the thick carpet toward the open balcony doors. "Business is business. You know that better than anyone. I taught you that. This, now, is more than business."

"Doesn't matter." He gave her another slight nudge to keep

her moving, his hand on her elbow preventing Liria from digging her heels into the carpet to slow her progress.

"Why not?" Liria asked, beginning to believe that he was still planning to kill her without a second thought.

"Because I can't live with the betrayal. Business is business, you're right, but betrayal is another matter entirely. And this, now, no matter what you want to believe, is just business."

"It wasn't a betrayal, it was just ..." Liria didn't finish her argument. She stumbled knowing that Mikel would pull the dagger back before it sliced into her flesh.

She was thankful that though she might not know Mikel now as well as she once did, his basic sense of fairness remained. And she was more than happy to prey upon what she perceived as his primary weakness.

Free, Liria already had her dagger in hand. She considered making a break for the door but discarded the idea. Celindria Dengannon already had identified what Liria was thinking and adjusted her positioning accordingly to block her.

Having no choice, Liria backed out of the living room, not stopping until her lower back hit the balcony railing. She looked over her shoulder for just a heartbeat, not wanting to take her eyes from Mikel for too long. She knew just how fast he could be.

A drop of a hundred feet waited for her. Maybe more. Unless ...

"Drop the dagger, Liria. There's no point in continuing this. You have nowhere to go," Mikel reasoned.

Liria snorted in disdain at that. "I'm supposed to trust you now. You held a dagger to my throat."

"I did," Mikel confirmed. "The difference between us being that when you had the chance, you stabbed me with your dagger. When I had the chance, I didn't." His expression hardened, eyes growing cold. This was the Mikel who had first caught Liria's attention when she arrived on the Crux. Hard. Certain. Strong. "At least not yet."

"Not the promise I wanted to hear," Liria replied.

"There's no point in giving you a promise, Liria. Not when I can't trust you."

She nodded at that. Not in a position to disagree with him. "And now that you're under the thrall of the Queen of the Crux, I can't trust you either."

"Of course you can trust me, Liria." Mikel's smile darkened. "You can trust that I will do what is right."

"That's what I'm afraid of." Liria shifted her focus for just a few heartbeats. "Keep him well for me, Celindria Dengannon. I expect him whole and healthy when I return for the Broken Bear."

With a final nod to Mikel, Liria placed one hand on the railing and leapt over, dropping over the side and into the early morning darkness without making a sound.

Drin rushed up to the railing. Looking over, she didn't quite believe what she had just witnessed.

Mikel joined her. Thoughtful. There was no sign of Liria. But that wasn't all that surprising. They couldn't see anything beyond the glow of the lanterns set into the stone by the door.

"Do you think she's dead?"

Mikel shook his head. "I doubt it. With Liria, it's never easy. And this was much too easy for her."

"Were you going to kill her?" Drin asked.

Mikel didn't answer right away. Finally pulling his eyes away from the darkness, he offered Drin a small smile that she knew so well. "No, I was just going to tie her up. Now I'm wondering if that was the right decision."

"It probably wasn't. Leaving her alive means she's still a threat to both of us."

Mikel wasn't in a position to argue. So he didn't. He acknowledged the truth of Drin's words with a sharp nod.

Drin nodded in turn. She understood the struggle Mikel faced, though she wasn't in favor of mercy. Her steely expression softening, she reached for Mikel on an impulse and hugged him.

"I can't say that I was expecting this kind of reception," he said with a smile in his voice.

Drin lifted her head and laughed. Then giving into an urge, her concern of the last few days replaced with a rush of happiness, she leaned up and kissed him.

The instant her lips touched his, an electricity surged that took both of them by surprise. A heat flowed between them that increased the intensity of their connection. Neither ever experiencing it before.

"What in the blazes is going on?"

Lucius Hanover stood in the center of the living room, a look of incredulity marring his features as he stared at the pair lost in one another on the balcony.

Drin and Mikel stepped apart reluctantly.

"Can I kill this one?" Mikel asked as he turned to face the Lord of House Hanover.

"I would be insulted if you didn't," Drin replied.

"Well, we can't have that, now can we?" Mikel murmured.

"Slumming it, are we? You would pick this thug before you would pick me?" Lucius demanded derisively. "What do you think you're ..."

Lucius stumbled backward, losing his feet as Mikel advanced toward him. On his backside, Lucius crab walked away with Mikel following, towering over him. Lucius kept his eyes focused on the remorseless gaze of the King of the Underworld, unable to gain any space to maneuver. That proved to be his doom.

His left hand knocked into an ottoman and sent him onto his back. When Lucius finally pushed himself back up and looked for his attacker, he saw nothing except for a very large fist coming right at him.

"Did you enjoy doing that?" Drin asked. She stood next to Mikel, staring down at the unconscious Lucius Hanover. A bruise already started to color the right side of his face. She wouldn't be surprised if Mikel broke Lucius' jaw with that single punch.

"Honestly, I did," Mikel admitted, giving Drin a wink. "I never much liked the pasty, privileged upstart."

"What do we do?"

"What do you mean?" Mikel wondered if she wanted him to throw Hanover over the railing after Liria.

When he looked up at her, she was showing him her wrist, the silver bracelet gleaming brightly.

His gaze narrowed. "This is what's keeping you here?"

"It is," Drin snapped. "It functions much like a Protector's Collar. Once affixed, it can't be removed." She sighed, taking a deep breath to calm himself, then offered Mikel a nod of thanks. "You came here for naught. Because of this bracelet, there is a restriction on where I can go on the Tor. Best that you leave. Otherwise, I fear that Malor Dragoran will be less gentle with you than he has been with me."

"I've seen something like this before," Mikel whispered, lost in thought. His memories coming to the surface, he grasped Drin's hand so he could get a better look at the ancient artifact.

"You have?"

"I have," he confirmed. "When I was younger I spent a lot of time working in the forges of the Giants of the Rime. I didn't see a bracelet like this. But I did watch as Cadmus crafted a Protector's Collar."

"So you can get this off me?" That thought thrilled Drin. Her excitement drowned an instant later.

"No. As you said, once affixed ... I don't know if it can be removed."

"Then why are you staring at it so intently. You need to go. You can't be here when Lucius wakes up. Or, worse, when Malor or Assindra make an appearance."

Mikel ignored her. Concentrating, he stared a bit longer at the silver.

"It will work, Lightcrafter. You need only try."

He nodded. Then stopped himself, not wanting to explain in that moment that Knute Frost Lord and the other Bearers of the Blade could communicate with him. That was a conversation that would have to wait.

Still holding Drin's hand with his right hand, he placed his left atop the bracelet.

"Mikel, what are you ..." The silver began to glow softly, then with a greater intensity. The metal resisted at first, though it was unable to do so for long. The Light Mikel sent into the artifact broke the bonds between object and person, returning the silver to its original state, the magic infused within it drawn back into Mikel and burned away.

When he pulled his hand back, the bracelet remained on Drin's wrist, but it was now only that. A bracelet. A piece of jewelry. The power and the restrictions contained within it removed.

"How did you do that?"

Mikel smiled, pleased that it had worked. "Another topic to discuss once we are free of the Ring. Come on."

Mikel gave Drin a gentle tug, pulling her toward the wall. Instead of taking the passageway that had brought him to her quarters, he had another route in mind. One that might confuse the hunters he assumed would come after them if they weren't on their way already.

Pushing with his boot on a slight indentation in the stone floor, another panel in the wall slid free that revealed a steel ladder and provided access to another secret tunnel.

Drin peeked through, looking up then down. She didn't see where the ladder led.

"Up you go," Mikel urged.

"You're sure about this?"

"Completely sure."

"Only because I trust you," Drin grumbled. She stepped through the door and began to climb, Mikel right behind her.

They were in complete darkness when the door closed behind them. Needing to move swiftly, Drin reached for the Talent.

A sphere of light formed just above her head, illuminating the ladder and the gloom around them for five yards in all directions.

Ecstatic that the natural magic flowed within her veins once more, Drin realized that she had another reason to thank Mikel when the time was right. And unlike her first few encounters with the King of the Underworld, she was already looking forward to it.

"You better not be looking at my ass," she warned.

"Then you should have kept us in the dark."

Drin smiled at his reply, but she was glad he couldn't see it.

"You can sense them?" she asked.

"I can," Mikel replied. Looking up. Not at her ass. Well, looking at her ass only because he needed to look up so that he could reach for the next rung. "Best to move as fast as you can."

Druden were hunting them.

The race to escape the Tor was on.

35

WORSE THAN A DRUDE

"You want to talk about what happened?" Mikel asked.

"What do you mean?" A lot had happened in the last few hours. Mikel needed to be more specific.

"After Liria went over the railing," he clarified.

"You kissed me," Drin replied, keeping her voice level. "It seems fairly straightforward."

"If I recall correctly, Queen Dengannon, you kissed me."

"That's very presumptuous of you, Broken Bear. You step too far."

Mikel smiled and snorted softly, shaking his head ever so slightly. Of all the names he had earned, that one, one of his first, had always been his favorite, although it was rarely used now.

And he liked it when she called him by that name, although she didn't need to know that.

There was much that Mikel could have said in reply, but he didn't, focusing instead on the map in his head and sticking to the route that he believed would give them the fastest path for escaping the Tor. Still, despite that challenge pressing down upon him, he felt the need to push back.

"I did kiss you, Queen Dengannon," Mikel admitted. "However, only after you kissed me first. I thought it best not to insult you."

"You would argue with me now?"

He heard the challenge in her voice. The soft humor as well. "I would argue with you always, Queen Dengannon. It is much too enjoyable an experience to not engage in."

The innuendo quieted Drin. Mikel was pleased that his response had its intended effect. And it gave him the few seconds he needed to confirm the route that he wanted to take.

"That is ... good to hear," she admitted in a thoughtful tone after they trotted another hundred yards down the poorly lit tunnel he selected, a small smile gracing her features.

After leaving the ladder that led away from her quarters, they followed a curling corridor that took them along the inside of the outer wall of the Ring and down on a comfortable slope, finally depositing them somewhere in the cellars of the fortress.

She knew what he was doing. Seeking to distract her from the peril they faced. And she appreciated his efforts. Though she believed he raised this issue for another reason as well.

Her brief transgression had offered a momentary release of the pressure and fear that had taken up residence on her shoulders. Yet now wasn't the time for such matters.

What they shared was an alliance based on mutual interest that would remain in place for only so long as it proved useful to them both. At least that's what she believed. Right then.

A hard truth lay between them. They were who they were. There could be no we. Ever.

Still, Drin couldn't ignore the fact that he had come for her. She had hoped that he would. But she had feared that it might be asking too much even of her Broken Bear.

She smiled more broadly.

Her Broken Bear.

She liked that.

She could use that against him at the right time.

He was right. She had kissed him. But only because he had come for her.

That rationalization helped Drin feel better about at least that smaller predicament.

Then she frowned. Another worry came to mind.

Why had he come for her? Because there always seemed to be more at play with Mikel. After all, her Broken Bear had used her as bait several times before.

Was this just another instance of that?

Was she simply a part of a larger game?

What motivated him to take the risk that he did?

What did he hope to gain?

That thought hardened her focus and strengthened her desire for clarity. As a result, Drin's smile tightened into a grimmer expression.

Escape first.

Then they could have the difficult conversation that was required to determine if the Queen of the Crux and the King of the Underworld could continue to work together when doing so allowed them both to gain what they required.

"I will always be honest with you, Queen Dengannon. You should know that by now."

"Just not completely honest."

"Old habits and all that," Mikel murmured quietly, his eyes never leaving the path they took.

Mikel's tone hinted that her pushing didn't faze him. She didn't know if she should be impressed by that or concerned that he showed only so much deference to her. The barest minimum and never more than that.

"Another topic that we will need to discuss."

"I serve at your pleasure, Queen Dengannon." Mikel

stopped abruptly. Just up ahead the corridor split. "Another time, perhaps? We have more immediate concerns."

Drin nodded. "Tell me." Drin was relying on him as their guide. She feared that using the Talent to search around them would give away their location to their pursuers.

Mikel didn't reply right away. He was concentrating instead on the image of the maze of passageways that ran beneath the Ring, grateful to Knute for sharing that information with him and staying in the back of Mikel's mind as he guided them unerringly through the fortress.

The Frost Lord helped them to reach their current location unseen. Even so, there were hunters on their heels.

"Druden," Mikel answered.

"How close?"

They could make a run for it. That was the first thought that crossed Mikel's mind. He chose against that option, however.

The Druden approached from the direction he and Drin had come, only a few hundred yards behind them and closing fast.

The corridor at their backs joined the one they were traveling through to form a junction that gave them two viable options for continuing their escape. Understanding that he and Drin had little chance of evading the Druden, Mikel viewed the junction from a different perspective. It offered them more space to fight without having to worry about being flanked.

Not the best battleground for challenging these monsters from the Spirit World, though certainly not the worst. And based on the map in his head, there was no better place than here to take the fight to their hunters.

"They're here." Mikel nodded back down the passageway. The gloom dominated the few lanterns valiantly seeking to brighten the darkness. That gloom darkened to a pitch black when the creatures passed.

"Only three?" Drin asked. "How very disappointing."

Mikel barked out a laugh. Not so much because her humor was funny but rather because it was so unexpected from the Queen of the Crux. "Yes, not much of a challenge."

"How would you like to manage this?" She pulled the dagger from the sheath on her hip. The only weapon she had been allowed upon her capture by Assindra.

Mikel already had the Blade of Light in his hand, the blazing steel burning through the gloom and gifting the Druden long shadows that stretched far back down the passageway.

"We don't hold back."

Drin understood his meaning. Reaching for the Talent, sparks of energy swirled around her free hand. Her gaze sharpened. More than pleased to finally have a chance to strike back.

She didn't wait, sending a cloud of flashing sparks surging toward the creatures.

Mikel used Drin's attack to get in among the Druden with his sword, dancing to a tune that only he could hear.

The Druden sought to avoid him. That proved to be no more than wasted effort, finding it difficult because of the tightness of the corridor and the constant flares of energy that sizzled toward them.

Stuck between a rock and a hard place, they had to choose between the lesser of the two threats.

The Druden succeeded in using the Curse to defend against the Magus' attack. The ancient scimitar proved to be more concerning.

With every touch of Mikel's steel, wispy folds of black drifted to the ground, dissolving into nothing before touching the stone. The very essence of these evil creatures cut away.

Weakening them.

Hurting them.

Watching from afar through the eyes of her servants, Assindra gave more of her power in the Curse to her hunters.

She was beginning to believe that even three of these monsters from the Spirit World could not stand against the Bearer of the Blade. Especially one who learned so quickly.

Accepting the gift from their master, the Druden countered the two distinct attacks with waves of black that rolled out from their sharpened fingertips. A single touch from that corrupt power was enough to drain the spirit from anyone unlucky enough to be caught within it.

"Mikel, this isn't working!"

Drin needed to shout to be heard above the deafening roar within the narrow corridor as the Talent and Curse clashed.

Mikel couldn't argue with her. They had caused the Druden some harm. But these three were difficult opponents. The injuries Mikel inflicted were not enough to force them from the fight. Worse, the Druden were getting stronger as the combat continued thanks to their master's aid.

Perhaps he could do something to change that.

"Be ready!" he yelled.

"What are you ..."

Already moving, Mikel didn't hear the rest of Drin's question. Leaving caution to the wind, he charged toward the Drude in the center of the corridor.

Its brethren sent bursts of dark magic at him that Drin blocked with small shields crafted of the Talent that deflected the Curse and left Mikel with an open path.

Raising his Blade above his head, he prepared to slice the creature in half.

When he was only ten feet away, he shifted his direction with a sharp cut and leapt for the wall to his left, catching the brick with his foot and then pushing off it. He used his momentum to lift himself into the air so that his head almost scraped the ceiling.

Mikel swept with his steel in a wide arc that ran parallel to the ground.

The Drude closest to him hissed. That hiss cut off when the Blade of Light completed its passage through its neck.

Yet rather than its head falling to the ground and its body collapsing, the monster simply faded away as the power contained within Mikel's Blade severed the creature's link to the Natural World.

Turning on his heel, he sprinted back toward Drin. He hoped that she understood what he was doing as the Druden glided after him.

Unconcerned by the bolts of Talent shooting toward them, the Druden reached for him with their claws.

Thankfully, Drin was ready.

Right before the Drude closest to him ripped into his back, a shimmering shield of power formed right at Mikel's heels. The Drude slammed into it. Then scraped with its claws, scrabbling desperately at the magical barrier.

"That was a very foolish thing to do," Drin chided, reaching out an arm and helping to slow Mikel down before he slammed into the far wall.

"Perhaps. Some would say that it was a very brave thing to do."

"I say foolish."

"Why am I not surprised?" he grumbled. "How long will the barrier hold?"

Looking over his shoulder, Mikel watched as the Druden made it clear that they were less than pleased by their change in fortune. The monsters were firing streams of the Curse at the shield. A bright flash drowning the hallway every time the two forces met.

"Not as long as I would like," Drin grumbled. "The Dark Magus controlling the Druden is too strong."

"Then let's hope it's just long enough. Come on." He trotted down the corridor to his left. "Best to make use of what time we have."

~

"HOW MUCH FARTHER?" Drin leaned her back against the rough brick of the wall, catching her breath. Her defense against the Druden continued to hold, making her think they might actually get away before those monsters found their way past her construction.

"A quarter mile," Mikel shrugged. The map Knute provided was not to scale, forcing him to guess based on his use of the Light.

"Then let's get going," Drin urged. They were much closer than she had anticipated. And that gave her a needed burst of energy.

Mikel didn't bother to say anything, simply setting off at the ground-eating pace that he used while in the Frozen Waste. Certain that if it was too much for Drin she would let him know.

He smiled at that thought, thinking that actually she wouldn't. She'd do all she could to stay with him, not complaining, refusing to demonstrate any form of weakness. That was just who she was.

Mikel liked that about her. Her innate toughness.

Although not all of her traits appealed to him. Like her attempts to lord it over him on occasion. He could do without that.

They had only gone another fifty yards when Mikel raised his hand and slowed his pace. Drin stopped next to him.

"What's the matter?"

"We're not alone," Mikel replied mysteriously. He pulled the Blade of Light from the sheath across his back.

"What do you mean? More Druden?"

He shook his head. "No, nothing from the Spirit World. Still, a lethal challenge all the same."

"Then what ..."

Mikel held up his hand then nodded down the hallway to their front. Drin shifted her gaze in that direction.

Most of the lanterns placed along this section of the wall had burned out long ago. Only a few provided any illumination. And that at no more than a sputter.

Mikel becoming more comfortable with the power that had been hidden within him, the brilliance of the Blade slowly grew brighter and illuminated the corridor for twenty yards in each direction.

"Quite the trick you've learned, Mikel."

Liria stood there. Seekers waited with her. The deep purple of the masked figures' eyes confirmed it.

"How many behind us?" Mikel asked softly of Drin.

"Two," Drin replied just as quietly.

"You can manage them?"

Drin didn't hesitate. "For a time, yes."

Mikel smiled then. Her innate toughness and refusal to back down when faced with a challenge shone just as brightly as the scimitar in his hand.

"Obviously you've learned some tricks as well," Mikel replied, "surviving that leap from the balcony."

"You don't sound all that surprised to see me."

Mikel snorted softly at that. "You've always been full of surprises, Liria. I won't believe you're dead until I see your body."

"Still angry with me?" she purred as she offered him the grin that had warmed his heart in a way that little else could when he was younger.

Now ...

Thoughts of someone else quashed whatever heat might have risen within him in the past.

"Angry, no." Mikel shook his head to emphasize his point. "Just disappointed. In myself. I didn't see who you truly were until it was almost too late."

"You don't have to blame yourself for that, Mikel. Love can do that to a person. Blind them to the realities in a relationship."

"Love can do more than that."

Liria nodded. "It can." She got a sense as to what he meant when she glanced into his very cold eyes. That look used to thrill her. Because it always presaged a characteristic in her former partner in crime that she found difficult to resist. That she rarely tried to resist.

Now, that look sent a shiver of unease down her spine. Never having been the focus of that intense gaze. Never having wanted to be the focus.

"You heard some of what I said to Queenie."

Mikel nodded, one lip curling slightly at the nickname she bestowed on Drin. He kept his gaze on Liria and the Seeker standing with her. Well aware of the risk of not doing so. "Enough."

"I spoke the truth, Mikel. I believe we can have again what we had before."

"Really?" His voice held more than just a hint of disbelief. "Forgive and forget?"

"Forgive," Liria corrected. "I know you don't forget." She took a half-step toward him. "Think of it more as forgive, then make up. We had quite a few disagreements when we were together. I won't deny it. But making up after each one was quite a lot of fun. Wouldn't you agree?"

Mikel nodded as he pretended to think about what Liria was offering him. All the while preparing for what he planned to do next.

"The barrier is down," Drin whispered to him. While listening to Mikel's conversation with Liria, she had grown increasingly concerned about how he might react to the woman, unable to observe the exchange. The entire time she kept her eyes on the pair of Seekers blocking her way. Unwilling to risk being distracted against such deadly foes.

Drin's acknowledgment was the catalyst he was waiting for. Mikel had no desire to deal with his current challenge and then have the Druden join them at the absolutely worst time.

"The past is the past, Liria," Mikel responded.

"Think of what we can have, Mikel," she urged with a suggestive smile, hoping to tempt him as she had in the past.

"I don't want what you're offering me."

"You need to give over," Drin said. "He's not interested. He's with me now."

Mikel's smile broadened upon hearing that from over his shoulder. His good humor deepened as he watched the change that swept over Liria. Her face tightened, anger coming to the forefront and emotion seeping in to cloud her thinking.

"And you have no power here, Quee ..."

The last of her words became a gasp and then a curse. Mikel glided forward and feinted a slice in her direction that sent her scrambling back.

Liria slipped when her heel caught the foot of the Seeker standing next to her. That single moment of clumsiness was all that Mikel required.

His primary focus the assassin, he pivoted, his blade still singing through the air.

The Seeker raised his dagger just in time, but it proved to be no match for the Blade of Light. The ancient steel burned right through the assassin's blade and continued on its arc until it was buried deep in flesh and bone.

Mikel tore the blade free then turned to face his former partner.

"Care to dance, Liria," Mikel asked. His cold eyes even colder.

HER FOCUS on the Seekers standing before her, Drin still listened intently to the conversation between Mikel and Liria. Gritting her teeth for most of it. Several times she had a pointed comment to offer. Yet she kept them all to herself until she couldn't any longer.

Pleased that Mikel wasn't taken in by the woman's lies.

Because as soon as she felt the barrier she constructed to hold back the Druden fail, the sand began flowing through the hourglass once again.

And she had no desire to be caught between Seekers and Druden.

Targeting the Seeker to her right, with that impulse driving her, she lunged with her dagger. Her attack failing, the assassin gliding away from her as she expected he would, she stepped back.

She could see little of the Seekers opposing her. Their clothes were a unique mesh that allowed them to fade into the gloom of the corridor. Only their purple eyes were clearly visible.

And those eyes appeared to be taunting her, as if they were amused by her attempt to defend herself.

That belief was confirmed when as one the pair of assassins pulled long daggers from the sheaths on their hips. A blade for each hand.

Her world shrank as the pair stepped apart then stepped forward at a slow walk.

She couldn't ignore the truth about these two.

They were formidable opponents.

Especially since they had something of a natural resistance to the Talent because of their distinctive training.

But not a complete resistance.

And they still had weaknesses just like any other adversary.

It was those weaknesses that Drin meant to play upon.

A sphere of energy took shape above her palm, which she threw down toward the brick at the Seekers' feet.

The blast of energy ripped the floor into sharp shards that pierced their shins. It also blinded the Seekers, black spots dancing before their eyes.

One of the Seekers never cleared those black spots as her natural response was to reach toward her wounds. Gasping. Shocked to feel a cold steel blade slide between her ribs. Not removed until she experienced a painful twist of the dagger that opened the gash even wider.

A wound from which she had no chance to recover.

The badly hurt Seeker dropped to her knees as her hands went to the wide hole in her side that spurted out blood. Not having the time to consider her fate as she slumped face forward toward the shattered brick.

"Do you have the courage to stand against me without your friend?" Drin asked in a quiet voice filled with resolve. She held a bloody dagger in front of her. Balanced on her toes, she was ready for the next combat to begin.

The Seeker facing off against her stood still as a statue, ignoring the bloody and painful wounds marring his lower legs.

She hadn't expected a response. She was quite familiar with the Seekers. Trained at a very young age to engage in the specialized work of the Order of the Assassins, she knew that he was expected to kill with a single strike. Without being seen. Without being heard. The assassin was taught that the greatest failure of a Seeker, short of failing to kill the assigned target, was discovery. That got Drin thinking. Was he there to kill her? She wasn't so sure, understanding her value if taken alive.

The Seeker demonstrated why he was hired a heartbeat later.

Dagger extended hilt first, the Seeker aimed to smash the steel knob against the Queen of the Crux's hand, relieving her of her dagger. Then, with his backswing, he'd crack her in the side of the head. Not too strongly. With just enough force to send her into a blissful unconsciousness that would ensure she couldn't use the Talent to defend herself.

The Seeker grunted in disbelief when he found himself stuck. A thin barrier of white energy wrapped around him. The hilt of his dagger just above where the Queen of the Crux's hand had been a moment before.

He struggled to break free. His natural resistance aided him, the Talent only holding him a second longer, yet that proved to be a second too long.

When finally he could move again, the Queen wasn't where she had been. Instead she was on his left side. And she was moving.

The cold steel punched through the soft flesh of his armpit and made him gasp. More in shock than pain.

When the blade was withdrawn, he didn't bother to reach for the wound, already knowing that his end was near.

He dropped to his knees, slumping forward and joining his partner as they both breathed their last.

Drin stared down at her work.

She did not enjoy killing. Yet at a young age she had learned from her uncle that there would be times when she would need to do what she didn't want to do.

This was one of those times.

She felt no remorse.

Rather she felt a burst of urgency, having sensed the Druden drawing closer as she searched around them with the Talent.

Her job done, wanting to get out from beneath the Tor as swiftly as possible, Drin turned. Dagger in one hand, natural magic sparking across the fingertips of her other, she stood ready to help Mikel remove the woman who was an albatross around his neck.

"I've missed this," Liria laughed as she stalked with an easy grace to either side of the corridor, drifting backward, seeking to increase the difficulty of Mikel's task.

"I'm afraid to ask," Mikel murmured. His eyes never left Liria. Placing his faith in Drin in a way that he would with only few other people, he trusted that he had nothing to fear with her standing against the two Seekers at his back.

Believing that he might be distracted, Liria lunged then stepped back quickly.

Mikel pivoted. Refusing to give ground, he wanted to keep the pressure on his former partner.

"The foreplay between us," Liria purred.

Mikel shook his head sadly. "You lost your chance years ago, Liria. What's done can't be undone. I'm not as easy as you think I am."

"So you say," she replied with a soft laugh and another stab. This one followed by a slash that missed Mikel's brow only because when he pivoted this time, he continued his motion, spinning away, reading Liria's full intention in her eyes. He had learned from experience that's where she revealed her secrets.

"Believe or don't believe. It matters little to me."

"You're lying, don't deny it," Liria snapped. She feinted a lunge this time. Stepping in even closer, she sought to slash across his thigh.

Remembering it as one of her favorite tactics, Mikel was ready for just such a move. A disabling strike.

Bringing his blade down with an impressive deftness, he parried Liria's dagger. Maintaining his momentum, he moved forward and shouldered into her, knocking her backward. He was quick to follow, tiring of the game and disliking how it felt as if she was leading him on as she used to when they were together.

"I didn't know you were into the rough stuff," Liria chuckled, her eyes blazing fiercely. Though with anger, desire, or both was unclear. "That opens a whole new world of possibility to us."

Liria got her dagger in place with scarcely a heartbeat to spare. Swiping at Mikel's steel, she deflected it right before it cut into her shoulder.

"I can tell you're enjoying this, Mikel," Liria growled in that way that used to send a spark of desire through him. Now, it just irritated him as one thought as clear as the ice that covered the rivers of the Frozen Waste constantly played through his mind while they dueled.

Liria had betrayed him.

She had left him for dead.

That went against all that he believed in.

The code that he lived by.

Fair play in all things. Even if it was to his own detriment.

A strange philosophy for someone in his position, he was more than willing to acknowledge that, but one that had served him well ever since he fled the Bitter Heights.

"You're wrong about that, Liria," Mikel replied in a voice that was barely above a whisper. "I'm doing what I must, no more than that."

His expression changed then, turning flinty, as he recalled some of the better memories of his time with Liria. All of that overshadowed by memories of their last job together. Here within the Tor in fact.

"And just what are you going to do to me?"

Liria's tone was suggestive. Aggressively so. Mikel knew she hoped to get under his skin. All the while not realizing that her efforts to do that had cooled his rage into a rock-hard resolve.

Mikel didn't bother to reply. Calling upon the power surging through him, the Blade of Light blinding, he slashed toward Liria in a broad arc.

Her attempt to defend herself proved futile. Mikel's ancient weapon sliced right through her blade as if it were nothing more than a piece of parchment.

Liria gasped, not believing her eyes. She saw her own death at the hand of the one who not so long before she believed would do everything in his power to protect her.

The touch of that ancient Blade on her neck felt strangely cool despite the energy flaring along its length.

And with that touch, the hard reality of her situation finally hit her.

Much to her regret, Liria finally understood that Mikel would be a much tougher nut to crack than she originally thought ... if she lived through the next few seconds.

"I had no choice but to do what Assindra wanted, Mikel," she offered in a conciliatory tone. "You have to believe me. If I had not done as she wanted, she would have killed me."

"Even if that's the truth, why should I care, Liria?"

Her voice quivered, incorporating as much emotion as she could manage with the steel forcing her to lift her chin. "That is not what the Mikel I knew would say. The Mikel I loved."

Mikel ensured that his emotions remained in check before replying. His voice was as cold as the Frozen Waste when he did. "That Mikel is gone, Liria, thanks in large part to you."

Acknowledging that she had misjudged the encounter, realizing that words would do her little good, and seeing nothing but her death in his eyes, she took a risk. She brought her knee up, aiming for his groin.

Mikel turned his hip, absorbing the blow on his thigh.

Still, it was enough for Liria to wriggle free from beneath his blade.

Liria scrambled back, seeking to put some space between them.

Mikel followed. Reaching out with his free hand when she tripped over the body of the dead Seeker lying behind her, he pushed her into the doorway that had been hidden within the gloom. Holding her against the stone, Blade back in place against her throat, Liria no longer had any opportunity to maneuver.

Out of the corner of his eye, Mikel glimpsed a large chamber just past the doorway, streaks of sunlight slicing into the cavernous expanse through slits cut into the rock far above.

The exit that he sought was just beyond that chamber. Then he and Drin could go back through the gate he had used to enter the Tor and they'd regain the safety of the wood.

But first, a bit of business required his attention.

His eyes locked onto Liria's. His former partner had nothing left to say. All her games played. Not quite comprehending how the fate that had befallen her had come to pass.

A single, simple slice.

That was all that it would take.

He would gain his revenge for her betrayal.

His fingers tightened on the hilt of the scimitar as he prepared to pass the judgment that Liria deserved.

"Mikel," Drin called.

He didn't hear her. So focused on Liria that he could acknowledge nothing else but the woman under his steel.

"Mikel!" Drin repeated with greater force. The voice of the Queen of the Crux broke through the haze that had enveloped his mind. "Do what you must but do it quickly." She waited a few seconds before offering one last piece of advice, wanting to make sure her words sunk in. "Just make sure you can live with whatever you decide."

Mikel didn't say anything. Thinking about what Drin said, her words stuck with him.

"You deserve to die, Liria," Mikel intoned. "Not even you can deny that. Just not today."

Reaching out with his free hand, he placed his fingertips on her forehead and did something that Kaduna had tried to teach him when he was younger. Mikel failed then because he couldn't touch the Talent, but he succeeded now. A thin stream of the Light sparked from his fingertips and sent Liria into a dreamless unconsciousness.

When she sagged against the wall, he helped her down to the floor. Glad to be rid of her.

Sighing, he took several deep breaths to calm the emotions that threatened to well up within him. Feeling more composed, believing that he made the right decision, he turned.

Drin stood next to him in the doorway, glancing out into the cavern beyond before shifting her focus back to him.

"You need to do a better job picking who you're going to spend time with."

The turmoil that had been boiling within him the instant Liria appeared fled in an instant at Drin's smile, making him smile as well. "With this face I have only so many options."

"More than you might think," Drin murmured under her breath.

Her eyes widened. Drin's expression shifted to surprise as Mikel rushed toward her and pulled her behind him a heartbeat before a spike of the Curse shrieked into the archway and struck Mikel full in the back.

"This is getting more than just a little ridiculous," Mikel grumbled under his breath. Even so, he had assumed that this would happen.

Complication piling upon complication.

It only made sense, after all. It seemed that complications had followed him ever since he had chosen to aid Celindria Dengannon in the Frozen Waste rather than leave her to the Mountain Trolls.

He and Drin stood in the entrance to the chamber that

would take them to the gate. Assindra waited for them, clapping her hands and nodding her head.

Whether because she viewed Mikel as brave or foolish for getting in the way of her strike, he couldn't say. And he really didn't want to ask.

He just wanted to get out from beneath the Tor.

Unfortunately, the only way to do that was to get past the Dark Magus who out of all of their hunters worried him the most. Not because of her power, but rather because of the look in her eyes.

There was an emptiness there. Some key emotion lacking. As if what drove her came from a place that was better left alone.

"I was the bait," growled Drin. "Again." Although this time she couldn't blame Mikel. She could only blame herself for not recognizing the truth until now.

Assindra had kidnapped her from the Crux. Drin assumed that the only reason she would do that was the most obvious reason. To give Malor Dragoran the political tool he needed to achieve his objective of bringing back together the Splintered Empire. Forcing her hand in marriage was a big step in that direction.

Yet Drin had been so taken with her own difficulties that she failed to see that was nothing more than one scheme masked by another.

Assindra didn't just want her. The Dark Magus wanted Mikel. Or more specifically the scimitar he now held in his hand.

And Drin was the lure.

That realization set her blood boiling.

She hated how she had been used.

She hated how she *allowed* herself to be used.

Drin's response?

Streams of the Talent came to life and played across her fingertips.

She might not be skilled enough or powerful enough to defeat Assindra in a contest of the Talent against the Curse, but she would make the Dark Magus work for her victory. That was a promise. She owed it to herself. More importantly, she owed it to Mikel.

"You thought you could hide from me, King of the Underworld," Assindra called.

Assindra took a few steps toward Mikel. Tainted energy sparked across her forearms and across her flowing blood-red dress. A reminder of what was to come if her demands were not met.

"Hide? No. Avoid?" Mikel gave Assindra a shrug and a lift of his eyebrows, as if to say that was the most logical course of action. "Well, you can't really blame me for that, now can you?"

"I commend you, Mikel. You put on a brave face." Assindra almost sounded sincere. Almost.

"I'm no braver than anyone else."

"Always quick with a witty reply." The sparks of black became streaks of tainted power that circulated around her palms. Assindra halted her advance when she was only ten yards away from her quarry. "Even though you know what I am ... and what I can do." She lifted her forearms away from her sides, the streaks now dancing to a more chaotic tune.

"You owe me a debt, Dark Magus," Drin stated in the voice of the Queen of the Crux. "You will pay for your crimes."

Assindra sighed. "Be quiet, child. You and I both know that you are no match for me. And even if Mikel sought to involve himself, he would only get in the way."

"I stopped your last attack. Why not your next?" Mikel asked.

Assindra's smile curled into a scowl. "You demonstrate a unique ability, Mikel, that is true. You also bear an artifact of almost indescribable worth. But you know little of either your skill or the scimitar you claimed. Until you do, all you can do is throw yourself around like a human shield. Not the most effective of strategies. Wouldn't you agree?"

Mikel couldn't fault the Dark Magus' logic, so he didn't bother to try. "Why so interested in me?" He sought to dig a bit more into Assindra's intentions, catching something in the back of her eyes that didn't so much worry him as intrigue him.

"For the weapon. You stole it for me. Then you stole it from me."

Mikel offered Drin a smile of apology, unable to miss her glare and understanding that this would be another topic of discussion between them assuming they survived this encounter. "I didn't have much of a choice. It didn't feel right giving you the Blade. The Blade wouldn't allow it."

"The Blade wouldn't allow it? That's your excuse?" Assindra demanded.

"Not an excuse. The truth." His eyes hardened then, responding to the energy flowing within him with a greater heat. The Light surged through his veins. Pulsing. Calling to him. It wanted to be released. "I am a thief. I won't deny it. But I follow my own set of rules."

"Now that's rich," Assindra snorted. "The King of the Underworld claims a morality that guides his decisions." She took one step closer to Mikel and Drin, her eyes glowing with a dark purpose. "And tell me, Mikel, what part of your code did you apply to make the decision that has brought us here? That has complicated my life and made it more difficult than it needed to be?"

"I wouldn't call it a code so much as guidelines," Mikel mused. Caught by her gaze, he read there what Assindra intended. He needed to counter her if he could. The corrupt power racing around her hands at a mesmerizing speed was close to being freed.

"Are you always this difficult?"

"Yes, he is," Drin replied, although this time with a touch of pride in her voice.

Mikel smiled then. "The guidelines are quite simple when it comes to you. Should I give a weapon of potentially immense power to the evil and most likely very unstable Dark Magus?" He lifted his hands as if he was weighing the question on a scale. When one arm dipped below the other, he answered. "I think not. Definitely not the responsible move."

"That decision only ensures you enjoy a very painful death."

"About that," Mikel said. "Why did you want me here?"

"The Blade of Light, you fool. We've already been over this."

"No, there's more to it than that. The Blade, yes, that makes sense. But you could have made another play for me at the Crux." He stepped forward then, giving Drin a look as he did so. Hoping she understood what he wanted from her, he stopped when he stood a few yards in front of Drin, thereby blocking Assindra from taking a direct shot at the Queen of the Crux. "Why here? Why me?"

"The valiant protector once more," Assindra chuckled. "You give yourself too much credit, King of the Underworld."

"What is it about me that so intrigues you, Dark Magus?" He motioned with the scimitar. "This is important. I understand that. What I don't understand is why it had to be me who took it." Mikel knew the answer. At least he thought so. But he wanted to hear it from her.

"You look for answers to questions that don't require them."

Mikel nodded as if he were contemplating the Dark Magus' response. He had expected just such a reply from her. Perhaps she didn't want to reveal the truth to him or ... admit it to herself. That last made the most sense to him. And he would have liked to press her more on that, but he doubted that it would be worth the effort. "Perhaps, but your eyes betray you."

"The only betrayal that occurred here is the one you committed," Assindra snarled. "You stole the Blade from me." She took another step closer. "I am done playing games. Give it to me! Now!"

"As you command," Mikel replied with a bow that would have done a courtier in the court of the Crux proud.

Here, it served another purpose by creating the opening that Drin needed. And she made the most of it.

Sizzling through the air above Mikel, shards of blazing energy shot from both her palms.

Surprised by the strength and the ferocity of the attack, Assindra was forced to take several steps back. Nevertheless, she responded with a deft touch, a thin barrier of shimmering black taking shape in front of her. The Talent struck with a resounding boom and little damaging effect.

"Mikel, I won't be able to keep this up for long!" Drin cried over the scream of the energy surging through the cavern as she maintained her attack.

She was pleased that she had caught the Dark Magus off guard. Disappointed that she could do little more than prevent her from attacking. And that for only a time as Drin admitted reluctantly that it wouldn't be long before Assindra got the better of her.

"*Any suggestions?*" Mikel asked, connecting with Knute.

"*You are the Lightcrafter. You can defeat the Dark Magus. None touched by the Curse can stand against you.*"

"*I am the Lightcrafter because you tell me I'm the Lightcrafter. That doesn't mean that I know what I'm doing.*"

Knute grumbled to himself for a few seconds, not having a good argument for the one Mikel offered. "*Let the Blade of Light guide you.*"

"*You're just as bad as Maximus,*" Mikel challenged, hoping that he would get more than just arcane advice. He wanted something more actionable. And quickly.

"There is nothing more I can tell you. This place," Knute said, *"no longer belongs to the Giants. An evil has taken root here. An evil that must be destroyed. You are the only one capable of doing that. You are the Lightcrafter."* The Frost Lord sighed in Mikel's mind, acknowledging the truth of his statement. *"But you're right. In name only. You are the Lightcrafter. For now. Because of that, you must rely on the Blade. Let the Blade guide you."*

"You want me to do that now? Fine. How do I do that?"

Knute chuckled softly. *"In time, we will talk more about what will be required of you. Right now, your concern is more immediate and more than just the Dark Magus. Focus on what you know needs to be done, not on what you don't know."*

"What are you talking about?" Mikel demanded, his aggravation plain.

"Look behind you."

Mikel glanced over his shoulder, then uttered a series of curses. Druden were gliding through the doorway at his back. In seconds, he and Drin would be caught in a vise.

"Let the Blade of Light guide you," Knute repeated. *"The Bearers have not always understood what is required of them or how to do what is required of them. Sometimes it is simply a matter of believing in the Blade. Even more, believing in themselves."*

Mikel didn't understand. But that mattered little in that moment. He needed to act. Now. Before he lost the chance.

Desperate, he did the only thing that came to mind.

He crouched down swiftly and slammed the hilt of the scimitar against the stone.

The blast of energy that erupted from the Blade of Light made the entire Tor shake and rumble. Massive stones fell from the ceiling above. Clouds of dust and grit billowed up when the rocks struck and shattered.

That shockwave of unstoppable power ripped through the Druden, burning the monsters made mostly of spirit into a flaky ash and banishing them to the Spirit World.

More importantly, the energy Mikel released demanded that Assindra focus on protecting herself. The Dark Magus, afraid of enjoying the same fate as the Druden, was forced to shield herself from the Light threatening to overwhelm her defenses.

Not waiting to see if that actually came to pass, Mikel grabbed Drin's arm and pulled her toward the gate behind the struggling Assindra.

36

A HELPING HAND

"Close the gate," Drin ordered through gritted teeth. The strain was becoming too much for her. She had scarcely an ounce of strength left as she pulled on the Talent and fought to hold back Assindra.

"I'm trying to do that." Mikel didn't bother to explain that he was also trying to protect her from those attacks that she couldn't defend against herself.

Having recovered from Mikel's shocking display, the Dark Magus blasted streak after streak of tainted power through the open doorway.

Mikel scrambled to stay out of Drin's way as she battled, though in truth now she spent most of her time defending against the punishing power Assindra fired at them.

Driven by her anger and embarrassment, the Dark Magus forced Drin farther back from the secret entrance to the Tor. The entrance that Assindra wanted to use as an exit so that she could finally claim what she believed rightfully belonged to her.

The Blade of Light.

The blazing weapon sang in Mikel's hands as he sliced

through the blackened shards of power that he feared would catch Drin at the worst possible time. And when he didn't recover fast enough to cut through the tainted magic that came at him like the floods that surged over the Crux's seawall, he held his sword before him. Standing strong, the ancient weapon consumed the Curse with a rapacious appetite.

They were holding their own. But Drin was right.

What they were doing wasn't enough.

Even with them working together so effectively, their current effort was unsustainable against a Dark Magus of Assindra's skill and strength.

"Try harder!" Worry laced Drin's command. She was weakening. She couldn't ignore that fact. Soon, she would make a mistake. And once she did ...

Drin didn't want to think about that.

All she could think about was maintaining her focus. Calling on what little reserve of strength she had left, she refused to give Assindra the satisfaction of the victory she craved.

"I can't get close to the door. I need to get there if we're to have any chance of ..." Mikel began but didn't finish his explanation as the hair on the back of his neck bristled. He ducked, sensing the spikes of white-hot energy the instant before they screamed right over his shoulder and through the doorway.

Disrupting Assindra's attack, the Dark Magus faltered for just a heartbeat. Caught off guard, she needed to adjust to this new combatant who had joined the fight against her.

Mikel smiled as he stood up again. Maximus had been true to his word, just as Mikel believed he would be. He and his Peikkos had kept Nat safe while he was rescuing Drin.

"You can't stay out of trouble, can you?" Nat asked as she stepped up next to Mikel, adding her power to Drin's efforts.

While the Queen of the Crux attacked with an enviable

precision, targeting the Dark Magus time and again, Nat adopted a more chaotic approach.

She sent spike after spike of magic through the doorway. Sometimes toward Assindra but more often seeking to strike close to her. Floor. Ceiling. Wall. It didn't matter. Nat didn't care about the destruction she caused, believing the resulting tumult of falling rock and clouds of crushed stone would help Mikel.

And it did.

With Assindra having no choice but to defend against attacks that were coming from two directions at once, she had no time to give any thought to the Bearer of the Blade.

Mikel was quick to take advantage of the haphazard clash. Sprinting forward he dodged around several shards of power that sizzled through the air, both the Talent and the Curse, before reaching the stone door.

As soon as he placed his hand on the rock, the magic within him surged out through his palm, runes of power flaring back to life.

"You will not escape me, thief! You will not ..."

Mikel didn't bother to listen to Assindra, who had noticed his approach but could do nothing to hinder him thanks to Drin and Nat. Instead, he relished the power racing through him, allowing that magic to teach him.

Rather than seeking to push the door closed physically, understanding that would be impossible, he used the Light to close the gate. The stone began to move. Slowly at first. Then with greater momentum. The runes flared with even greater intensity as Mikel applied more of the power that had been hidden within him.

Recognizing that she was losing her chance, Assindra reached for even more of the Curse. Sending a swirling cloud of black toward the closing door, she was anxious to emerge from beneath the Tor. Certain that catching her opponents in that prickly mist would ensure her success.

Drin and Nat held their ground despite the mounting strain, throwing shield after shield in front of the cloud. Each one destroyed. Yet each one gaining Mikel precious seconds by slowing the advance of the Dark Magus' creation.

Just a few feet away from breaking free, the cloud now spinning with the speed of a tornado, Assindra coming right behind it, Mikel added a burst of Light to his efforts.

That last bit of energy proved the difference. Assindra's shriek of anger was silenced when the stone slid back into place. The instant Mikel removed his hand, the runes faded back into the grey stone.

Grateful for his success, Mikel placed his forehead against the cool stone. He savored its rough touch, which reminded him that he was still alive and that he had a great deal more to learn.

Yet even with his eyes closed, he could still see Assindra's angry scowl and the look in her eyes that confirmed their confrontation had been delayed. Not settled.

"Will this hold her?" Drin's voice broke his concentration.

Mikel pushed himself off the stone and nodded to Drin, having already asked the same question of Knute, the former Bearer of the Blade always willing to offer his opinion when requested. "Yes, Assindra can't make it through this gate. Not if I don't open it for her. It's warded."

"And you know this how?"

Mikel didn't reply to her question, instead studying Drin's scowl. She had just escaped her prison and battled a Dark Magus to a draw – with a little bit of help admittedly, yet even after all that she clearly was less than pleased. "You certainly are testy."

"I have every right to be," Drin growled. "I was used as bait again."

Mikel nodded. "I can understand your displeasure about that."

"I'm displeased as well about my conversation with your former ... whatever she is to you."

"Former partner," Mikel clarified. He had been hoping that he could avoid this topic for a little while longer. At least until they were well away from the Tor and closer to the Trench.

"If that's what you want to call her," Drin snorted, thinking about the many ways *partner* could be defined. "We have a lot to talk about. It seems our lives, past and present, are entwined. So we will be speaking later. You can count on that."

Mikel had dodged that arrow. At least for a time. "I was afraid you were going to say that."

"The Broken Bear afraid to discuss certain matters?" Drin offered Mikel a raised eyebrow and a thin smile.

"With you, yes. You can be quite intimidating, Queen of the Crux."

That seemed to mollify Drin so Mikel shifted his focus when Nat stepped up to him. His smile faded when he saw her angry look.

"That was quite a risk you took," Nat stated in a deceptively calm voice.

"I didn't have much choice."

"You always have a choice."

"Then let me rephrase." Mikel wasn't sure what to think about how Nat had switched roles with him. Usually he was the one giving the lessons. Not taking them. "I didn't have any good choices."

"That's better." Nat tried to hide her concern for Mikel in her anger. "You were wrong by the way."

"Wrong about what?" Mikel asked, trying to keep up as Nat had a habit of switching between topics without any real transitions, forcing Mikel to stay on his toes.

"Having me stay here waiting for you."

"Really? We're going to talk about this now?"

"I can't think of a better time."

"I can." Mikel's tone suggested that he wasn't in the mood to engage in this conversation. A repeat of the one they had before he entered the Tor in search of the Queen of the Crux, who now stood to the side watching their encounter with a placid expression that did little to hide her intense interest.

"Admittedly, me being here proved to be a good decision. If I wasn't, I couldn't have saved you both as I just did." Nat's self-satisfied smirk confirmed how pleased she was with herself.

Mikel understood what was going on. Nat didn't need to rehash their argument. She just needed to confirm her success in her own mind, her own doubts about herself and her abilities never far from breaking through the shield she wove around herself. Even so, he offered a taste of the sarcasm she so enjoyed employing against him. "I'm glad your quick thinking and impressive skill didn't go to your head."

"Not at all," Nat confirmed.

"You feel better now?" Mikel asked.

"Much. Thanks."

"Can you sense them?" Drin asked. Intrigued at how the dialogue concluded between Mikel and Nat. Not quite sure she understood what happened but not having the time to think more deeply about it.

Mikel nodded. There were more Druden hunting them.

It seemed that Assindra had a limitless supply of the monsters from the Spirit World.

The difference being that now Mikel knew how to dispatch their hunters with extreme prejudice.

"We have some time. They were well behind the two I destroyed. They're going to need to head back through the Tor before they can come at us. By the time they do, we should have a lead on them."

"Do you have a way to get us back to the Crux safely?"

Mikel gave her a wry smile. "I have a way. How do you define safe?"

37

A PAINFUL TRUTH

"Not your finest moment, Assindra."

"You dare to challenge me?" Assindra puffed herself up, stare becoming a glare, voice as hard as the stone of Malor's throne, refusing to display any weakness to the King of the Tor.

"Challenge you?" Malor mulled that prospect for a time as if it were a foreign concept. "No. I'm not challenging you." He leaned toward her, forearms on his knees, as he smiled down from his seat of power. The smile of a predator preparing to strike. "I'm simply speaking the truth. Whether you care to hear it is of little concern to me. What does concern me is that all of your best-laid plans have come to nothing."

"You don't know of what you speak," Assindra hissed, back stiffening to the point of breaking. She sensed his anger. Yet he revealed nothing in his gaze other than a wolfish anticipation and a menace that appalled her.

Here, now, she couldn't deny the fact that she felt weak. That she was about to shatter into thousands of pieces. And in his presence of all places.

It was as if being close to Malor undid her. His very essence slithering through the many walls she had built around herself over the years. Those walls now no more than sand to be washed away.

When she first sought him out, believing that he could be the one to help her achieve the dream that had remained just beyond her grasp for so long, she had been fascinated by this quality of his. Attracted to it even. Malor demonstrated a strength and potency she had never seen in anyone else before. A strength that she didn't quite understand.

Now? She loathed this aspect of him.

Worse, she loathed herself.

Because in that moment she realized that not only had she misjudged him, but she also feared him.

She had allowed this to happen. She had placed herself in this position. She had allowed her curiosity and greed to get the better of her.

Yet why take herself to task for that now?

Her curiosity and greed had ruled her since she was a child. Those characteristics had led her to the power she exercised now. And perhaps these two traits of hers would allow her to navigate the danger staring down at her.

The danger that was Malor Dragoran.

"I know quite well of what I speak." The King of the Tor refused to acknowledge his own culpability in their failures. Because in his mind he never failed. Any setbacks he experienced resulted from the failures of others. Always.

Assindra his latest case in point.

So promising at the start. Now ...

Demonstrating her weakness just like all the others.

Malor fumed on the inside as he considered her failure. She had lost the lever needed to double the size of his Kingdom by once again joining the Crux to the Tor. Thereby recreating the Splintered Empire.

It was to be his first step as he expanded his power and his reach. The Giants of the Rime would be next.

And then?

All the Realms would be open to him. It was just a matter of deciding which direction to move first.

Although he did have one particular Realm in mind after he crushed the Frost Lord. Not because the Realm was critical to his plans, but rather because it gave him a chance to gain the revenge that he had craved for so long. To pay back those who had betrayed him.

That would all have to wait for a little while longer, however, because of the ineptitude of the woman who stood before him.

Assindra had lost the Blade of Light.

Again.

The artifact so important to what he wanted to accomplish. That he needed before all else.

What infuriated him all the more was that the ancient weapon had been in the Ring without his knowledge. It was right within his grasp. Yet it had slipped the trap before he could act.

He had sensed a disturbance within the Tor and had assumed that it was the Queen of the Crux regaining her use of the Talent when the magic in the bracelet vanished. Not realizing until it was too late the true cause of his unease.

But now he knew. And he also knew that the thief who had touched the Blade of Light was now a greater threat.

Malor wanted to reach out and place his hands around Assindra's neck, crushing the breath from her.

He didn't, despite how difficult it was for him to control himself.

Now wasn't the time to surrender to his urges. His desires. Not until he had the artifact, the ancient weapon needing to come before all else.

"You don't know of what you speak," Assindra argued, interrupting his thoughts. "Because if you did, you would know that I stood against two Magii."

"You are strong enough to defeat two Magii." Malor's disdain dripped from his words.

"With time," she growled. "I didn't have the time I needed."

"Why not?"

Assindra didn't reply right away because her thoughts weren't of the two Magii. Those young women were common enough concerns that she could deal with when next they met. She had little doubt of that.

No, it was the King of the Underworld who kept stepping to the forefront. She didn't know if she should be angry, impressed, or embarrassed that her thief freed the Queen of the Crux with such ease.

She decided that she was impressed.

Intrigued as well.

She could sense some power within the thief that tugged at her, and she didn't understand why.

This King of the Underworld or Broken Bear or Knife or Fox who had so many more names and fascinating qualities brought forth something from her past that she thought that she had forgotten.

But she couldn't now.

She couldn't ignore what her heart was telling her. And although she had little reason to believe what she suspected was the truth, she had no good cause to doubt it either.

"Because the thief has become something more than he was in the short time he has retained the Blade."

"What has he become?" Malor asked the question despite already knowing the answer, wondering how long it would take Assindra to realize the truth ... and then admit to it.

"A Bearer of the Blade."

"You did not consider the possibility of that happening when you selected your thief?"

"Why would I consider that possibility? He's not a Giant."

Malor chuckled then. A raspy sound. "So smart, so cunning, yet so blind."

"How dare you!" Assindra pushed all her rage into her voice, feeling even more inadequate under Malor's hard, calm glare. His eyes shocked her, having changed in just the last few seconds to ... she didn't know how to describe it.

What was there? What was it in his harsh gaze that sent a shiver of fear down her spine?

Looking at him now, Malor didn't appear to be the same man she had allied herself to. Shared her bed with. Planned to betray.

The man looming above her revealed a potency that she couldn't fully grasp. A potency that ...

Malor laughed, enjoying how Assindra struggled with what was right in front of her. "You do not see what you should see. So caught up in yourself and your own desires." He pushed himself back into his throne, understanding coming to him. "Or is it rather that you do not want to see?"

She couldn't quite believe what her senses and intuition were telling her. She didn't want to believe. "This can't be possible."

"More than possible," Malor confirmed, his laugh replaced by a flinty tone. "You need to open your eyes, Assindra. They have been blind for too long."

"I don't ..."

"You are surprised. That bothers me. Let us return to the Bearer."

"I had no idea that the thief could become a Bearer," Assindra spat, her frustration plain. "He was just a thief! I picked him because he was the best on the Crux."

"Yet he is more than a thief."

"The King of the Underworld, yes, but what does that have to do with ..."

"Not that, Assindra. You didn't sense it when you spoke with him? Fought with him?" Malor shook his head sadly. "That is what disappoints me the most. I thought you were stronger. More aware. More prescient. Apparently not."

"I just didn't think that after all this time ..." she began, stopping to gather her churning thoughts. Finally, she was able rip her gaze from Malor's, that proving to be more of a challenge than fighting the Queen of the Crux and the girl beneath the Tor. Her voice softened in a way that it hadn't since she was a young woman. Before the pressures of the path she had chosen bore down upon her. "He was supposed to be dead. I was told that he was dead."

"But you never confirmed it yourself."

"No," she admitted in a heavy sigh. "I never felt the need." The last said only to herself.

"Tell me about the thief who just stole the Queen of the Crux, Assindra." Malor leaned forward again, locking onto the Dark Magus' eyes and refusing to let go. "Tell me about your son."

38

BRAVING THE TRENCH

"So what's going on?"

Drin turned toward Nat, giving her a puzzled stare as they advanced toward the rim of the Trench through the long grass littered with wildflowers. "What do you mean?"

"You know exactly what I mean." She offered Drin a raised eyebrow. When Drin frowned Nat gave her a much-too-obvious wink. "What's going on between you and Mikel?"

"Between me and Mikel?" Nat's comment caught her off guard, her eyes widening just a little bit. She looked down for a moment, the long grass giving way to dirt and rock, collecting herself, before adopting a more composed expression. At least she hoped it was more composed.

"Yes, between you and Mikel. I'm not a fool. I can't help but see it. The looks. The smiles. The light touches on his arm." She stepped in closer to Drin, whispering, "So what's going on?"

"Nothing's going on," Drin stated in an even tone.

Nat snorted her disbelief. "Give me a little more credit, please. I was an orphan until Mikel took me in. Before that, I lived by my wits. And a large part of that was seeing all that was happening around me. Because if I didn't I'd run into trouble. And right now, I'm sensing trouble. Something has changed between you and Mikel."

Drin sighed, then shook her head and scrunched her lips together. She should have expected as much. Nat was much too aware and much too knowledgeable for someone of her age. Then again, it was that precociousness that Drin valued while they trained together. "Why do you want to know?"

"You know why I want to know," Nat prodded.

"Now you're just digging."

"It's allowed," Nat attested.

"Is it?" Drin challenged. "You do realize that I'm the Queen of the Crux?"

"You make that hard to forget. No worries there."

Drin ignored Nat's sarcasm. She could have taken offense. She chose not to. She understood from where Nat's concern was coming. "Mikel has proven to be a better friend and ally than I deserve. I value and am grateful for what he has done for me and the Crux. And it's that last that's most important. The Crux. Without his aid I lose the Crux. And if I lose the Crux, the Crux loses."

"That's quite an enlightened perspective you have," Nat said, her sarcasm even thicker this time.

"It's a realistic perspective. You know Mikel better than I do. But in the time that I've known him, I've learned that he does what he must for the people important to him and his interests. That's where his loyalty lies. And I have no doubt that Mikel aiding me comes from the belief that my ruling the Crux aids him. If he doesn't believe that, I'd still be in the Tor."

"You make a good point," Nat admitted grudgingly, hearing the truth in her words. "Still, there's more to my questioning than just that."

"How so?"

"I have a vested interest. I like what I have right now and I don't want you to mess it up for me." Nat said it quietly. Without any heat. Doing her best to hide her worry.

Drin tried to ease her student's concern while also bringing the conversation to a close. "You have nothing to fear, Nat. Mikel adores you. You're like a daughter to him. That much is obvious."

Nat's frown curled into a smile, pleased to hear it. Some of the tension she was feeling eased. Still, she had started this conversation for a reason, and she meant to see it through even as her walking companion attempted to set her on a different path.

"I know that but thank you for saying it." She leaned in even closer to Drin, her shoulder almost touching hers. "I still want an answer to my question. What's going on between you and Mikel?"

Drin chuckled softly. She should have expected this. Nat didn't give up on anything. Ever. It was obvious while she worked with her to master the Talent. It was obvious now. A trait to be admired. Unless you were on the other end of the hard stare Drin was receiving right then.

More disconcerting, she couldn't argue against the legitimacy of Nat's question.

Politics aside, what was going on between her and Mikel?

Nat was correct. Circumstances had changed between them since they escaped the Tor.

Maximus and the spirit army of the Peikkos guarded them as they made their way back through the Deep. Passing as quickly as they could on, over, and around the maze of roots that covered the forest floor. Despite their hunger, the Grim and Creepers had little desire to challenge those lost at the Bloody Gates. The creatures of the Deep coming close on occasion, though never so close as to cause any real concern. The spirits more than happy to remind the beasts that the heart trees belonged to them.

Having little to fear thanks to their escort, despite her concerns regarding the Crux Drin had allowed her mind to wander. Her thoughts landed time and time again on the topic that Nat had just raised.

Yet even with all her thinking on the matter, Drin hesitated to answer. Because though she had mulled a great deal about what seemed to be happening with Mikel, she had not reached any conclusions. And she really didn't want to talk about this with Nat until she did. Not knowing what she should say. Not knowing what she didn't want to say. Not knowing what she shouldn't say.

She and Mikel had grown closer during the last few days. That much was obvious. Often they talked for hours after dinner while they were nestled in the roots of a heart tree.

They spoke on matters they rarely if ever discussed with anyone else, revealing pieces of themselves that demonstrated a potentially dangerous openness. Neither knowing what to make of this newfound connection between them.

Maybe it was because they both felt comfortable in the company of Maximus and his fallen brothers and sisters. Protected in the gloom of the Deep. The real world not yet real again until they entered the sunlight once more. A brief vulnerability demonstrated because of their current circumstances.

Or was there more to it than that?

She didn't know. And her inability to reach any conclusions suggested that she might not want to know. At least not yet. Because her thoughts had taken her down a potentially treacherous path.

What was she supposed to do?

She was the Queen of the Crux.

And he was ...

What was he?

Because the title King of the Underworld didn't do him justice. Not anymore.

"We're here," Mikel called, pulling Drin from her thoughts and saving her from having to give Nat a response. At least for the time being, because the look Nat gave her confirmed that the conversation between them was far from over.

Mikel stopped not too far from the edge of the mile-long drop, the clouds hiding the Trench resembling a grey blanket. He had led them to a stone outcropping that served as the entrance to a gap along the cliffs. The ingeniously hidden path would take them to the base of the Trench without any of the canyon's residents aware of their presence.

"This is still your plan?" Drin asked, clearly not impressed. "We're going to walk across the floor of the Trench?"

Mikel shrugged. "You have a better idea?"

"I'm sure I can come up with one," Drin stated, though there was a strain of doubt audible in her voice. "How did you make it across the Trench the first time if you didn't take the Splintered Bridge?" That would have been her first choice. But Mikel was right. There was little chance of getting past the Tor soldiers guarding the eastern side of the span.

"Leonardo gave us one of his newest raptors."

"Raptor?" Drin was aware that Leonardo was doing a good bit of work for her uncle at the Splintered Bridge, but she didn't know what a raptor was.

"A glider," Nat explained.

"Then why can't we take the glider back?"

"Because there's no launcher on this side of the Trench and even if there was it wouldn't matter because Mikel crashed it when we landed on this side," Nat explained with a studied nonchalance.

"Crashed it?"

"I want to point out that we did make it to this side." Mikel felt the need to defend himself. "And we walked away from the landing."

"He crashed it," Nat confirmed, giving Mikel a smile that let him know she was enjoying the bite she was taking out of him. "He struggled quite a lot with the controls."

"I wouldn't have struggled so much if we weren't also evading attacks by Wyverns and black dragons."

"Wyverns and black dragons?" Drin couldn't quite believe what she was hearing. Then again, this was Mikel. So why was she surprised?

"Mikel has a knack for stirring up a hornet's nest even when there isn't a hornet's nest to be found," Nat continued.

"I do not ..."

Drin held up a hand, cutting off Mikel. "Are you two done?" Of course, she really couldn't disagree with Nat's claim, but that wasn't relevant to what they needed to do.

They both looked at her. Then they looked at one another. Through some silent communication they nodded.

"Good. So this glider can't fly?" Drin sought to clarify.

Nat and Mikel nodded again to confirm that fact.

"And that might be a good thing because Mikel clearly isn't very good at the controls."

Mikel didn't nod then. He frowned instead, having a different opinion, though based on Drin's flinty expression he kept it to himself.

"So with no raptor, we either need to cross at the Splintered Bridge ..."

"Which will be heavily guarded," Mikel interjected.

"Or we need to cross the cavern floor," Drin finished, clearly not pleased by Mikel's interruption.

"Correct."

Drin turned her sharp gaze to the King of the Underworld. "If you had so much difficulty coming across the Trench in a glider, why would crossing the Trench along the cavern floor be any easier?"

Mikel shrugged, feeling no need to color the truth. "It's not."

"Yet you seem confident," Drin poked.

Mikel shrugged again. "Just because it's difficult doesn't mean it can't be done."

"And you know this how?"

"How else do you think I keep track of all my businesses in the Kingdom of the Tor?"

~

"Is there a tunnel like this one on the other side?" Drin gazed across the mile-wide canyon, shocked by the color that lit up a rather barren landscape.

Tors wrapped in white and pink heather sprouted up from the rocky ground, their heads lost in the clouds far above. The bases pockmarked by a hollow blackness.

Caves.

Or rather nests.

Mikel had warned them to stay well clear of those black holes in the rock.

"Unfortunately not," Mikel replied as if that failure was of little concern. "Have no fear, though. We have other means for escaping the Trench."

He stepped up next to Drin, Nat at his shoulder.

"You're not going to tell us?" Drin wanted a bit more information before she risked her life crossing what for centuries had been known as a killing ground for anyone foolish enough to dare the Trench.

"Almost directly in line with us from where we stand now there's a crevice. That's our goal."

"No tunnel?" Drin didn't understand how they were supposed to climb out if there wasn't a passageway in the rock. Scaling the wall would be a fool's errand. Not only because of the height, but also because of the Wyverns.

"No tunnel. Something better."

"Something better than ..."

Mikel raised his hand, asking for silence. He was feeling uneasy. Which, in itself, was quite common. He felt like this every time he crossed the Trench. Yet now?

All was quiet. Not a hint of movement to be seen along the canyon floor. The only activity was the occasional Wyvern diving through the cloud cover far above. Thankfully, those beasts were few and far between and none showed any interest in this part of the Trench, which was several leagues farther south from where Mikel and Nat initially crossed.

A good sign, perhaps. Mikel would have preferred that Maximus and his brothers in arms escorted them to the other side, likely having the same effect on the denizens of the Trench as on the Grim and Creepers. Although willing, Maximus informed him that he could go no farther as he was bound to the Deep by blood and death.

Mikel shook his head ever so slightly as he studied what lay before him. He had used this route several times. Not once had it been like this. It was seemingly devoid of life, that in itself not uncommon, but with that came a sense of impending doom.

That last part was what worried him.

He didn't understand why he was so on edge. And he didn't like it when he didn't understand something.

Could it just be the timing?

He usually crossed mid-morning when the black dragons and Wyverns kept to their nests. The beasts were nocturnal unless disturbed.

It was late afternoon. Yet even so they should be able to cross to the other side before the animals that ruled this killing ground emerged from their dens.

Glimpsing Mikel's disquiet in the creases of worry around his eyes, Drin asked a question of Nat. "What do you sense?"

Nat stepped forward, making sure that she stayed within the shadows of the natural passageway they had followed from the top of the Trench all the way to the bottom.

Reaching for the Talent, she extended her senses exactly as Drin had taught her during their journey back to the Crux. Just one of many skills the Queen of the Crux had incorporated in her training.

Nat immediately sensed the Talent in play that wound its way along the base of the cavern. Mikel had explained that Magii had constructed the road centuries before. It served as the only safe passage through the Trench from north to south and still retained its vitality even after all these centuries.

Beyond that, Nat didn't identify any immediate threats. Nevertheless, the skin on the back of her neck was prickling. She didn't know why, and she didn't like it.

"There's nothing that I can identify that should worry me."

"But ..." Drin prodded.

"But I don't like it. It feels wrong."

Drin smiled, pleased by the thoroughness of Nat's efforts. "Another lesson for you. The Talent cannot and will not reveal everything. There are times when you need to go with your gut. Wouldn't you agree, Mikel?"

"I certainly don't disagree."

Drin scowled, his grin and wink irritating her. "Not helpful."

"I was just answering your question."

"Just ignore him," Nat sighed. "He can be like this at times."

"Acting the child? Yes, I'm much too familiar with this side of him."

"That's a nice way to put it," Nat murmured.

"I just answered Drin's question," Mikel protested, not sure how he got on the bad sides of his two traveling companions so quickly.

Drin felt out of sorts as well. It could simply be her proximity to the Trench and its residents. It could be something else entirely. She didn't know. But she did know she needed to get back to the Crux quickly. "Even with our reservations, do we cross?"

"We do," Mikel confirmed with a nod.

"And what's our best approach for doing that?"

"Carefully and quietly."

"That's not much of a plan," Drin charged.

"It's all in how you look at it," Mikel replied, his sardonic grin not instilling confidence in Drin or Nat.

Mikel swept his gaze from left to right then above before beginning his survey again. He was searching for any sign of movement within the caves dotting the bases of the stony spires they passed by. Grateful that all remained quiet as he, Nat, and Drin hiked across the floor of the Trench, making it a point to stay well clear of the dark hollows. There was no reason to do anything that might draw the attention of the predators resting in the gloom.

He judged that they were almost halfway across the canyon floor. Even so, the safety of the road was still a quarter mile away. The Magii-built route curled away from them and toward the far side to avoid several tors that jutted out of the ground all within one hundred yards of one another.

It had been an uneventful crossing. Just the way he liked it.

Nevertheless, the itch between his shoulder blades kept him on edge. Exactly like the prickling sensation on the back of Nat's neck, this was a feeling that he never ignored.

But what was the cause?

The black dragons and Wyverns had yet to demonstrate any interest in them.

So why the sense of approaching peril?

Unfortunately, the validity of his worry was revealed no more than ten yards farther across the Trench.

"We have a problem." Nat shifted her focus back toward the way they had come. She was composed though clearly concerned.

She had been using the Talent to search around them ever since they entered the Trench, seeking to fine-tune her skill while keeping an eye on their surroundings.

Nat was pleased that she had narrowed her focus to such a degree that she could identify the individual black dragons slumbering in their dens and the Wyverns perched in their well-hidden roosts that dotted the cavern walls.

However, she wasn't pleased by what she discovered.

"Druden." Drin identified them at the same time through her use of the Talent.

Nat pointed back toward the crevice that had taken them to the bottom of the Trench. Emerging right then from the same passageway they had used were three of the monsters from the Spirit World.

The first well ahead of the other two.

Drin cursed under her breath. How Assindra could summon these monsters from the Spirit World without a second thought she didn't understand, and she ... Drin pushed that useless thought from her mind. The here and now was what mattered.

"Do we fight them?" Drin asked.

"Not yet. Not until we have to." Mikel feared what would happen once the clash began. Three Druden were bad enough. He didn't want to add black dragons and Wyverns to the mix as well.

"To the road?" Drin suggested.

"As fast as we can," Mikel confirmed.

Drin and Nat took the lead, Mikel covering the rear, as they sprinted toward the route built by the Magii.

Mikel ignored the stirring he sensed within the caves. His focus was on the large stones that were evenly spaced along the cavern floor and growing bigger in size with every step they took.

They were almost there. Just a few hundred more yards.

"Mikel!" Drin shouted. Well ahead of him, about to step between the stones, she looked over her shoulder. She was worried that Mikel was falling farther behind them because of his protesting knee. Nat had just passed between the rocks to join her.

The Drude ahead of its other ilk was right on Mikel's heels and drawing dangerously closer.

Mikel sensed the hunter at his back as well. The musty, ancient evil of the Spirit World tickled his spine.

He had hoped to get just a hundred yards farther on and within the relatively safe confines of the road before this combat took place. But it wasn't to be. He would need to play the hand he had been dealt.

In the same motion he skidded to a stop and pulled the Blade of Light from the scabbard across his back.

As soon as his fingers wrapped around the hilt, the weapon blazed brightly to life.

Aware that the quiet of the canyon was coming to an end, Mikel wanted to end this combat before the traditional perils of the Trench emerged from their lairs.

That desire guiding him, he took a more aggressive approach than he might have otherwise. Rather than waiting for the Drude to reach him, he began the combat by sliding forward and slashing from shoulder to hip then back up.

The Drude tried to pull back, taken by surprise.

That miscalculation cost the Drude badly.

Where the blazing steel sliced through the Drude's essence, it shriveled then flaked away, the creature's spirit burning at the touch of the magicked weapon. The folds of black crisped to an ash then disappeared entirely before hitting the ground.

Angered, its fury demanding an immediate response, the

pain of its wound excruciating, the Drude swiped wildly with its claw.

That proved to be another mistake.

Anticipating the attack, Mikel brought his scimitar through the space in front of him with a whiplike speed and on an angled arc. The steel sliced through the monster's arm, severing the claw, the blade continuing on its path and cutting deeply into the Drude's neck.

The result was devastating.

For the Drude.

A bright flash erupted from the Blade, Mikel releasing a burst of the Light as soon as the sizzling steel connected that ripped through what was left of the Drude. The monster issued an ear-splitting keen that died when it exploded in a cloud of cinders.

Mikel was quite pleased by his success. He had no time to celebrate, however.

Two more Druden were coming for him.

"Stay between the stones!" Mikel didn't know if Nat and Drin heeded him. And he couldn't check to see where they were.

Not with Druden bearing down on him.

The monsters streaked across the cavern floor. Both less than a hundred yards away.

He would need to stand against them. He was too slow. If he ran, they'd take him down from behind.

And that was something that he would never allow.

His face hardening into a stony mask, he braced himself on the loose shale and dirt beneath his feet. One foot in front of the other. Blade of Light held in a two-handed grip. As if he was preparing to engage in a combat.

But he wasn't.

At least not in the form the Druden suspected.

Upon escaping the Tor, as he made his way through the

Deep, Mikel had engaged in a series of conversations with Knute and several of the other Bearers of the Blade who were now linked to him. The dialogue all in his head, he wasn't yet ready to share this unique form of communication with Drin and Nat. Not wanting to deal with the inevitable questions that would follow.

A great many of those conversations focused on how to battle the various threats he had come across or likely would in the days ahead. In particular, monsters such as those called from the Spirit World.

As the pair of Druden advanced toward him, claws extended, eyes gazing at him with an otherworldly hunger, desperate to claim his spirit, he put into practice what he had learned.

Calling to the Blade, linking the energy surging within him to the ancient artifact, he resisted the urge to slam the hilt of his weapon on the ground as he did while battling Assindra. A useful tactic and one that he was certain he would use again.

Just not now.

Now he wanted to send a message to these creatures from the Spirit World.

A very final one.

He didn't even need to point the blade. He just held it in front of his body. The Blade of Light directed by his thoughts. His desires. His needs.

And right then his need was quite simple.

The ancient weapon was more than happy to comply.

Despite the Druden now being only ten yards away and closing at an alarming rate, they got no closer.

Mikel couldn't help but smile.

At his command, a steady stream of light blasted out from the steel where the hilt crossed with the blade. Slamming into the Druden, illuminating them, the energy burned away the creatures crafted more of shadow and mist and left nothing behind except for the shrieks of agony that echoed in the Trench.

Mikel had no time to enjoy his victory, however, understanding exactly what would happen next.

The rush of power he released set off a cascade of side effects.

The ground rumbled as if an earthquake had struck. Loose stones fell from the sides of the tors and the Trench's walls. With loud crunches, several rocks larger than cottages shattered into thousands of smaller pieces when they struck the canyon floor.

Mikel had won his combat. At the same time, he had disturbed the beasts of the Trench. The black dragons and Wyverns were waking.

The ear-splitting cry from above confirmed it for him.

Not needing to look to know what was streaking down toward him, Mikel turned and raced for the stones. He was pleased to see Nat and Drin were already within the safe confines of the road. He was less than pleased to spy out of the corner of his eye the Wyvern diving down toward him from just behind his right shoulder.

He had a decision to make.

Try for the safety of the Magii-built road or fight?

He didn't ponder the question for long. The decision was made for him when he glimpsed the large shadows emerging from the base of the Tor just fifty yards to his right.

The largest shadow gifted him an extra burst of speed, his bad leg obeying him for once.

Now he knew why it had been so quiet in the Trench. The largest black dragon he had ever seen was racing out from its den. The other dragons taking their cues from this monstrous beast.

A chilling dread trickled down Mikel's spine. He was stuck. He had no chance of outpacing the Wyvern.

But if he turned to defend himself, he was dead.

And, even if he killed the Wyvern, he'd be serving himself up as a meal to the five black dragons already sprinting in his direction, the largest one in the lead.

"Run!"

Out of ideas, Mikel did as Nat instructed. Somehow he pushed himself to an even greater speed.

As he pounded across the rough surface, he believed that it was wasted effort. That he'd never get to the safety of the road before he was taken down from behind.

Until a streak of energy shot just a few feet above his head.

The Talent didn't hit the Wyvern squarely. Drin's spear crafted of magic clipped the Wyvern's wing as it tipped down toward Mikel, claws outstretched for the killing blow.

But that was enough.

The animal crashed to the cavern floor, skidding and tumbling through the dirt and rock, one wing charred, the leathery flesh ruined. The other bent at a terrible angle. Yet that was the least of the Wyvern's concerns.

The black dragons chasing Mikel pivoted to the injured beast, deferring to the monstrous brute that ended the Wyvern's shrieks of pain with a single bite that ripped the crea-ture in half.

Ignoring the pain in his knee and leg, blocking out the carnage behind him, his sprint now more a stumbling rush, Mikel kept his eyes focused on his goal.

Just fifty yards away.

Now thirty.

Ten yards.

He skidded between the stones then rolled when he lost his balance, Mikel asking too much of his injured leg. Taking several deep breaths, he pushed himself up. Sheathing his sword, forearms resting on one knee, he turned his head back the way he had come.

The largest of the black dragons had eaten its fill. The other black dragons were fighting over the remains of the Wyvern.

"Thank you," he gasped to Drin when she came to check on him, placing a hand on his shoulder and squeezing warmly.

"It was the least I could do. I owed you." Then she offered him a wry grin. "And I'm glad that you've finally decided to come to your senses and bend the knee."

DRIN DEBATED STEPPING off the path, tired of waiting. The last few hours gnawed at her. The urge to return to the Crux became almost unbearable as the dim grey of the Trench slowly shifted to a darker grey.

Mikel had said that the beasts of the Trench came awake at night. She didn't want to be here for that. However, they still hadn't moved from the road protected by the Talent.

That concern had built upon another.

She was free of Malor Dragoran.

Her Kingdom was not.

She feared what would happen if he sent more troops to the Splintered Bridge. If Assindra joined them and Drin wasn't there to assist her uncle ...

Drin didn't want to think about that.

She needed to get moving.

She needed to act.

Mikel held her back with a gentle grip on her elbow when she inched toward the magical boundary, shaking his head slightly.

"Not yet."

For more than an hour Mikel had been standing at the very edge of the stones that marked the boundary of their protected territory. Shifting his weight every so often because of the ache in his leg, his eyes never left the stretch of ground he was surveying.

The nook in the cliffs that was their objective was only a few hundred yards away. The shadowy crevice visible from where he was standing. Beckoning to him. It was their only path out of their predicament.

The Druden were no longer a problem. The dragons staring hungrily at their backs were an afterthought. Those beasts were unable to advance past the barrier that guarded the trail.

Still, he feared the Wyverns. Several of those animals glided a few hundred yards above the canyon floor in lazy circles. None of them diving in and out of the hanging clouds as was their practice. They were waiting. Ready to strike as soon Mikel and his friends stepped off the path.

With Drin's demonstration of prowess he believed that she could keep those beasts off them long enough to reach the crevice. What he feared more were the handful of black dragons resting in the shade of the tors. They would need to pass those beasts to escape the Trench.

"Why not?" Drin demanded. "Nat and I can handle the Wyverns. This could be our best chance. The dragons are dozing. And you said that when night fell the dragons hunted. I can't afford to lose an entire day stuck here. I need to get back to the Crux."

"Not dozing." Mikel ignored the angst he heard in her voice, understanding where it came from.

"What do you mean?" Drin asked.

"They're trying to play us," he replied with an appreciative nod. "Besides, there are more of these nasties watching us than just those we see."

"They're luring us?" Drin asked in disbelief. Could these animals truly display such cunning?

Mikel nodded. "And not just the black dragons. We see three of those beasts lazing in front of their dens. But there are quite a few more dens with a dragon waiting to rush out at us. Am I right, Nat?"

The young Magus nodded, searching around them constantly with the Talent and pinpointing the locations of all their hunters on this side of the road. "There are. Every hollow contains at least one dragon. In some more than one."

Mikel motioned toward the cliff face. "And there are a great many more Wyverns waiting to launch themselves from their nests."

Neither Drin nor Nat glimpsed anything other than jagged stone running all the way up to the clouds that hung far above them.

"I don't see anything."

"Do you see those notches that begin about three hundred yards up the cliffs?"

It took Drin and Nat a few seconds to identify them. It was difficult to do because they were so well camouflaged. Eyes locked onto one of those scratches in what appeared to be solid stone, a few seconds later they caught the barely visible hint of movement along the cliff face.

"More Wyverns," Nat whispered, a shiver of cold running through her. "Not just the ones flying above us." After her experience of gliding across the Trench, she had little love for the creatures and virtually no desire to battle them again.

Mikel nodded. "They're well concealed against the rock, but they're there. Only their heads are visible above the rim of their perches."

"So we're stuck between a rock and a hard place," Nat murmured. "Or in our particular case, between rock and dragon."

"There you go," Mikel confirmed with a smile, enjoying her dark humor.

"Then how are we supposed to cross?" Drin growled, realizing that the number of their hunters had increased ten-fold.

"A distraction," Mikel replied with a devilish grin.

"THIS IS NOT how I wanted to do this."

Drin could have said more, but she didn't. Saving her breath instead.

Sprinting out from between the stones, they had only gone half the distance to their objective before the black dragons rushed them. The crevice along the base of the wall seemed an ocean away despite being only a few hundred more yards of hard running.

A fist of dragons had joined the three pretending to nap in front of their nests. All of them intent on Drin and her companions, who were no more than appetizers considering how large some of these beasts were.

To say nothing of the Wyverns. Three times as many now circled above than before, a dozen of the flying beasts launching themselves from their perches as soon as she stepped past the stones and the protection of the trail.

All of the predators were eager to dive and claim their prize, though they demonstrated restraint, knowing better than to try to steal the prey from their much larger brethren.

"This is exactly how I wanted to do this," Mikel said with a wicked gleam in his eye. He glanced to his right. He had picked this specific time because all of the black dragons were on his right side. Those that had been napping had shifted their position in just the last half hour. Thanks to that bit of good fortune, he wouldn't have to worry about his left flank.

"It's not safe!" Drin yelled over her shoulder as Mikel drifted farther behind her. She hadn't liked his plan, but she didn't have a better one to offer in its place.

"It's the best chance we have. Trust me." Mikel never took his eyes from the black dragons rushing toward them, picking his victim based on which of the beasts led the pack. "Be ready!"

Mikel skidded to a stop then cut to his right. Breaking off from Nat and Drin as they sprinted toward the crevice, he charged toward the black dragon closest to him. Only twenty yards away and almost on him.

The beast roared, claws churning up dirt and rock. Maw opened wide to snap him up in one bite.

Mikel ignored the ravenous desire that radiated from the beast's menacing black eyes and concentrated solely on what he needed to do. This was his only chance to ensure that at least Drin and Nat made it out of the Trench even if he didn't.

Pulling his scimitar free from the scabbard across his back, the steel coming to life at his touch, he slid through the dirt and loose rock. Ducking the razor-sharp teeth that snapped at him, he passed right between the stunned dragon's legs, blazing Blade slicing through its soft underbelly without a hint of resistance.

With a terrible shriek, the fatally wounded black dragon crashed to the ground. The long gash opened wider when the beast's insides spilled free.

Covered in blood, Mikel pushed himself to his feet and began a stumbling sprint away from the dying animal and toward the crevice in the canyon wall.

Most of the dragons, overcome with hunger and bloodlust, shifted their focus to their dying brethren. Forgetting Mikel for the time being. Although not all. Two of the smaller beasts unwilling to wait for their larger brethren to eat their fill continued their pursuit.

Mikel cursed under his breath. His play had been successful in part, but there was no way he was going to escape the dragons right on his heels in addition to the Wyverns swooping down toward him.

Not unless ...

Mikel's grimace of disappointment shifted to a smile of delight.

Bursts of energy shot past both his shoulders. Blasting into the ground with a terrible force, clouds of dust and dirt mixed with shattered rock erupted around him, hiding him from his pursuers.

Some of the dragons and Wyverns avoided the worst of the shrapnel. The many that didn't suffered through the slivers and shards of stone that shredded them.

Three Wyverns crashed to the ground while one of the black dragons collapsed. All of them bloody messes. All of them unwilling meals for their onrushing brethren.

Grateful for the assistance, Mikel snuck into the crevice, joining Nat and Drin the instant before the closest Wyvern could take him down from behind, the enraged beast shrieking in frustration after its prey escaped.

A handful of the Wyverns were undaunted by their initial lack of success. Landing on the ground they poked their long, razor-sharp beaks into the crevice. Snapping viciously, they hoped to hook their victims and drag them out from their partially protected space.

Drin fired two bursts of magical spheres the size of marbles from her palms.

Each one was a direct hit.

Each one killed a Wyvern.

Best of all, the smoking bodies blocked the entrance to the crevice and bought them a few more seconds.

But only a few.

More of the Wyverns joined the fray. Eager to bite into their brethren's remains and them. Another feeding frenzy already beginning in front of the crevice. And now it was attracting the black dragons that were done gorging themselves.

"This couldn't have been your plan," Drin demanded through gritted teeth, hoping that she was right. Even so, she was prepared to send a few more blasts of power into the beastly scrum, hoping it would force them back.

"It's not. Just keep them off us for a little while longer."

Nat responded to his request by sending several of her own spheres of energy screaming through the crevice. One struck a Wyvern in the chest, killing the beast and adding to the feast. Her other throws were only glancing blows. Her range limited by the narrowness of their cubby hole and the speed with which her targets moved. A wing here. A clawed appendage there. Still, it was enough to add more chaos to the scramble of rapacious beasts seeking to poke their maws into the crevice.

Most important, it gave Mikel the time he needed. Reaching up, he pulled on what looked like a vine but proved to be something else entirely. It was a well-disguised rope. And when he did, a large net dropped free from where it had been hidden in a nook in the stone just above their heads.

"What is this?" Drin liked to believe that she was used to Mikel's surprises, but this one caught her off guard.

"Our way out of here." Mikel spread out the net and grabbed hold of the rope, explaining to Nat and Drin how to slip their arms and legs into the thick strands to ensure they wouldn't fall. "Courtesy of Leonardo," he added with a grin.

With a hard tug on the rope, they were off, shooting up the cavern wall at a stomach-dropping speed as they made use of the system of pulleys that the inventor had designed that extended all the way to the top of the Trench.

"You shouldn't be so pleased with yourself," Drin chided. "I'm not sure I'd call that a plan." The crevice wasn't fully protected in some places, but that didn't matter because they were going much faster than the Wyverns. The beasts on the ground only now began to launch themselves into the air, having no chance of catching up to them.

"It worked, didn't it?" Mikel wished that he could have come up with a cleverer reply, but he was exhausted and his leg was screaming at him. Once they got to the top, all he wanted to do was find a spot where they could settle down for the night.

"I expect better from you," Drin added, wanting to make her point. "Charging that black dragon was either the bravest thing I've ever seen or the most ill-advised."

Nat replied before Mikel could. "Definitely ill-advised. Close to foolish. If not plain old stupid."

39

CLOSER CONNECTION

"I have to agree with Nat," Drin said.

"Agree with her about what?" Reaching the top of the Trench just before darkness fell, Mikel led them deep into the woods to a spot that he was quite familiar with, ensuring that any overly persistent Wyverns couldn't get at them easily.

A small hunter's cottage that he used to store goods destined for passage across the Trench to the Tor was built between two heart trees, the construction so ingenious that it appeared to be a part of the system of curling and twisting roots that extended along the forest floor. The comfortable space was stocked with food and chopped wood for the stove.

After making a stew, he settled down next to the fire. Massaging his leg, he tried to loosen the tight muscles, knowing there was little that he could do about the damage in the joint that made it feel like his knee was filled with broken glass.

Drin sat down next to him. Nat was on the other side of the fire, turned away from them and wrapped in her bedroll. Already fast asleep, the excitement and adrenaline of the day had caught up to her.

"What you did with respect to that black dragon? Taking that beast on by yourself."

Mikel didn't say anything for a time, instead kneading the joint that seemed to burn as hot as the fire in front of him. "So you think I'm a fool?"

Drin shrugged, then she offered him a warm smile, displaying a side of herself that she usually kept well hidden. "Perhaps a brave fool."

Mikel leaned back into the bench he had pulled up close to the fire. "A brave fool?" He laughed softly. "I guess I can live with that."

"You know, when I first met you, I couldn't figure you out."

"How so?"

"At first I couldn't find any consistency in your decisions."

"That's not the first time I've been accused of that," Mikel replied softly.

"But then I realized that I was looking at you in the wrong way."

"You lost me there." Mikel turned slightly so he could look into Drin's eyes, fascinated by how they flashed in time with the dancing flames.

"When I first met you, I thought you were just like everyone else on the Crux. So I applied that frame to you."

"And now?"

"Now I see that you're nothing like most of the people on the Crux I have to deal with regularly."

"You mean the First Families."

"I do," Drin confirmed with a nod.

"I'll take that as a compliment."

"You should." Drin shook her head as she thought more about it. "The First Families do what they want to do. You do what you need to do."

"If you say so."

"I know so," Drin replied in a stronger voice, taking Mikel's comment as a challenge.

"I didn't need to come for you at the Tor." Mikel didn't know what he thought about Drin's argument. Whether he should view her interpretation of him in a positive or negative light.

"You did need to come for me," Drin stated with a rock-solid certainty.

"And why is that?"

Drin opened her mouth to reply, the words about to escape. She bit her tongue before she uttered them, realizing that she had wandered into potentially dangerous territory and not certain if she wanted to be there. Preferring to be cautious in matters such as these, she offered only a part of her reasoning.

"Because you seem to have this ingrained need to do what's right despite what it might cost you."

"Perhaps you could keep your perspective to yourself?" Mikel had never been comfortable talking about himself, and the Queen of the Crux seemed to have a unique talent for breaking down the walls he had built up over the years.

"Why?" Drin didn't understand Mikel's request since she offered her comment as a compliment.

"It could be bad for business. I have a reputation to uphold."

"Ah, yes," Drin sighed, laughing softly and leaning back into the bench before turning to look at Mikel from the side. He wasn't a handsome man. They would both agree on that. But there was a hidden strength to him. A steel spine and a generous heart. An attractive and rare combination. "The terrifying King of the Underworld."

"There you go," Mikel nodded.

"Quite the persona you've developed."

Mikel shrugged. "It was necessary. The cost of doing business."

Drin leaned in even closer to Mikel. "Is it that? Or is it something else entirely?"

"It's helped to eliminate a host of problems."

"And yet you still find yourself entangled in problems."

Mikel turned his head to the right. Locking eyes with Drin, he saw nothing else except for her since they were so close to one another. He studied her small smile and how the flickering flames played off her face. "Those problems tend to come from a single source."

Drin pursed her lips in amusement before replying. "You mean me." She wasn't offended. He was only speaking the truth.

"I do," Mikel confirmed. "Ever since you decided to take that stroll across the Frozen Waste, I haven't been able to get away from you."

"Because of your need to do what's right?" She could have asked a different question, a more personal question. She didn't, however.

Mikel took his time before responding, wondering how much he should say. Worried about Drin's reaction if he said too much, not knowing how she would take it if he told her all that was running through his mind. Rather than assume that risk, he decided to play it safe. "That's it exactly."

Drin let out a slow breath, realizing that she had been holding it while she waited for his reply. "I still have a hard time understanding this persona of yours."

"You've seen me in certain situations. Not in others that have required me to do things I might not have done otherwise."

"Perhaps. Perhaps not." Drin wasn't yet ready to let go of her argument. "You play this role of being mean, ruthless, deadly."

"I am all that," Mikel agreed. "It's not a role."

"Only if need be," Drin corrected. "You're also kind, trustworthy, loyal, and you care about others, particularly those who require assistance. I've seen it from you several times, and Nat has told me many a story about what you really do on the Crux."

"You need to stop."

"Why? Am I making you blush?"

"No, you'll make me angry if you keep this up. I put a lot of work into developing the character of the King of the Underworld. I'd hate to see all that time and effort go to waste."

"Maybe it's not you anymore," Drin wondered, not put off by Mikel's comment. Knowing what it truly was. "Maybe you're changing. Maybe you're less the King of the Underworld and more *my* Broken Bear," she suggested, placing her hand on his thigh just above his injured knee as she spoke.

Mikel stared at her hand. He wasn't certain what he thought about how she changed one of his monikers. That possessiveness both appealing and worrying.

Her hand still on his thigh, however ...

He tried to ignore it, even though he knew that he couldn't. "Maybe you're wrong." Not much of a response, but she had squeezed his thigh gently and distracted him, taking his mind down a path he never thought to travel with respect to Celindria Dengannon.

"Maybe I'm not."

"Why do you always think you're right?" Mikel sought to nudge the conversation back on balance, feeling like the scales had tipped in Drin's favor. "It's really irritating."

"I'm the Queen of the Crux," Drin explained. "I'm always right."

Mikel couldn't help but laugh softly, Drin joining in. Still, her comment remained stuck in his mind. "What if I don't want to change?"

"You might not have a choice."

"But you do have a choice about making noise and making me ill," Nat grumbled from beneath her blankets, unable to hold her peace any longer. Aggravated that her companions' constant prattle had woken her and was making it that much harder to get back to sleep. "So perhaps you could stop doing both?"

"Sorry," Mikel and Drin said at the same time.

Nat grumbled under her breath before she burrowed deeper into her bedroll.

Mikel and Drin sat together in silence for a time, enjoying the warmth of the flames.

"He's with me now," Mikel murmured, not yet ready to let the conversation go and feeling as if Drin had gotten the better of him in the first round.

"What?"

"He's with me now. That's what you said the last time we confronted Liria."

Drin nodded slightly, acknowledging the truth of his statement. "Have you not considered that I might have meant that comment in terms of your loyalty to me rather than the way you're thinking about it?"

"No, that was lost entirely on me." Mikel kept a straight face for as long as he could before the curl of a grin broke out.

Drin nodded then snorted quietly, turning toward him. Her eyes locked onto his dark orbs. Her lips less than a finger's breadth away from his. "You won't bend the knee if I asked you to?"

Mikel smiled at that, patting his bad knee and leg. "I couldn't if I wanted to."

"Convenient," Drin murmured.

"Isn't it though?"

"Have you not considered that there might be other ways to ... demonstrate your loyalty to me." Drin's eyes widened as she waited for Mikel to reply.

"There are?" The tone of Mikel's voice urged Drin to continue.

"There are," Drin confirmed.

Mikel nodded, hesitating at the crossroads they had reached. And what it could mean. For them both. Still, he couldn't help himself. "I'd be more than willing to *discuss* that with you."

"That's good to hear." She leaned into him then, her lips brushing his, that spark of energy back and shooting between them. "Because we really do need to *discuss* exactly what this is."

Mikel and Drin leaned in toward the other intent on continuing the discussion.

40

THE ONE

"I'm pleased to see that the saddle is working," Cadmus stated.

Scipio, the Frost Lord's master smith, stepped up next to Cadmus. They stood atop a snow-covered knoll in the Frozen Waste not too far from the Barrow. Their eyes drawn to the sky.

"Another excellent piece of work, Scipio." Cadmus clapped his friend on the back in appreciation.

Neither spoke to the other for quite some time. Still trying to come to grips with a sight neither had seen in their long lifetimes. In the lifetimes of several of their forebears as well.

A dragon rider.

Cadmus hadn't been certain that Mikel would agree to his proposal. But Mikel had taken one look at the ice dragon waiting for him atop the knoll then picked up the saddle that Scipio had made and approached Eisa.

The dragon Mikel had saved had grown to twice its size since then and didn't fuss except for a snort of discomfort when he tied the strap beneath her belly a bit too tight. Eisa nuzzled him when he loosened it.

And then he was in the air, Eisa taking flight with a few

powerful sweeps of her wings, Mikel riding on the ice dragon's back like it was the most natural thing in the world. As if he was meant to be there, Mikel acting the boy and whooping with a joy he usually restrained as he relished the freedom gifted to him.

"You think he could be the one?" Scipio asked, needing to look away. The ice dragon's acrobatics – sharp twists and curls, corkscrews, precipitous dives – were making him feel ill. Although it appeared as if the Steelheart enjoyed it, laughing and shouting with pleasure at every twist and turn. Eisa responded to his delight by maneuvering with even greater dexterity.

"I think we need to find out," Cadmus confirmed.

"And if he proves to be the one?"

Cadmus didn't respond for quite some time, unable to take his gaze away from the ice dragon and the Steelheart. "Then we know without a doubt that a great peril comes, and we must be prepared to stand against it."

BONUS MATERIAL

If you really enjoyed this story, I need you to do me a HUGE favor – please follow me on Amazon and BookBub. And if you have a few minutes, consider writing a review.

Keep reading for the first chapter from *Roar of the Broken Bear,* Book 3 in my series *Legend of the Dragon Lord.* Order Book 3 from my author website PeterWachtBooks.com. Also available on Amazon.

LEGEND OF
THE DRAGON
LORD

ROAR OF
THE
BROKEN
BEAR

AN EPIC FANTASY FICTION SERIES

PETER WACHT

Roar of the Broken Bear
By Peter Wacht

Book 3 of The Legend of the Dragon Lord

Published in the United States by Kestrel Media Group LLC.

ISBN: 978-1-950236-67-1

eBook ISBN: 978-1-950236-68-8

Library of Congress Control Number: 2025906494

 Formatted with Vellum

1. TAKING A CUT

"Everything in place?" Mikel asked. Every other step he glanced toward the roar of the water flowing below him.

"Yes, we're ready to go. Just in time too."

Teddy and Mikel walked along the southern shore of the Eastern River, one of the four rivers that ran fast and often rough until it struck the Crux and joined the maelstrom that was the Churn that surrounded the island.

With the darkness complete except for when the moon intermittently broke through the heavy clouds, they were careful with their steps along the rough ground. Neither willing to reveal themselves with lanterns despite the certainty that a fall meant a horrendous death.

They had selected this location not only because it was one of the narrowest points on the river -- no more than a few hundred yards separated them from the northern bank -- but also because they stood on a crag that rose more than one hundred feet above the rapids.

"Our target's approaching?"

Teddy nodded. "Samuel's crew has been tracking it. It'll be visible in a few minutes."

"Good to hear." Mikel placed a hand to his right, pushing off the boulder to climb between the two large rocks that blocked the rugged path, the call of the fast-flowing river just a clumsy slip away from claiming him. "I'm looking forward to this. It should be fun."

"You have a strange definition of fun," Teddy grumbled even as the giant of a man clapped Mikel on the back in friendship, although not so hard as to dislodge him as he climbed through the gap.

"You already knew that."

"I did, yet still I wonder."

"Wonder what?" Mikel stopped when they reached the highest point on the crag that jutted out into the river. Their current position reduced the distance to the far shore by fifty yards. Three towers stood tall among the rocks, each one ten yards away from the other. All of them invisible in the gloom of the night.

"Whether your definition of fun comes back and bites you in the ass more often than not."

"As long as it's not the knee." Mikel rubbed his aching joint, boot propped up on a rock. Scaling the rocks that made up the path aggravated his old injury, which was a constant source of pain. It was just a matter of how much pain.

Mikel gazed out into the darkness, tracking the steel cables bolted to the top of each stone tower before he lost them in the gloom. Perhaps Teddy was right. What they were about to attempt wasn't fun. However, he did believe that it was necessary. And he hoped that it would work. Not wanting to think any more than he already had about the consequences of failure.

"That I can understand," Teddy said as he took his place next to Mikel, sitting down on the rock and leaning his back against the base of the stand.

Sensing several more presences coming up behind him, Mikel turned then smiled.

He nodded to Samuel as the lanky fellow dressed all in black, just as he and Teddy were, walked past. Mikel appreciated Samuel's thoroughness. He counted a dozen daggers strapped to his body, and he was sure that the thief carried several more than just those hidden within his clothes and boots.

"Five minutes, no more," Samuel reported as he took up his assigned position by a tower.

Mikel stood straight again. He offered handshakes and pats on the back along with a few words of thanks and encouragement as well as questions about family to each of the men and women who walked past and joined him on what he hoped didn't prove to be a foolhardy expedition. Grateful for their courage and their trust in him.

Once they reached their assigned towers, Mikel's crew began to strap on the gear waiting for them. Silent. Focused. Determined. Running through their minds what would be required of them.

Mikel hoped that his outward calm helped to settle whatever nerves they might be feeling. They had one chance to make the attempt. If any of his crew missed their mark, the difference between success and failure no more than a heartbeat, then they would die.

Even so, when Mikel asked them to assume that risk, none had hesitated. None had said no. All had faith that they could do the job. All had faith in him.

A heartwarming and frightening trust, and Mikel felt that great weight on his shoulders. He had no time to dwell on it, however.

Teddy, sensing the change in Mikel and seeing how his expression shifted toward contemplation, decided to lighten the mood atop the crag by using his friend as his dartboard.

"So how is the Queen of the Crux?" Teddy's tone was light though sharp.

"Seriously? You're asking me that now?" Mikel sat down next to his friend, not missing how his crew continued to prepare themselves while their quiet conversations came to an end. All of them curious. That didn't surprise him. He couldn't say that it pleased him, however.

"We have a few minutes," Teddy replied with a shrug. "It's a worthwhile topic, don't you think? You have been spending a good bit of time with our beneficent Queen."

"Only because I have to," Mikel replied quietly. Shaking his head in annoyance, he really didn't want to have this discussion, but he saw no good way to avoid it. Not with so many eyes on him. Besides, he understood what Teddy was trying to do.

"Right." Based on Teddy's skeptical tone, clearly he didn't believe Mikel's claim. "Quite a lot of discussing going on in her private quarters at all hours of the night."

"It's the only place we can meet without being discovered, and it's the only time that either of us have." Mikel hoped that his argument didn't sound defensive. He couldn't tell. Although the smiles that he was receiving from Samuel and several others suggested that he had fallen short. So be it. Any embarrassment was worth the price if it helped with this job.

"And that's exactly my point." Teddy's broad grin threatened to break through the darkness and reveal their position. "When else are illicit rendezvouses supposed to occur?"

"It's not like that," Mikel growled. He refused to look at Teddy. Instead he focused his attention to the east, looking for any hint of the dark shadow that he knew was coming their way and would close this conversation. Unfortunately, he doubted that the target would come soon enough and dreaded that he would need to suffer through a few more minutes of Teddy's questioning.

"Not like what?" Teddy asked innocently.

"It's just business, Teddy. No more than that."

"Of course it is," Teddy confirmed with a sharp nod, the doubt in his voice impossible to miss.

Mikel shifted his gaze from the river to his friend, not appreciating the smug grin that greeted him. "Do you honestly believe that Celindria Dengannon would be interested in me in the way that you're suggesting?"

"It does sound quite ridiculous when you say it that way."

"Exactly."

"Nevertheless, stranger things have been known to happen."

Mikel took a deep breath, once again scanning the gloom for the shadow that would rescue him from this interrogation. "Teddy, you need to leave off. It's just business. Nothing more."

"So that's what they're calling it these days. Business?"

"Teddy ..." Mikel's voice was quieter, harder, his patience for his friend's teasing waning.

Teddy heard the change. He chose to ignore it, the grins of the men and women waiting by the towers egging him on. "The heart wants what the heart wants, my friend. You know that just as well as I do."

"That may be, but ..."

"I'm not suggesting anything ..."

"You are suggesting something," Mikel corrected.

Teddy ignored him again. "But you must know how it looks. You closeted with the Queen of the Crux almost every night. Privately. And you rarely return before first light. It suggests more than a business relationship."

"As I said, it is the only time we can talk privately." Mikel shook his head. He would almost be amused by Teddy's prodding if he wasn't the target. He could have ended the game. He chose not to, however, seeing how their conversation had captured the attention of his crew. Better that they were thinking about Mikel's difficulties rather than allowing their minds to concentrate on the risk they were about to assume.

"So now it's not business. It's *talking*."

Mikel didn't appreciate the emphasis Teddy placed on the last word. "Teddy, you're pushing your luck."

"I'm just explaining how it appears, Mikel. I'm by no means criticizing. I'm just trying to get a better sense of what's going on." He leaned in toward his friend conspiratorially, though he spoke loud enough for all to hear. "You know it just as well as I do. Often appearances are more important than reality. Truth is a fungible concept."

"That may be, but again, why would anyone even think that Celindria Dengannon would be interested in me?" Mikel's tone was less defensive this time, a hint of truth contained within his query. "You know the saying a face that only a mother could love?"

"You are the King of the Underworld, Mikel. I can see how that might attract her notice."

"You're reaching, Teddy."

"Perhaps, though as I said, stranger things and all that. You do raise a good point, however. You're not much to look at."

"On that we agree." Mikel laughed softly, as did the men and women waiting with him. He couldn't argue that point. His hulking presence tended to put people off though it was quite deceptive. Mikel was extraordinarily fast, particularly with a blade in hand, for someone with a bad knee. "I blame my uncommon looks on my many broken noses."

Teddy reached over and patted Mikel on the shoulder, shaking his head sadly. "I'm sorry to say it, Mikel, but someone must. All the broken noses actually are an improvement."

A louder round of laughter broke out on the crag, the sound smothered by the rush of whitewater far below them.

"Thank you for your honesty," Mikel snorted. "Although I would expect nothing less from you."

"Of course," Teddy replied, offering Mikel a nod. "I'm always happy to put you in your place."

"You do enjoy it," Mikel agreed.

"And I must admit as well that I have heard that some women are attracted to bruisers like you."

"You know, you would fit the parameters of a bruiser as well."

"That may be," Teddy nodded, understanding what Mikel was attempting to do, "but we're not talking about me. I'm not the one spending almost every night with the Queen of the Crux."

"I am not spending every night with the Queen of the Crux," Mikel sighed in exasperation.

"I didn't say every night," Teddy clarified, holding up a hand to halt the additional argument Mikel was about to offer. "I said *almost* every night."

"Thank you for that clarification," Mikel groused.

"My pleasure," Teddy replied, his broad smile somehow getting bigger. Obviously, he was pleased that he could poke at his friend at least for a little while longer. Of course, Mikel was making it a bit too easy for him, and he appreciated why. "You could be right, of course."

"I'm afraid to ask." Mikel shook his head, continuing to give his friend free rein and waiting to see what dart Teddy was going to throw at him next, because he could see how the banter between them continued to ease the strain his crew was feeling. They were about to attempt a maneuver that had never been attempted before, and Mikel preferred that they not think about their chances of success.

"No need, I'm happy to tell you." Teddy's comment gained a few soft chuckles from Samuel and the others. "She might not be attracted to you because you're a bruiser. Even though we can all agree that you are a bruiser. Isn't that right, Samuel?"

"It is indeed," Samuel replied, "but he could be called much worse. Terrible reputation that he has in certain circles."

"Very true, Samuel, a fact that can't be ignored," Teddy agreed. "Be that as it may, perhaps her interest in you isn't because you're a bruiser. Rather, perhaps she's interested in you because she perceives you as her knight in shining armor."

"An unfair description," Mikel challenged. "I've never worn shining armor in my life." That comment earned another round of laughter from his crew.

"Perhaps you should," Teddy suggested, "and a helmet to hide that many-times-broken nose of yours." The laughter around them only got louder. "During one of your late-night assignations. The Queen of the Crux might enjoy a little role ..."

"Teddy ..."

"Right, sorry," Teddy replied, raising his hands as a way of apologizing. He had noticed the spark in the back of Mikel's eyes and realized that he had been about to push a bit too far. "The image that I've conjured is quite unlikely and a bit disconcerting as well."

"More than disconcerting," Samuel offered in a chuckle. "Downright frightening."

"I couldn't agree more," Teddy said. "I'm simply suggesting that perhaps the Queen of the Crux keeps agreeing to your late-night assignations because you are, indeed, her knight in shining armor. You've saved her Kingdom what, twice now? And her life how many times?"

"You give me too much credit, Teddy. Right place, right time. No more than that."

"Perhaps, but right place, right time is a poor argument. You made a conscious decision. You know that just as she does. I simply throw out for your consideration the possibility that she views your decisions as more than just business decisions."

"You're seeing more than is actually there, Teddy." Even so, Mikel detected a kernel of truth in Teddy's words. A truth that he really hadn't wanted to consider.

"Perhaps." Teddy shrugged, his expression becoming more thoughtful. "Perhaps not. Even so, it's worth it just to have a little fun with you."

"I'm glad that I could offer you and the rest of the crew a few minutes of entertainment."

"We do appreciate it," Samuel said with a gap-toothed smile. "A good way to pass the time. Best not to think too hard on what we're about to do."

"As I said, happy to help," Mikel growled.

"Although I should offer a word of warning."

"Once again, Teddy, I'm afraid to ask."

"No need to ask. I'll just tell you."

"That's very kind of you."

Teddy ignored the heavy dose of sarcasm that laced Mikel's words. "Liria isn't going to like this."

"Like what?"

"Like this," Teddy repeated. "You having ... business relations ... with the Queen of the Crux."

"There are no relations between us," Mikel stated, a touch of defeat in his voice. Though Teddy was right.

Despite their history, despite the fact that he had every right to kill her, Liria still seemed to be interested in him. They were connected in some way that he didn't quite understand and that he had little desire to explore. Although, thinking about that some more, placing his former partner against Celindria Dengannon, upon initial review, he would give the edge to Liria. She was a dangerous woman. Yet there was a steel to the Queen of the Crux that ...

Mikel shook his head, seeking to clear it. He didn't have the time for his thoughts to follow that track, knowing exactly where it led. "It's just business ..."

"Exactly my point," Teddy cut in, offering Mikel a suggestive nod and wink. "Just business."

Mikel sighed, surrendering the fight. "You really are a pain in the ass. You know that?"

"You regret saving my life?"

"Every day," Mikel confirmed in a tired voice.

For a moment there was a silence between the two friends before they both broke out into a long laugh.

"What's so funny?" asked a new voice joining the conversation.

"We're just discussing the women in Mikel's life," Teddy explained. "He is struggling to navigate the challenges they bring with them, Leonardo."

"I can't help you with that. I've got enough challenges as it is, and I don't need to complicate my life any further." The young inventor sat down next to Mikel.

He was nervous. He always was right before he tested one of his new creations. Although this one was fairly straightforward, based almost entirely on physics. It was just a matter of getting the math right, and he believed that he had. He had checked his work several times. Of course, he wouldn't know for sure until the test in real-world conditions was complete.

"Can you help us with what we're about to do?" Mikel asked. "That's all that matters now."

"I can. Have no fear of that. All of my calculations are correct. It's just a matter ..."

"Of putting theory into practice," Teddy finished for him, having heard much the same before from Leonardo.

"Exactly," Leonardo confirmed with a nod.

"I never did," Mikel replied, seeking to settle the young inventor's nerves. "All well at the Splintered Bridge?"

Leonardo's expression brightened at the compliment. He

was grateful that Mikel had plucked him out of obscurity and given him the opportunity to make full use of his talents. And he relished the work that he was doing at the causeway that spanned the Trench and connected the Kingdom of the Crux to the Kingdom of the Tor.

At first, he had been reluctant to accept Mikel's commission because he had so many projects underway. Mikel hadn't pushed him, however. He had simply asked that Leonardo explore the possibility. Spend a few days there and see what he thought.

That gentle request from the King of the Underworld was exactly what Leonardo needed. He discovered quickly that aiding the Battle Lord and the soldiers of the Crux was the best possible testing ground for many of the ideas that swirled around in his head. At the moment, his thoughts on how to reconfigure for use against the soldiers of the Tor the invention he was about to test. Assuming, of course, that the test worked. Because if he lost his primary benefactor ...

"As well as can be," Leonardo replied, swiping at his long, curly hair to keep it out of his eyes. "General Booruz has his Tor soldiers attack with a frightening regularity. He doesn't seem to care about losses."

"It might not be Booruz," Mikel suggested. "It could be Dragoran. Probably is. Booruz has led the King of the Tor's army long enough to know that to keep leading it he needs to do as Dragoran wants. Regardless of the price paid."

"A fair assessment," Leonardo admitted. "So far we've held them. And I think we'll continue to do so. Only so many Tor soldiers can attack across the Splintered Bridge at one time, and we've got the tools now to make that exceedingly difficult for them."

"But ..." Mikel prodded. He caught Leonardo's worried expression, the young man holding something back.

"But that lasts only so long as the game remains the same."

"A good point," Teddy muttered. "Dragoran will not accept failure. Has he tried anything out of the ordinary? Any new strategy?"

"Not yet," Leonardo said. "Even so, the Battle Lord is worried."

"He's right to be worried," Mikel said. "Dragoran is many things, but he's not a fool. He won't allow the stalemate to continue forever."

"Which is why I'm here now. If what you two are about to do works, I might be able to use it on the Splintered Bridge."

"So that's why the Battle Lord gave you leave to join us. Research." Mikel couldn't fault Henri Dengannon for that. If Mikel was in his shoes, he would do much the same.

"Exactly so," Leonardo said with a smile. "When I told him why and who we were focusing our efforts on, he was more than happy to give me a few days."

"Yes, the Battle Lord does have a strong dislike for our current target," Teddy murmured.

"Deservedly so." Mikel pushed himself up, the shadow he was searching for finally appearing in the darkness. Faint, though growing steadily larger as it raced down the river. "We ready?"

Leonardo nodded and then got to his feet. "Yes, let me show you what I have for you. The ship will be here in just a few minutes."

"Why are you so nervous?"

"I'm not nervous." Even so, Marak couldn't help himself. An edginess deep in his bones forced him to stalk around the helm. Constantly glancing toward the far shores shrouded in darkness, he glimpsed nothing that caused him any concern beyond the lanterns lining the rail of the riverboat. He heard nothing but the rush of water beneath them, yet still he felt as if some unknown peril was about to strike.

"You are nervous. You're making me nervous." Junius stood at the helm of the riverboat, eyes passing over the large hooks situated at the bow and the stern that were designed to latch onto the steel cables that would pull them across the Churn.

He had captained for House Hanover for eight years, and he had known Marak for twice as long, serving with him in the Hanover Guard before he returned to his true love. The four rivers that became one at the Crux.

"You're right," Marak growled, stopping himself an almost physical effort. "I don't know." He lifted his hands to the star-filled sky as if he might receive an answer then began his prowl once more when no reply came.

"Another of your premonitions?" Junius asked. He wasn't making fun of Marak, his question serious. His friend became the leader of the five hundred soldiers sworn to serve the current Lord of House Hanover because of his grit and instincts.

Marak didn't stop his pacing, now squeezing the fingers of one hand with the fingers of the other. "Yes. I know we have little to fear, but ..."

"Still you fear." Marak nodded in understanding. His friend's anxiety didn't surprise him. Not when so much depended upon their mission.

"The curse of leadership, my friend." Marak clasped his hands behind his back, trying to exercise some control over the brittle energy pricking at him. "How far?"

"Ten leagues at most," Junius stated with the confidence of a man who had made this run dozens of times before and knew the river like the back of his hand.

Needing a break from his friend's infectious anxiety, Junius shifted his attention to the crew working the deck. There were only a handful at this hour of the morning, the sun not rising until they were closer to the Crux. Even so, his sailors went about their tasks with an efficiency that calmed him. They were masters of their jobs just as he was the master of his.

"Take heart, my friend," Junius prodded, turning the wheel ever so slightly to the starboard to account for the bend in the river they had entered. "No one knows that we are here. No one knows what we carry. And if anyone did, there is nothing they could do about it. Out here, we are safe."

Marak snorted out a laugh that really wasn't a laugh. "How can you be so certain of that? Lord Hanover has poked the King of the Underworld, and the King of the Underworld has punched back. He seems to know all that goes on in the shadows and he's never been shy about taking risks."

"In most shadows, yes, he probably does," Junius agreed. "But not these shadows." He motioned toward the surrounding gloom. "Even if he knows that we are here, he has no way to touch us." He reached out a hand and grasped his friend's shoulder, offering Marak some of his confidence if he was willing to accept it. "We are safe. The King of the Underworld could be watching us now. If he is, it doesn't matter. He couldn't get to us even if he wanted to. You have my word on that."

Marak sighed then nodded. Junius spoke the truth. He knew it. They were in the middle of the fast-flowing Eastern River. The only dangers they faced were the rough current and the rocks hidden just beneath the surface, both of which Junius had defeated time and time again.

He snorted out a real laugh this time. He wasn't nervous so much because of the King of the Underworld. He was more nervous because the cargo they carried was so essential to the success of the House. Lucius Hanover had made that abundantly clear to him.

"You're right, my friend." Marak gripped Junius' arm in thanks then leaned back against the railing, crossing his arms over his chest. "All is as it should be at the dock?"

Junius nodded. "Half of the Guard will meet us there. They will remove the cargo and take it to House Hanover. Then your job will be done. Truly, you have nothing to fear."

"I fear everything, Junius. The future of House Hanover hinges on what we carry."

Marak still hadn't decided if his Lord had made the right decision. He had been thinking about the deal agreed to ever since he stepped aboard the riverboat on the eastern side of the Trench. In retrospect, it seemed like the only decision that Lucius Hanover could have reached after making a series of other decisions that narrowed his options until he had none remaining.

Lucius Hanover had spent so much of the House treasury on the bribes and other schemes he put in place to gain the throne of the Crux that there was scarcely anything left. Yet still desperate for the throne, he had bound himself and the fortunes of his House, as well as the fortunes of those serving House Hanover, that much more tightly to Malor Dragoran.

The King of the Tor allowed Lucius to borrow thousands of golds all with the goal of unseating Celindria Dengannon. A risky play to begin with. And not just because Lucius Hanover had tied himself in a knot from which he would likely never be able to extricate himself.

Since assuming the throne, the Queen of the Crux had worked hard to solidify her hold on what had been her father's seat. The First Families acknowledged her rule, many supporting it, those against it or undecided about having a young woman guiding the future of the Crux keeping their mouths closed, in large part because of her ally who preferred to do his work from behind the curtain. An ally, some said, who was stronger than all the First Families combined.

"You have nothing to fear, Marak, I promise you that. As I said, no one can bother us out here. And once we dock, we'll be fine. It shouldn't take more than a few hours to unload the cargo. And with so many of the House Guard there, no one would be foolish enough to make a play for it."

"You seem to think that the King of the Underworld won't be watching for us when we reach the Hanover dock," Marak warned. Despite Junius' assurances, he was having a difficult time letting go of his concern.

"Why would he?" Junius scoffed. "We're nothing to him. Just one of dozens of riverboats making their way to the Crux. And again, he has no way to reach us, whether on the water or on land."

Marak frowned, not pleased by the captain's lack of perspective. Yet he had no good argument to broaden it. "As you know, Junius, the King of the Underworld has taken an interest in the Crown's fortunes."

"He'll lose interest once we bring this fortune across the Churn and our Lord Hanover works his golden magic. Have no worries about that. The King of the Underworld is first and foremost a businessman. He makes decisions with his brain, not his heart."

"You sure about this?" Mikel wasn't concerned so much as he disliked being one of the inventor's test subjects.

"Yes, completely," Leonardo stated with complete confidence. "It will work. I tried it myself."

"You tried it yourself?" Mikel's tone was dubious.

"On a smaller scale," Leonardo admitted as he nodded toward his invention. "And not here for obvious reasons. But yes, I tested it. It will do what's required so long as you do what's required."

Mikel and Leonardo stood atop one of four platforms built around a pyramidal tower constructed of wood and stone, essentially four ladders thick at the base that narrowed to a point where they were bound and bolted together with a steel cap set at the top. A long cable extended from the cap of each tower. Each cable was bolted to stone blocks on the far side of the river that ensured a downward angle for the four lines that were lost in the darkness.

Leonardo selected this section of the river not only because it was the narrowest, but also because their target would need to slow in order to navigate the turn safely.

"And if we do what's required of us, how do we know it will work? How do you know the cables won't snap?"

"They won't. I promise you that. The math is right. The greatest potential for error lies with you." Leonardo lifted his hands when he saw how his friend's expression stiffened. "No criticism intended. It is simply the truth. The timing must be perfect. Off by just a split-second when you and the others release ..." He shrugged his shoulders. Not to suggest that he didn't care. Rather to remind Mikel that it was out of his hands and in theirs. "The equipment will do what's demanded of it. Success will come down to your crew. Do you trust the men and women you selected?"

Mikel nodded without hesitation. "With my life."

"Then trust me as well. This is basic math and science. Nothing more. Physics. Force, acceleration, and momentum. You need only worry about staying on the cable until you no longer should be on the cable. If your crew remembers what we discussed, how to judge the release point, they'll be fine. And if they don't ..."

Mikel didn't need Leonardo to finish. Anyone off in their timing would end up in the river. A death sentence.

"I see it," Teddy called. He stood first in line on the platform just a few yards to the right of Mikel. The shadow they were waiting for was finally breaking free from the darkness.

"Let's get to it." About to put his latest creation to the test, Leonardo was all business. He was also now in command.

Three raiders, one lined up right after the other, stood on each platform, the pyramid at their backs. Grasping tightly to the steel bars with the leather grips Leonardo had crafted specifically for this assignment, they stared out into the darkness, tracking the large shadow as it approached from below.

Leonardo knelt at the very edge of the crag. He doubted that he could be seen with the darkness, but he didn't want to take the risk. Not after all the work that had gone into preparing for this moment.

He would be the one to release Mikel and his raiders at the desired intervals. It was on his shoulders to ensure all had a chance to reach their target, yet not at the risk of knocking one another from their line.

"On my count," Leonardo said, never taking his eyes from the shadow drifting along the river, reviewing his calculations in his mind, knowing that what he was about to do was more art than science now. The lives of the people about to soar off into the black in his hands. "First in line. Go!"

Mikel, Teddy, Samuel, and Ritzi pushed off the platform, picking up speed swiftly as they zipped down the line, knees tucked to their chests to reduce the drag. Eyes focused on the riverboat that was growing larger and curling toward them. Counting down in their heads when it was time to let go.

Tired of speaking with Junius, his friend's continuing assurances beginning to grate, Marak climbed down to the main deck so that he would have more space to continue with his pacing. Everything Junius said was correct. They had little to fear in the middle of the Eastern River. They had little to fear when they reached the Hanover dock. Yet he couldn't shake the premonition that plagued him.

Having reached the bow, crates of various sizes stacked in

the middle of the deck to keep the rails free, Marak turned so that he could make for the stern. As soon as he did, he jumped back a few inches. Startled. One of the biggest men he had ever seen stood before him.

"I know that I should have made a reservation, but are any cabins still available?" Before Marak could respond, not quite sure what was happening, he collapsed to the deck.

"Just as efficient as always," Mikel murmured quietly as he stepped up next to his friend and looked down at his work. Teddy knocked out the soldier with a single blow of his cudgel across the side of his head.

"I aim to please," Teddy replied softly, smiling at what he viewed as a clever pun. "Did everyone make it on board?"

"They did," Mikel confirmed with a pleased smile, ignoring his friend's attempt at humor. "Let's get to it. I've always wanted to be a pirate."

~

"That's the last of it," Samuel reported.

Once he and Mikel's other raiders gained control of the riverboat, Junius had been more than willing to steer to the far southern shore, recognizing that he had little choice. Especially when Mikel promised him that no one would come to harm unless they brought it upon themselves.

The riverboat captain had never met the King of the Underworld, but he knew one truth about him. His word was good, and that was all that mattered.

Junius served House Hanover. Still, he had no desire to throw away his life. The rest of his crew adopted the same perspective given the choice of behaving themselves or attempting to swim the rapids with heavy chains wrapped around their wrists and ankles. Marak and his soldiers didn't get a say. They were bound and gagged.

"Well done, my friend. You and your crew are to be commended." Four wagons were required to cart off the gold Malor Dragoran lent to Lucius Hanover to fund his multitude of efforts to destabilize the Crux.

"All in a day's work," Samuel replied. His broad smile revealed his pleasure. Not only that they had made such a score, but also that all of the men and women he led made it through the attack with barely a scratch. Only Hedley was hurt, spraining his ankle because he landed awkwardly when he let go of the steel bar. "Should I take all this to the usual place?"

"Yes, Nat will be waiting for you."

Samuel nodded. Before he walked away, he had a question that begged asking. "What do you have in mind for all that gold?"

"You mean after you and your crew receive your cuts as well as bonuses?"

Samuel's smile broadened all the more. Thieving had not paid so well as it did until he linked his fortunes to those of the Broken Bear. "Yes, and thank you for the additional consideration. My crew will appreciate your generosity."

"It's deserved. Everyone performed brilliantly." Mikel nodded toward the wagons that were already on the move, heading away from the river before turning west. "And to answer your question, I have several worthy causes that require funding. Now that Malor Dragoran has graciously agreed to support these endeavors, work can begin."

"He's going to love that," Samuel said as he strode toward the last wagon. "Once he finds out what happened, he's going to come after you."

"I certainly hope so," Mikel replied, his visage turning to ice. Dangerous, threatening, if only for a few seconds as his mind turned toward the last piece of business to be concluded before the sun broke the horizon. "The boat empty?"

Teddy nodded as he strode up the embankment from the shore. "Burn it?"

Marak and the soldiers sat farther up the bank beneath the few trees fighting to subsist among the rocks. Junius had permission to cut them loose once Mikel was gone and an hour had passed, Mikel having no doubt that the riverboat captain would keep his word despite whatever the Captain of the House Hanover Guard might demand of him.

Mikel shook his head in answer to Teddy's question.

"Cut it free?"

Mikel shook his head again.

"I can see the wheels turning. Tell me."

"No grand plan," Mikel shrugged. "I just have a feeling that we might need to make use of the riverboat captain's services at some point in the future, and he won't be of use to me if he doesn't have a riverboat."

Teddy chuckled softly. "Always scheming."

"I prefer to describe it as planning. It's like a game within a game within a game. Managing various pieces as you seek to create the outcome that you want."

"Scheming. Planning. Manipulating. What does it matter what we call it?"

"It doesn't. All that matters is perspective. That we see what is truly before us. Not what we want to see. That's the trick for winning the game, whatever that game might be."

"And what do you see?"

"An opportunity," Mikel replied, his smile becoming almost dastardly.

"I'm afraid to ask."

"You don't need to. You already know."

Teddy put his hands on his hips, studying Mikel. He had known him for more than a decade. Each one saving the other's life. Each one trusting the other with their lives. "Lucius Hanover is a small fish."

"That he is," Mikel agreed.

"You want to go after a bigger fish."

"That I do."

"And you have a plan in place already?"

"More like a scheme," Mikel replied, earning a laugh from his friend as they strode off after the wagons.

The end of the chapter.

To keep reading *Roar of the Broken Bear*, visit my author website at PeterWachtBooks.com or Amazon.

WHAT TO READ NEXT

THE REALMS OF THE TALENT AND THE CURSE

LEGEND OF THE DRAGON LORD

A Painful Truth (short story)*

Stealing the Light

Sacrificing the Queen

Roar of the Broken Bear

Rise of the Dragon Lord (Forthcoming 2026)

THE TALES OF CALEDONIA

(Complete 7-Book Series)

Blood on the White Sand (short story)*

The Diamond Thief (short story)*

The Protector

The Protector's Quest

The Protector's Vengeance

The Protector's Sacrifice

The Protector's Reckoning

The Protector's Resolve

The Protector's Victory

THE TALES OF THE TERRITORIES

(Complete 8-Book Series)

Stalking the Blood Ruby (short story)*

A Fate Worse Than Death (short story)*

Death on the Burnt Ocean

Monsters in the Mist

The Dance of the Daggers

Bloody Hunt for Freedom

A Spark of Rebellion

Shadows Made Real

Shadow's Reach

Storm in the Darkness

THE SYLVAN CHRONICLES

(Complete 9-Book Series)

The Legend of the Kestrel

The Call of the Sylvana

The Raptor of the Highlands

The Makings of a Warrior

The Lord of the Highlands

The Lost Kestrel Found

The Claiming of the Highlands

The Fight Against the Dark

The Defender of the Light

THE RISE OF THE SYLVAN WARRIORS

*Through the Knife's Edge (short story)**

THE FALLEN KNIGHT SERIES

*The Death of the Dragon (short story)**

The Dragon Awakens

Duel With a Dragon

Beware the Dragon

The Dragon Returns

JOIN PETER'S NEWSLETTER

This eBook is a prelude to the events in my epic fantasy series *The Tales of Caledonia* and is free to readers who receive my newsletter.

Join Peter's newsletter and get your FREE short story.
PeterWachtBooks.com